SOMEONE LIKE YOU
& THAT SUMMER

ALSO BY SARAH DESSEN

SARAH DESSEN

SOMEONE LIKE YOU & THAT SUMMER

PENGUIN BOOKS

SOMEONE LIKE YOU

I would like to gratefully acknowledge my agent, Leigh Feldman, and my editor, Sharyn November, for their help, humor, and determination in seeing this book to publication. Thank you.

PENGUIN BOOKS
An imprint of Penguin Random House LLC, New York

First published in the United States of America by Viking, 1998
Published by Puffin Books, an imprint of Penguin Random House LLC, 2000
Published by Speak, an imprint of Penguin Random House LLC, 2004

This omnibus edition published by Penguin, an imprint of Penguin Random House, 2019

Visit us online at penguinrandomhouse.com

THE LIBRARY OF CONGRESS HAS CATALOGED THE VIKING EDITION AS FOLLOWS:
Dessen, Sarah.
Someone like you / by Sarah Dessen.
p. cm.
Summary: Halley's junior year of high school includes the death of her best friend Scarlett's boyfriend, the discovery that Scarlett is pregnant, and Halley's own first serious relationship.
ISBN 0-670-87778-6 (hardcover)
[1. Pregnancy—Fiction. 2. Unmarried mothers—Fiction. 3. Friendship—Fiction.] I. Title.
PZ7.D455 So 1998 [Fic]—dc21 97-36437 CIP AC

Omnibus Edition ISBN 9780593113585

Printed in the United States of America

1 3 5 7 9 10 8 6 4 2

This one is for Bianca

Part I

THE GRAND CANYON

Chapter One

Scarlett Thomas has been my best friend for as long as I can remember. That's why I knew when she called me at Sisterhood Camp, during the worst week of my life, that something was wrong even before she said it. Just by her voice on the other end of the line. I knew.

"It's Michael," she said quietly. Her words crackled over distance. "Michael Sherwood."

"What about him?" The camp director, a woman named Ruth with short hair and Birkenstocks, shifted impatiently beside me. At Sisterhood Camp, we were supposed to be Isolated from the Pressures of Society in order to Improve Ourselves as Women. We weren't supposed to get phone calls. Especially not at midnight on a Tuesday, rousing you out of your creaky camp bed and through the woods to a room too bright and a phone that weighed heavily in your hand.

Scarlett sighed. Something was up. "What about him?" I repeated. The camp director rolled her eyes this time, thinking, I was sure, that this was no emergency.

"He's dead." Scarlett's voice was flat, even, as if she were reciting multiplication tables. I could hear clinking and splashing in the background.

"Dead?" I said. The camp director looked up, suddenly concerned, and I turned away. "How?"

"A motorcycle accident. This afternoon. He got hit by a car on Shortcrest." More splashing, and suddenly I realized she was washing dishes. Scarlett, always capable, would do housework during a nuclear holocaust.

"He's dead," I repeated, and the room seemed very small suddenly, cramped, and as the camp director put her arm around me I shook her off, stepping away. I pictured Scarlett at the sink in cutoffs and a T-shirt, her hair pulled back in a ponytail, phone cocked between her ear and shoulder. "Oh, my God."

"I know," Scarlett said, and there was a great gurgling noise as water whooshed down her sink. She wasn't crying. "I know."

We sat there on the line for what seemed like the longest time, the buzzing in the background the only sound. I wanted to crawl through the phone right then, popping out on the other side in her kitchen, beside her. Michael Sherwood, a boy we'd grown up with, a boy one of us had loved. Gone.

"Halley?" she said softly, suddenly.

"Yeah?"

"Can you come home?"

I looked out the window at the dark and the lake beyond, the moon shimmering off of it. It was the end of August, the end of summer. School started in one week; we'd be juniors this year.

"Halley?" she said again, and I knew it was hard for her to even ask. She'd never been the one who needed me.

"Hold on," I said to her in that bright room, the night it all began. "I'm on my way."

Michael Alex Sherwood died at 8:55 P.M. on August thirteenth. He was turning left onto Morrisville Avenue from Shortcrest Drive when a businessman in a BMW hit him dead on, knocking him off the motorcycle he'd only had since June and sending him flying twenty feet. The paper said he died on impact, the bike a total loss. It wasn't his fault. Michael Sherwood was sixteen years old.

He was also the only boy Scarlett had ever truly loved. We'd known him since we were kids, almost as long as we'd known each other. Lakeview, our neighborhood, sprawled across several streets and cul-de-sacs, bracketed only by wooden posts and hand-carved signs, lined in yellow paint: *Welcome to Lakeview—A Neighborhood of Friends*. One year some high-school students had gone around and crossed out the *r*s in *Friends*, leaving us a *Neighborhood of Fiends*, something my father found absolutely hysterical. It tickled him so much, my mother often wondered aloud if he'd done it himself.

The other distinguishing characteristic of Lakeview was the new airport three miles away, which meant a constant stream of airplanes taking off and landing. My father loved this, too; he spent most evenings out on the back porch, looking up excitedly at the sky as the distant rumblings got louder and louder, closer and closer, until the white nose of a plane would burst out overhead, lights blinking, seeming powerful and loud enough to sweep us all along with it. It drove our neighbor Mr. Kramer to high blood pressure, but my father reveled in it. To me, it was something normal. I hardly stirred, even when I slept, as the glass in my windows shook with the house.

The first time I saw Scarlett was the day she and her mother, Marion, moved in. I was eleven. I was sitting by my window, watching the movers, when I saw a girl just my age, with red hair and blue tennis shoes. She was sitting on the front steps of her new house, watching them cart furniture in, her elbows propped on her knees, chin in her hands, wearing heart-shaped sunglasses with white plastic frames. And she completely ignored me as I came up her front walk, stood in the thrown shade of the awning, and waited for her to say something. I'd never been good at friendships; I was too quiet, too mousy, and tended to choose bossy, mean girls who pushed me around and sent me home crying to my mother. Lakeview, *A Neighborhood of Fiends*, was full of little fiendettes on pink bicycles with Barbie carrying cases in their white, flower-appliquéd baskets. I'd never had a best friend.

So I walked up to this new girl, her sunglasses sending my own reflection back at me: white T-shirt, blue shorts, scuffed Keds with pink socks. And I waited for her to laugh at me or send me away or maybe just ignore me like all the bigger girls did.

"Scarlett?" a woman's voice came from inside the screen door, sounding tired and flustered. "What did I do with my checkbook?"

The girl on the steps turned her head. "On the kitchen counter," she called out in a clear voice. "In the box with the realtor's stuff."

"The box with—" The voice came back, uneven, as if its owner was moving around. "—the realtor's stuff, hmmm, honey I don't think it's here. Oh, wait. Yes. Here it is!" The woman sounded triumphant, as if she'd discovered the North-west Passage, which we'd just learned about at the end of the school year.

The girl turned back and looked at me, kind of shaking her head. I remember thinking for the first time how she seemed old for her age, older than me. And I got that familiar fiendette pink-bicycle feeling.

"Hey," she said to me suddenly, just as I was planning to turn back and head home. "My name's Scarlett."

"I'm Halley," I said, trying to sound as bold as she had. I'd never had a friend with an unusual name; all the girls in my classes were Lisas and Tammys, Carolines and Kimberlys. "I live over there." I pointed across the street, right to my bed-room window.

She nodded, then picked up her purse and scooted down a bit on the step, brushing it off with her hand and leaving just enough space for someone else about the same size. And then she looked at me and smiled, and I crossed that short expanse of summer grass and sat beside her, facing my house. We didn't talk right away, but that was okay; we had a whole lifetime of talking ahead of us. I just sat there with her, staring across the street at my house, my garage, my father pushing the mower past the rosebushes. All the things I'd spent my life learning by heart. But now, I had Scarlett. And from that day on, nothing ever looked the same.

The minute I hung up with Scarlett, I called my mother. She was a therapist, an expert on adolescent behavior. But even with her two books, dozens of seminars, and appearances on local talk shows advising parents on how to handle The Difficult Years, my mother hadn't quite found the solution for dealing with me.

It was 1:15 A.M. when I called.

"Hello?" Strangely, my mother sounded wide awake. It was all part of that professional manner she cultivated: *I'm capable. I'm strong. I'm awake.*

"Mom?"

"Halley? What's wrong?" There was some mumbling in the background; my father, rousing himself.

"It's Michael Sherwood, Mom."

"Who?"

"He's dead."

8

"Who's dead?" More mumbling, this time louder. My father saying *Who's dead? Who?*

"Michael Sherwood," I said. "My friend."

"Oh, goodness." She sighed, and I heard her telling my father to go back to sleep, her hand cupping the receiver. "Honey, I know, it's horrible. It's awfully late—where are you calling from?"

"The camp office," I said. "I need you to come get me."

"Get you?" she said. She sounded surprised. "You've still got another week, Halley."

"I know, but I want to come home."

"Honey, you're tired, it's late—" and now she was lapsing into her therapist voice, a change I could recognize after all these years—"why don't you call me back tomorrow, when you've had a chance to calm down. You don't want to leave camp early."

"Mom, he's *dead*," I said again. Each time I said the word Ruth, the camp director who was still standing beside me, put on her soothing face.

"I know, sweetie. It's awful. But coming home isn't going to change that. It will just disrupt your summer, and there's no point—"

"I want to come home," I said, talking over her. "I need to come home. Scarlett called to tell me. She needs me." My throat was swelling up now, hurting with its ache. She didn't understand. She never understood.

"Scarlett has her mother, Halley. She'll be fine. Honey, it's so late. Are you with someone? Is your counselor there?"

I took a deep breath, and all I could see in my mind was Michael, a boy I hardly knew, whose death now seemed to mean everything. I thought of Scarlett in her bright kitchen, waiting for me. This was crucial.

"Please," I whispered over the line, hiding my face from Ruth, not wanting this strange woman to feel any sorrier for me. "Please come get me."

"Halley." She sounded tired now, almost irritated. "Go to sleep and I'll call you tomorrow. We can discuss it then."

"Say you'll come," I said, not wanting her to hang up. "Just say you'll come. He was our *friend*, Mom."

She was quiet then, and I could picture her sitting in bed next to the sleeping form of my father, probably in her blue nightgown, the light from Scarlett's kitchen visible from the window over her shoulder. "Oh, Halley," she said as if I always caused these kinds of problems; as if my friends died every day. "All right. I'll come."

"You will?"

"I just said I would," she told me, and I knew this would strain us even further, a battle hard-won. "Let me talk to your counselor."

"Okay." I looked over at Ruth, who was close to dozing off. "Mom?"

"Yes."

"Thanks."

Silence. I would pay for this one for a while, I could tell. "It's all right. Let me talk to her."

So I handed the phone over to Ruth, then stood outside the door listening as she reassured my mother that it was fine, I'd be packed and ready, and what a shame, how awful, so young. Then I went back to my cabin, creeping onto my cot in the dark, and closed my eyes.

I couldn't sleep for a long time. I thought only of Michael Sherwood's face, the one I'd cast sideways glances at through middle school, the one Scarlett and I had studied in yearbook after yearbook. And later, the one in the picture that was tucked in the mirror in her bedroom, of Scarlett and Michael at the lake just weeks earlier, water glittering behind them. The way her head rested on his shoulder, his hand on her knee. The way he looked at her, and not at the camera, when I pushed the red button, the flash lighting them up in front of me.

My mother didn't look very happy when she pulled up at the front office the next afternoon. It was clear by this point that my experience at Sisterhood Camp had been a complete and utter disaster. Which was just what I'd predicted when I was dragged off against my will to spend the last two weeks of summer in the middle of the mountains with a bunch of other girls who had no say in the matter either. Sisterhood Camp, which was really called Camp Believe (my father coined the nickname), was something my mother had heard about at one of her seminars. She had come home with a brochure she tucked under my breakfast plate one morning, a yellow sticky note on it saying *What do you think?* My first reaction was *Not much, thank you,* as I stared down at the picture of two girls about my age running through a field together hand in hand. The basic gist was this: a camp with the usual swimming and horseback riding and lanyard making, but in the afternoons seminars and self-help groups on "Like Mother, Like Me" and "Peer Pressure: Where Do I Fit In?" There was a whole paragraph on self-esteem and values maintenance and other words I recognized only from the blurbs on the back of my mother's own books. All I knew was that at fifteen, with my driver's license less than three months away, I was too old for camp or values mainte-nance, not to mention lanyards.

"It will be such a valuable experience," she said to me that evening over dinner. "Much more so than sitting around the pool at Scarlett's getting a tan and talking about boys."

"Mom, it's summer," I said. "And anyway it's almost over. School starts in two weeks."

"You'll be back just in time for school," she said, flipping through the brochure again.

"I have a job," I told her, my last-ditch attempt at an excuse. Scarlett and I were both cashiers at Milton's Market, the gro-cery store at the mall down the street from our neighborhood. "I can't just take two weeks off."

"Mr. Averby says it's slow enough that he can get your shifts covered," she said simply.

"You called Mr. Averby?" I put down my fork. My father, who up until this point had been eating quietly and staying out of it, shot her a look. Even he knew how uncool it was for your mother to call your boss. "*God*, Mom."

"I just wanted to know if it was possible," she said, more to my father than me, but he just shook his head mildly and kept eating. "I knew she'd think of every reason not to go."

"Why should I go waste the last two weeks of summer with a bunch of people I don't know?" I said. "Scarlett and I have plans, Mom. We're working extra shifts to make money for the beach, and we—"

"Halley." She was getting irritated now. "Scarlett will be here when you get back. And I don't ask very much of you, right? This is something I really want you to do. For me, and also, I think you'll find, for yourself. It's only for two weeks."

"I don't want to go," I said, looking at my father for some kind of support, but he just smiled at me apologetically and said nothing, helping himself to more bread. He never got involved anymore; his job was to placate, to smooth, once it was all over. My father was always the one who crept to my doorway after I'd been grounded, sneaking me one of his special Brain Freeze Chocolate Milkshakes, which he believed could solve any problem. After the yelling and slamming of doors, after my mother and I stalked to our separate corners, I could always count on hearing the whirring of the blender in the kitchen, and then him appearing at my doorway presenting me with the thickest, coldest milkshake as a peace offering. But all the milk-shakes in the world weren't going to get me out of this.

So, just like that, I lost the end of my summer. By that Sun-

13

day I was packed and riding three hours into the mountains with my mother, who spend the entire ride reminiscing about her own golden camp years and promising me I'd thank her when it was over. She dropped me at the registration desk, kissed me on the forehead and told me she loved me, then drove off waving into the sunset. I stood there with my duffel bag and glowered after her, surrounded by a bunch of other girls who clearly didn't want to spend two weeks "bonding" either.

I was on what they called "scholarship" at Sisterhood Camp, which meant I had my way paid free, just like the four other girls I met whose parents just happened to be therapists. I made friends with my cabinmates, and we complained to each other, mocked all the seminar leaders, and worked on our tans, talking about boys.

But now I was leaving early, drawn home by the loss of a boy I'd hardly known. I put my stuff in the trunk of the car and climbed in beside my mother, who said hello and then not much else for the first fifteen minutes of the drive. As far as I was concerned, we'd come to a draw: I hadn't wanted to come, and she didn't want me to leave. We were even. But I knew my mother wouldn't see it that way. Lately, we didn't seem to see anything the same.

"So how was it?" she asked me once we got on the highway. She'd set the cruise control, adjusted the air-conditioning, and now seemed ready to make peace. "Or what you saw of it, that is."

"It was okay," I said. "The seminars were kind of boring."

"Hmm," she said, and I figured that I was pushing it. I knew my mother, though. She'd push back. "Well, maybe if you'd stayed the whole time you might have gotten more out of it."

"Maybe," I said. In the side mirror, I could see the mountains retreating behind us, bit by bit.

I knew there were a lot of things she probably wanted to say to me. Maybe she wanted to ask me why I cared about Michael Sherwood, since she'd hardly heard me mention him. Or why I'd hated the idea of camp right from the start, without even giving it a chance. Or maybe it was more, like why in just the last few months even the sight of her coming toward me was enough to get my guard up. Why we'd gone from best friends to something neither of us could rightly define. But she didn't say anything.

"Mom?"

She turned to look at me, and I could almost hear her take a breath, readying herself for whatever I might try next. "Yes?"

"Thanks for letting me come home."

She turned back to the road. "It's all right, Halley," she said to me softly as I leaned back in my seat. "It's all right."

My mother and I had always been close. She knew everything about me, from the boys I liked to the girls I envied; after school I always sat in the kitchen eating my snack and doing homework while I listened for her car to pull up. I always had something to tell her. After my first school dance she sat with me eating ice cream out of the carton while I detailed every single thing that had happened from first song to last. On Saturdays, when my dad pulled morning shift at the radio station, we had Girls' Lunch Out so we could keep up with each other. She loved fancy pasta places, and I only liked fast food and pizza, so we alternated. She made me eat snails, and I watched her gulp down (enjoying it more than she ever would admit) countless Big Macs. We had one rule: we always ordered two desserts and shared. Afterwards we'd hit the mall looking for sales, competing to see who could find the best bargain. She usually won.

She wrote articles in journals and magazines about our successful relationship and how we'd weathered my first year of high school together, and spoke at schools and parents' meetings about Staying in Touch with Your Teen. Whenever her friends came over for coffee and complained about their kids running wild or doing drugs, she'd just shake her head when they asked how she and I did so well.

"I don't know," she'd say. "Halley and I are just so close. We talk about *everything*."

But suddenly, at the beginning of that summer, something changed. I can't say when it started exactly. But it happened after the Grand Canyon.

Each summer, my parents and I took a vacation. It was our big splurge of the year, and we always went someplace cool like Mexico or Europe. This year, we took a cross-country road trip to California and then the Grand Canyon, stopping here and

16

there, sucking up scenery and visiting relatives. My mother and I had a great time; my father did most of the driving, and the two of us hung out, talking and listening to the radio, sharing clothes, making up songs and jokes as state lines and landmarks passed by. My father and I forced her to eat fast food almost every day as payback for a year's worth of arugula salad and prosciutto tortellini. We spent two weeks together, bickering sometimes but mostly just having fun, me and my parents, on the road.

As soon as I got home, though, three very big things happened. First, I started my job at Milton's. Scarlett and I had spent the end of the school year going around filling out applications, and it was the only place with enough positions to hire us both. By the time I got home from the trip, Scarlett had already been there two weeks, so she taught me the ropes. Second, she introduced me to Ginny Tabor, whom she'd met at the pool while I'd been gone. Ginny was a cheerleader with a wild streak a mile wide and a reputation among the football team for more than her cheers and famous midair splits. She lived a few miles away in the Arbors, a fancy development of Tudor houses with a country club, pool, and golf course. Ginny Tabor's father was a dentist, and her mother weighed about eighty pounds, chain-smoked Benson and Hedges 100's, and had skin that was as leathery as the ottoman in our living room. She threw money at Ginny and left us alone to prowl the streets of the Arbors on our way to the pool, or sneak out across the golf course at night to meet boys.

17

Which, in turn, led to the third big event that summer, when two weeks after coming home I broke off my dull, one-year romance with Noah Vaughn.

Noah was my first "boyfriend," which meant we called each other on the phone and kissed sometimes. He was tall and skinny, with thick black hair and a bit of acne. His parents were best friends with mine, and we'd spent Friday night together, at our house or theirs, for most of my lifetime. He'd been all right for a start. But when I was inducted into the new crazy world of Ginny Tabor, he had to go.

He didn't take it well. He sulked around, glowered at me, and still came over every Friday with his little sister and his parents, sitting stony-faced on the couch as I slipped out the door, yelling good-bye. I always said I was going to Scarlett's, but instead we were usually meeting boys at the pool or hanging out with Ginny. My mother was more sad about our breakup than anyone; I think she'd half expected I'd marry him. But this was the New Me, someone I was evolving into with every hot and humid long summer day. I learned to smoke cigarettes, drank my first beer, got a deep tan, and double-pierced my ears as I began to drift, almost imperceptibly at first, from my mother.

There's a picture on our mantel that always reminds me of what my mother and I were then. We're at the Grand Canyon, at one of those overlook sites, with it spread out huge and gaping behind us. We have on matching T-shirts, sunglasses, and big smiles as we pose, arms around each other. We have never, in any picture before or since, looked more alike. We have the same small nose, the same stance, the same goofy smile. We look happy, standing there in the sunshine, the sky spread out blue and forever in the distance. My mother framed that picture when we got home, sticking it front and center on the mantel where you couldn't help but see it. It was like she knew, somehow, that it would be a relic just months later, proof of another time and place neither of us could imagine had existed: my mother and I, best friends, posing at the Grand Canyon.

Scarlett was sitting on her front steps when we pulled up. It was early evening, just getting dark, and all up and down our street, lights were on in the houses, people out walking their dogs or children. Someone a few streets over was barbecuing, the smell mingling in the air with cut grass and recent rain.

I got out of the car and put my bag on the front walk, looking across the street at Scarlett's house, the only light coming from her kitchen and spilling out into the empty carport. She lifted one hand and waved at me from the stoop.

"Mom, I'm going to Scarlett's," I said.

"Fine." I still wasn't totally forgiven for this, not yet. But it was late, she was tired, and these days, we had to pick our battles.

I knew the way across the street and up Scarlett's walk by heart; I could have done it with every sense lost. The dip in the street halfway across, the two prickly bushes on either end of her walk that left tiny scratches on your skin when you brushed against them. It was eighteen steps from the beginning of the walk to the front stoop; we'd measured it when we were in sixth grade and obsessed with facts and details. We'd spent months calculating distances and counting steps, trying to organize the world into manageable bits and pieces.

Now I just walked toward her in the half-darkness, aware only of the sound of my own footfalls and the air conditioner humming softly under the side window.

"Hey," I said, and she scooted over to make room for me. "How's it going?"

It seemed like the stupidest thing to ask once I'd said it, but there really weren't any right words. I looked over at her as she sat beside me, barefoot, her hair pulled away from her face in a loose ponytail. She'd been crying.

I wasn't used to seeing her this way. Scarlett had always been the stronger, the livelier, the braver. The girl who punched out Missy Lassiter, the meanest, most fiendish of the pink-bike girls that first summer she moved in, on a day when they surrounded us and tried to make us cry. The girl who kept a house, and her mother, up and running since she was five, now playing mother to a thirty-five-year-old child. The girl who had kept the world from swallowing me whole, or so I'd always believed.

"Scarlett?" I said, there in the dark, and as she turned to me I saw her face was streaked with tears. For a minute, I didn't know what to do. I thought again of that picture tucked in her mirror, of her and Michael just weeks ago, the water so bright and shiny behind them. And I thought of what she had done all the millions of times I'd cried to her, collapsing at even the slightest wounding of my heart or pride.

So I reached over and pulled her to me, wrapping my arms around her, and held my best friend close, returning so many favors all at once. We sat there for a long time, Scarlett and me, with her house looming over us and mine right across the street staring back with its bright windows. It was the end of summer; it was the end of a lot of things. I sat there with her, feeling her shoulders shake under my hands. I had no idea what to do or what came next. All I knew was that she needed me and I was here. And for now, that was about the best we could do.

Chapter Two

Scarlett was a redhead, but not in an orangey, carrot-top kind of way. Her color was more auburn, deep and red mixed with browns that made her green eyes seem almost luminous. Her skin was pale, with masses of freckles for the first few years I knew her; as we grew older, they faded into a sprinkling across her nose, as if they'd been scattered there by hand. She was an inch and three-quarters shorter than me, her feet a size larger, and she had a scar on her stomach that looked like a mouth smiling from when she'd gotten her appendix out. She was beautiful in all the unconscious, accidental ways that I wasn't, and I was jealous more than I'd ever have admitted. To me, Scarlett was foreign and exotic. But she said she would have given anything for my long hair and tan in summer, for my thick eyelashes and eyebrows. Not to mention my father, my conventional family, away from Marion with her whims and fancies. It was an even trade, our envy of each other; it made everything fair.

We always believed we lived perfectly parallel lives. We went through the same phases at the same times; we both liked gory movies and sappy stuff, and we knew every word to every song on the old musical soundtracks my parents had. Scarlett was more confident, able to make friends fast, where I was shy and quiet, hanging back from the crowd. I was forever known as "Scarlett's friend Halley." But I didn't mind. Without her I knew I'd be hanging out in the bus parking lot with the nerds and Noah Vaughn. That was, I was sure, the destiny in store for me until the day Scarlett looked up from behind those white sunglasses and made a spot for me next to her for the rest of my life. And I was grateful. Because life is an ugly, awful place to not have a best friend.

When I pictured myself, it was always like just an outline in a coloring book, with the inside not yet completed. All the standard features were there. But the colors, the zigzags and plaids, the bits and pieces that made up me, Halley, weren't yet in place. Scarlett's vibrant reds and golds helped some, but I was still waiting.

For most of high school, we hadn't known Michael Sherwood that well, even though we'd grown up in the same neighborhood. He'd gone away the summer after middle school to California and returned transformed: tan, taller, and suddenly gorgeous. He was immediately *the boy* to date.

He went out with Ginny Tabor for about fifteen minutes, then Elizabeth Gunderson, the head cheerleader, for a few months. But he never seemed to fit in with that crowd of soccer-team captains and varsity jackets. He went back to his buddies from Lakeview, like his best friend Macon Faulkner.

Sometimes we'd see them walking down our street, between our two houses, in the middle of the night, smoking cigarettes and laughing. They were different, and they fascinated us.

By leaving the popular crowd, Michael Sherwood became an enigma. No one was sure where he fit in, and he was friendly with everyone, sort of the great equalizer of our high school. He was famous for his pranks on substitute teachers and was always asking to borrow a dollar in exchange for a good story; he told outlandish tales, half true at best, but they were so funny you got your dollar's worth. The one I remember he told me had to do with psychotic Girl Scouts who were stalking him. I didn't believe him, but I gave him two dollars and skipped lunch that day. It was worth it.

Each of us had our own story about Michael, something he'd done or said or passed down. More than anything, it was the things he *didn't* do that made Michael Sherwood so intriguing; he seemed so far from the rest of us and yet implicitly he belonged to everyone.

At the end of every school year there was the annual slide show, full of candid shots that hadn't made the yearbook. We all piled into the auditorium and watched as our classmates' faces filled the huge screen, everyone cheering for their friends and booing people they didn't like. There was only one picture of Michael Sherwood, but it was a good one: he was sitting on the wall by himself, wearing this black baseball hat he always wore, laughing at something out of the frame, something we couldn't see. The grass was so green behind him, and above that a clear stretch of blue sky. When the slide came up, the entire crowd in that auditorium cheered, clapping and hooting and craning their necks to look for Michael, who was sitting up in the balcony with Macon Faulkner, looking embarrassed. But that was what he was to us, always: the one thing that we all had in common.

The funeral was the next day, Thursday. I went across the street to Scarlett's after breakfast, in bare feet and cutoffs, carrying two black dresses I couldn't decide between. I'd only been to one funeral before, my grandfather's in Buffalo, and I'd been so little someone had dressed me. This was different.

"Come in," I heard Marion call out before I even had a chance to knock at the side door. She was sitting at the kitchen table, coffee cup in front of her, flipping through *Vogue*.

"Hey," I said to her as she smiled at me. "Is she awake?"

"Practically all night," she said quietly, turning the page and taking a sip of coffee. "She was on the couch when I got up. She really needs some rest, or she's just gonna crash."

I had to keep from smiling. These were the same words I heard from Scarlett about Marion on a regular basis; for as long as I'd known them their roles had been reversed. When Marion had been depressed and drinking heavily a few years back, it was Scarlett who came knocking at our front door in her nightgown at two A.M. because she'd found Marion passed out cold halfway up the front walk, her cheek imprinted with the ripples and cracks in the concrete. My father carried Marion into the house while my mother tried her best therapy schtick on Scarlett, who said nothing and curled up in the chair beside Marion's bed, watching over her until morning. My father called Scarlett "solemn"; my mother said she was "in denial."

"Hey." I looked over to see Scarlett standing in the doorway in a red shirt and cutoff long johns, her hair still mussed up from sleeping. She nodded at the dresses in my hand. "Which one you gonna wear?"

"I don't know," I said.

She came closer, taking them from my hands, then held each up against me, squinting. "The short one," she said quietly, laying the other on the counter next to the fruit bowl. "The one with the scoop neck always makes you look like you're twelve."

I looked down at the scoop-necked dress, trying to remember where I'd worn it before. It was always Scarlett who kept track of such things: dates, memories, lessons learned. I forgot everything, barely able to keep my head from one week to the next. But Scarlett knew it all, from what she was wearing when she got her first kiss to the name of the sister of the boy I'd met at the beach the summer before; she was our oracle, our common memory.

She opened the fridge and took out the milk, then crossed the room with a box of Rice Krispies under her arm, grabbing a bowl from the open dishwasher on her way. She sat at the head of the table, with Marion to her left, and I took my seat on the right. Even in their tiny family, with me as an honorary member, there were traditions.

Scarlett poured herself some cereal, adding sugar from the bowl between us. "Do you want some?"

"No," I said. "I ate already." My mother had made me French toast, after spending most of the early morning gossiping over the back fence with her best friend, Irma Trilby, who was known for her amazing azaleas and her mouth, the latter of which I'd heard all morning through my window. Apparently Mrs. Trilby had known Mrs. Sherwood well from PTA and had already been over with a chicken casserole to relay her regrets. Mrs. Trilby had also seen me and Michael and Scarlett more than once walking home from work together, and late one night she'd even caught a glimpse of Scarlett and Michael kissing under a streetlight. He was a sweet boy, she'd said in her nasal voice. He mowed their lawn after Arthur's coronary and always got her the best bananas at Milton's, even if he had to sneak some from the back. A nice boy.

So my mother came inside newly informed and sympathetic and made me a huge breakfast that I picked at while she sat across the table, coffee mug in hand, smiling as if waiting for me to say something. As if all it took was Michael Sherwood mowing a lawn, or finding the perfect banana, to make him worth mourning.

"So what time's the service?" Marion asked me, picking up her Marlboro Lights from the lazy Susan in the middle of the table.

"Eleven o'clock."

She lit a cigarette. "We're packed with appointments today, but I'll try to make it. Okay?"

"Okay," Scarlett said.

Marion worked at the Lakeview Mall at Fabulous You, a glamour photography store where they had makeup and clothes and got you all gussied up, then took photographs that you could give to your husband or boyfriend. Marion spent forty hours a week making up housewives and teenagers in too much lipstick and the same evening gowns, posing them with an empty champagne glass as they gazed into the camera with their best come-hither look. It was a hard job, considering some of the raw material she had to work with; not everyone is cut out to be glamorous. She often said there was only so much of a miracle to be worked with concealer and creative lighting.

Marion pushed her chair back, running a hand through her hair; she had Scarlett's face, round with deep green eyes, and thick blond hair she bleached every few months. She had bright red fingernails, smoked constantly, and owned more lingerie than Victoria's Secret. The first time I'd met her, the day they moved in, Marion had been flirting with the movers, dressed in hip-huggers, a macramé halter top that showed her stomach, and heels at least four inches high. She wasn't like my mother; she wasn't like *anyone's* mother. To me, she looked just like Barbie, and she'd fascinated me ever since.

"Well," Marion drawled, standing up and ruffling Scarlett's

hair with her hand as she passed. "Got to get ready for the salt mines. You girls call if you need me. Okay?"

"Okay," Scarlett said, taking another mouthful of cereal.

"Bye, Marion," I said.

"She won't come," Scarlett said once Marion was safely upstairs, her footsteps creaking above us.

"Why not?"

"Funerals freak her out." She dropped her spoon in her bowl, finished. "Marion has a convenient excuse for everything."

When we went upstairs to get ready I flopped on the edge of her bed, which was covered in clothes and magazines and mismatched blankets and sheets. Scarlett opened her closet and stood in front of it with her hands on her hips, contemplating. Marion yelled good-bye from downstairs and the front door slammed, followed by the sound of her car starting and backing out of the driveway. Through the window over Scarlett's bed, I could see my own mother sitting in the swing on our front porch, drinking coffee and reading the paper. As Marion drove past she waved, her "neighbor smile" on, and went back to reading.

"I hate this," Scarlett said suddenly, reaching into the closet and pulling out a navy blue dress with a white collar. "I don't have a single thing that's appropriate."

"You can wear my twelve-year-old dress," I offered, and she made a face.

"I bet Marion's got something," she said suddenly, leaving

the room. Marion's closet was legend; she was a fashion plate and a pack rat, the most dangerous of pairings.

I reached over and turned on the radio next to the bed, leaning back and closing my eyes. I'd spent half my life in Scarlett's room, sprawled across the bed with a stack of *Seventeen* magazines between us, picking out future prom dresses and reading up on pimple prevention and boyfriend problems. Right next to her window was the shelf with her pictures: me and her at the beach two years ago, in matching sailor hats, doing a mock salute at my father's camera. Marion at eighteen, an old school picture, faded and creased. And finally, at the end and un- framed, that same picture of her and Michael at the lake. Since I left for Sisterhood Camp, she'd moved it so it was in easy reach.

I felt something pressing into my back, hard, and I reached under to move it; it was a boot with a thick sole that resisted when I pulled on it. I shifted my position and gave it another yank, wondering when Scarlett had bought hiking boots. I was just about to yell out and ask her, when it suddenly yanked back, hard, and there was an explosion of movement on the bed, arms and legs flailing, things falling off the sides as some- one rose out of the mess around me, shaking off magazines and blankets and pillows in all directions. And suddenly, I found myself face to face with Macon Faulkner.

He glanced around the room as if he wasn't quite sure where he was. His blond hair, cut short over his ears, stuck up in tiny cowlicks. In one ear was a row of three silver hoops.

"Wha—?" he managed, sitting up straighter and blinking. He was all tangled up, one sheet wrapped around his arm. "Where's Scarlett?"

"She's down there," I said automatically, pointing toward the door, as if that was down, which it wasn't.

He shook his head, trying to wake up. I would have been just as shocked to see Mahatma Gandhi or Elvis in Scarlett's bed; I had no idea she even knew Macon Faulkner. We all knew *who* he was, of course. As a Boy with a Reputation, his neighborhood legend preceded him.

And what was he doing in her bed, anyway? It couldn't mean—no. She would have told me; she told me everything. And Marion *had* said Scarlett slept on the couch.

"Well, I think I can wear this," I heard Scarlett say as she came back down the hallway, a black dress over her arm. She looked at Macon, then at me, and walked to the closet as if it was the most normal thing in the world to have a strange boy in your bed at ten in the morning on a Thursday.

Macon lay back, letting one hand flop over his eyes. His boot, and his foot in it, had somehow landed in my lap, where it remained. Macon Faulkner's *foot* was in my *lap*.

"Did you meet Halley?" Scarlett asked him, hanging the dress on her closet door. "Halley, this is Macon. Macon, Halley."

"Hi," I said, immediately aware of how high my voice was.

"Hey." He nodded at me, moving his foot off my lap as if that was nothing special, then got off the bed and stood up, stretching his arms. "Man, I feel awful."

31

"Well, you should," Scarlett said in the same scolding voice she used with me when I was especially spineless. "You were incredibly wasted."

Macon leaned over and rooted around under the sheets, looking for something, while I sat there and stared at him. He was in a white T-shirt ripped along the hem and dark blue shorts, those clunky boots on his feet. He was tall and wiry, and tan from a summer working landscaping around the neighborhood, which was the only place I ever saw him, and even then from a distance.

"Have you seen—?" he began, but Scarlett was already reaching to the bedside table and the baseball cap lying there. Macon leaned over and took it from her, then put it on with a sheepish look. "Thanks."

"You're welcome." Scarlett pulled her hair back behind her head, gathering it in her hands, which meant she was thinking. "So, you need a ride to the service?"

"Nah," he said, walking to the bedroom door with his hands in his pockets, stepping over my feet as if I was invisible. "I'll see you there."

"Okay." Scarlett stood by the doorway.

"Is it cool? To go out this way?" he was whispering, gesturing down the hall to Marion's empty room.

"It's fine."

He nodded, then stepped toward her awkwardly, leaning down to kiss her cheek. "Thanks," he said quietly, in a voice I probably was not supposed to hear. "I mean it."

"It's no big deal," Scarlett said, smiling up at him, and we both watched him as he loped off, his boots clunking down the stairs and out the door. When I heard it swing shut, I walked to the window and leaned against the glass, waiting until he came out on the walk, squinting, and began those eighteen steps to the street. Across the street my mother looked up, folding her paper in her lap, watching too.

"I cannot believe you," I said out loud, as Macon Faulkner passed the prickly bushes and turned left, headed out of *Lakeview—Neighborhood of Friends.*

"He was upset," Scarlett said simply. "Michael was his best friend."

"But you never even told me you knew him. And then I come up here and he's in your *bed.*"

"I just knew him through Michael. He's messed up, Halley. He's got a lot of problems."

"It's so weird, though," I said. "I mean, that he was here."

"He just needed someone," she said. "That's all."

I still had my eye on Macon Faulkner as he moved past the perfect houses of our neighborhood, seeming out of place among hissing sprinklers and thrown newspapers on a bright and shiny late summer morning. I couldn't say then what it was about him that kept me there. But just as he was rounding the corner, disappearing from sight, he turned around and lifted his hand, waving at me, as if he knew even without turning back that I'd still be there in the window, watching him go.

*   *   *

When we got to the church, there was already a line out the door. Scarlett hadn't said much the entire trip, and as we walked over, she was wringing her hands.

"Are you okay?" I asked her.

"It's just weird," she said, and her voice was low and hollow. She had her eyes on something straight ahead. "All of it."

As I looked up I could see what she meant. Elizabeth Gunderson, head cheerleader, was surrounded by a group of her friends on the church steps. She was sobbing hysterically, a red T-shirt in her hands.

Scarlett stopped when we got within a few feet of the crowd, so suddenly that I kept walking and then had to go back for her. She was standing by herself, her arms folded tightly across her chest.

"Scarlett?" I said.

"This was a bad idea," she said. "We shouldn't have come."

"But—"

And that was as far as I got before Ginny Tabor came up behind me, throwing her arms around both of us at once and collapsing into tears. She smelled like hairspray and cigarette smoke and was wearing a blue dress that showed too much leg.

"Oh, my God," she said, lifting her head to take in me and then Scarlett as we pulled away from her as delicately as possible. "It's so awful, so terrible. I haven't been able to eat since I heard. I'm a wreck."

Neither of us said anything; we just kept walking, while

Ginny fumbled for a cigarette, lighting it and then fanning the smoke with one hand. "I mean, the time that we were together wasn't all that great, but I loved him *so* much. It was just circumstances—" and now she sobbed, shaking her head—"that kept us apart. But he was, like, everything to me for those two months. Everything."

I looked over at Scarlett, who was studying the pavement, and I said, "I'm so sorry, Ginny."

"Well," she said in a tight voice, exhaling a long stream of smoke, "it's so different when you knew him well. You know?"

"I know," I said. We hadn't seen much of Ginny since midsummer. After spending a few wild weeks with us, she'd gotten sent off to a combination cheerleading/Bible camp while her parents went to Europe. It was just as well, we figured. There was only so much of ongoing Ginny you could take. A few days later Scarlett had met Michael, and the second half of our summer began.

We kept following the line into the church, now coming up on Elizabeth. Ginny, of course, made a big show of running over to her and bursting into fresh tears, and they stood and hugged each other, crying together.

"It's so awful," a girl said from behind me. "He loved Elizabeth so much. That's his shirt she's holding, you know. She hasn't put it down since she heard."

"I thought they broke up," said another girl, and cracked her gum.

"At the beginning of the summer. But he still loved her. Any-

35

way, that Ginny Tabor is so damn shallow," said the first girl. "She only dated him for about two days."

Once inside, we sat toward the back, next to two older women who pulled their knees aside primly as we slid past them. Up at the front of the church there were two posters with pictures of Michael taped to them: baby snapshots, school pictures, candids I recognized from the yearbook. And in the middle, biggest of all, was the picture from the slide show, the one that had brought cheers in that darkened auditorium in June. I wanted to point it out to Scarlett, but when I turned to tell her, she was just staring at the back of the pew in front of us, her face pale, and I kept quiet.

The service started late, with people filing in and lining the walls, shuffling and fanning themselves with the little paper programs we'd been handed at the door. Elizabeth Gunderson came in, still crying, and was led to a seat with Ginny Tabor sobbing right behind her. It was strange to see my classmates in this setting; some were dressed up nicely, obviously used to wearing church clothes. Others looked out of place, awkward, tugging at their ties or dress shirts. I wondered what Michael was thinking, looking down at all these people with red faces shifting in their seats, at the wailing girls he left behind, at his parents in the front pew with his little sister, quietly stoic and sad. And I looked over at Scarlett, who had loved him so much in such a short time, and slipped my hand around hers, squeezing it. She squeezed back, still staring ahead.

The service was formal and short; the heat was stifling with all the people packed in so tightly, and we could barely hear the minister over the fanning and the creaking of the pews. He talked about Michael, and what he meant to so many people; he said something about God having his reasons. Elizabeth Gunderson got up and left ten minutes into it, her hand pressed against her mouth as she walked quickly down the aisle of the church, a gaggle of friends running behind her. The older women next to us shook their heads, disapproving, and Scarlett squeezed my hand harder, her fingernails digging into my skin.

When the service was over, there was an awkward murmur of voices as everyone filed outside. It had suddenly gotten very dark, with a strange breeze blowing that smelled like rain. Overhead the clouds had piled up big and black behind the trees.

I almost lost Scarlett in the crowd of voices and faces and color in front of the church. Ginny was leaning on Brett Hershey, the captain of the football team, as he led her out. Elizabeth was sitting in the front seat of a car in the parking lot, the door open, her head in her hands. Everyone else stood around uncertainly as if they needed permission to leave, holding their programs and looking up at the sky.

"Poor Elizabeth," Scarlett said softly as we stood by her car.

"They broke up a while ago," I said.

"Yeah. They did." She kicked a pebble, and it rattled off of something under the car. "But he really loved her."

I looked over at her, the wind blowing her hair around her

face, her fair skin so white against the black of Marion's dress. The times I caught her unaware, accidentally, were when she was the most beautiful. "He loved you, too," I told her.

She looked up at the sky, black with clouds, the smell of rain stronger and stronger. "I know," she said softly. "I know."

The first drop was big, sloshy and wet, falling on my shoulder and leaving a round, dark circle. Then, suddenly, it was pouring. The rain came in sheets, sending people running toward their cars, shielding themselves with their flimsy paper programs. Scarlett and I dove into her car and watched the water stream down the windshield. I couldn't remember the last time I'd seen it rain so hard.

We pulled out onto Main Street in Scarlett's Ford Aspire. Her grandmother had given it to her for her birthday in April. It was about the size of a shoe box; it looked like a larger car that had been cut in half with a big bread knife. As we crossed a river of water spilling into the road, I wondered briefly if we'd get pulled into the current and carried away like Wynken, Blynken, and Nod in their big shoe, out to sea.

Scarlett saw him first, walking alone up the street, his white dress shirt soaked and sticking to his back. His head was ducked and he had his hands in his pockets, staring down at the pavement as people ran past with umbrellas. Scarlett beeped the horn, slowing beside him.

"Macon!" she called out, leaning into the rain. "Hey!" He didn't hear her, and she poked me. "Yell out to him, Halley."

"What?"

"Roll down your window and ask him if he wants a ride."

"Scarlett," I said, suddenly nervous, "I don't even know him."

"So what?" She gave me a look. "It's pouring. Hurry up."

I rolled my window down and stuck my head out, feeling the rain pelting the back of my neck. "Excuse me," I said.

He didn't hear me. I cleared my throat, stalling. "Excuse me."

"Halley," Scarlett said, glancing into the rearview mirror, "we're holding up traffic here. Come on."

"He can't hear me," I said defensively.

"You're practically whispering."

"I am not," I snapped. "I am speaking in a perfectly audible tone of voice."

"Just yell it." Cars were going around us now as a fresh wave of rain poured in my window, soaking my lap. Scarlett exhaled loudly, which meant she was losing patience. "Come on, Halley, don't be such a wuss."

"I am not a wuss," I said. "God."

She just looked at me. I stuck my head back out the window.

"Macon." I said it a little louder this time, just because I was angry. "Macon."

Another loud exhalation from Scarlett. I was getting completely soaked.

"Macon," I said a bit louder, stretching my head completely out of the car. *"Macon!!"*

He jerked suddenly on the sidewalk, turning around and looking at me as if he expected us to come flying up the curb in our tiny car to squash him completely. Then he just stared, his shirt soaked and sticking to his skin, his hair dripping onto his face, stood and stared at me as if I was completely and utterly nuts.

"What?" he screamed back, just as loudly. *"What* is *it?"*

Beside me, Scarlett burst out laughing, the first time I'd heard her laugh since I'd come home. She leaned back in her seat, hand over her mouth, giggling uncontrollably. I wanted to die.

"Um," I said, and he was still staring at me. "Do you want a ride?"

"I'm okay," he said across me, to Scarlett. "But thanks."

"Macon, it's pouring." She had her Mom voice on, one I recognized. As he looked across me, I could see how red his eyes were, swollen from crying. "Come on."

"I'm okay," he said again, backing off from the car. He wiped his hand over his face and hair, water spraying everywhere. "I'll see you later."

"Macon," she called out again, but he was already gone, walking back into the rain. As we sat at the stoplight, he cut around a corner and disappeared; the last thing I saw was his shirt, a flash of white against the brick of the alley. Then he was gone, vanishing so easily it seemed almost like magic—there was no trace. Scarlett sighed as I rolled up my window, saying something about everybody having their ways. I was only watching the alleyway, the last place I'd seen him, wondering if he'd ever even been there at all.

Chapter Three

When I think of Michael Sherwood, what really comes to mind is produce. Deep yellow bananas, bright green kiwis, cool purple plums smooth to the touch. Our friendship with Michael Sherwood, popular boy and legend, began simply with fruits and vegetables.

Scarlett and I were cashiers at Milton's Market, wearing our little green smocks and plastic name tags: *Hello, I'm Halley! Welcome to Milton's!* She worked register eight, which was the No Candy register, and I worked Express Fifteen Items and Under right next to her, close enough to roll my eyes or yell over the beeping of my price scanner when it all got to be too much. It wasn't the greatest job by a long stretch. But at least we were together.

We'd seen Michael Sherwood come in to interview at the end of June. He'd been wearing a tie. He looked nervous and waved at me like we were friends as he waited for an application at the Customer Service Desk. He got placed in Fruits and Vegetables, his official title being Junior Assistant to Produce Day Manager, which meant that he stacked oranges, repacked fruit in those little green trays and sealed them with cling wrap, and watered the vegetables with a big hose twice a day. Mostly he laughed and had a good time, quickly making friends with everyone from Meat to Health and Beauty Aids. But it was me and Scarlett he was drawn to. Well, it was Scarlett, really. As usual, I was just along for the ride.

It started with kiwis. During his first week, Michael Sherwood ate four kiwi fruit for lunch each day. Just kiwis. Nothing else. He'd stick them on Scarlett's little scale in their plastic bag, smiling, then take them outside to the one little patch of grass in the parking lot and cut and eat them, one by one, by himself. We wondered about this. We never ate kiwis.

"He likes fruit," Scarlett said simply one day after he was gone, having smiled his big smile at her and made her blush. He came to my register once, but by the third day he was standing in line at Scarlett's, even when my overhead light was flashing OPEN NO WAITING.

I looked out at Michael, in his green produce apron, sitting in the sun with those tiny fuzzy fruits, and shook my head. It would always take at least fifteen minutes for Scarlett to stop blushing.

The next day, when he got to the front of the line with his kiwis and Scarlett was ringing him up, she said, "You must really like these things."

"They're awesome," he said, leaning over her little check and credit-card station. "Haven't you ever tried one?"

"Only in fruit salad," Scarlett said, and I was so distracted listening I rang up some rigatoni at two hundred dollars, screwing up my register altogether and scaring the hell out of the poor woman in my line, who was only buying that, some pineapple spears, and a box of tampons. Between voiding and ringing everything back out, I missed half of their conversation, and when I turned back Michael was walking outside with his lunch and Scarlett was holding one fuzzy kiwi in her hand, examining it from every angle.

"He gave it to me," she whispered. Her face was blazing red. "Can you believe it?"

"Excuse me, miss," someone in my line shouted, "are you open?"

"Yes," I shouted back. To Scarlett I said, "What else did he say?"

"I have these," said a tall, hairy man in a polka-dot shirt as he pushed his cart up, thrusting a pile of sticky coupons in my hand. He was buying four cans of potted meat, some air freshener, and two cans of lighter fluid. Sometimes you don't even want to think about what people are doing with their groceries.

"I think I'm going to take my break," Scarlett called to me, pulling the drawer from her register. "Since I'm slow and all."

"Wait, I'll be done here in a sec." But of course my line was long now, full of people with fifteen items, or eighteen items, or even twenty with a little creative counting, all staring blankly at me.

"Do you mind?" Scarlett said, already heading to the offices to drop off her drawer, that one kiwi in her free hand. "I mean . . ."

She glanced outside quickly, and I could see Michael on the curb with his lunch.

"It's okay," I said, turning back to Scarlett as I ran Hairy Man's check through the confirming slot. "I'll just take my break later, or something. . . ."

But she didn't hear me, was already gone, outside to the curb and the sunshine, sitting next to Michael Sherwood. My best friend Scarlett had traded a kiwi fruit for her heart.

I didn't get many breaks with her after that. Michael Sherwood wooed her with strange, foreign fruits and vegetables, dropping slivers of green melon and dark red blood oranges off at her register when she was busy. Later, when she looked up, there'd be something poised above her on her NO CANDY REGISTER sign; a single pear, perfectly balanced, three little radishes all in a row. I never saw him do it, and I watched her station like a hawk. But there was something magical about Michael Sherwood, and of course Scarlett loved it. I would have too, if it had ever happened to me.

That was the first summer when it wasn't just me and Scarlett. Michael was always there making us laugh, doing belly flops into the pool or sliding his arms around Scarlett's waist as she stood at the kitchen counter, stirring brownie mix. It was the first summer we didn't spend practically every night together, either; sometimes, I'd look across the street in early evening and see her shades drawn, Michael's car in the driveway, and know I had to stay away. Late at night I'd hear them outside saying good-bye, and I'd pull my curtain aside and watch as he kissed her in the dim yellow of the streetlight. I'd never had to fight for her attention before. Now, all it took was a look from Michael and she was off and running, with me left behind again to eat lunch alone or watch TV with my father, who always fell asleep on the couch by eight-thirty and snored to boot. I missed her.

But Scarlett was so happy, there was no way I could hold anything against her. She practically glowed twenty-four hours a day, always laughing, sitting out on the curb in front of Milton's with Michael, catching the grapes he tossed in her mouth. They hid out in her house for entire weekends, cooking spaghetti for Marion and renting movies. Scarlett said that after his breakup with Elizabeth at the end of the school year, Michael just didn't want to deal with the gossip. The day we went to the lake was the first time they'd risked exposure to our classmates, but it had been empty on the beaches, quiet, as we tossed the Frisbee and ate the picnic Scarlett packed. I sat with my *Mademoiselle* magazine, watching them swim together, dunking each other and laughing. It was later, just as we were leaving and the sun was setting in oranges and reds behind them, that I snapped the picture, the only one Scarlett had of them together. She'd grabbed it out of my hand the day I got them, taking my double copy, too, and giving it to Michael, who stuck it over the speedometer in his car, where it stayed until he traded the car a few weeks later for the motorcycle.

By the beginning of August, he'd told her he loved her. She said they'd been sitting at the side of her pool, legs dangling, when he just leaned over, kissed her ear, and said it. She'd whispered it as she told me, as if it was some kind of spell that could easily be broken by loud voices or common knowledge. *I love you.*

Which made it so much worse when he was gone so quickly, just two weeks later. The only boy who had ever said it to her and meant it. The rest of the world didn't know how much Scarlett loved Michael Sherwood. Even I couldn't truly have understood, much as I might have wanted to.

On the first day of school, Scarlett and I pulled into the parking lot, found a space facing the back of the vocational building, and parked. She turned off the engine of the Aspire, dropping her keychain in her lap. Then we sat.

"I don't want to do it," she said decisively.

"I know," I said.

"I mean it this year," she said, sighing. "I just don't think I have it in me. Under the circumstances."

"I know," I said again. Since the funeral, Scarlett had seemed to fold into herself; she hardly ever mentioned Michael, and I didn't either. We'd spent the entire first part of the summer talking about nothing but him, it seemed, and now he was out of bounds, forbidden. They'd planted a tree for him at school, with a special plaque, and the Sherwoods had put up their house for sale; I'd heard they were moving to Florida. Life was going on without him. But when he *was* mentioned, I hated the look that crossed her face, a mix of hurt and overwhelming sadness.

Now people were streaming by in new clothes, down the concrete path that led to the main building. I could hear voices and cars rumbling past. Sitting there in the Aspire, we held on to our last bit of freedom.

I sat and waited, shifting my new backpack, which sat between my feet, a stack of new shiny spiral notebooks and unsharpened pencils zipped away in its clean, neat compartments. It was always Scarlett who decided when it was time.

"Well," she said deliberately, folding her arms over her chest. "I guess we don't have much of a choice."

"Scarlett Thomas!" someone shrieked from beside the car, and we looked up to see Ginny Tabor, in a new short haircut and red lipstick, running past us holding hands with Brett Hershey, the football captain. Only Ginny could hook up with someone at a funeral. "School is this way!" she pointed with one red fingernail, then laughed, throwing her head back while Brett looked on as if waiting for someone to throw him something. She waggled her fingers at us and ran on ahead, dragging him behind her. I couldn't believe we'd spent so much time with her early that summer. It seemed like years ago now.

"God," Scarlett said, "I really hate her."

"I know." This was my line.

She took a deep breath, reached into the backseat for her

47

backpack, and pulled it into her lap. "Okay. There's really no avoiding it."

"I agree," I said, unlocking my door.

"Let's go then," she said grudgingly, getting out of the car and slamming the door behind her, hitching her backpack over one shoulder. I followed, merging into the crowd that carried us down through the teachers' parking lot to the courtyard in front of the main building. The first bell rang and everyone moved inside, suddenly thrown together in front of the doors and causing a major traffic jam of bodies and backpacks, elbows and feet, a tide I let carry me down the hallway to my home-room, keeping my eye on the back of Scarlett's red head.

"This is it," I said as we came up on Mr. Alexander's door, which was decorated with cardboard cutout frogs.

"Good luck," Scarlett called out, pulling open the door of her own homeroom and rolling her eyes one last time as she disap-peared inside.

Mr. Alexander's room already smelled of formaldehyde and he smiled at me, mustache wriggling, as I took my seat. The first day was always the same: they took roll, handed out schedules, and sent home about ten million different memos to your parents about busing and cafeteria rates and school rules. Beside me Ben Cruzak was already stoned and sleeping, head on his desk, with Missy Cavenaugh behind him doing her fin-gernails. Even the snake on Mr. Alexander's counter looked bored, after eating a mouse for the audience of science geeks who always hung out before first bell.

After about fifteen minutes of continuous droning over the intercom and a stack of memos an inch high on my desk, Alexander finally handed out our schedules. I could tell right away something was wrong with mine; I was signed up for Pre-calculus (when I hadn't even taken Algebra Two), French Three (when I took Spanish), and, worst of all, Band.

"Have a good day!" Alexander yelled above the bell as everyone headed toward the door. I went up to his desk. "Halley. Yes?"

"My schedule is wrong," I said. "I'm signed up for Band."

"Band?"

"Yes. And Pre-cal and French Three, and none of those are my classes."

"Hmmm," he said, and he was already looking over my head at the people streaming in, his first class. "Better go to your first class and get a pass to Guidance."

"But . . ."

He stood up, his mustache already moving. "Okay, people, take a seat and I'll be sending around a chart for you to fill in your chosen spot. This will be the seating chart for the rest of the semester, so I suggest you choose carefully. Don't tap on that glass, it makes the snake crazy. Now, this is Intro to Biology, so if you don't belong here . . ."

I walked out into the hallway, where Scarlett was leaning against the fire extinguisher waiting for me. "Hey. What's your first class?"

"Pre-cal."

"What? You haven't taken Algebra Two yet."

"I know." I switched my backpack to my other shoulder, already sick of school. "My schedule is so messed up. I'm signed up for Band."

"Band?"

"Yes." I stepped aside to let a pack of football players pass. "I have to go to Guidance."

"Oh, that sucks," she said. "I've got English and then Commercial Design, so I'll meet you after, okay? In the courtyard by the soda machines."

"I'm supposed to be in Band then," I said glumly.

"They can't force you to take Band," she said, laughing. I just looked at her. "They can't. Go to Guidance and I'll see you later."

The Guidance office was packed with people leaning against the walls and sitting on the floor, all waiting for the three available counselors. The receptionist, whose phone was ringing shrilly, nonstop, looked up at me with the crazed eyes of a rabid animal.

"What?" She had the kind of glasses that made her eyes seem wider than platters, magnified hundreds of times. "What do you need?"

"My schedule's all wrong," I said as the phone rang again, the row of red lights across it blinking. "I need to see a counselor."

"Right, okay," she said, grabbing the phone and holding one

finger up at me, like she was pushing a pause button. "Hello, Guidance office. No, he's not available now. Okay. Right, sure. Fine." She hung the phone up, the cord wrapped around her wrist. "Now, what? You need a counselor?"

"I got the wrong schedule. I'm signed up for Band."

"Band?" she blinked at me. "What's wrong with Band?"

"Nothing," I said as a kid carrying a clarinet case passed me, scowling. I lowered my voice. "Except I don't play an instrument. I mean, I've never been in Band."

"Well," she said slowly as the phone rang again, "maybe it's Introduction to Band. That's the beginning level."

"I never signed up for Band," I said a little bit louder, just to be heard over the phone. "I don't want to take it."

"Fine, well, then write your name on this sheet," she snapped, losing all patience whatsoever with debating the merits of musical training and grabbing the phone again in mid-ring. "We'll get to you as soon as we can."

I took a seat against the wall, under a shelf with a row of teenager-related books on it, with titles like *Sharing Our Differences: Understanding Your Adolescent* and *Peer Pressure: Finding Your Own Way*. My mother's second book, *Mixed Emotions: Mothers, Daughters, and the High School Years*, was there too, which just put me in a worse mood. If I'd really felt like torturing myself, I could have picked it up and read again how good and strong our relationship was.

It was hot in the room, and everyone was talking too loud,

crammed in together. A girl next to me was busy writing *Die Die Die* in all different colors on the cover of her notebook, a stack of Magic Markers beside her. I closed my eyes, thinking back to summer and cool pool water and long days with nothing to do except go swimming and sleep late.

I felt someone sit down beside me, leaning back against the wall close enough that their shoulder bumped mine. I pulled my arms across my chest, folding my knees against me. Then I felt a finger against my shoulder, *poke poke poke*. I opened my eyes, bracing myself for hours in Guidance Hell with Ginny Tabor.

But it wasn't Ginny. It was Macon Faulkner, and he was grinning at me. "What'd you do?" he asked.

"What?" The *Die Die Die* girl had switched to the back cover, methodically filling letter after letter with green ink.

"What'd you do?" he said again, then gestured toward the front desk. "It's only the first day and you're already in trouble."

"I am not," I said. "My schedule's messed up."

"Oh, sure," he said slowly, faking suspicion. He had on a baseball cap, his blond hair sticking out beneath, and a red T-shirt and jeans. He didn't have a backpack, just one plain spiral notebook with a pen stuck in the binding. Macon Faulkner was definitely not the school type. "You've probably already gotten into a fight and been suspended."

"No," I said, and I don't know if it was just the day I'd had or a sudden wave of Scarlett-like boldness, but I wasn't nervous talking to him. "I got signed up for all the wrong classes."

"Sure you did," he said easily. He settled back against the wall. "Now, you know how to handle yourself in there, right?"

I looked at him. "What?"

"How to handle yourself," He blinked at me. "Oh, please. You need big help. Okay, listen up. First, admit nothing. That's the most important rule."

"I'm not in trouble," I told him.

"Second," he said loudly, ignoring me, "try to divert them by mentioning anything about your therapist. For instance, say, 'My therapist always says I have a problem with authority.' Act real serious about it. Just the word 'therapist' will usually cut you some slack."

I laughed. "Yeah, right."

"It's true. And if that doesn't work, use the Jedi Mind Trick. But only if you really have to."

"The what?"

"The Jedi Mind Trick." He looked at me. "Didn't you ever see *Star Wars*?"

I thought back. "Sure I did."

"The Jedi Mind Trick is when you tell someone what you want them to think, and then they think it. Like, say I'm Mr. Mathers. And I say, 'Macon, you're already pushing the limits and it's only the first day of school. Is this any kind of way to start the year?' And you're me. What do you say?"

I shook my head. "I have no idea."

He rolled his eyes. "You say, 'Mr. Mathers, you're going to let this slide, because it's only the first day, it was an honest mistake, and the fire got put out as quickly as it was started.'"

"The fire?" I said. "What fire?"

"The point is," he said easily, flipping his hand, "that you just say that right back to him, very confidently. And then what does he say?"

"That you're crazy?"

"No. He says, 'Well, Macon, I'm going to let this slide because it's only the first day, it was an honest mistake, and the fire got put out as quickly as it started.'"

I laughed. "He will not."

"He will," he said, nodding his head. "It's the Jedi Mind Trick. Trust me." And when he smiled at me, I almost did.

"I'm really not in trouble." I handed him my schedule. "Unless that trick works on getting out of this stuff, I don't think I can use it."

He squinted at it. "Pre-calculus." He looked up at me, raising his eyebrows. "Really?"

"No. I barely got through Algebra."

He nodded at this; obviously we now had common ground. "French, P.E. . . . Hey, we're in the same P.E. period."

"Really?" Macon Faulkner and me, playing badminton. Learning golf strokes. Watching each other across a gymful of bouncing basketballs.

"Yep. Third period." He kept reading, then reached up to take

54

off his hat, shake his hair free, and put it back on backwards. "Science, English, blah, blah. . . . Oh! Looky *here*."

I already knew what was coming.

"Band," he said, smiling big. "You're in Band."

"I am *not* in Band," I said loudly, and that same kid with the clarinet looked over at me again. "It's a big mistake and no one believes me."

"What do you play?" he asked me.

"I don't," I said. I was trying to be indignant but he was so cute. I had no idea why he was even talking to me.

"You look like the flute type," he said thoughtfully, stroking his chin. "Or maybe the piccolo."

"Shut up," I said, surprising myself with my boldness.

He was laughing, shaking his head. "Maybe the triangle?" He held up his hand, pretending to hold one, and struck it wistfully with an imaginary wand.

"Leave me alone," I moaned, putting my head in my hands and secretly hoping more than anything that he wouldn't.

"Oh, now," he said, and I felt his hand come around my shoulder, squeezing it, and I wanted to die right there. "I'm just razzing you."

"This has been the worst day," I said as he took his arm back, sliding it across my shoulders. "The worst."

"Faulkner." The voice was loud, quieting down the entire room, and as I looked up I saw Mr. Mathers, the junior class head counselor, standing by the front desk, a folder in his hands. He didn't look happy. "Come on."

"That's me," Macon said cheerfully, standing up and grabbing his notebook. He tapped the side of his head with a finger, winking at me. "Remember. Jedi Mind Trick."

"Right," I said, nodding.

"See ya later, Halley," he said. He took his time walking over to Mr. Mathers, who clamped a hand on his shoulder and led him down the hallway. I couldn't believe he'd even remembered my name. The *Die Die Die* girl was staring at me now, as if by my short encounter with Macon Faulkner I was suddenly more important or worth noticing. I definitely *felt* different. Macon Faulkner, who before had said less than seven words to me total in my entire lifetime, had just appeared and talked to me for, like, minutes. As if we were friends, buddies, after only one day of knowing each other formally. It gave me a weird, jumpy feeling in my stomach and I thought suddenly of Scarlett, standing at register eight at Milton's, blushing down at a kiwi fruit.

"Hal—Hal Cooke. Is there a Hal Cooke here?" someone was saying in a bored voice from the front desk, and whatever elation I was experiencing screeched to a halt. It is times like the first day of school that I curse my parents for not naming me Jane or Lisa.

I stood up, grabbing my backpack. The counselor by the front desk, a huge African-American woman in a bright pink suit, was still trying to make out my name. "Halley," I said as I got closer. "It's Halley."

"Umm-hmmm." She turned around and gestured for me

to follow her down the hall past two offices to door number three. As I passed the middle door I thought I heard Macon's voice from behind the half-shut door, the low rumbling of Mr. Mathers mixing in. I wondered if his trick was working.

I had almost forgotten him altogether when I finally emerged, bruised and tired, with my new schedule in my hand, standing dazed outside the Guidance office as the bell ending second period rang and people suddenly began pouring out of classrooms and hallways. I went to the Coke machine to find Scarlett.

"Hey," she called out to me over the crowd of people pushing forward with their quarters and dollar bills, mad for soda. She waved two Cokes over her head, and I followed them until I found her against the far wall, the same one Michael Sherwood had his picture snapped against for the slide show.

She handed me a Coke. "How's Band?"

"Great," I said, opening my can and taking a long drink. "They say I'm a prodigy already at the oboe."

"Like hell," she said.

I smiled. "I got out of it, thank God. But you won't believe who I talked to in the Guidance office."

"Who?"

A loud booing noise went up at the Coke machine, drowning us out, and someone was sent to find the janitor. It always broke at least once each day, causing a minor mutiny. I waited until the crowd had calmed down, walking off jangling their change, before I said, "Macon Faulkner."

"Really?" She opened her backpack, rummaging through to find something. "How's he doing?"

"He was already in trouble, I think."

"Not surprising." She put her drink down. "God, I feel so rotten all of a sudden. Like just bad."

"Sick?"

"Kind of." She pulled out a bottle of Advil, popped the top, and took two. "It's probably just my well-documented aversion to school."

"Probably." I watched her as she leaned back against the brick wall, closing her eyes. In the sun her hair was a deep red, almost unreal, with brighter streaks running through it.

"But anyway," I said, "it was so weird. He just sat right next to me, just like that, and started talking my ear off. Like he knew me."

"He does know you."

"Yeah, but only from that one day of the funeral. Before then we'd never even been introduced."

"So? This is a small town, Halley. Everyone knows everyone."

"It was just weird," I said again, replaying it in my head, from the poking on my shoulder to him saying my name as he walked away, grinning. "I don't know."

"Well," she said slowly, reaching behind her head to pull her hair up in a ponytail, "maybe he likes you."

"Oh, stop it." My face started burning again.

"You never know. You shouldn't always assume it's so impossible."

The bell rang and I finished off my Coke, tossing it in the recycling bin beside me. "On to third period."

"Ugh. Oceanography." She put on her backpack. "What about you?"

"I have—" I started, but someone tapped my shoulder, then was gone as I turned around, the classic fake-out. I turned back to Scarlett and saw Macon over her shoulder, on his way to the gym.

"Come on," he yelled across the now-empty courtyard to me. "Don't want to be late for P.E."

"—P.E.," I finished sheepishly, feeling the burn of a new blush on my face. "I better go."

Scarlett just looked at me, shaking her head, like she already knew something I didn't. "Watch out," she said quietly, pulling her backpack over her shoulders.

"For what?" I said.

"You know," she said, and her face was so sad, watching me. Then she shook her head, smiling, and started to walk away. "Just be careful. Of P.E. and all that."

"Okay," I said, wondering if she had visions of me being nailed by errant Wiffle balls or blinded by flying badminton birdies, or if it was only just Macon, and everything he reminded her of, that made her so sad. "I will," I said.

She waved and walked off, up the hill to the Sciences building, and I turned and went the other way, pushing open the gym doors to that smell of mildew and Ben-Gay and sweaty mats, where Macon Faulkner was waiting for me.

P.E. became the most important fifty minutes of my life. Regardless of illness, national disaster, or even death, I would have shown up for third period, in my white socks and blue shorts, ready at the bell. Macon missed occasionally, and those days I was miserable, swatting around my volleyball halfheartedly and watching the clock. But the days he was there, P.E. was the best thing I had going.

Of course I acted like I hated it completely, because it was worse than being a Band geek to actually like P.E. But I was the only one in the girls' locker room who didn't complain loudly as we dressed out at 10:30 A.M. for another day of volleyball basics. All I had to do was walk out of the dressing room, nonchalant, acting like I was still half-asleep and too out of it to notice Macon, who was usually over by the water fountain in nonregulation tennis shoes and no socks (for which he got a minus-five each day of class). I'd sit a few feet over from him, wave, and pretend I wasn't expecting him to slide the few feet across the floor to sit beside me, which he always did. Always. Usually those few minutes before Coach Van Leek got organized with his clipboard were the best part of my day, every day. With a few variations, they went something like this:

Macon: What's up?
Me: I'm so beat.

Macon: Yeah, I was out late last night.

Me: (like I was ever allowed out past eight on school nights)
Me, too. I see you're not wearing socks today, again.

Macon: I just forget.

Me: You're gonna fail P.E., you know.

Macon: Not if you buy me some socks.

Me: (laughing sarcastically) Yeah, right.

Macon: Okay. Then it's on your head.

Me: Shut up.

Macon: You ready for volleyball?

Me: (like I'm so tough) Of course. I'm going to beat your
butt.

Macon: (laughing) Okay. Sure. We'll see.

Me: Okay. We'll see.

I lived for this.

Macon was not in school to Get an Education or Prepare for
College. It was just a necessary evil, tempered by junk food and
perpetual tardies. Half the time he showed up looking like he'd
just rolled out of bed, and he was forever getting yelled at by
Coach for sneaking food into P.E.: Cokes slipped in his backpack, Atomic Fireballs and Twinkies stuffed in his pockets. He
was the master of the forged excuse.

"Faulkner," Coach would bark when Macon showed up, ten
minutes late, with no socks and half a Zinger sticking out of his
mouth, "you'd best have a note."

"Right here," Macon would say cheerfully, drawing one out

of his pocket. We'd all watch attentively as Coach scrutinized it. Macon never looked worried. He failed all of P.E.'s notoriously easy quizzes, but he could copy any signature perfectly on the first try. It was a gift.

"It's all in the wrist," he'd tell me as he excused himself for another funeral or doctor's appointment with a flourish of his mother's name. I kept waiting for him to get caught. But it never happened.

He didn't seem to have a curfew; all I knew about his mom was that she didn't dot her *is*. I didn't even know where he lived. Macon was wild, different, and when I was with him, caught up in it all, I could play along like I was, too. He told me about parties where the cops always came, or road trips he up and took in the middle of the night, no planning, to the beach or D.C., just because he felt like it. He showed up on Mondays with wild stories, T-shirts of bands I'd never heard of, smeared entry stamps from one club or another on the back of his hands. He dropped names and places I'd never heard, but I nodded, committing them to memory and repeating them back to Scarlett as if I knew them all myself, had been there or seen that. Something in him, about him, with his easy loping walk and sly smile, his past secret and mysterious while mine was all laid out and clear, actually documented, intrigued me beyond belief.

Scarlett, of course, just shook her head and smiled as she listened to me prattle on, detailing every word and gesture of our inane sock-and-volleyball conversations. And she sat by without saying anything whenever he didn't show up and I sulked at lunch, picking at my sandwich and saying it wasn't like I liked him anyway. And sometimes, I'd look up at her and see that same sad look on her face, as if Michael Sherwood had suddenly reared up from wherever she'd carefully placed him, reminding her of the beginning of summer when she was the one with all the stories to tell.

Meanwhile, all through September, things were happening. My father's radio show on T104 had gotten an overhaul and format change over the summer and was suddenly The Station to Listen To. In the morning I heard his voice coming from cars in the parking lot or at traffic lights or even at the Zip Mart where Scarlett and I stopped before school for Cokes and gas. My father, making jokes and razzing callers and playing all the music I listened to, the soundtrack to every move I made. *Brian in the Morning!* the billboard out by the mall said; *He's better than Wheaties!* My father thought this was hysterical, even better than *A Neighborhood of Fiends*, and my mother accused him of always taking the long way home just to look at it. His was the voice I heard no matter where I went, inseparable from my life away from our house. It was somewhat unsettling that listening to my *father* was suddenly cool.

The worst was when he talked about me. I was in the Zip Mart before school one day, and of course they had T104 on; people were calling in sharing their most embarrassing moments. About half my school was buying cigarettes and cookies and candy bars, that early morning sugar and nicotine rush. I was at the head of the line when I heard my name.

"Yeah, I remember when my daughter Halley was about five," my father said. "Man, this is like the funniest thing I ever saw. We were at this neighborhood cookout, and my wife and I . . ."

Already my face was turning red. I could feel my temperature jump about ten degrees with each word he said. The clerk, of course, picked this moment to change the register tape. I was stuck.

"So we're standing there talking to some neighbors, right next to this huge mud puddle; it had been raining for a few days and everything was still kind of squishy, you know? Anyway, Halley yells out to me, 'Hey, Dad, look!' So my wife and I look over and here she comes, running like little kids do, all crooked and sideways, you know?"

"Damn," the clerk said, hitting the register tape with his fist. It wasn't going in. I was in hell.

"And I swear," my father went on, now chuckling, "I was thinking as she got closer and closer to that mud puddle, *Man, she's going in.* I could see it coming."

Behind me somebody tittered. My stomach turned in on itself.

"And she hits the edge of that puddle, still running, and her feet just—they just flew out from under her." Now my father dissolved in laughter, along with, oh, about a thousand commuters and office workers all over the tri-county area. "I mean,

she skidded on her butt, all the way across that puddle, bumping along with this completely shocked look on her face, until
she, like, landed right at out feet. Covered in mud. And we're
all trying not to laugh, God help us. It was the funniest thing I
think I have ever seen. *Ever.*"

"That'll be one-oh-nine," the clerk said to me suddenly. I
threw my dollar and some change at him, pushing past all the
grinning faces out to the car, where Scarlett was waiting.

"Oh, man," she said as I slid in. "How embarrassed are *you*
right now?"

"Shut up," I said. All day I had to listen to the mud jokes and
have people nudge me and giggle. Macon christened me
Muddy Britches. It was the worst.

"I'm sorry," my father said to me, first thing that night. I ignored him, walking up the stairs. "I really, really am. It just
kind of came out, Halley. Really."

"Brian," my mother said. "I think you should just keep Halley's life off limits. Okay?"

This from the woman who wrote about me in two books. My
parents both made their livings humiliating me.

"I know, I know," he said, but he was smiling. "It was just so
funny, though. Wasn't it?" He giggled, then tried to straighten
up. "Right?"

"Real funny," I said. "Hysterical."

This was just one example of how my parents were suddenly,
that fall, making me crazy. It wasn't just the statewide shame
on the radio, either. It was something I couldn't put my finger

65

on or define clearly, but a whole mishmash of words and incidents, all rolling quickly and building, like a snowball down a hill, to gather strength and bulk to flatten me. It wasn't what they said, or even just the looks they exchanged when they asked me how school was that day and I just mumbled *fine* with my mouth full, glancing wistfully over at Scarlett's, where I was sure she was eating alone, in front of the TV, without having to answer to anyone. There had been a time, once, when my mother would have been the first I'd tell about Macon Faulkner, and what P.E. had become to me. But now I only saw her rigid neck, the tight, thin line of her lips as she sat across from me, reminding me to do my homework, no I couldn't go to Scarlett's it was a school night, don't forget to do the dishes and take the trash out. All things she'd said to me for years. Only now they all seemed loaded with something else, something that fell between us on the table, blocking any further conversation.

I knew my mother wouldn't understand about Macon Faulkner. He was the furthest I could get from her, Noah Vaughn, and the perfect daughter I'd been in that Grand Canyon picture. This world I was in now, of high school and my love affair with P.E., with Michael Sherwood gone, had no place for my mother or what she represented. It was like one of those tests where they ask what thing doesn't belong in this group: an apple, a banana, a pear, a tractor. There wasn't anything she could do about it. My mother, for all her efforts, was that tractor.

Chapter Four

Macon finally asked me out on October 18 at 11:27 A.M. It was a monumental moment, a flashbulb memory. I hadn't had a lot of incredible events in my life, and I intended to remember every detail of this one.

It was a Friday, the day of our badminton quiz. After I handed in my paper, I pulled out my English notebook and started to do my vocabulary, at the same time keeping a close eye on Macon as he chewed his pencil, stared at the ceiling and struggled with the five short questions of the same test Coach had been giving out for the last fifteen years.

A few minutes later he got up to hand in his test, sticking his pencil behind his ear as he passed me. I braced myself, reading the same vocab word, *feuilleton*, over and over again, like a spell, trying to draw him over to talk to me. *Feuilleton, feuilleton*, as he handed his test to Coach, then stretched his arms over his head and started back toward me, taking his time. *Feuilleton, feuilleton*, as he got closer and closer, then grinned as he passed me, heading back to where he'd been sitting. *Feuilleton, feuilleton*, I kept thinking hopelessly, the word swimming in front of my eyes. And then finally, on the last *feuilleton*, the sound of his notebook sliding up next to me, and him plopping down beside it. And just like that, I felt that goofy third-period P.E. rush, like the planets had suddenly aligned and everything was okay for the next fifteen minutes while I had him all to myself.

"So," he said, lying back on the shiny gym floor, his head right next to my leg, "who invented the game of badminton?"

I looked at him. "You don't know?"

"I'm not saying that. I'm just asking what you said."

"I said the right answer."

"Which is?"

I just shrugged. "You know. That guy."

"Oh, yeah." He nodded, grinning, running a hand through his damp hair. "Right. Well, that's what I said too, Muddy Britches."

"Well, good for you." I turned the page of my English notebook, pretending I was concentrating on it.

"What are you doing this weekend?" he said.

"I don't know yet." We had this conversation every Friday; he always had big plans, and I always acted like I did.

"Big date with old Noah?"

"No," I said. Noah's P.E. class had come in for a volleyball tournament with ours, and of course when he grunted hello to me I had to explain who he was. Why I said he'd been my boyfriend I had no idea; I'd been trying to live it down ever since.

"What about you?" I asked him.

"There's this party, I don't know," he said. "Over in the Arbors."

"Really."

"Yeah. It might be lame, though."

I nodded, because that was always safest, then lied, which was second best. "Oh, yeah. I think Scarlett might have mentioned it."

"Yeah, I'm sure she knows about it." Scarlett was our middle ground. "You guys should come, you know?"

"Maybe we will," I said, having already made up my mind we would be there even if God himself tried to stop us. "If she wants to. I don't know."

"Well," he said, looking up at me with a shock of blond hair falling across his forehead, "even if she can't make it, you should come."

"I can't come by myself," I said without thinking.

"You won't be by yourself," he said. "I'll be there."

"Oh." That was when I looked at the clock, over his head, marking this moment forever. The culmination of all those badminton matches and volleyball serves, of laps run around the gym in circles. This was what I'd been waiting for. "Okay. I'll be there."

"Good." He was smiling at me, and right then I would have agreed to anything he asked, as dangerous as that was. "I'll see you there."

The bell rang then, loud and jarring and bounding off the walls of the huge, hollow gym as everyone stood up. Coach Van Leek was yelling about bowling starting on Monday and how we should all come ready to learn the five-step approach, but I wasn't hearing him, or anyone, as Macon grabbed his notebook and stood up, sticking out a hand to me to pull me to my feet. I just looked up at him, wondering what I could be getting myself into, but it didn't matter. I put my hand in Macon's, feeling his fingers close over mine. I let him pull me toward him, to my feet, and my eyes were wide open.

After school Scarlett and I went to her house, where Marion was busy getting ready for a big date with an accountant she'd met named Steve Michaelson. She was painting her fingernails and chain-smoking while Scarlett and I ate potato chips and watched.

"So," I said, "what's this Steve guy like anyway?"

"He's very nice," Marion said in her gravelly voice, exhaling a stream of smoke. "Very serious, but in a sweet way. He's the friend of a friend of a friend."

"Tell her the other thing," Scarlett said, popping another chip in her mouth.

"What thing?" Marion shook the bottle of polish.

"You know."

"What?" I said.

Marion held up one hand, examining it. "Oh, it's just this thing he does. It's a hobby."

"Tell her," Scarlett said again, then raised her eyebrows at me so I knew something good was coming.

Marion looked at her, sighed, and said, "He's in this group. It's like a history club, where they study the medieval period together, on weekends."

"That's interesting," I said as Scarlett pushed her chair out and went to the sink. "A history club."

"Marion." Scarlett ran her hands under the faucet. "Tell her what he *does* in this club."

"What? What does he do?" I couldn't stand it.

"He dresses up," Scarlett said before Marion even opened her mouth. "He has this, like, medieval alter-ego, and on the weekends he and all his friends dress up in medieval clothes and become these characters. They joust and have festivals and sing ballads."

"They don't joust," Marion grumbled, starting on her other hand.

"Yes, they do," Scarlett said. "I talked to him the other night. He told me everything."

"Well, so what?" Marion said. "Big deal. I think it's kind of sweet, actually. It's like a whole other world."

"It's, like, crazy," Scarlett said, coming back to the table and sitting down beside me. "He's a nut."

"He is not."

"You know what his alter-ego name is?" she asked me. "Just guess."

I looked at her. "I cannot imagine."

Marion was acting like she couldn't hear us, engrossed in buffing a pinky nail.

"Vlad," Scarlett said dramatically. "Vlad the Impaler."

"It's not the Impaler," Marion said snippily, "it's the Warrior. There's a difference."

"Whatever." Scarlett was never happy with anyone Marion dated; mostly they were men who stared at her uncomfortably as they passed out the door on weekend mornings.

"Well," I said slowly as Marion finished her left hand and waved it in the air, "I'm sure he's very nice."

"He is," she said simply, getting up from the table and walking to the stairs, fingers outstretched and wiggling in front of her. "And Scarlett would know it too, if she ever gave anyone a fair chance."

We heard her go upstairs, the floor creaking over our heads as she walked down the hall to her room. Scarlett picked up the dirty cotton balls, tossing them out, and collected the polish and the remover, putting them back in the basket by the bathroom where they belonged.

"I've given lots of people chances," she said suddenly, as if Marion was still in the room to hear her. "But there's only so much faith you can have in people."

We sat in her bedroom and watched as Steve arrived, in his Hyundai hatchback, with flowers. He didn't look much like a warrior or an impaler as he walked Marion to the car, holding her door open and shutting it neatly behind her. Scarlett didn't look as they drove off, turning her back on the window, but I pressed my palm against the glass, waving back at Marion as they pulled away.

When I went home later, my mother was in the kitchen reading the paper. "Hi there," she said. "How was school?"

"Fine." I stood in the open kitchen doorway, my eyes on the stairs.

"How was that math test? Think you did okay?"

"Sure," I said. "I guess."

"Well, the Vaughns are coming over tonight for a movie, if you want to hang around. They haven't seen you in a while."

Noah Vaughn was in eleventh grade and he still spent his Friday nights watching movies with his parents and mine. I couldn't believe he'd ever been my boyfriend. "I'm going over to Scarlett's."

"Oh." She was nodding. "Okay. What are you two doing?"

I thought of Macon, of that clock in the gym, of the momentous day I'd had, and held back everything. "Nothing much. Just hanging out. I think we're going out for pizza."

A pause. Then, "Well, be in by eleven. And don't forget you're mowing the lawn tomorrow. Right?"

My mother, deep into writing a book about teens and responsibility, had decided I needed to do more chores around the house. *It enhances the sense of family,* she'd said to me. *We're all working toward a common goal.*

"The lawn," I said. "Right."

I was halfway up the stairs when she said, "Halley? If you and Scarlett get bored, come on over. The more the merrier."

"Okay," I said, and I thought again how she always had to have her hands in whatever I did, keeping me with her or herself, somehow, with me, even when I fought hard against it. If

I'd told her about Macon, I could hear her voice already, asking questions: *Whose party was it? Would the parents be there? Would there be drinking?* I imagined her calling the house, demanding to speak to the parents like she had at the first boy-girl party I'd ever gone to. I knew I had to keep him to myself, as I'd slowly begun to keep everything. We had secrets now, truths and half-truths, that kept her always at arm's length, behind a closed door, miles away.

Scarlett and I pulled up at the party at nine-thirty, which we figured was fashionably late since there were already lines of cars up and down the street, parked haphazardly on the curbs and against mailboxes. It was Ginny Tabor's house, Ginny Tabor's party, and the first thing we saw when we walked up the driveway was Ginny Tabor, already drunk and sitting on the back of her mother's BMW with a wine cooler in one hand and a cigarette in the other.

"*Scarlett!*" she screamed at us as we came up on the front porch, which was white and chocolate brown like the rest of the house. The Tabors lived in what looked like a big gingerbread house, all Tudor and eaves and flower boxes.

Ginny was still yelling at Scarlett as she jumped off the back of the car, dragging Brett Hershey by the hand.

"Hey, girl!" Ginny said as she came closer, stumbling a bit, past a big fountain that was in the middle of the circular driveway. She was in a red dress and heels, too fancy for just a Friday night beer bash. "You're just the person I want to talk to."

Beside me I heard Scarlett sigh. She had a cold and hadn't wanted to come out anyway. It was only because I'd begged her, not wanting to make an entrance by myself, that she'd gotten up off the couch where she'd been comfortable with her tissue box and the television. And that was only after I'd had to dodge Noah Vaughn, who sat sulking in our kitchen as I said good-bye, glaring at me, as if he'd expected me to suddenly decide to be his girlfriend again. His little sister, Clara, clung to my legs and begged me to stay, and my mother reminded me again to bring Scarlett over if I wanted. I half expected them to tie me down and force me to be with them, keeping me from what I was sure would be the most important night of my life.

I only hoped that Macon could appreciate what I'd been through to meet him.

I kept trying to look for him without being obvious, while Ginny threw her arms around Scarlett. Brett stood by looking uncomfortable. He was a steely kind of guy, an All-American jock, with broad shoulders and a crew cut.

"This has been the *best* night. You would not believe the stuff that has happened," Ginny said into Scarlett's face, and I could smell her breath from where I was standing. "Laurie Miller and Kent Hutchinson have been in the guest bedroom like all night, and the neighbors already called the police once. But our housekeeper is chaperoning, so they couldn't do anything but tell us to keep it down."

"Really." Scarlett sniffled, reaching in her pocket for a tissue.

"And Elizabeth Gunderson is here, with all those girls she's been hanging out with since Michael died. They're all up in the attic drinking wine and crying. I heard they had some shrine set up to him, but I'm not sure if that's just a rumor." She took another swig of her wine cooler. "Isn't that weird? Like they're trying to bring him back or something."

"We should go in," I said, grabbing the back of Scarlett's shirt and pulling her behind me. Inside, the music had stopped suddenly, and I could hear a girl laughing. "We're looking for someone."

"Who?" Ginny shouted after us, as Brett wrapped his arms around her waist, holding her back. The music came back on inside, bass thumping, as we got closer. She yelled something I couldn't make out, words half slurred and unfinished, as we went inside.

I pushed the half-open door with my hand, then stepped in and promptly bumped right into Caleb Mitchell and Sasha Benedict, who were lip-locked next to the grandfather clock. In the living room, I could see some people dancing, others lying across the couch in front of the TV, an MTV VJ talking soundlessly on the wide screen. Further back, in the den, a group of girls were playing quarters, bouncing a coin across the coffee table. I didn't see Macon anywhere.

"Come on," Scarlett said, and I followed her down the hall into the kitchen, where a bunch of people were perched on the bright white counters and sitting at the table, smoking cigarettes and drinking. Liza Corbin, who had been the biggest geek before a summer of modeling school and a nose job, was perched on some linebacker's lap, head thrown back against his shoulder, laughing. Another girl from my homeroom was sitting on the floor, knees pulled up to her chest, holding a wine cooler and looking kind of green. Scarlett walked down a side hallway and pushed open a door, surprising a Hispanic woman inside who was sitting on a twin bed watching a *Falcon Crest* rerun and doing needlepoint.

"Sorry," Scarlett said as the woman looked up at us, eyes wide, and we closed the door again. She shook her head, smiling. "That must be the chaperone."

"Must be," I said. I was beginning to think this whole night had been a mistake; we'd seen just about every member of the football team, all the cheerleaders, about half the school tramps, and no Macon anywhere. I felt stupid in the clothes I'd so carefully picked out to seem thrown on at random, as if I went to parties to meet boys all the time.

We went upstairs, still looking, but he wasn't there. I felt like a fool, searching for him when he was probably miles away, on the way to the beach or D.C., just because he felt like it.

I could tell something big was happening before we even got back downstairs; it was too quiet, and I could hear someone screaming. As I peered around the corner, I saw Ginny in the living room, standing over a pile of broken glass on the carpet. A red stain that matched her dress was seeping into the thick, white pile. She was unsteady, her face flushed, one finger pointed at the door.

"That's it, get *out!*" she screamed at the group of people

huddled around her, who all stepped back a couple of feet and kept staring. "I *mean* it. *Now!!!*"

"Uh-oh," Scarlett said from behind me. "I wonder what happened."

"Someone broke some precious heirloom," a girl in front of us, who I recognized from P.E., said in a low voice. "Wedgwood or crystal or something, and spilled red wine all over the carpet."

Ginny was down on her hands and knees now, blotting the carpet with a T-shirt, while a few of her friends stood around uncertainly, offering cleaning tips. The crowd around the living room started to shift toward the door.

"This is lame," some girl in a halter top said over her shoulder as she passed us. "And there's no beer left anyway."

Her friend, a redhead with a pierced nose, nodded, flipping her long hair back with one hand. "I heard there's a frat party uptown tonight. Let's go up there. It's gotta be better than all these high-school boys."

One by one Ginny's friends drifted off, gathering their cigarettes and purses and backing out of the room. Brett Hershey, ever the gentleman, had found a brush and dustpan and was cleaning up the glass while Ginny sat down on the carpet, crying, as the house got quieter and quieter.

I just looked at Scarlett, wondering what we should do, and she glanced into the living room and called out in a cheerful voice, "Bye, Ginny. See you Monday."

Ginny looked up at us. Her mascara had run, leaving black

smudges under her eyes. "My parents are going to kill me," she wailed, patting at the stained carpet helplessly. "That glass was a wedding gift. And there's no way I can cover this."

"Soda water," Scarlett said as I inched open the door, hoping for a clean getaway. Ginny just looked up at us, confused. "And a little Clorox. It'll take it right out."

"Soda water," Ginny repeated slowly. "Thanks."

We slipped out the door, letting it fall shut behind us. Someone had left an empty six-pack container on the fountain, and a bottle was floating in its sparkling water and knocking against its sides, clinking, as we passed.

"What a drag," Scarlett said as we came up on her car. She was being quietly respectful of my sulking. "Really."

"I should have known better," I said. "Like he was really asking me to meet him."

"It sounded like he was."

"Whatever," I said, getting in the car as she started the engine. "I'm probably better off."

"I know *I* am," she said cheerfully, pulling out onto the street, the big houses of the Arbors looming on either side of us. "Now I don't have to hear the sordid details of P.E. every day."

"Leave me alone." I leaned my head against the cool glass of the window. "This sucks."

"I know," she said softly, reaching over and patting my leg. "I know."

When we got home we sat out on the front steps, drinking

Cokes and not talking much. Scarlett blew her nose a lot and I tried to salvage what was left of my pride, making lame excuses neither one of us believed.

"I never really liked him," I said. "He's too wild anyway."

"Yeah," she said, but I could feel her smiling in the dark. "He's not your type."

"He isn't," I went on, ignoring her. "He needs to be dating Ginny Tabor. Or Elizabeth Gunderson. Someone with a reputation to match his. I was so stupid for even thinking he'd look twice at someone like me."

She leaned back against the door, stretching out her legs. "Why do you say stuff like that?"

"Stuff like what?" Across the street I could see Noah Vaughn pass in front of our window.

"*Someone like you.* Any guy would be damn lucky to have you, Halley, and you know it. You're beautiful and smart and loyal and funny. Elizabeth Gunderson and Ginny are just stupid girls with loud voices. That's it. You're special."

"Scarlett," I said. "Please."

"You don't have to believe me," she said, waving me off. "But it's true, and I know you better than anyone. Macon Faulkner would be damn lucky if *you* chose *him*." She sneezed again, fumbling around for a Kleenex. "Shoot, I'll be right back. Hold on."

She went inside, the door creaking slowly shut behind her, and I sat back against the steps, staring up at my brightly lit house and the dark sky above it. Inside, my father was probably popping popcorn and drinking a beer, while my mother and Mrs. Vaughn talked too much during the movie so you couldn't hear anything. Noah was still sulking, for sure, and Clara was probably already curled up asleep on my bed, to be carried to the car later. I knew those Friday nights by heart. But my mother didn't understand why I couldn't spend the rest of my life on that couch with Noah, a bowl of popcorn in my lap, with her on my other side. Why just the thought of it was enough to make me feel like I couldn't breathe, or too sad to even look her in the eye.

Then, suddenly, I noticed someone walking up the street toward my house, dodging through the McDowells' yard and through their hedge, then darting across the sidewalk and down the far end of my front yard. I sat up straighter, watching the shadow slip past the row of trees my mother was trying to nudge into growing against the fence, stepping smoothly over the hole where my father had sprained his ankle mowing the lawn the summer before. I got up off the steps and crept across the street, coming up on the side of my house.

Whoever it was finally came to a stop under my side bedroom window, then stood looking up at it for a good long while before bending down, picking up something, and tossing it. I heard a *ping* as it bounced off the glass and I moved closer, close enough to see the person more clearly as he tossed up another rock, missing altogether and hitting the gutter, which was loose and rattled loudly. I was also close enough to hear the voice now, a hushed whisper.

"Halley!" Then a pause, and another ping of a rock hitting the glass. "Halley!"

I moved behind the tree that shaded my bedroom in summer, a mere two feet away from Macon Faulkner, who seemed determined to break my window or at least weaken it to the point of spontaneous collapse.

"Halley!" He stepped closer to the house, craning his neck.

I crept up behind him, silent, and tapped him on the shoulder just as he was launching another rock; he jerked to face me, not quite completing the throw, so it rained back down on him, bouncing off his head and landing between us on the ground.

"Shoot," he said, all flustered. He'd almost jumped out of his skin. "Where did you come from?"

"Why are you trying to break my window?"

"I'm not. I was trying to get your attention."

"But I wasn't home." I said.

"I didn't know that," he said. "You scared the crap out of me."

"Sorry," I said, and I couldn't believe he was here, in my yard, like some kind of ghost I'd conjured up with wishful thinking. "How'd you know this was my window anyway?"

"Just did," he said simply. I was noticing that he didn't usually explain what he didn't have to. He was still a little shaken but now he grinned at me, his teeth white, like this was not unusual or amazing. "Where were you?"

"When?"

"Earlier. I thought you were coming to that party."

"I was there," I said, trying to sound casual. "I didn't see you."

"Oh," he said confidently, "that's a lie."

"I was," I said. "We just got home."

"I have been there since seven o'clock," he said loudly, talking over me, "and I was looking for you, and waiting, and you stood me up—"

"No, you stood *me* up," I said in a louder voice, "and I have Scarlett to vouch for it."

"Scarlett? She wasn't there either."

"Yes, she was. She was with me." I looked back across the street, where she was standing on the steps, one hand shielding her eyes, looking over at us. I waved, and she waved back, then sat down and blew her nose.

"I was upstairs," he said. "I never saw you."

"Where upstairs?"

"In the attic."

"Oh," I said. "We didn't go there."

"Why not?"

I just looked at him. "Why would we?"

"I don't know," he said, out of arguments. "I did."

A light came on upstairs in my room, and I heard the window sliding open. My father stuck his head out, looking around, and I pushed Macon into the shadow of the house, then stepped back into the brightness of the side porch light.

"Hi," I called out, startling my father, who jerked back and slammed his head on the window. "It's just me."

"Halley?" He turned around, rubbing his head, and said into the house, "It's just Halley, Clara, go back to sleep. It's fine."

Macon was looking up at my father; if he had glanced down, he could have made him out easily.

"I was looking for something," I said suddenly. I hadn't lied to my father very much, so I was grateful for the dark. "I dropped a bracelet of Scarlett's out here and we were looking for it."

My father craned his neck, looking around. "A bracelet? Is Scarlett down there?"

"Yes," I said, and the lies just rolled out of me, on and on, "I mean, no, she was but we found it and she went back to her house. Because she's got this cold and all. So I was just, um, getting ready to follow her. When you opened the window."

In front of me, Macon was quietly snickering.

"Isn't it about time for you to be in?" my father said. "It's almost ten-thirty."

"I'll be home by eleven."

"You two should come over now. We've got this great movie on that Noah brought and I just made popcorn."

"That sounds great, but I better get back across the street," I said quickly, stepping back under the shield of the tree behind me. "I'll see you in the morning."

He snapped his fingers. "That's right! Don't you have a morning date with—" and here he paused, dramatically—"the Beast?"

I was about to die.

84

"The Beast?" Macon whispered, grinning. Above us, my father was making growling noises.

The Beast, of course, was my father's pet name for his mower, his most prized possession. He was so embarrassing.

"Yeah," I said, willing him with all my power to go away. "I guess."

"Okay, then," he said, starting to pull the window shut and having to bank it with the side of his hand at the point where it always stuck. "Don't creep around out there, okay? You scared Clara to death."

"Right," I said as the window clicked shut, and I could see my room behind him until the light cut off. I stood there, breathing heavily, until I was sure he was gone.

"You," Macon said, stepping out where I could see him, "are such a liar."

"I am not," I said. "Well, not usually. But he would have freaked if he'd seen you."

"You want me to leave?" He stepped closer to me, and even in the dark I knew every inch of his face from all those hours of P.E., studying him across a badminton net.

"Yes," I said loudly, and he pretended to walk off but I grabbed his arm, pulling him back. "I'm kidding."

"You sure?"

"Yes." And for a minute it was like I wasn't even myself anymore; I could have been any girl, someone bold and reckless. There was something about Macon that made me act different, giving that black outline some inside color, at last. I was still holding his arm, my face hot, and in the dark I might have been Elizabeth Gunderson or Ginny Tabor or even Scarlett, any girl that things happen to. And as he leaned in to kiss me, I thought of nothing but how unbelievable it was that this was all happening, in my side yard, the most familiar of places.

Just then a car came screeching around the corner, music blaring. It passed my house, horn beeping, and then turned onto Honeysuckle, where it sat idling.

"I gotta go," Macon said, kissing me again. "I'll call you tomorrow."

"Wait—" I said as he pulled away, holding my hand until he had to let go of it. "Where are you going?"

"Faulkner!" I heard a voice yell from down the street. "Where are you?"

"Bye, Halley," he whispered, smiling at me as he slipped easily around the side of the house, disappearing into the darkness of my backyard. I leaned around the corner, watching him as he ducked beneath the kitchen window, where Noah Vaughn was standing. His face was stony, solemn, as he stared at me, holding a Coke in his hand. He couldn't see what I saw: Macon, my last glimpse, vanishing into thin air.

The next morning my father was grinning when I came outside. He loved this. "Well, hey there, lawn girl. Ready to take on the Beast?" Then he made the growling noise again.

"You're not funny," I said.

"Sure I am." He chuckled. "Better get started before it gets any warmer. It'll take you a good two hours, at least."

"Shut *up*," I said, which just made him laugh harder. My father believes our lawn is impossible; over the years it had sent yard services and neighborhood mowing boys running for their lives. My father, the only one who could navigate it safely, saw himself as a warrior, victorious among the grass clippings.

"Okay, here's the thing," he said, now suddenly serious. "There's the Hole between the junipers that got me last summer, as well as a row of tree roots by the fence that were made specifically to pull you to the side and cut your motor. Not to mention the ruts in the backyard and the series of hidden tree stumps. But you'll do fine."

"Just let me get it over with." I leaned down and started the mower, pushing it to the front curb, with him still behind me chuckling.

It was hot, loud, and too bright out in that yard. I got sleepy, then careless, and hit the Hole, which of course I'd forgotten; my ankle twisted in it and I fell forward, the mower flying out from under me and sputtering to a stop. By this time my father had gone to the fence by the driveway and was busy talking lawns or golf or whatever with Mr. Perkins, our neighbor. Neither one of them noticed me do a faceplant in the grass, then kick the mower a few feet out of pure vengeance.

I heard a horn beep and turned to see a red pickup truck sliding to a stop by the curb, a green tarp thrown over something in the truck bed. It was Macon.

"Hey," he said, getting out of the truck and slamming the door. "How's it going?"

"Fine," I said. "Actually, it's not. I just fell down." I looked over at my father, who was staring right back at us.

"That your dad?" Macon said.

"Yep," I said. "That's him."

Macon looked around the yard, at the small patch I'd done so far and the high grass that lay ahead all around us, spurred on by a straight week of rain. "So," he said confidently, "you want some help?"

"Oh, you don't want to . . ." I said, but he was already walk-ing back to the truck, pulling the tarp aside to reveal a mower twice the size of mine, which he wheeled off a ramp on the back. He had on his BROADSIDE HOME AND GARDEN baseball hat, which he flipped around backwards, readying for action.

"You don't understand," I said to him as he started checking the gas, examining the wheels, "this lawn is, like, impossible. You practically need a map to keep from killing yourself."

"Are you underestimating my ability as a lawn-service provider?" he asked, looking up at me. "I sincerely *hope* that you are not."

"I'm not," I said quickly, "but it's just . . . I mean, it's really hard."

"Psssh," he said, fanning me off with one hand. "Just stand back, okay?" And then he stood up, pulled the cord, and the mower roared to life and started across the lawn with Macon guiding it. It sucked up the grass, marking a swath twice as wide as I'd been managing with the Beast. I turned around to look at my father, who was staring at Macon as he glided over the tree roots and past the Hole, and edged the fence perfectly.

"Halley," my father said from behind me, yelling over the roar of the mower, "this is supposed to be *your* job."

"I'm working," I said quickly, starting up my own mower, which puttered quietly like a kid's toy as I pushed it along between the juniper bushes. "See?"

I didn't hear what he said as Macon passed us again, the mower annihilating the grass and leaving a smooth, green trail behind him. He nodded at my father, all business, as he turned the corner and disappeared around the side of the house, the roar scaring all the birds at the feeder on the back porch into sudden flight.

"Who is that kid?" my father said, craning his neck around the side of the house.

"What?" I was still pushing my mower, circling the trees by the fence. The smell of cut grass filled the air, sweet and pungent.

"Who is he?"

I cut off the mower. In the backyard I could see Macon mowing around the hidden tree stumps. My father saw it too, his face shocked. "He's my friend," I said.

There must have been some giveaway in how I said it because suddenly his face changed and I could tell he wasn't thinking about the lawn anymore.

My mother came out the front door, holding her coffee

cup. "Brian? There's some strange boy mowing the lawn."

"I know," my father said. "I'm handling it."

"I thought that was Halley's job," she said like I wasn't even there. "Right?"

"Right," he said in a tired voice. "It's under control."

"Fine." She went back inside, but I could see her standing in the glass door, watching us.

"This was supposed to be your job," he said, as if reading off a script she'd written.

"I didn't *ask* him to do it," I said as the mower roared around the corner of the house, edging the garage. "We were talking about it last night and I guess he just remembered. He works mowing lawns, Dad. He just wanted to help me out."

"Well, that doesn't change the fact that it was your responsibility." It was an effort, but he was fading.

The mower was roaring toward us now as Macon finished off the patch by the front walk. Then he came closer, until the noise was deafening, before finally cutting it off. We all stood there in the sudden silence, looking at each other. My ears were ringing.

"Macon," I said slowly, "this is my dad. Dad, this is Macon Faulkner."

Macon stuck his hand out and shook my father's, then leaned back against the mower, taking off his hat. "Man, that is one tough yard you have there," he said. "Those tree stumps out back almost killed me."

My father, hesitant, couldn't help but smile. He wasn't sure how my mother would want him to react to this. "Well," he said, easing back and sticking his hands in his pockets, "they've brought down a few in their time, let me tell you."

"I can believe it," Macon said. I looked over his head, back toward the house, and saw my mother standing in the doorway, still watching. I couldn't make out her expression. "This thing is equipped with sensors and stuff, so it makes it easier."

"Sensors?" my father stepped a little closer, peering down at the mower's control console. He was clearly torn between doing the Right Thing and his complete love of garden tools and accessories. "Really."

"This thing here," Macon explained, pointing, "shows how far you've gone. And then anything over a height the blade can handle pops up here, on the Terrain Scope, so you can work around it."

"Terrain Scope," my father repeated dreamily.

Then we all heard it; the front door opening and my mother's voice, shattering the lawn reverie with a shrillness she had never been able to control. "Brian? Could you come here a moment, please?"

My father started to back away from Macon, toward the house, his eyes still on the mower. "Coming," he called out, then turned to face her, climbing the steps. I could see her mouth moving, angrily, before he even got to the porch.

"Thanks," I said to Macon. "You saved me."

"No problem." He started pushing the mower back to the curb. "I gotta get this thing back, though. I'll see you later, right?"

"Yeah," I said, watching him climb back into the truck. He took his hat off and tossed it onto the seat. "I'll see you later."

He drove off, beeping the horn twice as he rounded the corner. I walked as slowly as I could up the driveway and front walk to the porch, where my mother was waiting.

"Halley," she said before I even hit the first step, "I thought we had an understanding that it was your job to mow the lawn."

"I know," I said, and my father was studying some spot over my head, avoiding making eye contact, "he just wanted to help me out."

"Who is he?"

"He's just this guy," I said.

"How do you know him?"

"We have P.E. together," I said, opening the door and slipping inside, making my getaway. "It's no big deal."

"He seems nice enough," my father offered, his eyes on the lawn.

"I don't know," she said slowly. I started up the stairs, pretending not to hear her, turning away to keep my secrets to myself. "I just don't know."

Part II

SOMEONE LIKE YOU

Chapter Five

"I need you," Scarlett said to me as I was busy weighing produce for a woman with two screaming babies in her cart. "Meet me in the ladies' room."

"What?" I said, distracted by the noise and confusion, oranges and plums rolling down my conveyer belt.

"Hurry," she hissed, disappearing down the cereal aisle and leaving me no chance to argue. My line was long, snaking around the Halloween display and back into Feminine Products. It took me a good fifteen minutes to get to the bathroom, where she was standing in front of the sinks, arms crossed over her chest.

"What's wrong?" I said.

She just shook her head.

"What?" I said. "What is it?"

She reached behind the paper towel dispenser and pulled out a small white stick-shaped object with a little circle on the end of it. As she held it out, I saw that in the little circle was a bright pink cross. Then, all at once, it hit me.

"No," I said. "No way."

She nodded, biting her lip. "I'm pregnant."

"You can't be."

"I am." She shook the stick in front of me, the plus sign blurring. "Look."

"Those things are always wrong," I said, like I knew.

"It's the third one I've taken."

"So?" I said.

"So what? So nothing is wrong three times, Halley. And I've been sick every morning for the last three weeks, I can't stop peeing, it's all there. I'm pregnant."

"No," I said. I could see my mother in my head, lips forming the word: *denial.* "No way."

"What am I going to do?" she said, pacing nervously. "I only had sex one time."

"You had *sex?*" I said.

She stopped. "Of *course* I had sex. God, Halley, try to stay with me here."

"You never told me," I said. "Why didn't you tell me?"

She sighed, loudly. "Gosh, Halley, I don't know. Maybe it was because he *died* the next day. Go figure."

"Oh, my God," I said. "Didn't you use protection?"

"Of course we did. But something happened, I don't know. It came off. I didn't realize it until it was over. And then," she said, her voice rising, "I thought there was no way it could happen the first time. It couldn't."

"It came off?" I didn't understand, exactly; I wasn't very clear on the logistics of sex. "Oh, my God."

"This is nuts." She pressed her fingers to her temples, hard, something I'd never seen her do before. "I can't have a baby, Halley."

"Of course you can't," I said.

"So, what, I have to get an abortion?" She shook her head. "I can't do that. Maybe I should keep it."

"Oh, my God," I said again.

"Please." She sat down against the wall, pulling her legs up against her chest. "Please stop saying that."

I went over and sat beside her, putting my arm around her shoulders. We sat there together on the cold floor of Milton's, hearing the muffled Muzak playing "Fernando" overhead.

"It'll be okay," I said in my most confident voice. "We can handle this."

"Oh, Halley," she said softly, leaning against me, the pregnancy stick lying in front of us, plus sign up. "I miss him. I miss him so much."

"I know," I said, and I knew now it was my job to hold us together, my turn to see us through. "It'll be okay, Scarlett. Everything is going to be fine."

But even as I said it, I was scared.

That evening, we had a meeting at Scarlett's kitchen table. Me, Scarlett, and Marion, who didn't know anything yet and ate her dinner incredibly slowly as we edged around her. She had a date with Steve/Vlad at eight, so we were working with a time frame.

"So," I said, looking right at Scarlett, who was overstuffing the napkin holder with napkins, "it's almost eight."

"Is it?" Marion turned around and looked at the kitchen clock. She reached for her cigarettes, pushed her chair out from the table, and said, "I better start getting ready."

She started to leave, and I shot Scarlett a look. She looked right back. We battled it out silently for a few seconds before she said, very quietly, in a voice flat enough to ensure anyone wouldn't, "Wait."

Marion didn't hear her. Scarlett shrugged her shoulders, like she'd tried, and I stood up and got ready to call after her. I could hear Marion heading up the stairs, past the creaky third one, when Scarlett sighed and said, louder, "Marion. Wait."

Marion came back down and stuck her head into the kitchen. She'd had to get two two-hundred-and-fifty-pound women glamorous that day at Fabulous You, one of whom wanted lingerie shots, so she was worn out. "What?"

"I have to talk to you."

Marion stood in the doorway. "What's going on?"

Scarlett looked at me, as if this was some kind of relay race and I could carry the baton from here. Marion was starting to look nervous.

"What?" she asked, looking from Scarlett to me, then back to Scarlett. "What is it?"

"It's bad," Scarlett said, and started crying. "It's really bad."

"Bad?" Now Marion looked scared. "Scarlett, tell me. Now."

"I can't," Scarlett managed, still crying.

"Now." Marion put one hand on her hip. It was my mother's classic stance but it looked out of place on Marion, as if she was wearing a funny hat. "I mean it."

Then Scarlett just spit it out. "I'm pregnant."

Everything was really quiet all of a sudden, and I suddenly noticed that the faucet was leaking, *drip drip drip.*

Then Marion spoke. "Since when?"

Scarlett fumbled for a minute, getting her bearings. She'd been expecting something else. "When?"

"Yes." Marion still wasn't looking at either of us.

"Ummm . . ." Scarlett looked at me helplessly. "August?"

"August," Marion repeated, like it was the clue that solved the puzzle. She sighed, very loudly. "Well, then."

The doorbell rang, all cheerful, and as I glanced out the front window I could see Steve/Vlad on the front porch carrying a bunch of flowers. He waved at us and rang the bell again.

"Oh, God," Marion said. "That's Steve."

"Marion," Scarlett began, stepping closer to her, "I didn't mean for it to happen—I used something, but . . ."

"We'll have to talk about this later," Marion told her, running her hands through her hair nervously, straightening her dress as she headed for the door. "I can't—I can't talk about this now."

Scarlett wiped her eyes, started to say something, and then turned and ran out of the room, up the stairs. I heard her bedroom door slam, hard.

Marion took a deep breath, composed herself, and went to

the front door. Steve was standing there, smiling in his sports jacket and Weejuns. He handed her the flowers.

"Hi," he said. "Are you ready?"

"Not quite," Marion said quickly, smiling as best she could. "I have to get something—I'll be right down, okay?"

"Fine."

Marion went upstairs and I heard her knocking on Scarlett's door, her voice muffled. Steve came in the kitchen. He looked even blander under bright light. "Hello there," he said. "I'm Steve."

"Halley," I said, still trying to listen to what was happening upstairs. "It's nice to meet you."

"Are you a friend of Scarlett's?" he asked.

"Yes," I said, and now I could hear Scarlett's voice, raised, through the ceiling overhead. I thought I could make out the word *hypocrite*. "I am."

"She seems like a nice girl," he said. "Halley. That's an unusual name."

"I was named for my grandmother," I told him. Now I could hear Marion's voice, stern, and I babbled on to cover it. "She was named for the comet."

"Really?"

"Yes," I said, "she was born in May of 1910, when the comet was coming through. Her father watched it from the hospital lawn while her mom was in the delivery room. And in 1986, when I was six, we watched it together."

"That's fascinating," Steve said, like he really meant it.

"Well, I don't remember it that well," I said. "They say it wasn't very clear that year."

"I see," Steve said. He seemed relieved to hear Marion coming down the stairs.

"Ready?" she called out, all composure, but she still wouldn't look at me.

"Ready," Steve said cheerfully. "Nice to meet you, Halley."

"Nice to meet you, too."

He slipped his arm around Marion as they left, his hand on the small of her back as they headed down the front walk. She was nodding, listening as he spoke, holding her car door open. As they pulled away she let herself look back and up, to Scarlett's bedroom window.

When I went upstairs, Scarlett was on the bed, her legs pulled up against her chest. The flowers Steve had brought Marion were abandoned on the dresser, still in their crinkly cellophane wrapper.

"So," I said. "I think that went really well, don't you?"

She smiled, barely. "You should have heard her. All this stuff about the mistakes she'd made and how I should have known better. Like doing this was some way of proving her the worst mother ever."

"No," I said, "I think my mother's got that one pegged."

"Your mother would sit you down and discuss this, rationally, and then counsel you to the best decision. Not run out the door with some warrior."

"My mother," I said, "would drop dead on the spot."

She got up and went to the dresser mirror, leaning in to look at herself. "She says we'll go to the clinic on Monday and make an appointment. For an abortion."

I could see myself behind her in the mirror. "Is that what you decided to do?"

"There wasn't much of a discussion." She ran her hands over her stomach, along the waist of her jeans. "She said she had one, a long time ago. When I was six or seven. She said it's no big deal."

"It'd be so hard to have a baby," I said, trying to help. "I mean, you're only sixteen. You've got your whole life ahead of you."

"She did, too. When she had me."

"That was different," I said, but I knew it really wasn't. Marion had been a senior in high school, about to go off to some women's college out west. Scarlett's father was a football player, student council president. He left for a Big East school and Marion never saw or contacted him again.

"Keeping me was probably the only unselfish thing Marion's ever done in her life," Scarlett said. "I've always wondered why she did."

"Stop it," I said. "Don't talk like that."

"It's true," she said. "I've always wondered." She stepped back from the mirror, letting her hands drop to her sides. We'd spent our lifetimes in this room, but there had never been anything, ever, like this. This was bigger than us.

"It'll be all right," I told her.

"I know," she said quietly, looking into the mirror at herself and me beyond it. "I know."

It was going to be done that Friday. We never talked about it openly; it was whispered, never called by name, as a silence settled over Scarlett's house, filling the rooms to the ceiling. To Marion, it was already a Done Deal. She went to the clinic counseling sessions with Scarlett, handling all the details. As the week wound down, Scarlett grew more and more quiet.

On Friday, my mother drove me to school. I'd told her Scarlett had something to do and couldn't take me; then, we pulled up behind her and Marion at a stoplight near Lakeview. They didn't see us. Scarlett was looking out the window, and Marion was smoking, her elbow jutting out the driver's side window. It still didn't seem real that Scarlett was even pregnant, and now the next time I saw her it would be wiped clean, forgotten.

"Well, there's Scarlett right there," my mother said. "I thought you said she wasn't going to school today."

"She isn't," I said. "She has an appointment."

"Oh. Is she sick?"

"No." I turned up the radio, my father's voice filling the car. *It's eight-oh-four A.M., I'm Brian, and you're listening to T104, the only good thing about getting up in the morning. . . .*

"Well, there must be something wrong if she's going to the doctor," my mother said as the light finally changed and Scarlett and Marion turned left, toward downtown.

103

"I don't think it's a doctor's appointment," I said. "I don't know what it is."

"Maybe it's the dentist," she said thoughtfully. "Which reminds me, you're due for a cleaning and checkup."

"I don't know," I said again.

"Is she missing the whole day or just coming in late?"

"She didn't say." I was squirming in my seat, keeping my eye on the yellow school bus in front of us.

"I thought you two told each other everything," she said with a laugh, glancing at me. "Right?"

I was wondering exactly what that was supposed to mean. Everything she said seemed to have double meanings, like a secret language that needed decoding with a special ring or chart I didn't have. I wanted to shout, *She's having an abortion, Mom! Are you happy now?* just to see her face. I imagined her exploding on the spot, disappearing with a puff of smoke, or melting into a puddle like the Wicked Witch of the West. When we pulled into the parking lot, I was never so glad to see school in my life.

"Thanks," I said, kissing her on the cheek quickly and sliding out of the car.

"Come home right after school," she called after me. "I'm making dinner and we need to talk about your birthday, right?"

Tomorrow was my sixteenth birthday. I hadn't even had much time to think about it. A few months ago, it had been the only thing I had to look forward to: my driver's license, freedom, all the things I'd been waiting for.

"Right. I'll see you tonight," I said to her, backing up, losing myself in the crowd pushing through the front doors. I was walking through the main building, headed outside, when Macon fell into step beside me. He always seemed to appear out of nowhere, magic; I never saw him coming.

"Hey," he said, sliding his arm over my shoulders. He smelled like strawberry Jolly Ranchers, smoke, and aftershave, a strange mix I had grown to love. "What's up?"

"My mother is driving me nuts," I said as we walked outside. "I almost killed her on the way to school today."

"She drove you?" he said, glancing around. "Where is Scarlett, anyway?"

"She had an appointment or something," I said. I felt worse, much worse, lying to him than I had to my mother.

"So," he said, "don't make plans for tomorrow night."

"Why?"

"I'm taking you somewhere for your birthday."

"Where?"

He grinned. "You'll see."

"Okay," I said, pushing away the thought of the party my mother was planning, complete with ice-cream cake and the Vaughns and dinner at Alfredo's, my favorite restaurant. "I'm all yours."

The bell rang, and he walked with me toward homeroom

until someone called his name. A group of guys I'd met uptown with him a few days before, with longer hair and sleepy eyes, were waving him over toward the parking lot. No matter how well I thought I was getting to know him, there was always some part of himself he kept hidden: people and places, activities in which I wasn't included. I got a phone call each evening, early, just him checking in to say hello. What he did after that, I had no idea.

"I gotta go," he said, kissing me quickly. I felt him slide something in the back pocket of my jeans as he started to walk away, already blending with the packs of people. I already knew what it was, before I even pulled it out: a Jolly Rancher. I had a slowly growing collection of candy at home, in a dish on my desk. I saved every one.

"What about homeroom?" I said. For all my pretend rebellion I'd never missed homeroom or skipped school in my life. Macon had a scattered attendance rate at best, and I didn't even ask him about his grades. All the women's magazines said you couldn't change a man, but I was learning this the hard way.

"I'll see you third period," he said, ignoring the question altogether. Then he turned and started toward the parking lot, tucking his one hardly cracked notebook under his arm. A group of girls from my English class giggled as they passed me, watching him. We'd been big news the last two weeks; a month ago I'd been Scarlett's friend Halley, and now I was Halley, Macon Faulkner's girlfriend.

At the end of second period, someone knocked on the door of my Commercial Design class and handed Mrs. Pate a slip of paper; she read it, looked at me, and told me to get my stuff. I'd been summoned to the office.

I was nervous, walking down the corridor, trying to think of anything I'd done that could get me in trouble. But when I got there the receptionist handed me the phone and said, "It's your mother."

I had a sudden flash: my father, dead. My grandmother, dead. Anyone, dead. I picked up the phone. "Hello? Mom?"

"Hold on," I heard someone say, and there were some muffled noises. Then, "Hello? Halley?"

"Scar—?"

"Shhhh! I'm your mother, remember?"

"Right," I said, but the receptionist was busy arguing with some kid over a tardy slip and not even paying attention. "What's going on?"

"I need you to come get me," she said. "At the clinic."

I looked at the clock. It was only ten-fifteen. "Is it over? Already?"

"No." A pause. Then, "I changed my mind."

"You what?"

"I changed my mind. I'm keeping the baby."

She sounded so calm, so sure. There was nothing I could think of to say.

"Where's Marion?" I said.

"I told her to leave me here," she said. "I said she was mak-

107

ing me nervous. I was supposed to call her to come get me after."

"Oh," I said.

"Can you come? Please?"

"Sure," I said, and now the receptionist was watching me. "But, Mom, I think you have to tell them to give me a pass or something."

"Right," Scarlett said, all business. "I'm going to put my friend Mary back on the phone. I'm at the clinic on First Street, okay? Hurry."

"Right," I said, wondering how I was getting anywhere, since I had no car.

There were some more muffled noises, Scarlett giving instructions, then the same voice I'd heard earlier came back on. "This is Mrs. Cooke."

"Hold on," I said. I held out the phone to the receptionist. "My mom needs to talk to you."

She tucked her pen behind her ear and took the receiver. "Hello?"

I concentrated on the late sign-in sheet on the counter in front of me, trying not to look twitchy.

"She does? Okay, that's fine. No, it's no problem. I'll just give her a pass. Thank you, Mrs. Cooke." She hung up and scribbled out a pass. "Just show this to the guard as you leave the parking lot. And keep it to show your teachers so your absence is excused."

"Right," I said as the bell rang and the hallway outside started to fill up. "Thanks."

"And I hope the surgery goes well," she said, eyeing me carefully.

"Right," I said, backing into the door to push it open. "Thanks."

I stood outside of P.E., waiting for Macon. As he passed, on his way to dress out, I grabbed his shirt and pulled him back.

"Hey," he said, grinning. I still felt that rush whenever he looked so happy to see me. "What's up?"

"I need a favor."

"Sure. What is it?"

"I need you to skip P.E. with me."

He thought for about a second, then said, "Done. Let's go."

"Wait." I pulled him back. "And I need a ride somewhere."

"A ride?"

"Yeah."

He shrugged. "No problem. Come on."

We walked up to the parking lot and got into his car; he pushed a pile of stereo parts out of my seat. The car smelled slightly smoky and sweet, the same smell that followed him, faintly, wherever he went. He was always in a different car, which was also something he never felt it necessary to explain. So far I'd seen him in a Toyota, a pickup, and some foreign model that smelled like perfume. All of them had candy wrappers littering the floors and stuffed in the ashtrays.

Today he was in the Toyota.

"Wait a sec," I said as he started the engine. "This isn't going to work. You don't have a pass to get out."

"Don't worry about it," he said casually, grabbing something from his visor, scribbling on it, and starting up the hill toward the guardhouse. The security guy, an African-American guy we called Mr. Joe, came out with his clipboard, looking bored.

"Macon," I hissed as we slid to a stop. I doubted even the Jedi Mind Trick would fool Mr. Joe. "This will not work; you should just go back—"

"Hush," he said, rolling down the window as Joe came closer, the sun glinting off his store-bought security guard badge. "What's up, Joe?"

"Not much," Joe said, looking in at me. "You got a pass, Faulkner?"

"Right here," Macon said, handing him the scrap of paper he'd pulled down from the visor. Joe glanced at it, handing it back, then looked in at me.

"What about you?"

"Right here," Macon said cheerfully, taking my pass and handing it over. Joe examined it carefully, taking much longer than he had with Macon's.

"Y'all drive safe," Joe said, handing my pass back. "I mean it, Faulkner."

"Right," Macon said. "Thanks."

Joe grumbled, ambling back to his stool and mini-TV in the

guardhouse, and Macon and I pulled out onto the road, free.

"I cannot believe you," I said as we cruised toward town, playing hooky on a Friday. It was my first time, and everything looked different, brighter and nicer, the world of eight-thirty to three-thirty on a school day, a world I never got to see.

"I told you not to worry," he said smugly.

"Do you have a whole stack of those passes, or what?" I pulled at the visor and he laughed even as he grabbed my hand, stopping it.

"Just a few," he said. "Definitely not a stack."

"You are so bad," I said, but I was impressed. "He didn't even hardly look at your pass."

"He likes me," he said simply. "Where are we going, anyway?"

"First Street."

He switched lanes, hitting his turn signal. "What's on First Street?"

I looked over at him, so cute, and knew I'd have to trust him. We both would. "Scarlett."

"Okay," he said easily. And as I looked over, the scenery was whizzing past houses and cars and bright blue sky, on and on. "Lead the way."

Scarlett was sitting on a bench in front of the clinic with a heavyset woman in a wool sweater and straw hat.

"Hey," I said as we pulled up beside them. Now, closer, I

could see the woman had a little dog in her lap with one of those cone collars on its head to keep it from biting itself. "Are you okay?"

"I'm fine," she said quickly, grabbing her purse off the bench. To the woman she said, "Thanks, Mary. Really."

The woman petted her dog. "You're a good girl, honey."

"Thanks," Scarlett said as I unlocked the door and she slid into the backseat. "I paid her five bucks," she explained to me. The dog in the woman's lap looked at us and yawned. To Macon, in a lower voice, Scarlet said, "Go. Now. Please."

Macon hit the gas and we left Mary behind, pulling out of the shopping center and into traffic. Scarlett settled into the backseat, pulling her hands through her hair, and I waited for her to say something.

After a few stoplights she said quietly, "Thanks for coming. Really."

"No problem," Macon said.

"No problem," I repeated, turning back to look at her, but she was facing the window, staring out at the traffic.

When Macon stopped at the Zip Mart and got out to pump gas, I turned around again. "Hey."

She looked up. "Hey."

"So," I said. I wasn't sure quite where to start. "What happened?"

"I couldn't do it," she blurted out, as if she'd only been waiting, holding her breath, for me to ask. "I tried, Halley, really. I knew all the arguments—*I'm young, I have my whole life ahead of me, what about college*—all that. But when I lay down there on that cot and stared at the ceiling, just waiting for them to come do it, I just realized I couldn't. I mean, sure, nothing is going to be normal for me anymore. But how normal has my life *ever* been? Growing up with Marion sure wasn't, losing Michael wasn't. Nothing ever has been."

I watched Macon as he stood in line inside, tossing a pack of Red Hots from hand to hand. Two months ago, when Michael died, I hadn't even known him. "It isn't going to be easy, at all," I said. I tried to imagine us with a baby, but I couldn't picture it, seeing instead just a blur, a vague shape in Scarlett's arms. Impossible.

"I know." She sighed, sounding like my mother. "I know everyone will think I'm crazy or even stupid. But I don't care. This is what I want to do. And I know it's right. I don't expect anyone to really understand."

I looked at my best friend, at Scarlett, the girl who had always led me, sometimes kicking, into the best parts of my life. "Except for me," I said. "I understand."

"Except for you," she repeated, softly, looking up to smile at me. And from that moment, I never questioned her choice again.

We spent the whole day just driving around, eating pizza at one of Macon's hideouts, looking for some guy he knew for a reason that was never quite clear, and just listening to the radio, killing time. Scarlett called Marion and said she'd taken a cab home. Everything, for now, was taken care of.

Macon dropped us off a few streets over from our houses, so I could pretend I'd taken the bus, then drove off, beeping the horn as he turned out of sight. Scarlett steadied herself and went to wait for Marion, and I walked in the door and found a strange, uneasy silence, as well as my father, who darted out of sight the second he saw me. But not fast enough: Milkshakes. Big Time.

"I'm home," I called out. The house smelled like lasagna, and I suddenly realized I was starving, which distracted me until my mother stepped out of the kitchen, holding a dishtowel. Her face had taken on that pointy, angular look, a dead giveaway that I was in trouble.

"Hi there," she said smoothly, folding the towel. "How was school today?"

"Well," I said, as my father passed by quickly again, into the kitchen, "It was . . ."

"I would think very hard before answering if I were you," she interrupted me, her voice still even and calm. "Because if you lie to me, your punishment will only be worse."

Busted. There was nothing I could do.

"I saw you, Halley, today at about ten forty-five, which I believe is when you're supposed to be in gym class. You were in a car, pulling out of the First Street Mall."

"Mom," I said. "I can—"

"No." She held up her hand, stopping me. "You're going to let me finish. I called your school and was told, to my surprise, that I had just spoken with someone to have you sent home due to a family emergency."

I swallowed, hard.

"I cannot *believe* that you would lie like this to me." I looked at the floor; it was my only option. "Not to mention," she went on, "cutting class and running around town with some boy I don't know, and Scarlett, who of all people should know better. I called Marion at work and she was equally furious."

"You told Marion that Scarlett was with us?" I said. So she knew; she knew before Scarlett would even have a chance to explain.

"Yes, I did," she snapped. "We agreed if this was a new trend for you two, it needed to be nipped in the bud, right now. I will not have this, Halley. You've been pushing it with Ginny and camp all summer, but today was the last straw. I'm not going to let you openly defy me when it suits you. Now go upstairs and stay there until I tell you to come down."

"But . . ."

"Go. Now." She was shaking, she was so mad. There'd been that strange uneasiness all summer, the rippling of irritation— but this was the real deal. And she didn't even know half of it yet.

I went up to my room and straight to the window, grabbing

my phone. I dialed Scarlett's number and just as it started ringing I saw Marion's car coming down the street. Scarlett answered right as she turned into the driveway.

"Watch out," I said quickly, whispering, "we're busted. And Marion knows you didn't do it."

"What?" she said. "No, she doesn't. She thinks I took a cab home."

"No," I said, and I could hear my mother coming up the stairs, down the hall, "my mother called her. She knows."

"She what?" Scarlett said, and I could see her garage door opening.

"Halley, *get off that phone!*" my mother said from outside my door, rattling the handle because thank God it was locked. "I mean *now!*"

"Gotta go," I said, hanging up quickly, and from my window I could see Scarlett in her kitchen, holding her phone and staring up at me as Marion burst in, her finger already pointing. My mother was outside my own door, her voice meaning business, but I saw only Scarlett, trying to explain herself in the bright light of her kitchen before Marion reached and yanked at the shade, making it fall crooked, sideways, and shutting me out.

Chapter Six

I had to sit and wait for my punishment. I could hear my parents downstairs conferring, my father's voice low and calm, my mother's occasionally bouncing off the walls, peaking and plummeting. After an hour she came upstairs, stood in front of me with her hands on her hips, and laid down the law.

"Your father and I have discussed it," she began, "and we've decided you should be grounded for a month for what happened today. You are also on phone restriction indefinitely. This does not count your birthday tomorrow; the party will go on as planned. But as far as anything else goes, you may go to school and to work but not anywhere else."

I was watching her face, how it transformed when she was angry. The short haircut that always framed her face looked more severe, all the angles of her cheekbones hollowing out. She looked like a different person.

"Halley."

"What?"

"Who was the boy who was with you today? The one who was driving?"

Macon flashed into my head, smiling. "Why?"

"Who is he? Was he the boy who cut the lawn that day?"

"No," I said. My father had either forgotten Macon's name or was choosing, wisely, to stay out of this. "I mean, it's not him, it was my—"

"He took you off campus and I need to know who he was. Anything could have happened to you, and I'm sure his parents would like to know about this as well."

The thought alone was mortifying. "Oh, Mom, no. I mean, he's nobody. I hardly know him."

"You obviously know him well enough to leave school with him. Now what's his name?"

"Mom," I said. "Please don't make me do this."

"Is he from Lakeview? I must know him, Halley."

"No," I said, and thought *You don't know everyone I know. Not everyone is from Lakeview.* "You don't."

She took a step closer, her eyes still on me. "I'm losing patience here, Halley. What's the boy's name?"

And I hated her at that moment, hated her for assuming she knew everyone I did, that I was incapable of life beyond or without her. So I stared back, just as hard. Neither of us said anything.

Then the phone rang, suddenly, jarring me where I sat. I started to reach for it, remembered about phone restriction, and sat back. I knew it was Macon. It rang on and on as she stood there watching me, until my father answered it.

"Julie!" he yelled from downstairs. "It's Marion."

"Marion?" my mother said. She picked up the phone next to

my bed. "Hello? Hi, Marion. . . . Yes, Halley and I were just discussing what happened. . . . What? Now? Okay, okay . . . calm down. I'll be right over. Sure. Fine. See you in a minute."

She hung up the phone. "I have to go across the street for a few minutes. But this conversation is not over, understand?"

"Fine," I said, but I knew already things would have changed by the time she got back.

Marion met her at the end of the walk, by the prickle bush, where they stood talking for a good five minutes. Actually Marion talked, standing there nervously in a mini-dress and wedge heels, chain-smoking, while my mother just listened, nodding her head. From across the street I could see Scarlett in her own window, watching them as well; I pressed my palm against my window, our special signal, but she didn't see me.

Then my mother walked inside with Marion, shut the door, and stayed for an hour and a half. I expected to see a ripple, a shock wave shaking the house when my mother was told the news; instead, it was quiet, like the rest of the neighborhood on a Friday night. At seven the Vaughns arrived, and by eight I could smell popcorn from downstairs. The phone rang only once more, right at eight o'clock; I tried to grab it but my father answered first and Macon hung up, abruptly. A few minutes later I heard the blender whirring as my father did his part to mend fences.

At eight-fifteen Marion walked my mother to the door, standing on the stoop with her, arms crossed against her chest. My mother hugged her, then crossed back to our house, where my father and the Vaughns were already watching a movie with a lot of gunfire in it. A few minutes later she came up the stairs and knocked at my door.

When I opened it she was standing there with a bowl of popcorn and, of course, a milkshake. It was so thick with chocolate it was almost black, foaming over the edge of the glass. Her face was softer now, back to its normal state. "Peace offerings," she said, handing them to me, and I stepped back and let her in.

"Thanks." I took one suck off the straw in the shake but nothing budged.

"So," she said, sitting on the edge of my bed, "why didn't you tell me about Scarlett?"

"I couldn't," I said. "She didn't want anyone to know."

"You thought I'd be mad," she said slowly.

"No," I said. "I just thought you'd freak out."

She smiled, reaching over for a handful of popcorn. "Well, to be truthful, I did."

"She's going to keep it, right?" I asked.

She sighed, reaching back to rub her neck. "That's what she's saying. Marion is still hoping she'll change her mind and put it up for adoption. Having a baby is hard work, Halley. It will change her life forever."

"I know."

"I mean, of course it's nice to have someone that's all yours, that unconditional love, but with being a mother there are responsibilities: financial, emotional, physical. It will affect her education, her future, everything. It's not a smart decision to take all that on now. And I'm sure that some of this is an attempt to hold on to a part of Michael, an extension of the mourning process, but a baby goes way beyond that." She was on a roll now, her voice getting louder and smoother.

"Mom," I pointed out, "I'm not Scarlett."

She was taking a breath, readying herself for another point, but now she stopped, sighing. "I know you're not, honey. It's just frustrating to me because I can see what a mistake she's making."

"She doesn't think it's a mistake."

"Not now, no. But she will, later. When she's tied down to a baby and you and all her other friends are going off to college, traveling abroad, living other lives."

"I don't want to go abroad," I said quietly, taking a handful of popcorn.

"My point is," she said, putting her arm around my shoulder, "that you have an entire life ahead of you, and so does Scarlett. You're too young to take on anyone else's."

From downstairs there was a hail of movie gunfire, then my father's chuckling. Another Friday night, at home with the Vaughns. My life before Macon.

"So, about what happened today," she said, but she'd lost the fire, the anger that had brought her up here earlier, ready to draw and quarter me. "We can't just let this go, honey. Your punishment will have to stand, even if you thought you were helping Scarlett."

"I know," I said. But it was clear; by the pure fact of not being pregnant, I'd escaped the worst of her wrath. Scarlett had saved me, again.

She stood up, brushing off her slacks. I could see her at Scarlett's kitchen table, a place that I considered mine, negotiating Marion and Scarlett to some kind of truce. My mother was good at all kinds of peace except my own.

"Why don't you come down and watch the movie?" she said. "The Vaughns haven't seen you for so long. Clara thinks you're just fabulous."

"Clara's five, Mom," I said. I tried another sip of the shake, then gave up and stuck it on my bedside table.

"I know." She stood at my open door, leaning against the frame. "Well, you know. If you change your mind."

"Okay."

She started to leave, then stopped in the doorway and said in a low voice, "Marion says that boy you were with is named Macon. She says he's your boyfriend."

Marion and her big mouth. I lay down on my bed, turning my back to her and pulling my knees up to my chest. "He's just this guy, Mom."

"You never mentioned it to me," she said, as if I had to, as if that was required.

"It's no big deal." I couldn't look at her, couldn't risk it. Her voice sounded sad enough. I had my eyes on the window, where the lights of a plane were coming closer, red and green blinking, the noise not quite loud yet.

Another sigh. Sometimes I wondered if she'd have breath left to speak. "Okay, then. Come down if you feel like it."

But she lingered there, maybe thinking I figured she'd left, as that plane came closer and closer, the lights brighter, the sound growing louder and louder and finally starting to shake the house, the panes in the window rattling. I could see its broad belly, coasting overhead, white like a whale. And in the din of its passing, the shaking and thundering and noise, my mother slipped out of the doorway and down the stairs. When I turned back over, in sudden silence, she was gone.

Chapter Seven

At work, in the middle of a typical terrible Saturday rush, Macon stepped up to my station and grinned at me.

"Hey," he said. "Happy birthday."

"Thanks," I said, taking as long as I could to scan his Pepsi and four candy bars. Scarlett reached over to poke him and he waved to her.

"So," he said, "How'd it go this morning? Did you pass, or what?"

I looked at him. "Of course I did."

He laughed, throwing his head back. "Halley with a license, look out. I'm staying off the roads for a while."

"You're funny," I said, and he grinned.

"You didn't answer the phone last night," he said, leaning over my register and lowering his voice. "I called, you know."

"That," I said, hitting the total button, "is because I got busted."

"For what?"

"What do you think?"

He thought back. "Oh. Skipping school? Or helping Scarlett go AWOL?"

"Both." I held out my hand. "That'll be two fifty-nine."

He handed me a five, pulling it out of his back pocket all wrinkled. "How bad did you get it?"

"I'm grounded."

"For how long?"

"A month."

He sighed, shaking his head. "That's too bad."

"For who?"

The woman behind him was murmuring under her breath, irritated.

As I handed him his change he grabbed my fingers, holding them, then leaned over the register and kissed me fast, before I even had a chance to react. "For me," he said, and with his other hand slipped a candy bar into the front pocket of my Milton's apron.

"Really?" I said, but he just grabbed his bag and walked off, turning back to smile at me. Everyone in my line was watching, grumpy and impatient, but I didn't care.

"Really," he said, taking a few steps still facing me, smiling. Then he turned and walked out of Milton's, just like that, leaving me speechless at my register.

"Man," Scarlett said as my next customer stepped up, slapping a carton of Capris on the belt. "There's something wrong with that boy."

"I know," I said, still feeling his kiss on my lips, saving me from all the Saturdays ahead. "He likes me."

* * *

That evening we had my party at Alfredo's: my parents and me, Scarlett, and of course the Vaughns. Scarlett sat next to me; the way she told it, my mother had saved her baby. She said when Marion had come storming in she'd already made another appointment for the next day and planned to sit outside the operating room, chair blocking the door, if that was what it took to see it was done. They had a huge blowout, and she said she'd been packing a bag, ready to leave to go somewhere, anywhere, when my mother appeared at the front door in her red cardigan sweater like Mr. Rogers, ready to handle everything. She held Scarlett's hand and passed her tissues, calmed Marion down, and then mediated through the twists and turns of what Scarlett had done. In the end, it was decided: Scarlett would go through with the pregnancy, but would honor Marion's wishes of seriously considering adoption. This was the truce.

"I'm telling you," she said to me again as I ate my pasta, "your mother is a miracle worker."

"She grounded me an entire month," I said, keeping my voice low. "I can't even go out later."

"This is a very nice party," she said. "Noah looks especially happy for you."

"Shut up." I was already sick of my birthday.

"I'd like to propose a toast." My mother stood up at her seat, holding her glass of wine, with my father smiling from where he sat beside her. "To my daughter Halley, on her sixteenth birthday."

"To Halley," everyone else echoed. Noah still wouldn't look me in the eye.

"May this year be the best yet," my mother went on, even though everyone had already drank. She was still standing. "And we love you."

So everyone clinked their glasses again, and drank again, and my mother just stood there with her cheeks flushed, smiling at me, as if yesterday had never happened.

When we got home we opened presents. I got some clothes and money from my parents, a book from the Vaughns, and a silver bracelet from Noah, who just stuffed the box in my hand when no one was looking and ignored me for the rest of the evening. Scarlett gave me a pair of earrings and a keychain for my new car keys, and when she left to go home she hugged me tight, suddenly emotional, and told me how much she loved me. As I hugged her back I tried again to picture her with a baby, or even just pregnant. It was still hard.

I was getting ready for bed around eleven when I heard it. The slow, even rumble of a car passing slowly on the street, then pausing, the engine humming. I went to the window and watched, my eyes on the stop sign that faced my house. A few seconds later the car slid back into sight, facing my window, and blinked its lights. Twice.

I put on my shoes and crept down the stairs in my pajamas and jacket, past my mother's half-open bedroom door, past where my father was dozing on the couch in front of the TV. I opened the back door, mindful to go slow because of the creak it made halfway. I slipped outside, across the deck, and down around the house to the side yard, past the juniper

127

bushes, to the sidewalk and across the street.

"Hey," Macon said as I leaned into his window. "Get in."

I went around and climbed into the passenger seat, pulling the door shut behind me. It was warm inside, the dash lights giving off a bright green glow.

"Ready for your present?" he asked.

"Sure." I sat back in my seat. "What is it?"

"First," he said, putting the car in gear, "we have to go someplace."

"Go someplace?" I took a panicked look at my house. It was bad enough to sneak out, but the further away I got the better chance I had of getting caught. I could see my father sticking his head in my room to say good night, seeing me gone. "I probably shouldn't."

He looked at me. "Why not?"

"I mean, I'm already in trouble," I said, and I sounded like a wimp even to myself, "and if I got caught—"

"Oh, come on," he said, already starting to head out of Lakeview. "Live a little. It's your birthday, right?"

I looked up at my dark house. I had just an hour left of my birthday, and I had the right to celebrate at least that much of it the way I wanted.

"Let's go," I said to him and he smiled, hitting the gas as we took the corner, tires squealing a little bit, carrying me away.

He took me all the way out to Topper Lake, a good twenty minutes from my house. We stopped about halfway and I drove, watching him as he squirmed, just like my dad, as the speedometer edged higher and higher.

"You nervous?" I asked him as we went across the bridge, the water black and huge all around us.

"No way," he said. But he was, and I laughed at him. I was barely doing the speed limit.

We passed all the boat ramps and docks, all the tourist traps, and finally went down a long dirt road that wound through woods and potholes and NO TRESPASSING signs into complete darkness. In the distance I could see the radio towers of my father's station, blinking red and green against the sky.

We got out of the car and I followed him through the dark, his hand holding mine. I could hear water but I couldn't make out where exactly it was.

"Watch your step up here," he said as we climbed a steep hill, up and up and up with me barely able to keep from falling. I was cold in my pajamas and jacket, disoriented, and out of breath by the time the ground beneath my feet got more smooth and stable. I still had no idea where I was.

"Macon, where are we going?" I said.

"Almost there," he called out over his shoulder. "Walk right behind me now, okay?"

"Okay." I kept my eyes ahead, on the blond of his hair, the only thing I could make out in the dark.

And then, suddenly, he stopped dead in his tracks and said, "Here we are."

I wasn't sure where *here* was, since I still couldn't see any-

129

thing. He sat down, dangling his legs over the edge in front of us, and I did the same. I could still hear water, louder now.

"So what is this?" I said, shivering in my jacket.

"Just this place I know," he said. "Me and Sherwood found it, a couple of years back. We used to come out here all the time."

It was one of the only times he'd mentioned Michael, ever, in the whole time I'd known him. Michael had been on my mind a lot lately, with the baby. Scarlett said she had to get up her nerve to write his mom; whether she had moved to Florida or not, she had a right to know about a grandchild. "I bet you miss him," I said.

"Yeah." He leaned back against the thick concrete behind us. "He was a good guy."

"If I lost Scarlett," I said, not knowing if I was going too far or saying the wrong thing, "I don't know what I'd do. I don't think I could live without her."

"Yeah," he said, there in the dark. He turned his head, not looking at me. "You think that, at first."

So we sat there, in the pitch black, the sound of water rushing past, and I thought of Michael Sherwood. I wondered how this year would have been different if he hadn't taken that road that night, if he was still here with us. If Scarlett would be keeping that baby, if I'd ever have met Macon or come this far.

"Okay," he said suddenly, looking down at his glowing watch. "Get ready."

"Ready for what?"

"You'll see." He slid his arm around my waist, pulling me

closer, and I felt his warm lips on my neck. Right as I turned my head to kiss him, there was a loud whooshing noise and the world suddenly lit up bright all around us. It was blinding at first, and frightening, like a camera flash going off right in my face and turning the world starry. I pulled back from Macon and saw that I was sitting on a thin strip of white concrete, surrounded by DANGER DO NOT ENTER signs, my feet dangling over the edge into the air. Macon grabbed my waist as I leaned forward, still dazed and blinking, to peer over the edge and finally see the water I'd been hearing gushing past a full mile below. It was like opening your eyes and finding yourself suddenly in midair, falling. The dam was groaning, opening, as I twisted in Macon's arms, suddenly terrified, all the noise and light and the world so far below us.

"Macon," I said, trying to pull away, back toward the path. "I should—"

But then he pulled me back in, kissing me hard, his hands smoothing my hair, and I closed my eyes to the light, the noise, the water so far below, and I felt it for the first time. That exhilaration, the whooshing feeling of being on the edge and holding, the world spinning madly around me. And I kissed him back hard, letting loose that girl from the early summer and the Grand Canyon. At that moment, suspended and free-falling, I could feel her leaving me.

Chapter Eight

"Okay, let's see. . . . Food cravings."

"Check."

"Food aversions."

"Ugh. Check."

"Headaches."

"Check."

"Moodiness," I said. "Oh, *I'll* answer that one. Check."

"Shut up," Scarlett said, grabbing the book out of my hands and flopping back in her seat. We were in her car, before first bell; since I'd gotten my license, she let me drive every day. She was eating saltines and juice, the only things she could keep down, while I tried to eat my potato chips quietly and unobtrusively.

"Just wait," I said, popping another one in my mouth. "The book says morning sickness should end by the beginning of Month Four."

"Oh, well, isn't *that* special," she snapped. She had been moodier than hell lately. "I swear those chips smell so bad, they're going to make me *puke.*"

"Sorry," I said, rolling down my window and making a big

show of holding them outside, my head stuck sideways to eat free and clear of the confines of the car. "You know the doctor said it's normal to feel sick a lot of the time."

"I know what she said." She stuck another saltine in her mouth, swigging some juice to wash it down. "This is just crazy. I've never even *had* heartburn before and now I do, like, all the time, my clothes look terrible on me, I'm sweating constantly for some weird reason and even when I'm starving, everything I look at makes me feel sick. It's ridiculous."

"You'll feel better at Month Five," I said, picking up the book, which was called *So You're Pregnant—What Now?* It was our Bible, consulted constantly, and my job was usually to quote from it to rally and strengthen both of us.

"I wish," she said in a low voice, turning to glower at me with a face I hadn't even seen before Month Two, ever, "that you would *shut up* about Month Four."

I shut up.

Macon was waiting for me outside my homeroom, leaning against the fire extinguisher. Since my birthday, things had changed between us, almost imperceptibly; everything was a little bit more serious. Now just the sight of him gave me a sense of looking down and finding myself in midair, dangling lost above the world.

"Hey," he said as I came closer, "where have you been?"

"Arguing with Scarlett," I said. "She's so cranky lately."

"Oh, come on. Cut her some slack. She's pregnant." I'd told

him the night of my birthday. He was the only one besides my parents, Marion, and us who knew.

"I know. It's just hard, that's all." I stepped a little closer to him, lowering my voice. "And keep quiet about that, okay? She doesn't want anyone to know yet."

"I didn't tell anyone," he said. Behind me people were crowding into my homeroom, bumping backpacks and elbows against me. "Sheesh, what kind of a jerk do you think I am, anyway?"

"A big one," I said. He wasn't laughing. "She just wants to wait until she has to tell people. That's all."

"No problem," he said.

"Faulkner!" someone yelled from behind us. "Get over here, I gotta talk to you."

"In a second," Macon yelled back.

"You said you were going to homeroom today," I reminded him. "Remember?"

"Right. I gotta go." He kissed me on the forehead, quickly, and started to walk off before I could stop him. "I'll see you third period."

"Wait," I said, but he had vanished in the shifting bodies and voices of the hallway. I only saw the top of his head, the red flash of his shirt, before he was gone. Later, when I was hunting for a pencil in my backpack pocket and found a handful of Hershey's Kisses, I wondered again how he did so much without my noticing.

Later that morning I was in Commercial Design, the only

class I had with Scarlett, looking for some purple paper in the supply room. I heard someone behind me and turned around to see Elizabeth Gunderson shuffling through a stack of orange paper. She'd been slumming since Michael's death, quitting the cheerleading team, chain-smoking, and taking up with the lead singer for some college band who had a pierced tongue and a goatee. All of her copycat friends were following suit, casting off their J. Crew tweeds for ripped jeans and black clothes, trying to look morose and morbid in their BMWs and Mercedes.

"So, Halley," she said, moving closer to me, a sheaf of orange tucked under one arm. "I heard you're going out with Macon Faulkner."

I glanced out to the classroom, to Scarlett, who was bent over the table, cutting and pasting letters for our alphabet project. "Yeah," I said, concentrating on the purple paper in my hand, "I guess I am."

"He's a nice guy." She reached across me for some bright red paper. "But just between us, as your friend, I think I should warn you to watch out."

I looked up at her. Even with her ripped jeans and styled-to-look-stringy hair, Elizabeth Gunderson was still the former head cheerleader, the homecoming queen, the girl with the effortless looks and perfect skin, straight out of *Seventeen* magazine. She was not like me, not at all. She didn't even know me.

"I mean," she went on, stepping back and tucking her paper under her arm, "he can be real sweet, but he's treated a lot of girls pretty badly. Like my friend Rachel, he really used her and then never talks to her anymore. Stuff like that."

"Yeah, well," I said, trying to get around her but she wasn't moving, just standing there with her eyes right on me.

"I got to know him really well when I was with Michael." She said his name slowly, so I'd be sure to get it. "I just didn't know if you knew what he was like. With girls and all."

I didn't know what to say, how to defend myself, so I just stepped around her, knocking my shoulder against a shelf just to slip by.

"I just thought you should know, before you get too involved," she called after me. "I mean—*I* would want to know."

I burst out into the classroom. When I looked back she was still watching me, standing by the paper cutter talking with Ginny Tabor, who practically had radar for these kinds of confrontations. I threw my paper down next to Scarlett and pulled out my chair.

"You would not believe what just happened to me," I said. "I was in the supply room, and—"

I didn't get any further than that, because she suddenly pushed her chair back, clapped a hand over her mouth, and ran toward the bathroom.

"Scarlett?" Mrs. Pate, our teacher, was a little high-strung; outbursts made her nervous. She was supervising the paper cutter, making sure no one lost any fingers. "Halley, is she okay?"

"She's got the flu," I said. "I'll go check on her."

"Good," Mrs. Pate said, redirecting her attention to Michelle Long, who was about to sever at least half her hand with slapdash cutting behavior. "Michelle, wait. Look at what you're about to do. Can you see that? *Can* you?"

I found Scarlett in the last stall against the wall, kneeling on the floor. I wet some paper towels at the sink and handed them to her, then said, "It's gonna get better."

She sniffled, wiping her eyes with the back of her sleeve. I felt so sorry for her. "Are we alone?" she asked.

I walked down the row of stalls, checking underneath for feet, and saw none. It was just us, the deep blue cinderblock of the girls' bathroom, and a dripping faucet.

She leaned back on her heels, dabbing her face with the wet paper towel. "This," she said in a choked voice, sniffling, "is the worst."

"I know," I said, telling myself not to talk about Month Four or the joy of birth or the little life inside of her, all things that had failed me in the past. "I know."

She wiped her mouth with the back of her hand, closing her eyes. "It's like, whenever I used to see pregnant women, they always looked happy. Glowing, right? Or on TV, in those big dresses, knitting baby afghans. No one ever tells you it makes you fat and sick and crazy. And I'm only three months along, Halley. It's just going to get *worse*."

"The doctor said—" I started, but she cut me off, waving her hand.

"It's not about that," she said softly, and she was crying

137

again. "It would be different if Michael was here or I was married with a husband. Marion doesn't even want me to have this baby, Halley. It's not like she's being that supportive. This is all me, you know? I'm on my own. And it's scary."

"You are not on your own," I said forcefully. "I'm here, aren't I? I've been holding your head while you get sick and bringing you saltines and letting you crab like crazy at me. I'm doing everything a husband or anyone would do for you."

"It's not the same." In the fluorescent light her face seemed paler than ever. "I miss him so much. This fall has been so hard."

"I know it," I said. "You've been really strong, Scarlett."

"If he was here, I don't even know what might have happened between us. We were only together for a summer, you know? Maybe he would have turned out to be a major jerk. I'll never know. But when it gets like this, and I'm miserable, all I can think is that he might have made everything okay. That he was the only one who understood. Ever."

I knelt down next to her. "We can do this," I said firmly. "I know we can."

She sniffled. "What about childbirth classes? What about when I have to give birth and it hurts, and all that? What about money? How am I going to support a whole other person scanning groceries at Milton's?"

"We've already talked about that," I said. "You have that trust your grandparents put aside, you'll use that."

"That's for college," she moaned. "Specifically."

"Oh, fine," I said, "you're right. College is much more important right now. This is your *baby*, Scarlett. You have to hold it together because it needs you."

"My baby," she repeated, her voice hollow in the cool deep blue of the stall. "My baby."

Then I heard it: the creak of a door opening, not the outside door either but closer, just behind me. I turned, already dreading what I'd see. A set of feet I'd somehow missed, belonging to somebody who now had heard everything. But it was worse than that. Much worse.

"Oh, my God," Ginny Tabor said as I turned to face her, standing there in a white sweater, her mouth a perfect O. "Oh, my God."

Scarlett closed her eyes, lifting her hands to her face. I could hear the lights buzzing. No one said anything.

"I won't tell anyone," Ginny said quickly, already backing up to the door, her eyes twitchy and weird. "I swear. I won't."

"Ginny—" I started. "It's not—"

"I won't tell," she said in a louder voice, backing up too far and banging against the door, her hand feeling wildly for the knob. "I swear," she said again, slipping out as it fell closed between us, a flash of white all I saw before she was gone.

By lunch we were getting strange looks as we walked to Macon's car. Everyone seemed to be eyeing Scarlett's stomach, as if since second period she'd suddenly be showing, the baby ready to pop out at any minute. We ate lunch in the Toyota, parked in the Zip Mart lot around back by the Dumpsters.

"It's weird," Scarlett said, finishing off her second hot dog, "but since I know everybody knows now, I'm starving."

"Slow down on those hot dogs," I said nervously. "Don't get overconfident."

"I feel fine," she said, and Macon reached over and squeezed my leg. All through P.E. I'd agonized about how it was all my fault, Ginny Tabor faking me out, then spreading Scarlett's secret like wildfire across the campus. "And I'm not mad at you, so stop looking at me like you're expecting me to fly into a rage at any second."

"I'm so sorry," I said for at least the twentieth time. "I really am."

"About what?" she said. "This isn't about you, it's about Ginny and her huge mouth. Period. Forget about it. At least it's over now."

"God," I said, and Macon rolled his eyes. I'd already planned several ways I could kill Ginny with my bare hands. "I really am *sorry*."

"Shut up and pass those chips back here," Scarlett said, tapping my shoulder.

"Better pass them," Macon told me, grabbing them out of my lap. "Before she starts eating the upholstery."

"I'm hungry," Scarlett said, her mouth full. "I'm eating for two now."

"You shouldn't be eating hot dogs, then," Macon said, turning to face her. "At least not all the time. You need to eat fruit and vegetables, lots of protein, and yogurt. Oh, and vitamin C is important, too. Cantaloupe, oranges, that kind of thing. Green peppers. Loaded with C."

We just looked at him.

"What?" he said.

"Since when are you Mr. Pregnancy?" I asked him.

"I don't know," he said, embarrassed now. "I mean, I'm not. It's just common knowledge."

"Cantaloupe, huh?" Scarlett said, finishing off the bag of chips.

"Vitamin C," Macon said, starting up the car again. "It's important."

By the time we got back from lunch, everyone was definitely staring, entire conversations dissolving as we passed. Macon just kept walking, hardly noticing, but Scarlett's face was pinched. I wondered if we'd see those hot dogs coming up again.

"Oh, please," Macon said as we passed the Mouth herself, Ginny Tabor, standing with Elizabeth Gunderson, both of them staring, thinking, I knew, of Michael. "Like they've never seen a pregnant woman before."

"Macon," I said. "You're not helping."

Scarlett kept walking, facing straight ahead, as if by only concentrating she could make it all go away. I wondered what was more shocking, in the end; that Scarlett was pregnant, or that the baby was Michael's. Of course girls got pregnant at our school, but they usually dropped out for a few months and then returned with baby pictures in their wallets. Some carried their babies proudly to the school day care, where little kids climbed on the jungle gym on the right side of the courtyard, running to the fence to watch their mothers go by on their way to class. But for girls like us, like Scarlett, these things didn't happen. And if they did it was taken care of in secret, discreetly, and only rumored, never proven.

This was different. If we'd started to forget Michael Sherwood, any of us, it would be a very long time before we would again.

Chapter Nine

Then, in the middle of everything, we began losing my Grandma Halley.

It had actually started months earlier, in the late spring. She became forgetful; she would call me Julie, confusing me with my mother, forgetting even her own name. She kept locking herself out of her house, misplacing her key. My mother even convinced her to wear one on a string around her neck, but nothing worked. The keys just slipped away into cracks and crevices, sidewalks and street corners, thin air.

It got worse. She walked out of the Hallmark store with a greeting card she forgot to pay for, setting off all the alarms, which scared her. She started calling in the middle of the night, all anxious and upset, sure we'd said we were coming to visit the next day, or the previous one, when no plans had actually been made. For those calls her voice was unbalanced and high, scaring me as I handed the phone over to my mother, who would pace the kitchen floor, reassuring her own mother that everything was fine, we were all okay; there was nothing to be afraid of. By the end of October, we weren't so sure.

I'd always been close to my Grandma Halley. I was her namesake and that made her special, and I'd spent several summers with her when I was younger and my parents went on trips. She lived alone in a tiny Victorian house outside of Buffalo with a stained-glass window and a big, fat cat named Jasper. Halfway up her winding staircase was a window, and from the top sill she hung a bell from a wire. I always touched it with my fingers as I passed, the chiming bouncing off the glass and the walls around me. It was that bell that always came to mind before her face, or her voice, when I heard her name.

My mother had Grandma Halley's sparkling eyes, her tiny chin, and sometimes, if you knew when to listen for it, her singsong laugh. But my Grandma Halley was kind of wild, a little eccentric, more so in the ten years since my grandfather had died. She gardened in men's overalls and a floppy sun hat, and made up her scarecrows to resemble neighbors she didn't like, especially Mr. Farrow, who lived two doors down and had buck teeth and carrot-red hair, which fit a scarecrow nicely. She ate only organic food, adopted twenty kids through Save the Children, and taught me the box step when I was in fifth grade, the two of us dancing around the living room while her record player crackled and sang.

She was born in May of 1910, as Halley's Comet lit up the sky of her small town in Virginia. Her father, watching with a crowd from the hospital lawn, considered it a sign and named her Halley. It was the comet that always made her seem that much more mystical, different. Magic. And when I was named after her, it had made me a little magical too, or so I hoped.

The winter I was six, we made a special trip to visit her for the comet's passing. I remember sitting outside in her lap, wrapped in a blanket. There'd been so much hype, so much excitement, but I couldn't see much, just a bit of light as we strained to make it out in the sky. Grandma Halley was quiet, holding me tight against her, and she seemed to see it perfectly, grabbing my hand and whispering, *Look at that, Halley. There it is.* My mother kept saying no one could see it, it was too hazy, but Grandma Halley always told her she was wrong. That was Grandma Halley's magic. She could create anything, even a comet, and make it dance before your eyes.

Now my mother was suddenly distracted, making calls to Buffalo and having long talks with my father after I went to bed. I busied myself with school, work, and Macon; with my grounding over, I slipped off to see him for a few hours whenever I could. I went with Scarlett to the doctor, read to her from the pregnancy Bible, reminding her to get more vitamin C, to eat more oranges and green peppers. We were adjusting to the pregnancy; we had no choice. And after our being the scandal for a couple of weeks, Elizabeth Gunderson's tongue-pierced boyfriend fooled around with her best friend Maggie, and Scarlett and the baby were old news.

But each time Grandma Halley called again, scared, I'd watch my mother's face fold into the now-familiar frown of concern. And each time I'd think only of that comet overhead, as she held me in close to her, all those years ago. *Look at that. There it is.* And I'd close my eyes, trying to remember, but seeing nothing, nothing at all.

By the middle of November, Marion had been dating Steve the accountant for just about as long as I'd been seeing Macon. And slowly, he was beginning to show his alter ego.

It started around the third or fourth date. Scarlett noticed it first, nudging me as we sat on the stairs, talking to him and waiting for Marion to come down. He always showed up in ties and oxford shirts, nice sports jackets with dress pants or chinos, and loafers with tassels. But this night, suddenly, there was something different. Around his neck, just barely visible over his tie, was a length of brown leather cord. And dangling off the cord was a circular, silver *thing.*

"It is not a medallion," I hissed at Scarlett after he excused himself to go to the bathroom. "It's just jewelry."

"It's a medallion," she said again. "Did you see the symbols on it? It's some kind of weird warrior coin."

"Oh, stop."

"It is. I'm telling you, Halley, it's like his other side can't be held down any longer. It's starting to push out of him, bit by bit."

"Scarlett," I said again, "he's an accountant."

"He's a freak." She pulled her knees up to her chest. "Just you wait."

Marion was coming down the stairs now, her dress half-zipped, reaching to put in one earring. She stopped in front of us, back to Scarlett, who stood up without being asked and zipped her.

"Marion," she said in a low voice as we heard the toilet flush and the bathroom door open, "look at his neck."

"At his what?" Marion said loudly as he came around the corner, neat in his sports jacket with the leather cord still visible, just barely, over his collar.

"Nothing," Scarlett muttered. "Have a good night."

"Thank you." Marion leaned over and kissed Steve on the cheek. "Have you seen my purse?"

"Kitchen table," Scarlett said easily. "Your keys are on the counter."

"Perfect." Marion disappeared and came back with the purse tucked under her arm. "Well, you girls have a good night. Stay out of trouble and get to bed at a decent hour." Marion had been acting a little more motherly, more matronly, since she'd taken up with conservative warrior Steve. Maybe she was preparing to be a grandmother. We weren't sure.

"We will," I said.

"Gosh, give us some credit," Scarlett said casually. "It's not like we're gonna go and get pregnant or anything."

Marion shot her a look, eyes narrowed; Steve still didn't know about the baby. After only a month and a half, Marion figured it was still a bit early to spring it on him. She still wasn't dealing with it that well herself, anyway. She hardly ever talked about the baby, and when she did, "adoption" was always the first or last word of the sentence. Steve just stood there by the door, grinning blandly, distinctly unwarriorlike. It was my hope that he *would* metamorphose into Vlad, right before our eyes.

"Have a good night," I called out as they left, Marion still mad and not looking back, Steve waving jauntily out the door.

"Sheesh," Scarlett said. "What a weirdo."

"He's not that bad."

She leaned back against the step, smoothing her hands over her stomach. Though she wasn't showing yet, just in the last week she'd started to look different. It wasn't something I could describe easily. It was like those stop-action films of flowers blooming that we watched in Biology. Every frame something is happening, something little that would be missed in real time—the sprout pushing, bit by bit, from the ground, the petals slowly moving outward. To the naked eye, it's just suddenly blooming, color today where there was none before. But in real time, it's always building, working to show itself, to become.

Cameron Newton was probably the only person in school who was getting weirder looks than Scarlett that fall. He'd transferred in September, which was hard enough, but he was also one of those short, skinny kids with pasty white skin; he always wore black, which made him look half dead, or half alive, depending on how optimistic you were. Either way, he was having a tough time. So it didn't seem unusual that he was drawn across Mrs. Pate's Commercial Design class to Scarlett.

I'd missed one morning of school because of a doctor's appointment, and when we came in the next there was Cameron Newton, sitting at our table.

"Look," I said, whispering. "It's Cameron Newton."

"I know," she said cheerfully, lifting a hand to wave to him. He looked nervous and stared down at his paste jar. "He's a nice guy. I told him he should sit with us."

"What?" I said, but it was already too late, we were there and Cameron was looking up at us, in his black turtleneck and black jeans. Even his eyes looked black.

"Hey, Cameron," Scarlett said, pulling out the chair next to him and sitting down. "This is Halley."

"Hi," I said.

"Hello." His voice was surprisingly deep for such a small guy, and he had an accent that made you lean in and concentrate to understand him. He had very long fingers and was busy working with a lump of clay and a putty knife.

"Cameron's spent the last five years in France," Scarlett told me as we got settled, pulling out all of our alphabet letters and getting them organized. "His father is a famous chef."

"Really," I said. Cameron was still making me a little nervous. He had the jumpy, odd quality of someone who'd spent a lot of time alone. "That's neat."

Scarlett kicked me under the table and glared at me, as if I was making fun of him, which I definitely wasn't. Cameron got up suddenly, pushed out his chair, and stalked into the supply room. He walked like a little old man, slowly and deliberately. As he passed the paper cutter, a group of girls there dissolved into laughter, loud enough so I was sure he heard.

"You didn't tell me you made friends with Cameron Newton," I said in a low voice.

"I didn't think it was that big a deal," Scarlett said, cutting out an O. "Anyway, it was the coolest thing. I was here yesterday by myself, right? And Maryann Lister and her friends were talking about me. I could hear every word, you know, all about Michael and the baby and how I was a slut, blah blah blah."

"They said that?" I said, swiveling in my chair to find Maryann Lister, who just stared back at me, startled, until I turned away.

"I don't care now," she said. "But yesterday I'd been sick all morning and I was kind of blue and you weren't here and it just got to me, you know? So I start blubbering right here in Commercial Design, and I'm trying to hide it but I can't and right when I'm just feeling completely pathetic, Cameron scoots his chair over and puts this little piece of clay on the table in front of me. And it's Maryann Lister."

"It's what?"

"It's Maryann Lister. I mean, it's this perfect little head with her face on it, and the details were just amazing. He even had that little mole on her chin and the pattern of the sweater she was wearing."

"Why did he do that?" I said, glancing back to the supply room where Cameron was pacing the aisles, putty knife in hand, looking for something.

"I had no idea. But I just told him it was nice, and pretty, and he kind of ignored me and then handed me his history book. And he just puts it in my hand, but I still didn't know what he wanted me to do with it, so I handed it back to him. And right then she and her friends said something about him and me, like we would be perfect for each other or something."

"I hate her," I grumbled.

"No, but listen." She was laughing. "So Cameron, totally solemn, takes the book, centers the little clay Maryann on the table in front of us, and then lifts the book up, drops it, and flattens her. Just like that, *smoosh*. It was so funny, Halley. I mean, it just about killed me. And then I took the book and pounded her, and he did, and we just pummeled her into nothing. I'm telling you, he's a riot."

"A riot," I said as Cameron came out of the paper room with another wad of clay in his hands. He looked straight ahead as he walked, as if he was on a mission. "I don't know."

"He is," Scarlett said with certainty as he came closer. "Just wait."

I spent the rest of that week in Commercial Design getting to know Cameron Newton. And Scarlett was right: he *was* funny. In a weird, under-his-breath-as-if-totally-not-meaning-to way that made you think you shouldn't laugh, even when you wanted to. He was incredibly artistic, truly gifted even; he could make a clay face of anyone in minutes, completely accurate down to the last detail. He did Scarlett beautifully, the curve of her face and smile, her hair spilling across her shoulders. And he did me, half smiling, my face tiny and accurate. He had a way of being able to capture the world, perfectly, in miniature.

So Scarlett took Cameron in, the way she'd taken me in all those years ago. And Cameron grew on me as well; his low, quiet voice, his all-black ensembles, his strange, jittery laugh. I had nothing in common with Cameron Newton except for the one thing that counted: Scarlett. And that, alone, was enough to make us friends.

My mother still wasn't happy about Macon. There were things he did that she couldn't pin on him directly, but she was suspicious. Like the calls he made to me every night: when I didn't answer he either hung up or wouldn't leave a message. Sometimes he called late at night, the phone seeming to ring incredibly loud, just once, before I could grab it. Often she'd pick it up, and I could hear her, half-asleep, breathing on the other end.

"I got it," I'd say, and she'd slam it down. Macon would laugh, and I'd huddle deeper under the covers, and whisper so she couldn't hear.

"Your mom hates me," he'd say. He seemed to enjoy it.

"She doesn't even know you."

"Ah," he'd say, and I could feel him grinning on the other

end. "And to know me, as you have discovered, is to *love* me."

Because of this, and other frustrations, she started making new rules.

"No phone calls after ten-thirty," she said one morning, over her coffee cup. "Your friends should know better."

"I can't stop them from calling," I said.

"Tell them you'll get your phone taken away," she said curtly. "Okay?"

"Okay." But of course the calls didn't stop. I never was able to fully fall asleep, with one hand always on the phone. All this just to say good night to Macon, from wherever he was.

There were other things, too. Some nights, when Macon knew I couldn't see him, he'd drive by and just beep or sit idling at the stop sign across from my window. I knew he was waiting for me, but I could never go. I knew he knew that, too. But he still came. And waited.

So I'd just lie there, smiling to myself, goofily secure in the knowledge that he was thinking about me for those few rumbling minutes before he hit the gas and screeched away. This always brought on the light at the Harpers' next door, and Mr. Harper, neighborhood watch chairman, standing on his porch, glaring down the street. I don't know why Macon did it; he knew I was on thin ice anyway, that my parents were strict, a concept he clearly could not understand. Every time I heard a beep or a squealing of tires, I felt that same pull in my stomach, half exhilaration, half dread. And always my mother would look up from her book, her paper, her plate and look at me as if it was me behind that wheel, me hitting the gas, me terrorizing the neighbors.

Because of this, I had to devise new ways for him to pick me up. I'd leave the house most weekend nights, bound for Scarlett's, and cut through the woods behind her pool to meet him on Spruce Street. And from there, we went everywhere and anywhere. Slowly, I was beginning to see bits and pieces of the rest of his life.

One night, after a few hours of driving around, we pulled into a parking lot at the bottom of a huge hill. It faced a tall apartment building lit up with row after row of bright lights. The highest floor was all windows, and I could see people moving around, holding wine glasses and laughing, like a party on top of the world.

"What's this?" I said as we got out of the car and climbed the hill, then a winding flight of stairs with a thick iron rail.

"This," Macon said as we came to a row of glass doors, and a lobby with cream-colored walls and a huge chandelier, "is home."

"Home?" He held the door for me. When I stepped inside, the first thing I smelled was lilacs, just like the perfume my mother wore on special occasions. I looked at my watch: 11:06. I had fifty-four minutes to curfew.

Macon led the way to the elevator, hitting a triangle-shaped button with the back of his hand. The door slid open with a soft beep. The elevator was carpeted in deep green pile and even had a little bench against the far wall if you got tired of standing. He hit the button for P and we started moving.

"You live in the penthouse?" I turned in a circle, watching myself in the four mirrored walls.

"Yep," he said, his eyes on the numbers over my head. "My mother's into power trips." This was the first time he'd talked about her, ever. All I knew about was what I'd heard, years ago, when she'd lived in our neighborhood. She sold real estate and had been married at least three times, the last to a developer of steak houses.

"This is amazing," I said. "This elevator is nicer than my whole house." The beep sounded again as the doors slid open, onto another, smaller lobby. As we got out I saw, through a slightly open door, people moving, mingling, and voices mixed with the clinking of glasses and piano music.

"Down here," Macon said, leading me around a corner to what looked like a linen closet or maid's room. He pulled a key-chain out of his pocket, unlocked it, and reached in to turn on a light. Then he stood there, holding it, waiting for me. "Well, come on," he said, reaching over to snap me on the side in the one spot where I was absolutely the most ticklish, "we haven't got all night."

The room itself was pretty small, painted a light sky blue; there was a single bed, neatly made, and a dresser and desk that looked brand-new. Beyond another door on the opposite wall, I could hear someone playing the piano. On a chair, at the end of the bed, there was a TV with something taped to the screen.

"This is your room?" I said, taking a few steps to the TV to get a better look at what was stuck to it. It looked like a photograph.

"Yep." He opened the door to the party, just a crack, then peeked out and shut it again. "Wait here," he said. "I'll be right back."

I sat down on the bed, facing the TV, and leaned forward to get a good look at the photograph. I thought how familiar it looked, and the setting, before it finally hit: it was me. Me, at the Grand Canyon with my mother, the same picture that sat framed on our mantel. But she wasn't in this picture, had somehow been cut out neatly, leaving only me with my arm reaching nowhere, cut off at the elbow.

I pulled the picture off the TV, turning it over. I was still holding it when Macon came back in, carrying two glasses and a plate of finger food.

"Hey," he said, "I hope you like caviar, because that's about the best thing they had out there."

"Where did you get this?" I asked him, holding up the picture.

He just looked at me, and I swear he blushed, even if only for a second. "Somewhere."

"Where?" It wouldn't have surprised me a bit to go home and find that frame on the mantel empty, everything else untouched and in its proper place. He was that slick.

"Somewhere," he said again, handing me a wine glass and the paper plate.

"Where, Macon?" I said. "Come on."

"Scarlett. I took it—borrowed it—from Scarlett. It was stuck to her mirror."

"Oh," I said. I flipped it over again. "You could have asked me for one."

"Yeah," he said, popping something small and doughy into his mouth and not looking at me.

"Well," I said, kissing his cheek where it was smooth and soft and smelled slightly cool, like aftershave. "I'm glad you like me enough to steal my picture."

Outside the music was still playing. In Macon's tiny room, we were like stowaways.

"You don't spend much time here, do you?" I asked him.

"Nope." He sat up and drained his glass. "Can you tell?"

"Yeah. It doesn't even look like anyone lives here. Where *do* you stay, Macon?"

"I don't know. I used to stay at Sherwood's a lot. They had an extra room, his dad was always out of town. His mom never cared. And I got other friends, other places. You know."

"Sure," I said, but I didn't. It was completely foreign to me, this nomadic existence, traveling from place to place, crashing wherever was convenient. I thought of my own room, filled to the brim with my trophies and pictures, my spelling-bee ribbons and schoolbooks, everything that made up who I was.

157

The only place in the world that had been all mine, always.

I looked over and he was watching me, then leaning over to kiss me as I closed my eyes and lay back, feeling his arms slide around me. With the party music in the background, and voices outside passing louder and softer, he kissed me and kissed me, the bed settling comfortably under us. The sheets smelled like him, sweet and smoky. Macon was a good kisser—not that I had much to compare him to—but I just knew. I tried not to think of all the practice he'd had.

Then, after what seemed like blissful hours, I saw his watch glowing and the time on it: 12:09.

"We have to go," I said suddenly, sitting up. My shirt was all twisted and out of place and my mouth felt numb. "I'm late."

"Late?" he said, all discombobulated and confused. "For what?"

"For my curfew." I grabbed my coat and jammed my feet into my shoes while he jumped up and turned on the light beside the bed, which had somehow been turned off though I couldn't remember when. "God," I said, shaking my head. "I'm dead."

We ran out of the elevator downhill to the parking lot, jumping into his car and squealing around corners and through stop signs, finally pulling up to the corner of my street at exactly 12:21. I could see the light from Scarlett's house, where I was supposed to be, through the trees.

"I gotta go," I said, opening the door. "Thanks."

"I'll call you tomorrow," he called out through the car window. I could see him smiling in the dark.

"Right," I said, smiling back as precious seconds went by. I waved, one last time, then cut through the trees and popped out by Scarlett's pool. I heard him beep as he drove off.

I walked up Scarlett's back steps, through the door and into the kitchen, where she was sitting at the table eating a hot-fudge sundae, with *So You're Pregnant—What Now?* propped up against the sugar bowl in front of her.

"You're late," she said distractedly as I passed through, heading straight for the front door. She had a smear of chocolate sauce on her chin.

"I know," I said, wiping it off with my finger as I passed her. "I'll see you tomorrow."

"Right." She went back to her book and I opened the front door and headed up the walk, across the street.

My mother was waiting for me inside, by the stairs. As I shut the door behind me I could hear Macon's engine rumbling, testing fate again. Bad timing.

"You're late," she said in an even voice. "It's past curfew."

"I know," I said, revving up for my excuse, "but Scarlett and I were watching this movie, and I lost track of time."

"You weren't with Scarlett." This was a statement. "I could see her sitting in her living room by herself, all night. Nice try, Halley."

Outside, Macon was still there, rumbling. He didn't know how much worse he was making it.

"Where were you?" she said to me. "Where did you go with him?"

"Mom, we were just out, it was nothing."

"Where did you go?" Now her voice was getting louder. My father appeared at the top of the stairs, watching.

"Nowhere," I said, as Macon's revving got louder and louder, and I clenched my fists. There was no way to stop it. "We were at his house, we were just hanging out."

"Where does he live?"

"Mom, it doesn't matter."

She had her stony face on, that look again, like a storm crossing over. "It does to me. I don't know what's gotten *into* you lately, Halley. Sneaking around, creeping in the door. Lying to me to my face. All because of this Macon, some boy you won't introduce to us, who we don't even know."

The rumbling got louder and louder. I closed my eyes.

Her voice rose too, over it. In the alcove, it seemed to bounce all around me. "How can you keep lying to us, Halley? How can you be so dishonest?" And she caught me off guard, sounding not mad, not furious, just—sad. I hated this.

"You don't understand," I said. "I don't want to—" and then the engine was tacking up higher and higher, louder and louder, God he wanted me to get caught, he didn't understand, as the tires squealed and screeched, burning, and he took off down the street, racing, stopping to beep as he rounded the corner. All this I knew, without even looking, as well as I knew Mr. Harper's light was already on, he was already out there in his slippers and bathrobe, cursing the smoke that still hung in the air.

"Did you hear that?" my mother said, twisting to look up at my father, who just nodded. "He could *kill* someone driving like that. Kill someone." Her voice was shaky, almost scared, just like Grandma Halley's.

"Mom," I said. "Just let me—"

"Go to bed, Halley," my father said in a low voice, coming down step by step. He took my mother by the arm and led her into the kitchen, flicking on the light as they went. "Now."

So I went, up to my room, my heart thumping. As I passed the mirror in the hallway I glanced at myself, at a girl with her hair tumbling over her shoulders, in a faded jeans jacket, lips red from kissing. I faced my reflection and committed this girl to memory: the girl who had risen out of that night at Topper Lake, the girl who belonged with Macon Faulkner, the girl who broke her mother's heart, never looking back. The girl I was.

Chapter Ten

"Look at this," Scarlett said, passing me the magazine she was holding. "By Month Four, the baby is learning to suck and swallow, and is forming teeth. And the fingers and toes are well defined."

"That's surprising," I said, "considering it's existing only on hot dogs and orange juice." It was the next day, and we were at the doctor's office for the fourth-month checkup. Scarlett had always been phobic of stethoscopes and lab coats and needed moral support, so I'd been pardoned from my most recent grounding, for (1) lying about being with Macon and (2) breaking curfew. I was becoming an expert at being grounded; I could have written books, taught seminars.

"I'm eating better, you know," she said indignantly, shifting her position on the table. She was in one of those open-back gowns, trying to cover her exposed parts. Behind her, on the wall, was a totally graphic poster with the heading *The Female Reproductive System*. I was trying not to look at it, instead focusing on the plastic turkey and Pilgrims tacked up around it; Thanksgiving was two weeks away.

"You're still not getting enough green leafy vegetables," I told her. "Lettuce on a Big Mac doesn't count."

"Shut up." She leaned back, smoothing her hand over her stomach. In just the last few weeks she was finally starting to show, her waist bulging just barely. Her breasts, on the other hand, were getting enormous. She said it was the only perk.

There was a knock on the door, and the doctor came in. Her name tag said Dr. Roberts and she was carrying a clipboard. She had on bright pink running shoes and blue jeans, her hair in a twist on the back of her head.

"Hello there," she said, then glanced down at her notes and added, "Scarlett. How are you today?"

"Fine," Scarlett said. She was already starting to wring her hands, a dead giveaway. I concentrated on the *Life* magazine in my lap; the cover story was on Elvis.

"So you're about sixteen weeks along," Dr. Roberts said, reading off the chart. "Are you having any problems? Concerns?"

"No," Scarlett said in a low voice, and I shot her a look. "Not really."

"Any headaches? Nosebleeds? Constipation?"

"No," Scarlett said.

"Liar," I said loudly.

"You hush," she snapped at me. To the doctor she said, "She doesn't know anything."

"And who are you?" Dr. Roberts turned to face me, tucking her clipboard under her arm. "Her sister?"

"I'm her friend," I said. "And she's scared to death of doctors, so she won't tell you anything."

"Okay," the doctor said, smiling. "Now, Scarlett, I know all of this is a little scary, especially for someone your age. But you need to be honest with me, for the good of yourself and your baby. It's important that I know what's happening."

"She's right," I chimed in, and got another death look from Scarlett. I went back to Elvis and kept quiet.

Scarlett twisted the hem of her gown in her hands. "Well," she said slowly, "I have heartburn a lot. And I've been dizzy lately."

"That's normal," the doctor said, easing Scarlett onto her back and sliding her hand under the gown. She ran her fingers over Scarlett's stomach, then put her stethoscope against the skin and listened. "Have you noticed an increase in your appetite?"

"Yes. I'm eating all the time."

"That's fine. Just be sure you keep up your proteins and vitamin C. I'll give you a handout when you leave today, and we can discuss it further." She took off her stethoscope and consulted the file again, tapping the clipboard with her finger. "Blood pressure is fine, we've gotten the urine sample already. Is there anything you'd like to talk about? Or ask me?"

Scarlett shot me a look, but I didn't say anything. I just turned the page, reading up on national politics, and pretended I wasn't listening.

"Well," Scarlett said quietly. "I have one. How bad does it hurt?"

"Does what hurt?"

"Delivery. When it comes. Is it really bad?"

Dr. Roberts smiled. "It depends on the situation, Scarlett, but I'd be lying if I said it was painless. It also depends on the course of childbirth you want to take. Some women prefer to go without drugs or medication; that's called 'natural childbirth.' There are birthing classes you can take, which I will be happy to refer you to, that teach ways of breathing that can help with the delivery process."

"But you're saying it hurts."

"I'm saying it depends," Dr. Roberts said gently, "but honestly, yes, it hurts. But look at how many people have gone through it and lived to tell. We're all here because of it. So it can't be that bad. Right?"

"Right," Scarlett said glumly, putting her hand on her stomach.

"You're gonna need major drugs," I said as we left, climbing into the car en route to our Saturday twelve-to-six shifts at Milton's. I was driving, and she settled into the passenger seat, sighing. I said, "They should just totally knock you out. Like with a baseball bat."

"I know," she said, "but that's bad for the baby."

"The bat?"

"No, the drugs. I think I should take a birthing class or something. Learn how to breathe."

"Like Lamaze?"

"Yeah, or something like that." She shuffled through the handouts the doctor had given us, packets and brochures, all with happy pregnant women on their covers. "Maybe Marion could go with me."

"I'm sure she would," I said. "Then she'd get to be there when it came. That would be cool."

"I don't know. She's still talking about adoption like it's for sure going to happen. She's already contacted an agency and everything."

"She'll come around."

"I think she's saying the same thing about me." We pulled into Milton's parking lot, already packed with Saturday shoppers. "Sooner or later, one of us will have to back down."

Later that afternoon, after what seemed like thousands of screaming children and gallons of milk, hundreds of bananas and Diet Coke two-liters, I looked down my line and saw my mother. She was reading *Good Housekeeping*, a bottle of wine tucked under one arm, and when she saw me she waved, smiling. My mother still got some small thrill at seeing me at work.

"Hi there," she said cheerfully when she got to the front of the line, plunking the bottle down in front of me.

"Hi," I said, scanning it and hitting the total button.

"What time do you get off tonight?"

"Six." Behind me I could hear Scarlett arguing with some man over the price of grapes. "It's seven eighty-nine."

"Let's go out for dinner," she said, handing me a ten. "My treat."

"I don't know," I said. "I'm real tired."

"I want to talk to you," she said. My line was still long, people shifting impatiently. Like me, they had no time for my mother's maneuvering. "I'll pick you up."

"But, Mom," I said as she grabbed her wine and change from my hands and started toward the door. "I don't—"

"I'll see you at six," she called out cheerfully, and left me stuck there face to face with a fat man buying two boxes of Super Snax and a bottle of Old English. Lately to get to me she'd had to hit hard and fast, rushing me, then tackling to the ground. For the rest of the afternoon, all I could think about was what she had planned, what trick was up her sleeve.

She picked me up at six, waiting in the loading zone with the engine running. When I got in the car, she looked over at me and smiled, genuinely happy, and I felt a pang of guilt for all the dreading I'd been doing all afternoon.

We went to a little Italian place by our house, with checkered tablecloths and a pizza buffet. After a half a slice of pepperoni and some small talk about Milton's and school, she leaned across the table and said, "I want to talk to you about Macon."

The way she said it you'd think she knew him, that they were friends. "Macon."

"Yes." She took a sip of her drink. "To be honest, Halley, I'm not happy with this relationship."

Well, I thought, *you're not in it*. But I didn't say anything. I could tell already this wasn't going to be a discussion, a dialog, or anything involving my opinion. I was an expert at my mother. I knew her faces, her tones of voice, could translate the hidden, complex meanings of each of her sighs.

"Now," she began, and I could tell she'd worked on this, planned every word, probably even outlined it on a legal pad for her book, "since you've been hanging around with Macon you've gotten caught skipping school, broken your curfew, and your attitude is always confrontational and difficult. Honestly, I don't even recognize you anymore."

I didn't say anything and just picked at my pizza. I was losing my appetite, fast. She kept on; she was on a roll.

"Your appearance has changed." Her voice was so loud, and I sunk lower in my seat; this wasn't the place for this, which was exactly why she'd picked it. "You smell like cigarettes when you come home, you're listless and distracted. You never talk about school with us anymore. You're distant."

Distant. If she couldn't keep me under her thumb, I was far away.

"These are all warning signs," she went on. "I tell parents to watch out for them every day."

"I'm not doing anything," I said. "I was only twenty minutes late, Mom."

"That's not the issue here, and you know it." She got quiet as the waiter came by with more bread, then lowered her voice and continued. "He's not good for you."

Like he was food. Not a green pepper or an orange, but a big sticky Snickers bar. "You don't even know him," I said.

"That's because you refuse to discuss him!" She wadded up her napkin and threw it down on her plate. "I have given you endless chances to prove me wrong here. I have tried to dialog—"

"I don't want to dialog,'" I snapped. "You've already made up your mind anyway, you hate him. And this isn't about him, anyway."

"This is what I know," she said, leaning closer to me. "He drives like a maniac. He's not from Lakeview. And you are willing to do anything for him, including but probably not limited to lying to me and your father. What I *don't* know is what you're doing with him, how far things have gone—if there are drugs involved or God knows what else."

"Drugs," I repeated, and I laughed. "God, you always think everything is about *drugs*."

She wasn't laughing. "Your father and I," she said, finally lowering her voice, "have discussed this thoroughly. And we've decided you cannot see him anymore."

"*What?*" I said. "You can't do that." My stomach was tight and hot. "You can't just decide that."

"Well, Halley, with your actions lately you've given us no other choice." She sat back in her chair, crossing her arms. This wasn't going the way she wanted, I could tell. This wasn't her office and I wasn't a patient and she couldn't just tell me what to do. But I didn't know what she'd expected. That she was do-

ing me a favor? "Halley, I don't think you understand how easy
it is to make a mistake that will cost you forever. All it takes is
one wrong choice, and . . ."

"You're talking about Scarlett again," I said, shaking my
head. I was tired of this, tired of battling and putting up fronts,
of having to think so hard about my next move.

"No," she said. "I am talking about you falling in with the
wrong crowd, getting influenced to do something you aren't
ready to do. That you don't *want* to do. You don't know what
Macon's involved in."

I hated the way she kept saying his name.

"There's a lot of dangerous stuff out there," she said. "You're
inexperienced. And you're like me, Halley. You have a tendency not to see people for what they really are."

I sat there and looked at my mother, at the ease in her face as
she told me how I felt, what I thought, everything. Like I was a
puzzle, one she'd created, and she knew the solution every
time. If she couldn't keep me close to her, she'd force me to be
where she could always find me.

"That's not true," I said to her slowly, and already I knew I'd
say something ugly, something final, even as I stood up, pushing back my chair. "I'm not getting influenced, I'm not inexperienced, and *I am not like you.*"

It was the last thing that did it. Her face went blank, shocked,
like I'd reached out and slapped her.

You wanted distance, I thought. *There you go.*

She sat back in her chair, keeping her voice low, and said, "Sit down, Halley. Now."

I just stood there, thinking of running out the door, losing myself in Macon's secret network of pizza parlors and arcades, side streets and alleys, riding up to that penthouse room and stowing away, forever.

"Sit *down*," she said again. She was looking over my head, out to the parking lot. She was blinking, a lot, and I could hear her taking deep, deep breaths.

I sat down, pulling in my chair, while she dabbed at her mouth with a napkin and waved over the waiter. We got the check, paid, and went out to the car without a word between us. All the way home I stared out the window, watching the houses slip past and thinking back to the Grand Canyon, vast and uncrossable, like so many things were now.

When we pulled into our driveway we passed Steve, who was getting out of his Hyundai in front of Scarlett's house. He was carrying flowers, his usual, and wearing yet another tweedish, threadbare jacket with patches on the elbows. But this time I didn't need Scarlett to point out the newest sign of Vlad's emergence: boots. Not just regular boots either, but big, leather, clunky boots with a thick heel and buckles that I imagined must be clanking loudly with each step, although my window was up and I couldn't hear them. Warrior boots, poking out from beneath his pants leg as if they'd just walked over the heads of dead opponents. He waved cheerfully as we passed, and my mother, still irritated, lifted her hand with her fake neighborhood wave.

We still hadn't said a word to each other as we came into the kitchen where my father was on the phone, his back to us. As he turned around, I could tell instantly something was wrong.

"Hold on," he said into the receiver, then covered it with his hand. "Julie. It's your mother."

She put down her purse. "What? What is it?"

"She fell, in her house—she's hurt bad, honey. The neighbors found her. She'd been there for a while."

"She fell?" My mother's voice was high, shaky.

"This is Dr. Robbins." He handed her the phone, adding, "I'll use the other phone and start calling about flights."

She took the phone from him, taking a deep breath as he squeezed her shoulder and headed down the hall, toward her office. I stood in the open doorway and held my breath.

"Hello, this is Julie Cooke. . . . Yes. Yes, my husband said . . . I see. Do you know when this happened? Right. Right, sure."

All this time, each word she said, she was looking right at me. Not like she was even aware of it or could see me at all. Just her eyes on me, steady, as if I was the only thing holding her up.

"My husband is calling about flights right now, so I'll be there as soon as I can. Is she in pain? . . . Well, of course. So the surgery will be tomorrow at six, and I'll just—I'll get there as soon as I can. Okay. Thanks so much. Good-bye." She hung up the phone, turning her back to me, and then just stood there, one hand still on the receiver. I could see her tense back, the shoulder blades poking out.

"Your grandmother's hurt," she said in a low voice, still not turning around. "She fell and broke several ribs, and she'll have to have surgery on her hip in the morning. She was alone for a long time before anyone found her." She choked on this last part, her voice wavering.

"Is she gonna be okay?" Down the hall I could hear my father's voice, asking questions about departures and arrivals, coach or first class, chances of standby. "Mom?"

I watched her shoulders fall and rise, one deep breath, before she turned around, her face composed and even. "I don't know, honey. We'll just have to see."

"Mom—" I started, wanting to somehow fix this, whatever I'd opened between us by not wanting to share Macon with her. By not wanting to share *me* with her.

"Julie," my father's voice came booming from down the hall, always too loud for small spaces, "there's a flight in an hour, but you have a long layover in Baltimore. It's the best we can do, I think."

"That's fine," she said evenly. "Go ahead and book it. I'll throw a bag together."

"Mom," I said, "I just—"

"Honey, there's no time," she said quickly as she passed me, reaching to pat my shoulder, distracted. "I've got to go pack."

So I sat on my bed, in my room, with my math homework in

my lap and the door open. I heard the closet door opening and shutting, my mother packing, my father's low, soothing voice. But it was the silences that were the worst, when I craned my neck, hoping for just one word or sound. Anything would have been better than imagining what was happening when everything was muffled, and I knew she had to be crying.

She came in and hugged me, ruffling my hair like she always had when I was little; she said not to worry, she'd call later, everything was okay. She'd forgotten about what I'd said, about what had happened at dinner. Just like that, with one phone call, she was a daughter again.

Chapter Eleven

With my mother gone, it was like I'd been handed a Get Out of Jail Free card. My father's morning show was still riding an Arbitron rating high, which meant he was busy almost every afternoon or evening with promotional events. In the past few months, he'd already lost an on-air bet with the traffic guy that resulted in him having to perform an embarrassing (and thank God, not complete) striptease at a local dance club, attended about a hundred contest-winner cocktail parties, and wrestled a man named the Dominator at the Hilton for charity. That one had left him bruised, battered, and with nose splints for a full week, which he'd loved. He'd discussed his drainage problems, complete with a million booger jokes, every morning while I cringed on the way to school.

The phone rang constantly, usually a nervous-sounding man named Lottie who organized my father's every waking moment, lining up another trip to the mall, meeting, or Wacky Stunt. My father, who my mother insisted was too old and too educated for any of this nonsense, hardly even saw me, much less kept careful track of what I was doing. At most, we passed each other late at night, as I walked past his bedroom to brush my teeth. We came to an unspoken understanding: I'd behave, show up when I was supposed to, and he wouldn't ask questions. It was only four days, after all.

Of course, I was always with Macon. Now he could pick me up for school and take me to work or home in the afternoons; Scarlett, who used to drive me, was as busy as my father. She was working extra shifts at Milton's so she could buy baby clothes and nursery items; plus, she was spending a lot of time with Cameron, who made her laugh and rubbed her feet. Finally, our guidance counselor, Mrs. Bagbie, had convinced her to join a fledgling Teen Mothers Support Group that met at school two afternoons a week. She hadn't wanted to go, but she said the other girls—some pregnant, some already with kids—made her feel a little less strange. And Scarlett, as I knew, could make friends anywhere.

Macon and I had fun. Monday we didn't go to school at all, spending the entire time just driving around, eating at McDonald's, and hanging out by the river. When the school called that night my father wasn't home, and I easily explained that I'd been sick and my mother was out of town. Macon had already mastered her signature, signing with a flourish every note I needed.

She called every night and asked me the basic questions about school and work, whether my father was remembering to feed me. She said she missed me, that Grandma Halley was going to be all right. She said she was sorry we'd argued, and she knew it was hard for me to break it off with Macon, but someday I would understand it was the right thing. At the other end of the line, phone in hand, I agreed and watched him back out of the driveway, lights moving across me, then heard him beep as he drove away. I told myself I shouldn't feel guilty, that she'd played dirty, changing the rules to suit her. Sometimes it worked; sometimes not.

The night before my father and I were leaving to go to Buffalo for Thanksgiving, Macon brought me home from work. The house was dark when we pulled up.

"Where's your dad?" he said as he cut off the engine.

"I don't know." I grabbed my backpack out of the back of the car and opened my door. "Doing radio stuff, probably."

As I leaned over to kiss him good-bye, he pulled back a bit, his eyes still on my dark house. Across the street Scarlett's front porch light was already on, and I could see Marion in front of the TV in the living room, her shoes off, feet up on the coffee table. In the kitchen Scarlett was standing at the stove, stirring something.

"Well," I said to Macon, sliding my hand around his neck. "I guess I'll see you when I get back."

"Aren't you going to ask me to come in?"

"In?" I drew back. He'd never asked before. "Do you want to?"

"Sure." He reached down and opened his door, and just like that we were walking up the driveway, past my mother's mums, to the front steps. The paper was on the porch and a few leaves were blowing around, making scraping noises. It was getting ready to rain.

177

I fished around in my backpack for my keys, then unlocked the door and pushed it open just as there was a loud rumbling overhead. Even without looking up I could feel the plane coming closer, the thin line of windowpanes on either side of the door already vibrating.

"Man," Macon said. "That's loud."

"It's bad around this time," I told him. "There are lots of early evening flights." The house was completely dark inside, and I felt across the wall for the light switch. Right as the light came on overhead there was a popping noise, a flash, and we were in the dark again.

"Hold on," I said, dropping my backpack as he stepped in behind me, a few leaves blowing in across his feet. "I'll find another light."

And then I felt his arms wrap around me from behind, his hand, cool, on my stomach, and in the dark of my parents' alcove he kissed me. He didn't seem to have any problem negotiating the dark of the empty house, walking me backwards to the living room and the couch, pushing me down across my mother's needlepoint pillows. I kissed him back, letting his hand slide up my shirt, feeling the warmth of his legs pressing against mine. Another plane was rumbling in the distance.

"Macon," I said, coming up for air after a few minutes, "my father could be home any second."

He kept kissing me, his hand still exploring. Obviously this wasn't as much of a threat to him as it was to me.

"Macon." I pushed him back a little. "I'm serious."

"Okay, okay." He sat up, bumping back against another stack of pillows. My mother was into pillows. "Where's your sense of adventure?"

"You don't know my father," I said, like he was some big ogre, chasing boys across the yard with a shotgun. I was running enough risk just having him there; my father finding us alone in the dark would be another story altogether.

I got up and went into the kitchen, flicking on lights as I went. All the familiar things looked different with him trailing along behind me. I wondered what he was thinking.

"Do you want something to drink?" I said, opening the fridge.

"Nah," he said, pulling out a chair from the kitchen table and sitting down.

I was bending into the fridge, searching out a Coke, when I suddenly heard my father's voice, as if he'd stepped up right behind me. I swear I almost stopped breathing.

"Well, we're over here at the new Simpson Dry Cleaners, at the Lakeview Mall, and I'm Brian and I gotta tell you, I've seen a lot of dry cleaners before but this place is different. Herb and Mary Simpson, well, they know a little bit about this business, and . . ."

I felt my face get hot, blood rushing up in sheer panic, even after I realized it was just the radio and turned around to see Macon smiling behind me, his hand still on the knob.

"Not funny," I said, pulling over a chair to sit down next to him. He turned the volume down and I could only hear my father murmuring, something about same-day service and starch.

He said he wanted to see my room, and I knew why, but I took him up there anyway, climbing up the steps in the dark with him holding my hand. He walked around my bed, leaning into my mirror to examine the blue ribbons I'd gotten in gymnastics years ago, the pictures of Scarlett and me from the photo booth at the mall, mugging and smiling for the camera. He lay across my bed like he owned it. And as he leaned to kiss me, I had my eyes open, looking straight over his head to the top of my bookcase, at the Madame Alexander doll Grandma Halley had given me for my tenth birthday. It was Scarlett O'Hara, in a green-and-white dress and hat, and just seeing it for that second before I closed my eyes gave me that same pang of guilt, my mother's face flashing across, telling me how wrong this was.

Outside, the planes kept going over, shaking my windows. Macon kept sliding his hand under my waistband, pushing farther than he had before, and I kept pushing him back. We'd turned on my clock radio, low, to keep track of my father's whereabouts, but after a while it cut off and it was just us and silence, Macon's lips against my ear coaxing. His voice was low and rumbly and right in my ear, his fingers stroking the back of my neck. It all felt so good, and I would feel myself forgetting, slipping and losing myself in it, until all of a sudden—

"No," I said, grabbing his hand as he tried to unsnap my jeans, "this is not a good idea."

"Why not?" His voice was muffled.

"You know why not," I said.

"No, I don't."

"Macon."

"What's the big deal?" he asked me, rolling over onto his back, his head on my pillow. His shirt was unbuttoned; one hand was still on my stomach, fingers stretched across my skin.

"The big deal is that this is my house and my bed, and my father is due home at any time. I could get so busted."

He rolled over and turned up the radio again, my father's voice filling the room. *"So come on down here to Simpson's Dry Cleaners, we've got some prizes and great deals, and cake —there's cake, too?—how can you say no to cake? I'm Brian, I'm here till nine."* He just lay there, watching me, proving me wrong.

"It's just not a good idea," I said, reaching over and turning on the light. All around me my room jumped into place, the familiar parameters of my life: my bed, my carpet, my stuffed animals lined up across the third shelf of my bookshelf. There was a little green pig in the middle that Noah Vaughn had bought me for Valentine's day two years before. Noah had never slid his hand further than my neck, had never found ingenious ways to get places I was trying zealously to guard. Noah Vaughn had been happy just to hold my hand.

"Halley," Macon said, his voice low. "I'm into being patient and waiting and all, but it's been almost three months now."

"That's not that long," I said, picking at the worn spot in my comforter.

"It is to me." He rolled a little closer, putting his head in my lap. I had a sudden flash, out of nowhere, that he had done this before. "Just think about it, okay? We'll be careful, I promise."

"I think about it," I said, running my fingers through his hair. He closed his eyes. And I *did* think about it, all the time. But each time I was tempted, each time I wanted to give up my defense and pull back my troops, I thought of Scarlett. Of course I thought of Scarlett. She'd thought she was being careful, too.

He left not long after that. He didn't want to stay and watch TV or just hang out and talk. Something was changing, something I could sense even though I'd never been here before, like the way baby turtles know to go to the water at birth, instinctively. They just *know.* And I already knew I'd lose Macon, probably soon, if I didn't sleep with him. He kissed me goodbye and left, and I stood in my open door and watched him go, beeping like he always did as he rounded the corner.

As I lost sight of him, I thought of that sketched black outline, the colors inside just beginning to get filled in. The girl I'd been, the girl I was. I told myself the changes had come fast and furious these last few months, and one more wasn't that big of a deal. But each time I did I thought of Scarlett, always Scarlett, and that new color, that particular shade, which I wasn't ready to take on just yet.

When I went over to Scarlett's to say good-bye, there was food out on the kitchen table and counters, and she was squatted on the floor with a bucket and sponge, scrubbing the inside of the fridge.

"Can you smell it?" she said before I'd even opened my mouth. She hadn't even turned around. Pregnancy was making every one of her senses stronger, more intense, and I swear sometimes she seemed almost clairvoyant.

"Smell what?"

"You can't smell it?" Now she turned around, pointing her sponge at me. She took a deep breath, closing her eyes. "That. That rotting, stink kind of smell."

I breathed in, but all I was getting was Clorox from the bucket. "No."

"God." She stood up, grabbing onto the fridge door for support. It was harder for her to get to her feet now, her stomach throwing her off balance. "Cameron couldn't smell it either—he said I was being crazy. But I swear, it's so strong it's making me gag. I've had to hold my breath the whole time I've been doing this."

I looked over at the pregnancy Bible, which was lying on the table, open to the chapter on Month Five, which was fast approaching. I flipped through the pages as she bent down over the vegetable crisper, nose wrinkled, scrubbing like mad.

"Page seventy-four, bottom paragraph," I said out loud, following the words with my finger. "And I quote: 'Your sense of smell may become stronger during your pregnancy, causing an aversion to some foods.'"

"I cannot believe you don't smell that," she muttered, ignoring me.

"What are you going to do, scrub the whole house?" I said as she yanked out the butter dish, examined it, and dunked it in the bucket.

"If I have to."

"You're crazy."

"No," she said, "I'm pregnant and I'm allowed my eccentricities; the doctor said so. So shut up."

I pulled out a chair and sat down, resting my arm on the table. Every time I was in Scarlett's kitchen I thought back to the years we'd spent there, at the table, with the radio on. On long summer days we'd make chocolate-chip cookies and dance around the linoleum floor with our shoes off, the music turned up loud.

I sat down at the table, flipping through Month Five. "Look at this," I said. "For December we have continued constipation, leg cramps, and ankle swelling to look forward to."

"Great." She sat back on her heels, dropping the sponge in the bucket. "What else?"

"Ummm . . . varicose veins, maybe, and an easier or more difficult orgasm."

She turned around, pushing her hair out of her face. "Halley. Please."

"I'm just reading the book."

"Well, you of all people should know orgasms are not my big concern right now. I'm more interested in finding whatever is rotting in this kitchen."

I still couldn't smell anything, but I knew better than to argue. Scarlett was handling things now, and I was proud of her; she was eating better, walking around the block for a half hour every day because she'd heard it was good for the baby, and reading everything she could get her hands on about child rearing. Everything, that is, except the adoption articles and pamphlets that Marion kept leaving on the lazy Susan or on her bed, always with a card from someone interested in Discussing the Options. Scarlett was playing along because she had to, but she was keeping the baby. Like everything else, she'd made her choice and she'd stick to it, everyone else be damned.

"Scarlett?" I said.

"Yeah?" her voice was muffled; she had her head stuck under the meat and cheese drawer, inspecting.

"What made you decide to sleep with him?"

She drew herself out, slowly, and turned to face me. "Why?"

"I don't know," I shrugged. "Just wondered."

"Did you sleep with Macon?"

185

"No," I said. "Of course not."

"But he wants you to."

"No, not exactly." I spun the lazy Susan. "He brought it up, that's all."

She walked over and sat down beside me, pulling her hair back with her hands. She smelled like Clorox. "What did you say?"

"I told him I'd think about it."

She sat back, absorbing this. "Do you want to?"

"I don't know. But he does, and it's not that big a deal to him, you know? He doesn't understand why it is to me."

"That's bullshit," she said simply. "He knows why."

"It's not like that," I said. "I mean, I really like him. And I think for guys like him—like that—it isn't that big of a deal. It's just what, you know, you *do*."

"Halley." She shook her head. "This isn't about *him*. It's about *you*. You shouldn't do anything you're not ready for."

"I'm ready," I said.

"Are you sure?"

"Were *you* ready?" I said.

That stopped her. She smoothed her hands over her stomach; it looked like she'd swallowed a small melon, or a pumpkin. "I don't know. Probably not. I loved him, and one night things just went farther than they had before. Afterwards I realized it was a mistake, in more ways than one."

"Because it came off," I said.

"Yeah. And for other reasons, too. But I can't preach to you,

186

because I was sure I was doing the right thing. I didn't know he'd be gone the next day. Like, literally *gone*. But you have to consider that."

"That he might die?"

"Not die," she said softly, and there was that ripple again, the one that still came over her face whenever she spoke of him, and I suddenly realized how long it had really been. "I mean, I loved Michael so much, but—I didn't know him that well. Just for a summer, you know. A lot could have happened this fall. I'll never know."

"I can tell he wants to. Like soon. He's getting more pushy about it."

"If you sleep with him, it will change things," she said. "It has to. And if he goes, you'll have lost more than just him. So be sure, Halley. Be real sure."

Chapter Twelve

Grandma Halley was staying in a place called Evergreen Rest Care Facility. Some of the people were bedridden, but others could get around; women in motorized wheelchairs zoomed past us down the corridors, their purses clamped against their laps. Everything smelled fruity and sharp, like too much cheap air freshener. It seemed like every open piece of wall had a Thanksgiving decoration taped to it, turkeys and Pilgrims and corn husks, and you got the sense that holidays there were imperative, important, because there wasn't much else to look forward to.

I'd slept for most of the trip up, since my father wanted to leave at four A.M. to get the jump on all the other travelers. My father was always concerned with "getting the jump" when we traveled, obsessed with outsmarting other motorists; once in the car, he flipped the radio dial constantly, checking out his competition, something that drove me crazy since I never got to hear any music.

Before we left I lay awake most of the night, listening for cars outside. I was sure Macon would come by, even just to beep, to say good-bye again. He knew I was upset about my grandmother, but it made him uncomfortable; family stuff was not really his department. I didn't want to leave things the way we had, unresolved, and I pictured him in the few places I knew he went, with the few friends of his I'd met, and tried to tell myself he cared about me enough not to look elsewhere for what I wasn't giving him.

The first thing I thought when I walked into Grandma Halley's room was how small she looked. She was in bed, her eyes closed, and a square of sunlight was falling across her face from the window. She looked like a doll, her face porcelain and unreal, like the Madame Alexander Scarlett O'Hara she'd given me.

"Hi there." My mother stood up from a chair by the window. I hadn't even seen her. "How was the trip?"

"Fine," I said as she came over and kissed me.

"Fine," my father said, putting his arm around her waist. "We made great time. Really got the jump on everyone."

"Come outside," she said softly. "She's had a hard night and she really needs her rest."

Out in the corridor a pack of women in wheelchairs was passing, laughing and talking, and next to Grandma Halley's room, behind a half-closed door, I could see someone hooked up to a machine, a tube in his nose. The room was dark, the shades drawn.

"So how's everything?" my mother said to me, pulling me close. "I've missed you guys so much."

"How are you?" my father said, noticing as I did how tired

189

she looked, her face older and more drawn, as if just time in this place could age you.

"I'm okay," she said to him, her arm still around me. I was uncomfortable, my arm clamped in an odd position against my side, but this was important to her, so I didn't move. "She's doing much better today. Every day she just improves by leaps and bounds." Every few words she squeezed my shoulder again for emphasis.

When we went back inside I only spoke with Grandma Halley for a few minutes. At first, when she opened her eyes and saw me there was no flicker of recognition, no instant understanding that I was who I was, and that scared me. As if I had already changed into another girl, another Halley, features and voice and manners all shifting to make me unrecognizable.

"It's Halley, Mother," my own mother said softly from the other side of the bed, looking across at me encouragingly, since she couldn't squeeze my shoulder and pass this off as better than it was.

And then I saw it, flooding across my grandmother's antique, careful features: she found me in the strange face looking down at her. "Halley," she said, almost scolding, as if I was an old friend playing a trick on her. "How are you, sweetheart?"

"I'm good. I've missed you," I said, and I took her hand, so small in mine, and wrapped my fingers around it. I could feel the bones in it working, moving to grab hold, as I carefully squeezed it, emphasizing, reassuring, that everything would be all right.

*   *   *

Later, we watched Grandma Halley eat turkey and cranberry Jell-O off an orange plastic, cornucopia-decorated tray. The halls at Evergreen were packed with other relatives now, making pilgrimages; at one point when I passed the room next door, the man with the tubes and machines had a crowd around his bed, all talking softly and huddled together. Outside, in the hallway, a little girl in a pinafore and Mary Janes was playing hopscotch across the linoleum tiles. The halls had a different smell now, of air freshener mingled with hundreds of types of perfumes and hair spray, the outside world suddenly mixed in.

That evening we went to a hotel downtown and paid a flat twenty bucks each for a Thanksgiving buffet, rows and rows of steam tables full of mashed potatoes and gravy and cranberry sauce and pumpkin pie. Everyone was dressed up and eating at little tables, like a huge family broken up into pieces. My father ate three plates' worth and my mother, her face tired and lined from lack of sleep, talked the entire time, nonstop, as if enough words could make it less strange, less different from every other Thanksgiving we'd ever had. She asked me tons of questions, just to keep the conversation going, about Scarlett and school and Milton's. My father told a long story about some listener who'd stripped naked and run down Main Street for concert tickets, the station's latest coup. I picked at my mashed potatoes, smooth as silk, and wondered what Macon was doing, if he even had a turkey dinner or just a Big Mac in his empty room and another party without me. I missed him, just like I missed the lumpy potatoes my mother made every Thanksgiving.

We settled into Grandma Halley's house, me in my old room from all those summers, my parents down the hall in the guest room with the blue flowered wallpaper. Nothing much had changed. The cat was still fat, the pipes still wheezed all night, and each time I passed the bell in the staircase window I touched it automatically, without thinking, announcing myself to the empty stairwell.

In the evenings I reread the few magazines I'd brought or called Scarlett. She'd cooked an entire traditional dinner for Cameron (whose family ate early) and Marion and Steve/Vlad, who showed up, she told me, in dress pants, with his clanking boots and medallion necklace and what she said could only be described politely as a tunic.

"A what?" I said.

"A tunic," she said simply. "Like a big shirt, with a drawstring collar, that hung down past his waist."

"He tucked it in, right?"

"No," she said. "He just wore it. And I swear Marion hardly even noticed."

This fascinated me. "What did you say?"

"What could I say? I told him to sit down and gave him a bowl of nuts. I don't know, Marion's crazy for him. She wouldn't care if he showed up butt naked."

I laughed. "Stop."

"I'm serious." She sighed. "Well, at least dinner went well. Cameron kept the conversation going, and I was highly complimented on my potatoes. Not that I could eat them. My back has been killing me and I've been feeling nauseous since last week. Something is rotting in the kitchen. Did I tell you that?"

"Yeah, you did," I said. "Did they have lumps?"

"What?"

"The potatoes. Did they have lumps?"

"Of course they did," she said. "They're only good if they have lumps."

"I know it," I said. "Save me a bowl, okay?"

"Okay," she said, her voice crackling across the line, reassuring as always. "I will."

I got to know my Grandma Halley a little better that weekend, and it wasn't through the few short visits I spent by her bedside, holding her hand. She was still in pain from her surgery and a little confused; she called me Julie more than once, and told me stories that trailed off midway, fading out in the quiet. And all the while my mother was there behind me, or beside me, finishing the sentences my grandmother couldn't, and trying to make everything right again.

In my bedroom at Grandma Halley's, there was an old cabinet made out of sweet-smelling wood with roses painted across the doors. One night when I was bored I opened it up, and inside were stacks of boxes, photographs, letters, and odds and ends, little things my grandmother, who was an intense pack rat, couldn't bear to throw away. There were pictures of her as a teenager in fancy dancing dresses posing with gaggles of other girls, all of them smiling. Her hair had been long and dark, and she wore it twisted up over her head, with flowers woven across the crown. There was one box full of dance cards with boys' names signed in them, each dance numbered off. I found a wedding picture of her and my grandfather bending over a cake, the knife in both their hands. It all fascinated me. I read the letters she wrote to her mother during her first trip abroad, where she spent four pages describing an Indian boy she met in the park, and every word he said, and how blue the sky was. And the later letters about my grandfather, how much she loved him, letters that were returned to her postmarked and neatly tied with string when her own mother died.

I went downstairs and found my mother at the kitchen table, drinking a cup of tea and sitting in Grandma Halley's big green chair by the window. She didn't hear me come in and jumped when I touched her shoulder.

"Hey," she said. "What are you still doing up?"

"I've been reading all this stuff of Grandma Halley's," I said, sliding in beside her. "Look at this." And I showed her the dance card I had tied to my wrist, and the wedding picture of them dancing past the band, and my birth announcement, carefully saved in its own envelope. Hours had passed as I'd sat going through my grandmother's life, stored in boxes and envelopes, neatly organized as if she'd meant for me to find it there all along.

"Can you believe she was ever so young," my mother said, holding the wedding picture to the light. "See the necklace she's wearing? She gave that to me on my wedding day. It was my 'something borrowed.'"

"She fell in love with an Indian boy the summer she was nineteen," I told her. "In a park in London. He wrote to her for two years afterwards."

"No kidding," she said softly, her fingers idly brushing across my hair. "She never told me."

"And you know that bell she keeps in the window halfway up the stairs? Grandpa bought her that at a flea market in Spain, when he was in the service."

"Really?"

"You should read the letters," I said, looking down at my own name on the birth announcement: *Welcome, Halley!*

She smiled at me, as if remembering suddenly when moments like this between us were not noticed for the very fact of how rare they were.

"Honey," she said, gathering up my hair in her hands, "I'm sorry about that night at the restaurant. I know it's hard to understand why we can't let you see Macon. But it's for the best. Someday you'll understand that."

"No," I said. "I won't." And then, just as easily as it had closed, the distance opened up between us. I could almost see it.

She sighed, letting my hair drop. She felt it, too. "Well, it's late. You should get to bed, okay?"

"Yeah, okay." I got up and walked toward the stairs, past the framed front page of the local paper, announcing the comet's arrival. HALLEY MAKES ANOTHER VISIT, it said.

"I remember when the comet came through," I said, and she walked up behind me, reading over my shoulder. "I sat in Grandma's lap and we watched it together."

"Oh, honey, you were so little," she said easily. "And it really wasn't clear at all. You didn't see anything. I remember."

And that was it; it was so easy for her. My own *memories* did not even belong to me.

But I knew she was wrong. I had seen that comet. I knew it as well as I knew my own face, my own hands. My own heart.

The next morning we locked up the house, fed the cat and left money for the petsitter, then piled into the car for one last visit with Grandma Halley. Evergreen was quiet then, with the visitors already having hit the road, getting the jump on each other. My father said his good-bye quickly and went out to the parking lot to stand by the car, eyes on the freeway ramp, his head ducked against the wind. Inside, behind the sealed-for-your-own-safety windows, we couldn't even hear it blowing.

I sat for a long time next to Grandma Halley's bed, her hand in mine, with my mother on the other side. She was coherent, but barely; she was tired, the drugs made her woozy, and she kept closing her eyes. Her cheek was dry when I kissed it, and as I pulled back she put her hand against my face, her fingers smooth and cool, smiling at me but saying nothing. I remembered the girl in the pictures, with the roses and the long dancing dresses, and I smiled back.

I waited in the hallway while my mother said good-bye. I stood against the wall, under the clock, and listened to it ticking. Inside, my mother's voice was low and even, and I couldn't make out any words. Next door, the man with the tubes was alone again, the equipment by his bed beeping in the dark. The TV over his bed was showing only static.

Finally, after about twenty minutes, I walked back to the half-open door. My mother had her back to me, one hand on Grandma Halley's, and as I looked closely I could see Grandma Halley had fallen asleep, her eyes closed, breath even and soft. And my mother, who had spent the entire holiday weekend almost manic with reassurance, squeezing my shoulder and smiling, forcing conversation, was crying. She had her head down, resting against the rail of the bed, and her shoulders shook as she wept, with Grandma Halley sleeping on, oblivious. It scared me, the same way I'd been scared the night I came home from Sisterhood Camp and found Scarlett in tears on her porch, waiting for me. There are some things in this world you rely on, like a sure bet. And when they let you down, shifting from where you've carefully placed them, it shakes your faith, right where you stand.

Chapter Thirteen

Now that it was Month Five, there was no hiding anymore that Scarlett was pregnant. With her stomach protruding and her face always flushed, even the drab green Milton's Market apron couldn't keep her secret. The first week of December, she got called in to talk to Mr. Averby. I went along for moral support.

"Now, Scarlett." Mr. Averby looked over his desk and smiled at us. He was about my dad's age, with a bald spot he tried to cover with creative combing. "I couldn't help but notice that you have some, uh, news."

"News?" Scarlett said. She had this little game she played with people; she liked to make them say it.

"Yes, well, what I mean is that it's come to my attention—I mean, I've noticed—that you seem to be expecting."

"Expecting," Scarlett said, nodding. "I'm pregnant."

"Right," he said quickly. He looked like he might start sweating. "So, I just wondered, if there was anything we should discuss concerning this."

"I don't think so," Scarlett said, shifting her weight in the chair. She could never get comfortable anymore. "Do you?"

"Well, no, but I do think that it should be acknowledged, because there might be problems, with the position, that someone in your condition might have." He was having a hard time getting it out, clearly, that he was worried about what the customers might think of a pregnant sixteen-year-old checkout girl at Milton's, Your Family Supermarket. That it was a bad example. Or bad business. Or something.

"I don't think so," Scarlett said cheerfully. "The doctor says it's fine for me to be on my feet, as long as it's not full time. And my work won't be affected, Mr. Averby."

"She's a very good worker," I said, jumping in. "Employee of the Month in August."

"That's right." Scarlett grinned at me. She'd already told me she wouldn't quit for anything, not even to save Milton's embarrassment. And they couldn't fire her. It was against the law; she knew that from her Teen Mothers Support Group.

"You *are* a very good worker," Mr. Averby said, and now he was shifting around in his seat like he couldn't get comfortable either. "I just didn't know how you felt about keeping up your hours now. If you wanted to cut back or discuss other options or—"

"Nope. Not at all. I'm perfectly happy," Scarlett said, cutting him off. "But I really appreciate your consideration."

Now Mr. Averby just looked tired, beaten. Resigned. "Okay," he said. "Then I guess that's that. Thanks for coming in, Scarlett, and please let me know if you have any problems."

"Thanks," she said, and we stood up together and walked out

of the office, shutting the door behind us. We made it through Bulk Foods and Cereal before she started giggling and had to stop and rest.

"Poor guy," I said as she bent over, still cackling. "He never knew what hit him."

"Nope. He thought I'd be glad to leave." She leaned against the rows of imported coffees, catching her breath. "I'm not ashamed, Halley. I know I'm doing the right thing and they can't make me think any different."

"I know you are," I said, and I wondered again why the right thing always seemed to be met with so much resistance, when you'd think it would be the easier path. You had to fight to be virtuous, or so I was noticing.

As December came, and everything was suddenly green and red and tinseled, and holiday music pounded in my ears at work, "Jingle Bells" again and again and *again*, I still hadn't made any real decision about Macon. The only reason I was getting out of it was the pure fact that we hadn't seen each other much, except in school, which was the one place I didn't have to worry about things going too far. I was working extra holiday shifts at Milton's and busy with Scarlett, too. She needed me more than ever. I drove her to doctor's appointments, pushed the cart at Baby Superstore while she priced cribs and strollers, and went out more than once late in the evening for chocolate-raspberry ice cream when it was crucially needed. I even sat with her as she wrote draft after draft of a letter to Mrs. Sherwood at her new address in Florida, each one beginning with *You don't know me, but*. That was the easy part. The rest was harder.

Macon was busy, too. He was always ducking out of school early or not showing up at all, calling me for two-minute conversations at all hours where he always had to hang up suddenly. He couldn't come to my house or even drop me off down the street because it was too risky. My mother didn't mention him much; she assumed her rules were being followed. She was busy with her work and arranging Grandma Halley's move into another facility, anyway.

"It's just that he's different," I complained to Scarlett as we sat on her bed reading magazines one afternoon. I was reading *Elle*; she, *Working Mother*. Cameron was downstairs making Kool-Aid, Scarlett's newest craving. He put so much sugar in it, it gave you a headache, but it was just the way she liked it. "It's not like it was."

"Halley," she said. "You read *Cosmo*. You know that no relationship stays in that giddy stage forever. This is normal."

"You think?"

"Yes," she said, flipping another page. "Completely."

There were still a few times that month, as Christmas bore down on us, when I had to stop him as his hand moved further toward what I hadn't decided to sign over just yet. Twice at his house, on Friday nights as we lay in his bed, so close it seemed inevitable. Once in the car, parked by the lake, when it was cold and he pulled away from me suddenly, shaking his head in the dark. It wasn't just him, either. It was getting harder for me, too.

"Do you love him?" Scarlett asked me one day after I told her of this last incident. We were at Milton's, sitting on the loading dock for our break, surrounded by packs upon packs of tomato juice.

"Yes," I said. I'd never said it, but I did.

"Does he love you?"

"Yes," I said, fudging a bit.

It didn't work. She took another bite of her bagel and said, "Has he told you that?"

"No. Not exactly."

She sat back, not saying any more. Her point, I assumed, was made.

"But that's such a cliché," I said. "I mean, *Do you love me.* Like that means anything. Like if he did say it, then I should sleep with him, and if he didn't, I shouldn't."

"I didn't say that," she said simply. "All I'm saying is I would hope he did before you went ahead with this."

"It's just three words," I said casually, finishing off my Coke. "I mean, lots of people sleep together without saying, 'I love you.'"

Scarlett sat back, pulling her legs as best she could against her stomach. "Not people like us, Halley. Not people like us."

*　　*　　*

My mother, who is serious and businesslike about most things, is an absolute fanatic about the holidays. Christmas begins at our house the second the last bite of Thanksgiving dinner is eaten, and our Christmas tree, decorated and sagging with way too many ornaments, does not come down until New Year's Day. It drives my father, who always loudly proclaims himself a Christmas atheist, completely bananas. If it was up to him, the tree would be dismantled and out at the curb ten seconds after the last gift was opened—a done deal. Actually, if given his choice, we wouldn't have a tree, period. We'd just hand each other our gifts in the bags they came in (his chosen wrapping paper), eat a big meal, and watch football on TV. But he knew when he married my mother, who insisted on a New Year's Eve wedding, that he wouldn't get that. Not even a chance.

I figured Grandma Halley's being sick would make the holidays a little less important this year, or at least distract my mother. I was wrong. If anything, it was more important that this be the Perfect Christmas, the Best We've Ever Had. She took a day, maybe, after we got home from Thanksgiving before the boxes of ornaments came out, the stockings went up, and the planning was in full swing. It was dizzying.

"We have to get a tree," she announced around the fourth night of December. We were at the dinner table. "Tonight, I was thinking. It would be something nice to do together."

My father did it for the first time that year, a combination of a sigh and something muttered under his breath. His sole holiday tradition: The Christmas Grumble.

"The lot's open until nine," she said cheerfully, reaching over me for my plate.

"I have a lot of homework," I said, my standard excuse, and my father kicked me under the table. If he was going, I was going.

The lot was packed, so it took my mother about a half hour, in the freezing cold, to find the Perfect Tree. I stood by the car, more frustrated by the minute, as I watched her walk the aisles of spruces with my father yanking out this one, then that one, for her inspection. Overhead, what sounded like the same Christmas tape we had at Milton's played loudly; I knew every word, every beat, every pause, mouthing along without even realizing it.

"Hi, Halley." I turned around and saw Elizabeth Gunderson, standing there holding hands with a little girl wearing a tutu and a heavy winter coat. They had identical faces and hair color. I hadn't seen her much lately; after the scandal with her boyfriend and best friend, she'd been away for a couple of weeks "getting her appendix out"; the rumor was she'd been in some kind of hospital, but that was never verified either.

"Hey, Elizabeth," I said, smiling politely. I was not going to make a mute fool of myself again.

"Lizabeth, I want to go look at the mistletoe," the little girl said, yanking her toward the display by the register. "Come *on.*"

"One second, Amy," Elizabeth said coolly, yanking back. The little girl pouted, stomping one ballet slipper. "So, Halley, what's up?"

"Not much. Doing the family thing."

"Yeah, me, too." She looked down at Amy, who had let go of her hand and was now twirling, lopsidedly, between us. "So, how are things with Macon?"

"Good," I said, just as coolly as I could, my eyes on Amy's pink tutu.

"I've been seeing him out a lot at Rhetta's," she said. "You know Rhetta, right?"

The correct answer to this, of course, was "Sure."

"I've never seen you over there with him, but I figured I was just missing you." She tossed her hair back, a classic Elizabeth Gunderson gesture; I could still see her in her cheerleading uniform, kicking high in the air, that hair swinging. "You know, since Mack and I broke up, I've been spending a lot of time over there."

"That's too bad," I said. "I mean, about you and Mack."

"Yeah." Her breath came out in a big white puff. "Macon's been so great, he really understands about that kind of stuff. You're so lucky to have him."

I watched her, forgetting for the moment about being cool and friendly, about maintaining my facade. I tried to read her eyes, to see beyond the words to what might really be happening at Rhetta's, a place I'd never been. Or been invited to. Elizabeth Gunderson obviously hadn't been grounded, her life controlled by her mother's hand. Elizabeth Gunderson could *go* places.

"Elizabeth!" We both looked over to see a man standing by a BMW, a tree lashed to the roof. The engine was running. "Let's go, honey. Amy, you, too."

"Well," Elizabeth said as Amy ran over to the car, "I guess I'll see you tomorrow in class, right?"

"Right."

She waved, like we were friends, and her dad shut the door behind her. As they pulled away, their headlights flooded my face, making me squint, and I couldn't tell whether she was watching me.

"We found one!" I heard my mother say behind me. "It's just about perfect and it's a good thing because your father was almost completely out of patience."

"Good," I said.

"Was that one of your friends from school?" she said as Elizabeth's car pulled out.

"No," I said under my breath. The Christmas Mumble.

"Do I know her?"

"No," I said more loudly. She thought she knew everyone. "I *hate* her, anyway."

My mother took a step back and looked at me. As a therapist, this was almost permission for her to pick my brain.

"You hate her," she repeated. "Why?"

"No reason." I was sorry I'd said anything.

"Well, here's the damn tree," my father said in his booming radio voice; a few people looked over. He walked up and thrust it between us so I got a face full of needles. "Best of the lot, or so your mother is convinced."

"Let's go home," my mother said, still watching me through the tree. You'd think she'd never heard me say I hated anyone before. "It's getting late."

"Fine," my father said. "I think we can stuff this in the back, if we're lucky."

They went around to the back of the car and I sat in the front seat, slamming the door harder than I should have. I did hate Elizabeth Gunderson, and I hated the fact God gave me virginity just so I'd have to lose it someday and I even hated Christmas, just because I could. In September I'd told Scarlett that Macon belonged with someone like Elizabeth, and maybe I'd been right. I wasn't ready to think about the other yet: that it wasn't that I wasn't right for Macon, but that maybe he wasn't right for me. There *was* a difference. Even for someone who things didn't come so easy for, someone like me.

The next afternoon, when I was supposedly at work and Macon and I were over at his house, his hand crept back again to our familiar battleground. I grabbed it, sat up, and said, "Who's Rhetta?"

He looked at me. "Who?"

"Rhetta."

"Why?"

"I just want to know."

He sighed loudly, dramatically, then flopped back across the bed. "She's just this friend of mine," he said. "She lives over on Coverdale."

"You go over there a lot?" I knew I sounded petty and jealous, but there was no other way to handle this. I was prepared, soon, to hand over something valuable to him. I needed to be sure.

"Sometimes." He traced my belly button with one finger, absently. To him, this was obviously no big deal. "How'd you know about her?"

"Elizabeth Gunderson," I said. I was watching his face closely for a sign, any suspicious ripple at the sound of her name.

"Yeah, she's over there sometimes," he said casually. "She and Rhetta are friends, or something."

"Really."

"Yeah." I was watching him, and he just stared back, suddenly catching on, and said, "What, Halley? What's your problem?"

"Nothing," I said. "I just thought it was weird you never mentioned it. Elizabeth said she'd seen you there a lot."

"Elizabeth doesn't know anything."

"She acts like she does," I said.

"So? Is that my fault?" He was getting angry. "God, Halley, it's *nothing*, okay? Why is this important now?"

"It isn't," I said. "Except half the time I don't know where you are or what you're doing and then I hear from Elizabeth you're off somewhere you never told me about hanging out with her."

"I'm not hanging out with her. I'm at the same place she is, sometimes. I'm not used to being accountable to anyone. I can't tell you what I'm doing every second, because half the time I don't even know *myself*." He shook his head. "It's just the way I am."

Back in the beginning, when P.E. was my life and nothing had happened between us yet, it wasn't like this. Even two months ago, when I'd spent my afternoons just driving around with him, listening to the radio under a bright blue fall sky, there hadn't been these issues, these awkward silences. We didn't talk or laugh as much anymore, or even just play around. Everything had narrowed to just going to his house, parking out by the lake and battling for territory while arguing about trust and expectations. It was like dealing with my mother.

"Look," he said, and he slid his arm around my waist, pulling me close against him. "You've just got to trust me, okay?"

"I know," I said, and it was easy to believe him as we lay there in the early winter darkness, him kissing my forehead, my bare feet entwined with his. It all felt good, real good, and this is what people *did;* all people, except me. I felt closer than ever to telling him I loved him, but I bit it back. He had to say it first, and I willed him to just as I'd willed him to come over to me in P.E. when it all began.

Feuilleton, feuilleton, I thought hard in my head as he kissed

209

me. *Feuilleton, feuilleton.* Kissing him felt so good and I closed my eyes, feeling his skin warm against mine, breathing him in.

Feuilleton, feuilleton, as his hand crept down to my waistband. *I love you, I love you.*

But I didn't hear it, just like I always hadn't. I pushed his hand back, trying to keep kissing him, but he pulled away, shaking his head.

"What?" I said, but I knew.

"Is it me?" he asked. "I mean, is it just you don't want to do it with me?"

"No," I said. "Of course not. It's just—it's a big deal to me."

"You said you were thinking about it."

"I am." *Every damn second,* I thought. "I am, Macon."

He sat back, his hands still around my waist. "What happened with Scarlett," he said confidently, "that's, like, an impossibility. We'll be careful."

"It's not about that."

He was watching me. "Then what is it about?"

"It's about me," I told him, and by the way he shifted, looking out the window, I could tell that wasn't the right answer. "It's just the way I am."

We had come to the same place we always did, a place I knew well. Just standing across the battle line, eye to eye, no further than where we'd started. A draw.

Christmas was coming, and everyone seemed suddenly giddy. All the mothers came into Milton's in sweatshirts with wreaths and reindeer on them and even my boss, congested Mr. Averby, wore a Santa hat on the day before Christmas. My parents went to party after party, and I lay in bed and listened to them as they came home, half drunk and silly, their voices muffled and giggly downstairs. Grandma Halley's move to the rest home was all set, and my mother was going up there in early January to help. I thought of my grandmother in that tiny room, small in her bed, and pushed the thought away.

We had our tree, all the presents beneath it, and the Christmas cards lined up on the mantel. We had lights strung up across the porch and Christmas knickknacks on every free bit of table or wall space. My father kept breaking things. First, with a too-bold arm movement, he sent the chubby smiling porcelain Santa off the end table and into the wall, and later one of the three Wise Men from the crèche under the tree rolled across the floor and was flattened, easily, as he walked through the room. *Crunch.* This happened every year, which explained why all of our Christmas sets were short something—a baby Jesus, one reindeer, the tallest singing caroller. The Christmas Victims.

Scarlett and I did our shopping together at the mall, in the evenings; she bought an ABBA CD for Cameron, his favorite, and I got Macon a pair of Ray-Ban sunglasses, since he was always losing his. The mall was crowded and hot and even the little mechanical elves in the Santa Village seemed tired.

I felt like I saw Macon less and less. He was always running off with his friends, his phone calls shorter and shorter. When he did pick me up or we went out it wasn't just us anymore; we were usually giving someone a ride here or there, or one of his friends tagged along. He was constantly distracted, and I stopped finding candy in my pockets and backpack. One day in the bathroom I overheard some girl saying Macon had stolen her boyfriend's car stereo, but when I asked him he just laughed and shook his head, telling me not to believe everything I heard in the bathroom. When he called me now, from noisy places I wondered about, I got the feeling it was only because he felt he had to, not because he missed me. I was losing him, I could feel it. I had to act soon.

Meanwhile, my mother was so happy, sure that things were good between us again. I'd catch her smiling at me from across the room, pleased with herself, as if to say, *See, wasn't I right? Isn't this better?*

On Christmas Eve, after my parents had left for another party, Macon came over to give me my present. He'd called from the gas station down the street and said he only had a minute. I met him outside.

"Here," he said, handing me a box wrapped in red paper. "Open it now."

It was a ring, silver and thick, that looked like nothing I would have picked out for myself. But when I slid it on, it looked just right. "Wow," I said, holding up my right hand. "It's beautiful."

"Yeah. I knew it would be." He already had the sunglasses; I wasn't good at keeping secrets. He'd convinced me to give him his present the day I got it, begging and pleading like a little kid. They were only half his present, but he didn't know that yet.

"Merry Christmas," I said, leaning over and kissing him. "And thanks."

"No problem," he said. "It looks good on you." He lifted up my hand and inspected my finger.

"So," I asked, "what are you doing tonight?"

"Nothing much." He let my hand drop. "Just going out with the fellas."

"Don't you have to do stuff with your mom?"

He shrugged. "Not tonight."

"Are you going over to Rhetta's?"

A sigh. He rolled his eyes. "I don't know, Halley. Why?"

I kicked at a bottle on the ground by my feet. "Just wondered."

"Don't start this again, okay?" He glanced down the road. One mention of this and he was already twitchy, ready to go.

But I couldn't stop. "Why don't you ever take me there?" I said. "Or any of the places you go? I mean, what do you guys do?"

"It's nothing," he said easily. "You wouldn't like it. You'd be bored."

"I would not." I looked at him. "Are you ashamed of me or something?"

"No," he said. "Of course not. Look, Halley. Some of the places I hang out I wouldn't *want* you to go. It's not your kind of place, you know?"

213

I was pretty sure this was an insult. "What does that mean?"

"Nothing." He waved me off, frustrated. "Forget it."

"What, you think I'm too naive or something? To hang out with your friends?"

"That's not what I said." He sighed. "Let's not do this. Please?"

I had a choice here: to let it go, and wonder if that what was what he meant, or keep at him and be sure. But it was Christmas, and the lights on the tree in our front window were twinkling and bright. I had a ring on my finger, and that had to mean something.

"I'm sorry," I said. "I really like my ring."

"Good." He kissed me, smoothing back my hair. "I gotta go, okay? I'll call you."

"Okay."

He kissed me again, then went around to the driver's side of the car, his head ducked against the wind. "Macon."

"What?" He was half in the car, half out.

"What are you doing for New Year's?"

"I don't know yet. Why?"

"Because I want to spend it with you," I said. Even as I said it I hoped he understood what I was saying, how big this was. What I was giving him. "Okay?"

He stood there, watching my face, and then nodded. "Okay. It's a plan."

"Merry Christmas," I said again as he got in the car.

"Merry Christmas," he called out, then turned on the engine, gunning it, and backed out of the driveway. At the bottom he flashed his lights and beeped, then screeched away noisily, bringing on Mr. Harper's front light.

So that was that. I'd made my choice and now I had to stick to it. I told myself it was the right thing, what I wanted to do, yet something still felt uneven and off-balance. But it was too late to go back now.

Then I heard Scarlett's voice.

"Halley! Come here!"

I whirled around. She was standing in her open front door, hand on her stomach, waving frantically. Behind her I could see Cameron, a blotch of black against the yellow light of the living room.

"Now! Hurry!" She was yelling as I ran across the street, my mind racing: something was wrong with the baby. The baby. The baby.

I got to her front stoop, panting, already in crisis mode, and found her smiling at me, her face excited. "What?" I said. "What is it?"

"This." And she took my hand and put it on her stomach, toward the middle and down, and I felt her skin, warm under my hand. I looked up at her, wondering, and then I felt it. A ripple under my hand, resistance—a kick.

"Did you feel that?" she said, putting her hand over mine. She was grinning. "Did you?"

"Yeah," I said, holding my hand there as it—the baby— kicked again, and again. "That's amazing."

"I know, I know." She laughed. "The doctor said it should happen soon, but when it did, it just freaked me out. I was just sitting on the couch and *boom*. I can't even explain it."

"You should have seen her face," Cameron said in his low, quiet voice. "She almost started crying."

"I did not," Scarlett said, elbowing him. "It was just—I mean, you hear about what it's like to feel it for the first time, and you think people are just dramatic—but it was really *something*, you know. Really something."

"I know," I said, and we sat down together on the stoop. I looked at Scarlett, her face flushed, fingers spread across the skin of her belly, and I wanted to tell her what I'd decided. But it wasn't the time, so just I put my hand over hers, feeling the kicks, and held on.

Chapter Fourteen

My mother spent the whole day of New Year's Eve madly cleaning the house for her annual New Year's Anniversary Party. She was so distracted it wasn't until late afternoon, as I lifted my legs so she could get to a patch of floor by the TV, that she concerned herself with me.

"So what are your plans tonight?" she asked, spraying a fog of Pledge on the coffee table and then attacking it with a dustcloth. "You and Scarlett going to watch the ball drop in Times Square?"

"I don't know," I said. "We haven't decided."

"Well, I've been thinking," she said, working her way over to the mantel, and then around the Christmas tree, which regardless of my father's loudest grumbling was still standing, dropping what seemed like mountains of needles anytime anyone passed it. "Why not just stay here and help me out? I sure could use it."

"Yeah, right," I said. I honestly thought she was joking. I mean, it was New Year's Eve, for God's sake. I watched her as she sanitized the bookcase.

"The Vaughns will be here, and you can keep an eye on Clara

217

for us, and you and Scarlett always like helping out at the party—"

"Wait a second," I said, but she kept moving, dusting knick-knacks like her life depended on it. "I have plans tonight."

"Well, you don't sound like you do," she said in a clipped voice, lifting up the Grand Canyon picture and dabbing at it with the cloth, then setting it back on the mantel. "It sounds like you and Scarlett don't even know what you're doing. So I just thought it would be better—"

"No," I said, and then suddenly realized I sounded more forceful than I should, more desperate, as I felt the net start to close around me. "I can't."

I half expected her to spin around, rag in hand, point at me and say, *You're going to sleep with him tonight!* proving she had somehow managed to read my mind, and once again making my choice for me before I had a chance to think for myself.

"I just think you and Scarlett can watch TV and hang out over here as easily as you can over there, Halley. And I would feel better knowing where you were."

"It's New Year's Eve," I said. "I'm sixteen. You can't make me stay home."

"Oh, Halley," she said, sighing. "Stop being so dramatic."

"Why are you doing this?" I said. "You can't just come in here at five o'clock and forbid me to go out. It's not fair."

She turned to look at me, the dust rag loose in her hand. "Okay," she said finally, really watching me for the smallest flicker of wavering strength on my part. "You can go to Scarlett's. But know that I am trusting you, Halley. Don't make me regret it."

And suddenly, it was so hard to keep looking at her. After all these months of negotiating and bartering, putting up strongholds and retreating, she'd used her last weapon: trust.

"Okay," I said, and I fought that sudden pull from all those days at the Grand Canyon and before. When she was my friend, my best friend. "You can trust me."

"Okay," she said quietly, still watching me, and I let her break her gaze first.

As I got dressed to go out that night I stood in front of the mirror, carefully studying my face. I blocked out the things around my reflection, the ribbons from gymnastics, honor-roll certificates, pictures of me and Scarlett, markers of the important moments in my life. I rubbed my thumb over the smooth silver of the ring Macon had given me. This time, I had only myself and what I would remember, so I concentrated, taking a picture I could keep always.

I stopped at Scarlett's house on the way to Spruce Street, where Macon was picking me up. This was one of the first New Year's Eve we hadn't spent together; I'd made my decision, but for some reason I still felt guilty about it.

"Take these," Scarlett said to me when I came in, stuffing something into my hand. Marion came around the corner, smoking, her hair in curlers, just as I dropped a condom right on the floor by her foot. She didn't see it and kept going, stepping over the half-assembled stroller—none of us could understand the directions—and I snatched it up, my heart racing.

"Um, I don't think I'll need this many," I said. She'd given me at least ten, in blue wrappers. They looked like the mints hotels give you on your pillow. I could see Cameron sitting at the kitchen table. He was cutting up a roll of refrigerated cookie dough into little triangles and squares. Scarlett had been scarfing cookies like crazy lately; usually she didn't even wait until the dough was cooked, just eating it by the handful out of the wrapper.

"Just take them," Scarlett said. "Better to be safe than sorry." One of my mother's favorite sayings.

She was looking at me as we stood there in the kitchen, as if there was something she wanted to say but couldn't. I pulled out a chair, sat down, and said, "Okay, spit it out. What's the problem?"

"No problem," she said, spinning the lazy Susan. Cameron was watching us nervously; he'd recently branched into wearing at least one thing that wasn't black—Scarlett's idea—and had on a blue shirt that made him look very sudden and bright. "I'm just—I'm just worried about you."

"Why?"

"I don't know. Because I know what you're doing, and I know you think it's right, but—"

"Please don't do this," I said to her quickly. "Not now."

"I'm not doing anything," she said. "I just want you to be careful." Cameron got up from the table and scuttled off toward the stove, his hands full of dough. He was blushing.

"You said you'd support me," I said. "You said I'd know when it was right." First my mother, now this, thrown across my path to keep me from moving ahead.

She looked at me. "Does he love you, Halley?"

"Scarlett, come on."

"Does he?" she said.

"Of course he does." I looked at my ring. The more times I said it, the more I was starting to believe it.

"He's said it. He's told you."

"He doesn't have to," I said. "I just know." There was a crash as Cameron dropped a cookie sheet, picked it up, and banged it against the stovetop, mumbling to himself.

"Halley," she said, shaking her head. "Don't be a fool. Don't give up something important to hold onto someone who can't even say they love you."

"This is what I want to do," I said loudly. "I can't believe you're doing this now, after we've been talking about this for weeks. I thought you were my friend."

She looked at me, hard, her hands clenched. "I am your *best* friend, Halley," she said in a steady voice. "And that is why I am doing this."

I couldn't believe her. All this talk about trusting myself, and

221

knowing when it was time, and now she fell out from beneath me. "I don't need this now," I said, getting up and shoving my chair in. "I have to go."

"It's just not right," she said, standing up with me. "And you know it."

"Not right?" I said, and I already knew something hateful was coming, before the words even left my lips. "But with you it was right, Scarlett, huh? Look at how *right* you were."

She took a step back, like I'd slapped her, and I knew I'd gone too far. From the stove I could see Cameron looking at me, with the same expression I saved for Maryann Lister and Ginny Tabor and anyone who hurt Scarlett.

We just stood there, silent, facing off across the kitchen, when the doorbell suddenly rang. Neither of us moved.

"Hello?" I heard a voice say, and over Scarlett's shoulder I saw Steve, or who I thought was Steve, coming into the room. The transformation, clearly, was complete. He was wearing his cord necklace, his boots, his tunic shirt, thick burlaplike pants, what appeared to be a kind of cape, and he was carrying a sword on his hip. He stood there, beside the spice rack, a living anachronism.

"Is she ready?" he said. He didn't seem to notice us outright staring at him.

"I don't know," Scarlett said softly, taking a few steps back toward the stairs. She wouldn't look at me. "I'll go see, okay?"

"Great."

So Vlad and I stood there together, both of us fully evolved, in Scarlett's kitchen at the brink of the New Year. I heard Scarlett's voice upstairs, then Marion's. On the table in front of me I could see the pregnancy Bible, lying open to Month Six. She'd highlighted a few passages in pink, the pen lying beside.

"I have to go," I said suddenly. Vlad, who was adjusting his sword, looked up at me. "Cameron, tell Scarlett I said good-bye, okay?"

"Yeah," Cameron said slowly. "Sure."

"Have a good night," Vlad called out to me as I got to the back door. "Happy New Year!"

I got halfway across the backyard before I turned around and looked back at the house, the windows all lit up above me. I wanted to see Scarlett in one of them, her hand pressed against the glass, our old secret code. She wasn't there, and I thought about going back. But it was cold and getting late, so I just kept walking to Spruce Street, Macon's car idling quietly by the mailbox, and what lay ahead.

The party was at some guy named Ronnie's, outside of town. We had to go down a bunch of winding dirt roads, past a few trailers and old crumbling barns, finally pulling up at a one-story, plain brick house with a blue light out front. There were a few dogs running around, barking, and people scattered across the stoop and the yard. I didn't recognize anyone.

The first thing I thought when I stepped inside, past a keg set up at the front door, was what my mother would think. I was sure the same things would jump out at her: the fake oak paneling, the coffee table crammed with full ashtrays and beer bottles, the yellow and brown shag carpet that felt wet as I walked over it. This house wasn't like Ginny Tabor's, where you knew in its real life it was a home, with parents and dinner and Christmas.

A bunch of people were lined up on the couch, drinking, and beside them the TV was on with just static, a soundless blur. I couldn't hear, the music was so loud, and I kept having to step over people sitting on the floor and backed against the walls, as I followed Macon to the kitchen.

He seemed to know everybody, people reaching out to slap his shoulder as he passed, his name floating over my head in different voices. At the keg he filled up a cup for me, then himself, while I tried to make myself as small as possible to fit in the tiny space behind him.

Macon handed me my beer and I sucked most of it down right away out of nervousness. He grinned and filled it again, then motioned me to follow him down a hallway, past a trash can overflowing with beer cans, to a bedroom.

"Knock-knock," he said as we walked in. A guy was sitting on the bed, and there was a girl with him, leaning over the side. The room was small and dark, with just a candle lit on the headboard, one with cabinets and shelves, like in my parents' room.

"Hey, hey," said the guy on the bed, who had short hair and a tattoo on his arm. "What's up, man?"

"Not much." Macon sat down at the foot of the bed. "This is Halley. Halley, this is Ronnie."

"Hi," I said.

"Hello." Ronnie had very sleepy eyes and his hair was short and spiky, black, his voice low and gravelly. He slid his hand across the bed to the leg of the girl beside him, who gave up on whatever she was looking for on the floor and started to lift her head out of the shadows.

"I lost my damn earring," she said, as her hair slid across her face, and I could make out her mouth. "It rolled under the bed and I can't reach it." As she sat upright, her features all falling into place, she looked at me, and I looked right back. It was Elizabeth Gunderson.

"Hey," she said to Macon, doing that hair swing, so out of place here. "Hi, Halley."

"Hi." I was still staring at her. She was wearing a T-shirt that was too big on her and shorts, obviously not what she'd come to the party in. Elizabeth Gunderson worked fast.

Ronnie reached down beside the bed, on the floor, and picked up a purple bong, which he handed to Macon. I sucked down the rest of my beer, just to have something to do, as he took the hit and handed it back.

"You want one?" Ronnie asked me, and I could feel Elizabeth watching me as she lit a cigarette. I wondered what her father, with his Ralph Lauren looks and BMW, would think if he could see her. I wondered what my father would think of me. As she watched me, in the dark, I could have sworn she was smiling.

225

"Sure," I said, pushing the thought of my father away as quickly as it came. I handed Macon my empty cup and took the bong, pressing it to my mouth the way I'd seen it done at other parties. He lit it and I breathed in, the smoke curling up toward my mouth, thicker and thicker, until there was a sudden rush of air and my lungs were full, hot. I held it until it hurt and then blew it out, the smoke thick against my teeth.

"Thanks," I said to Ronnie, handing it back as Macon slid his hand across my back. He'd been wrong. I could fit in here. I could fit in anywhere.

After a while Ronnie and Macon went outside to do something and left me and Elizabeth alone in the dark together. He handed me his beer as he left, which I downed half of because I was suddenly so thirsty, my tongue sticking to my lips. I'd never been stoned before, so I didn't know what to think about what I was feeling. I wasn't about to ask Elizabeth Gunderson, who had taken three bong hits before I lost count and was now stretched out across the bed, smoking, examining her toes. I was still perched at the foot, looking at the shag carpet which was suddenly fascinating, and wondering why I'd never tried this before.

"So," she said suddenly, rolling over onto her stomach. "When's Scarlett due, anyway?"

"May," I said, and my voice sounded strange to me. "The second week, or something."

"I can't believe she's having Michael's baby," she said. "I mean, I didn't even know they'd hooked up."

I licked my lips again, taking a tiny sip of beer, then looked around Ronnie's room, at the towels hung over the window for a curtain, at the *Penthouse* magazine by my foot, at the litter box that was by the door. I didn't see any cat.

Then I remembered I was talking to Elizabeth, so I thought back to what we'd been saying, which was hard, and then said, "They didn't hook up. They went out all summer."

"Did they?" Elizabeth said. Her voice didn't sound strange at all. "I had no idea."

"Oh, yeah," I said, taking another precious sip of my beer, which was warm and flat. "They were really in love."

"I didn't know," she said slowly. "They must have been awfully secretive about it. I saw Michael a lot last summer, and he never mentioned her."

I didn't know what to say to that. I had the feeling we were getting into sticky territory, so I changed the subject. Scarlett didn't belong in this room, in this place, any more than my mother did. "So is Ronnie your boyfriend?"

She laughed, like she knew something I didn't. "Boyfriend? No. He's just—Ronnie."

"Oh."

"It's funny that she's keeping the baby," Elizabeth said, pulling Scarlett right back between us. "I mean, it's going to ruin her life."

I was looking at that litter box, wondering about the cat again. "No, it won't. It's what she wants to do."

"Well," she said, and there was that hair flip as she sat up,

227

pulling another cigarette out of the pack on the headboard. "If it was me, I'd just kill myself before I'd have a baby. I mean, I'd know enough to realize there was no way I could handle it."

I decided, at that moment, that I truly hated Elizabeth Gunderson. It was all clear to me now; she was evil. She lived her life to swoop down and catch me off guard, dropping bombs and walking off, leaving them to explode in my face.

"You're not Scarlett," I said.

"I know it." She got off the bed, tucking her cigarettes in her pocket. "Thank God for that, right?" She walked to the door, brushing past me, and pushed it open. "You coming?"

"No," I said, looking back at her, "I think I'll just—" But she was already gone, the door left half-open with light spilling in, and I was alone.

I sat there on the bed by myself for a long time, the music drifting in from the hallway along with voices and noise, girls giggling, the bathroom door slamming. I lost all track of time and I was sure hours had passed, that I'd missed the New Year altogether, when Macon finally slipped back through the door, locking it behind him.

"Hey," he said. I could only see his teeth in the dark, just a mouth coming toward me. "You okay?"

I leaned forward, determined to make out his face. As he got closer I was relieved to see he looked the same. My Macon. My boyfriend. Mine. "What time is it?"

"I don't know." He looked at his watch, glowing green in the dark. "Eleven-thirty. Why?"

"I just wondered," I said. "Where have you been?"

"Mingling." He handed me the beer in his hand, which tasted good and cold going down. I'd lost track of how many I'd had. I felt liquid and warm, and I curled up against him on the bed, kissing his neck as he wrapped his arms around me. As I closed my eyes the world began to spin in the dark, but he held me tight, his hand already moving up my leg, to my waistband. This was it.

I kept kissing him, trying to lose myself in it, but the room was hot and small and the bed smelled bad, like sweat. As we went further and further, I kept thinking that this wasn't how I'd imagined it would be. Not here, in a smelly bed, when my head was spinning and I could hear each flush of the toilet in the room next door. Not here, in a room with a dirty litter box and *Penthouse* magazine on the floor, where Elizabeth Gunderson had preceded me. Not here.

I started to get nervous, jumpy, and as Macon kept on, unsnapping my jeans, the noise from the bathroom only got louder, and outside some girl was coughing, and I felt something pressing against my bare back, something hard. When I reached around I felt it cool against my palm, and held it up over Macon's head to the dim light. It was an earring, a gold teardrop; the one Elizabeth had lost. Scarlett had the same pair.

"Wait," I said suddenly to Macon, pushing him up and away from me. We were very close, almost there, and I could hear him groan even as I squirmed out from beneath him.

"What?" he said. "What's wrong?"

"I feel sick," I told him, and it wasn't really true until I said it, and then I thought of all those beers and that bong hit and being here in this sweaty stinky bed and the reeking litter box. "I think I need some air."

"Come on," he said, sliding his hand up my back but it felt cold and creepy, suddenly, "lay back down. Come here."

"No," I said, jerking away from him and standing up, but I was off-balance and everything slanted off to one side. I leaned against the door, fumbling with the lock. "I think—I think I need to go home."

"Home?" He said it like it was a dirty word. "Halley, it's early. You can't go home."

I couldn't get the door open, the lock slipping past my fingers as I tried to find it, and suddenly I could feel everything on its way up, slowly. "I have to go," I said. "I think I'm going to be sick."

"Wait," he said. "Just calm down, okay? Come here."

"No," I said, and I was crying suddenly, scared in this strange place and I hated him for doing this to me, hated myself, hated my mother and Scarlett for being right, all along. And then I heard it: voices, counting down. *Ten, nine, eight,* and I was sick and lost and the lock wouldn't budge even as I felt everything coming up, the first taste in my mouth, and then finally the door was somehow open and I was running, *seven, six, five,* down the hallway, busting past the people crammed and chanting the numbers in the kitchen and living room and out into the cold, down the steps and the driveway *four, three, two* and into the woods and then, as the *one* came and everyone cheered, I was finally, violently, sick, alone on my knees in the woods, as the New Year began.

Chapter Fifteen

He didn't speak to me for the first part of the ride home. He was mad, as if I'd elaborately planned getting sick. When he found me in the woods I was half asleep, wishing I was dead, with leaves stuck to my face. He put me in the car and peeled out down the driveway, going way too fast and fishtailing as we headed out onto the main road.

I was huddled against my window, my eyes closed, hoping I wouldn't get sick again. I felt terrible.

"I'm sorry," I said after about five miles, as the lights of town started to come into view. Every time I thought of that litter box, and those sheets, my stomach rolled. "I really am."

"Forget it," he said, and the engine growled as he changed gears, careening around a corner.

"I wanted to," I told him. "I swear, I was going to. I just drank too much."

He didn't say anything, just turned with a screech onto the highway that led to my house, gunning the engine.

"Macon, please don't be like this," I said. "Please."

"You said you wanted to. You made this big deal about spending New Year's with me and what that meant, and then you just change your mind." We were coming up on the main intersection to my neighborhood now, the stoplight shining green ahead.

"It's not like that," I said.

"Yes, it is. You never really wanted to, Halley. You can't just play around like that."

"I wasn't playing around," I said. "I wanted to. It just wasn't right."

"It felt fine to me." The light was turning yellow but he kept pushing it, and we were going faster and faster, the mall shooting by in a blaze of lights.

"Macon, slow down," I said, as we came up to the intersection, faster and faster. The light turned red but I knew already we weren't stopping.

"You just don't get it," he said, punching the gas as we got closer, under the light now, and I turned to look at him, wondering what was coming next. "You're just so—"

I was wondering what he was going to say, what word could sum me up right then, when I saw the lights come across his face, blaringly yellow, and suddenly he was brighter, and brighter, and I asked him what was happening, what was wrong. I remember only that light, so strong as it spilled across my shoulders and lit up his face, and how scared he looked as something big and loud hit my door, sending glass shattering all across me, little sparks catching the light like diamonds as they fell, with me, into the dark.

Chapter Sixteen

This is what I remember: the cold. The wind was blowing in my face and it was shivery cold, like ice. I remember red lights, and someone's voice moaning. Crying. And lastly, I remember Macon holding my hand, tightly between his, and saying it finally, in the wrong place at the wrong time, but saying it. *I love you. Oh, God, Halley, I'm sorry. I love you, I'm right here, just hold on. I'm right here.*

When the ambulance came, I kept telling them to just take me home, that I'd be okay, just take me home. I knew how close I was, all the landmarks. I'd traveled that intersection a thousand times in my life; it was the first big road I'd crossed alone.

I tried to keep track of Macon, his hand or his face, but in the ambulance, on the way to the hospital, I lost him.

"He had to stay at the accident scene," a woman with red hair kept telling me in a steady voice, each time I asked. "Lie back and relax, honey. What's your name?"

"Halley," I said. I had no idea what had happened to me; my leg hurt, and one of my eyes was swollen shut. I couldn't move my fingers on my left hand, but it didn't hurt. That was strange.

SOMEONE LIKE YOU

"That's a pretty name," she said as someone shot something into my arm, a slight prick that made me flinch. "Real pretty."

At the hospital they put me in a bed with a sheet pulled around it and suddenly people were hovering all over me, hands reaching and grabbing. Someone came and leaned into my ear, asking me my phone number and I gave her Scarlett's. Even then, I knew how much trouble I would be in with my parents.

After a while a doctor came and told me I had a sprained wrist, lacerations on my back, stitches to bind the cut by my right eye, and two bruised ribs. The pain in my leg was just bruising, she said, and because I'd also banged my head they wanted to keep me overnight. She said again and again how I was very, very lucky. I kept asking about Macon, where he was, but she wouldn't answer, telling me to get some sleep, to rest. She'd come back later to check on me. Oh, and by the way— my sister was waiting outside.

"My sister?" I said, as they parted the curtains and Scarlett came in, looking like she'd just rolled out of bed. She had her hair pulled back in a ponytail and was wearing the long flannel shirt I knew she slept in. Her stomach was bigger than it had been just hours ago, if that was possible.

"Jesus, Halley," she said, stopping short a few feet from the bed and looking at me. She was scared but trying not to show it. "What *happened* to you?"

"It was an accident," I said.

"Where's Macon?" Scarlett said.

235

"I don't know." I felt like I was going to cry, suddenly, and now everything was beginning to hurt all at once. "Isn't he outside?"

"No," she said, and now her mouth was moving into a thin, hard line, her words clipped. "I didn't see him."

"He had to stay at the accident," I told her. "He said he'd be right here. He was really worried."

"Well, good," she snapped. "He almost killed you."

I closed my eyes, hearing only the beeping of some machine in the next room. It sounded just like the bell halfway up Grandma Halley's stairs, chiming.

"I didn't do it," I said to her after a long silence. "In case you were wondering."

"I wasn't," she said. "But I'm glad."

"When my parents find out about this, I'm dead meat," I said, and I was so sleepy it was hard to even get the words out. "They'll never let me see him again."

"He's not even here, Halley," she said softly.

"He's at the accident," I said again.

"That was over an hour and a half ago. The cop was in the waiting room, too. I talked to him. Macon left."

"No," I said, fighting off the sleep even as it crept over me. "He's on the way."

"Oh, Halley," she said, and she sounded so sad. "I'm so, so, sorry." But she was getting fuzzier and fuzzier and the beeping quieter, as I drifted away.

*   *   *

When I woke up next, the first thing I saw was a quarterback going out for a pass on the TV over my head. The ball was flying, curving through the air, as he just reached up, grabbed it, and began to dodge through the bodies and helmets, running, while the crowd screamed behind him. When he hit the end zone he spiked the ball, high-fived one of his teammates, and the camera zoomed into his smiling face, his fist pumping overhead. Touchdown.

"Hi there," I heard my mother say, and I turned to see her sitting beside me, her chair pulled close. "How are you feeling?"

"Okay," I said. My father was on the other bed in my room, still in the tacky Mexican shirt he always wore for the New Year's party. "When did you get here?"

"Just a little while ago." I looked at the clock on the wall as she reached over and brushed my hair out of my face, smoothing her fingers over the bandage on my eye. It was three-thirty. A.M.? P.M.? I wasn't sure. "Halley, honey, you really, really scared us."

"I'm sorry," I said, and it was work just to talk, I was so tired. "I ruined your party."

"I don't care about the party," she said. She looked tired too, sad, the same face she'd had that whole week we were with Grandma Halley. "Where were you? What happened?"

"Julie," my father said from the next bed, his voice thick. "Let her sleep. It's not important now."

"The policeman said you were with Macon Faulkner," she went on, and she sounded uneven, as if she was running over broken ground. "Is that true? Did he do this to you?"

"No," I said, and it was coming back to me now, the cold and the bright light and all the stars, falling. I was so drained, I closed my eyes. "It was just—"

"I knew it, I knew it," she said, and she was still holding my good hand, squeezing it now, hard. "God, you just can't listen to me, you just can't understand that I might be right, I might know what's best, you always have to prove it to yourself, and look what happens, look at this. . . ." Her voice was getting softer and softer, or maybe I was just slipping off. It was hard to say.

"Julie," my father said again, and I could hear him coming around the bed, his steps moving closer. "Julie, she's sleeping. She can't even hear you, honey."

"You promised me you wouldn't see him," she whispered, close to my ear now, her voice rough. "You *promised* me."

"Let it go," my father said. Then, again, so soft I could hardly hear it, "Let it go."

I was half asleep, wild thoughts tangled in with the sounds around me, pulling me away. But right before I fell off entirely, or maybe I was already dreaming, I heard a voice close to my ear, maybe hers, maybe Macon's, maybe just one I made up in my head. *I'll be right here*, it said as I drifted off into sleep. *Right here.*

Chapter Seventeen

January was flat, gray, and endless. I spent New Year's Day in the hospital and then went home with everything aching and took to my bed for the next week, staring out the window at Scarlett's house and the planes overhead. My mother took complete control of my life, and I let her.

We didn't talk about Macon. It was understood that something had happened to me that night before the accident, something big, but she didn't ask and I didn't offer. Instead she rebandaged my eye and wrist, and gave me my pills, bringing me my meals on a tray. In the quiet of my house with her always so close by, Macon seemed like a dream, something barely visible, hardly real. It hurt too much to even picture him.

But he was trying to get in touch with me. My first night home I heard him idling at the stop sign, our old signal, and I lay staring at my ceiling and listened. He left after about ten minutes, turning the corner so that his headlights traced a path across my walls, lighting up a slash of my mirror, a patch of wallpaper, the smiling face of my Madame Alexander doll.

Then he beeped the horn, one last chance, and I turned again to the night sky and closed my eyes.

I didn't know what to think. That night was a mad blur, beginning with my fight with Scarlett and ending being cold cold cold on the side of the road. I was hurt and angry and I felt like a fool, for my wild notions, for turning even on Scarlett, the only one who really mattered, when she tried to tell me the truth.

Sometimes when I lay in bed that week I still felt for the ring he'd given me, forgetting they'd cut it off at the emergency room. It was on my desk, in a plastic baggie, next to the saucerful of candy I'd never touched. He wasn't what I'd thought he was; maybe he never had been. I wasn't what I'd thought *I* was, either.

Of course, some of us had already formed our opinions.

"He's such a *jerk*," Scarlett said after the first week, as we sat at my kitchen table playing Go Fish and eating grapes. We never discussed our argument on New Year's Eve; it made both of us uncomfortable. "And today he kept asking about you at school. He would *not* leave me alone. Like he couldn't come over and visit you himself."

"He came by again last night," I said. "He sits out there like he's waiting for me to sneak out."

"If he gave a crap, he'd be at your door on his knees, begging for forgiveness." She made a face, shifting in her seat. Now she really was huge; she couldn't even sit against the table, her walk reduced to what could only be politely called a waddle.

"I'm so hormonal right now I could kill him with my bare hands."

I didn't say anything. You can't just turn your heart off like a faucet; you have to go to the source and dry it out, drop by drop.

It was around midnight a few nights later when I heard something *ping* off my bedroom window. I lay in bed, listening to pebble after pebble bounce off until I finally went and opened it up, sticking my head out. I could barely see Macon in the shadows of the side yard, but I knew he was there.

"Halley," I heard him whisper. "Come out. I have to talk to you."

I didn't say anything, watching my parents' window for the sudden light that meant they'd heard too, and I almost hoped they had.

"Please," he said. "Just for a second. Okay?"

I shut the window without answering, then walked down the back stairs and even let the screen door slam a little bit behind me. I didn't care about being careful anymore.

He was in the side yard, by the juniper bushes, and as I came around the corner he walked toward me, stepping out of the shadows. "Hey."

"Hi," I said.

A pause. He said, "How are you feeling? How's your wrist?"

"Better."

He waited, like he expected me to say more. I didn't.

"Look," he began, "I know you're mad that I didn't show up

241

at the hospital, but I had a good reason. Your parents would've been upset enough without having to see me. Plus I had to walk to a phone and get a ride because my car was totaled, and . . ."

As he talked I just watched his face, wondering what it was that I'd ever thought was so magical about him. I had been fascinated by the things he'd shown me, but they were all just sleight of hand, quarters pulled from children's ears. Anyone can do that trick, if they know how. It's nothing special.

He was still talking. ". . . and I've been coming by all week 'cause I wanted to explain, but you wouldn't come out and I couldn't call you, and . . ."

"Macon," I said, holding up my hand. "Just stop, okay?"

He looked surprised. "I didn't mean to hurt you," he said, and I wondered which hurt he meant, exactly. "I just freaked out. But I'm sorry, Halley, and I'll make it up to you. I need you. I've been miserable ever since this happened."

"Yeah?" I said, not believing a word.

"Yeah," he said softly, and reached out to put his arms around my waist, brushing my bruised ribs and hurting me again. "I've been going crazy."

I stepped back, out of his reach, and crossed my arms against my chest. "I can't see you anymore," I said to him.

He blinked, absorbing this. "Your parents will get over that," he said easily, and I knew he'd said this many times before. Everything, each line I'd held close to my heart, had been said a million times to a million other girls under their windows and in their side yards, on back streets and in backseats, in dark rooms at parties, with the door locked tight.

"This isn't about my parents," I said. "This is about me."

"Halley, don't do this." He ducked his head, that old hangdog P.E. look. "We can work this out."

"I don't think so," I said. The truth was I knew, after all those flat January days, that I deserved better. I deserved *I love you*s and kiwi fruits and flowers and warriors coming to my door, besotted with love. I deserved pictures of my face in a million expressions, and the warmth of a baby's kick under my hand. I deserved to grow, and to change, to become all the girls I could ever be over the course of my life, each one better than the last.

"Halley, wait," he called out after me as I backed away. "Don't go."

But I was already gone, working a little magic of my own, vanishing.

I didn't see her right away as I came inside the back door, easing it shut behind me. Not until I turned around, in the dark, and the room was suddenly bright all around me. My mother, in her bathrobe, was standing with her hand on the light switch.

"So," she said, as I stood there blinking. "Things are right back to the way they were, I see."

"What?"

"Wasn't that our friend Macon?" She said it angrily. "Does he ever come around in broad daylight? Or does he only work under cover of darkness?"

"Mom, you don't understand." I was going to tell her then that he was gone, maybe even that she was right.

"I understand that even that boy almost *killing* you is not enough for you to learn a lesson. I cannot believe you would just go right back out there to him, like nothing had changed, after what happened to you. After what he *did*."

"I had to talk to him," I said. "I had to—"

"We have not discussed this because you were hurt, but this is *not* going to happen. Do you understand? If you don't have the sense to stay away from that boy, I will keep you away from him."

"Mom." I couldn't believe she was doing it again. She was taking this moment, this time when I was strongest, away from me.

"I don't care what I have to do," she said, her voice low and even. "I don't care if I have to send you away or switch schools. I don't care if I have to follow you myself twenty-four hours a day, you will *not* see him, Halley. You will not destroy yourself this way."

"Why are you just assuming I'm going back to him?" I asked her, just as she was drawing in breath to make another point. "Why don't you ask me what I said to him out there?"

She shut her mouth, caught off guard. "What?"

"Why don't you ever wait a second and see what I'm plan-

244

ning, or thinking, before you burst in with your opinions and ideas? You never even give me a *chance*."

"Yes, I do," she said indignantly.

"No," I said. "You don't. And then you wonder why I never tell you anything or share anything with you. I can never trust you with anything, give you any piece of me without you grabbing it to keep for yourself."

"That's not true," she said slowly, but it was just now hitting her, I could see it. "Halley, you don't always know what's at stake, and I do."

"*I will never learn,*" I said to her slowly, "*until you let me.*"

And so we stood there in the kitchen, my mother and I, facing off over everything that had built up since June, when I was willing to hand myself over free and clear. Now, I needed her to return it all to me, with the faith that I could make my own way.

"Okay," she said finally. She ran a hand through her hair. "All right."

"Thank you," I said as she cut the light off, and we started upstairs together, her footsteps echoing mine. It was still all settling in, this deal we'd made. It was like learning another way of something instinctive, like walking or talking. Changing something you already thought you'd mastered and figured out on your own.

As we got to the top of the stairs, to split off into our different directions, she stopped.

"So," she said softly. "What did you tell him?"

Outside, across the street, I could see Scarlett's kitchen light, yellow in the dark. "I told him he wasn't what I'd thought he was," I said. "That he let me down, and I couldn't see him anymore. And I said good-bye."

I knew there was probably a lot she wanted to ask or say, but she only nodded. We would have to learn this slowly, making the rules up as we went. It was undiscovered country, as wide as the Grand Canyon, as distant as Halley's Comet.

"Good for you," she said simply, and then she went inside her room, shutting the door quietly between us.

You can't just plan a moment when things get back on track, just as you can't plan the moment you lose your way in the first place. But standing there alone on the landing, I thought of Grandma Halley and how she'd held me close against her lap as we watched the sky together. I'd always thought I couldn't remember, but suddenly in that moment, I closed my eyes and saw the comet, finally, brilliant and impossible, stretching above me across the sky.

Part III

GRACE

Chapter Eighteen

"Oh, honey, you look so wonderful! Brian, come in here with the camera, you've got to see this. Stand here, Halley. No—here, so we get the window behind you. Or maybe—"

"Mom," I said, reaching behind me again for the itchy tag that had been scratching my neck since I'd put the damn dress on, "please. Not now, okay?"

"Oh, but we've *got* to take pictures," she said, waving me over by the potted plant in the corner of the kitchen, "some of you alone, and some when Noah comes."

Noah. Every time I heard his name, I couldn't believe I'd gotten myself into this. Not just the prom, not just a too-poofy dress with a tag that would drive me insane, but the prom with the dress with the tag with Noah Vaughn. I was in hell.

"Oh my goodness," my mother said, looking over my shoulder, one hand moving up to cover her mouth. She looked like she might cry. "Look at *you!*"

I turned around to see Scarlett, much as I'd left her upstairs minutes ago, except maybe larger, if that was possible. She was at nine months almost exactly, her belly protruding up and outward so it was always the very first thing you noticed when she came into a room. Her dress had been made especially by Cameron's mother, a seamstress, who was so happy Cameron was actually going to the prom that she spent hours, *days*, making the perfect maternity prom dress. It was black and white, with a semi-drop neck that showed off Scarlett's impressive bosom, an empire waist, and it fell gently over her knees. She really did look good, if huge. But it was the smile on her face, wide and proud, that made it perfect.

"Ta-da!" she said, sweeping her arms over herself and back down again, as if she was a prize on a game show. "Crazy, huh?"

She just stood there, grinning at me, and I had to smile back. Since we'd decided we would go to the prom and fulfill our *Seventeen* daydreams, nothing had been normal. But then, nothing had been normal, or even close to normal, for a while.

Since January, something had changed. It was all subtle, hard to see with the naked eye, but it was there. The way my mother held her tongue when I knew she was dying to offer an opinion, to dominate a conversation—to be my mother. She'd take a breath, already gathering words, and then stop, let it out, and look hard at me as something passed between us, imperceptible to the rest of the world. She'd backed off just enough, focusing on other things: selling Grandma Halley's house and visiting her often, as well as the new book she'd started writing about her experiences being a daughter again. Maybe I'd be in this one. Maybe not.

As for Macon, I hadn't talked to him much since that night in my side yard. He seemed to be coming to school even less, and when he did I was skilled at avoiding him. But I still felt a pang whenever I saw him, the way I still felt a soreness in my wrist every morning, or a pain in my ribs when I lay a certain way at night. In March, when I heard his mother had kicked him out, I worried. And in mid-April, when I heard he was dating Elizabeth Gunderson, I cried for two days straight.

I made myself concentrate on something more important: the baby. I saw it, small and hardly recognizable, when we had the ultrasound during Month Six. It had hands and feet and eyes and a nose. The doctor knew the sex, but Scarlett didn't want to know; she wanted it to be a surprise.

We had a baby shower at my house, inviting Cameron and his mother, the girls from the Teen Mothers Support Group, and even Ginny Tabor, who bought the baby a huge stuffed yellow duck that quacked when you squeezed it. But something was wrong with it, and it quacked whenever you picked it up, and then wouldn't shut up until you took its head off, an option we never had with Ginny herself. Cameron's mother sewed a beautiful layette set, and my parents gave Scarlett ten babysitting coupons, for whenever she needed a break. For my gift, I had blown up a recent picture of me and Scarlett, sitting on her front steps together. Scarlett's belly was huge, and she had her hands folded over it, her head on my shoulder. I had it framed and Scarlett immediately hung it over the baby's crib, where she or he would see it every day.

"The three of us," she said, and I nodded.

And then we just waited, circling in a holding pattern, while the due date got closer and closer.

We planned. We bought a baby name book and made lists of good ones: something simple, not bringing to mind someone else, like Scarlett's, or needing a paragraph of explanation, like mine. We both knew how far a name could take you.

We went to Lamaze classes, me sitting in a long row of fathers, her head in my lap. We were the youngest ones there. We breathed and we pushed, and I tried to tell myself that I could handle this when it happened, that I could do it. Scarlett was scared and tired, with all that huffing and puffing, and I always nodded at her, confident.

And Marion had come around. She acted like she was firm on adoption until about Month Seven, early March, when I walked in on her in the nursery. The sun was slanting through the window, warm and bright, bouncing off the yellow walls, and the constellations Cameron had painted on the ceiling. Everything was ready: the clothes all folded in the drawers, the crib and changing table in place, the stroller finally assembled (with the help of a neighbor, who was an engineer and the only one who could figure out the instructions). She was just standing there, arms crossed, surveying it all with a smile on her face. And I knew it then. There'd never been a question of where this baby was going or who it belonged with. Of course, when she saw me she turned around and scowled, muttering something about paint fumes, and hurried out. But that was Marion. I knew what I had seen.

And lastly, I walked with Scarlett to the mailbox as she carried the letter we'd worked and re-worked, all these months. *Dear Mrs. Sherwood,* it began, *You don't know me, but I have something to say.* She dropped it in, the mailbox door clanked, and there was no going back. If we heard from her, we heard from her. If not, this baby had enough love to carry on.

And now, on May twelfth, we were going to the prom. I was doing this for Scarlett; it was important to her. When Cameron asked her, I had to go, too. Which is how I ended up with Noah Vaughn.

Actually, it was my mother's fault. She brought up the prom one Friday night when the Vaughns were over, Mrs. Vaughn lit up like the sun, and it went from there. *Of course I keep telling Halley she should go,* my mother said, *I mean, it's the prom. Well, Noah, I can't believe you haven't mentioned this,* said Mrs. Vaughn. *Well, Halley's best friend is going, you know Scarlett, but Halley hasn't been asked,* said my mother, and now I was realizing what was happening, how awful this could be, as Noah watched me from across the table and my father giggled at his plate. *But Noah doesn't have a date either,* said Mrs. Vaughn, *so I don't see why you two couldn't* ... And then my mother, who had learned something, looked across the table, realizing too late, and said quickly, *Actually I think Halley might have plans that weekend,* but of course now it *was* too late, way too late, and Mrs. Vaughn was already clapping her hands together excitedly, and smiling big, and my mother kept trying to get me to look at her but I wouldn't. All I could see was Noah across the table, eating a slice of pizza, with cheese all over his chin.

Of course Scarlett was ecstatic. She dragged me out to buy a dress and shoes, and insisted we get ready together. And I went along, trying not to complain, because I knew somehow that this was the end of something for her, before the baby came and everything changed.

"Smile!" my mother said, stepping back across the kitchen with her camera's red light blinking. My father was leaning against the kitchen door, making faces at me. "Oh, you two look just great. So glamorous!"

Scarlett put her arm over my shoulder, pulling me closer, tighter in for the shot. I saw the red in her hair, her easy smile, the small sprinkling of freckles across her nose.

"Okay!" my mother said, now against the far wall, crouching down. "Now say prom night!"

"Prom night!" Scarlett said, still smiling.

"Prom night," I said, more softly, my eyes on her, and not the camera, as the flash popped bright all around me.

I could tell that Noah was drunk the minute he crossed the living room holding the corsage.

"Hi," he said as he got close, reaching out with the pin toward my bodice, his breath hot and sweet. "Hold still."

"I'll get it," I said, taking it from him before he stabbed me while Mrs. Vaughn, who obviously hadn't gotten close to him lately, and my mother, who looked like she might bust with happiness, watched from across the room. Beside us Cameron was carefully attaching Scarlett's corsage, a group of pink roses and baby's breath, to her ample bustline. Cameron looked very small and very dapper in his tuxedo and cranberry-colored cummerbund and socks. Very European, my mother had said when he arrived, with Noah in his rented tux and too-short pants with gym socks peeking out beneath. I stuck my corsage on, barely missing poking myself in my haste, and settled in for another round of pictures.

"Wonderful!" Mrs. Vaughn said, circling us with the video camera while Noah snaked his arm around my waist. The liquor had obviously emboldened him. "Halley, smile!"

"One more," my mother said, going through at least another roll of film, flash after flash. "What a great night you'll have! Terrific!"

Marion was there, with one of those disposable cameras, taking picture after picture of Scarlett in her dress. She was going to a medieval tournament with Vlad that night, and was already dressed for the part in a long velvet dress with puffy sleeves that made her look like Guinevere, or maybe Sleeping Beauty. She'd gotten into Vlad's weekend hobby, bit by bit, and she seemed to like it, tagging along to tournaments and drinking mead while he jousted. Scarlett was embarrassed, but Marion just said being someone else was kind of nice, every once in a while.

"Scarlett," she called out, waving one hand over her head. "Over here, honey. Perfect. Perfect!"

After we'd been satisfactorily documented, we finally got out the door and to the limousine, on loan from the hotel where Cameron's father worked. Cameron, for all his quirkiness, really knew how to make an evening. I couldn't exactly say the same for *my* date.

"Where's the bar?" Noah slurred as soon as we shut the door and drove off. "There's supposed to be a bar in these things, right?"

Scarlett was just eyeing him, settling her dress around her, and I said, "He's wasted. Ignore him."

"I am not," Noah said indignantly. Already he'd talked more to me, total, than he had in the entire year and a half we'd been broken up. "But there *is* supposed to be a bar."

"I'm sure they just took it out," Cameron said quietly. "Sorry."

"Don't be sorry," Scarlett said to him, squeezing his arm. "We don't care."

"I don't need it anyway," Noah said loudly, pulling a plastic juice container from his inside pocket. "Got it all taken care of, right here."

I just looked at him. "Noah," I said. "Please."

"Wow," Scarlett said as he opened the container and guzzled down a bit, dribbling on his shirtfront. "That sure is classy."

"Works for me," Noah said snippily. He stuck it back in his pocket, wiping his mouth, and put his arm over my shoulder, which I shrugged off as best I could.

By the time we got to the prom, Noah was completely

loaded. The limo dropped us off in the bus parking lot, by the cafeteria, and I just started to walk inside, leaving him to stumble along behind me. He'd downed the last swallow of his stash, dropped the container on the sidewalk, and reached out to grab me; instead, he got my dress, tearing it at the waist. I felt cool air on my back and legs and stopped walking.

"Ooops," he said as I turned around. He had something white and shiny, formerly part of my dress, in his hands and he was giggling. "Sorry."

"You jerk," I snapped, grabbing behind me to bunch the fabric together, covering myself. Now I was at the prom with Noah Vaughn *and* half-naked. There was no end to my shame.

"Halley, what's going on?" Scarlett called from the front entrance to the cafeteria. I could see Melissa Ringley, prom chairwoman, sitting at a table watching me. "Hurry up."

"Go in without me," I said. "I'll be right there."

"Are you sure?"

"Yes."

She shrugged, handing Melissa their tickets, and she and Cameron disappeared inside. I could hear music playing, loud, and people kept walking past, on their way in. I backed into the shadow of the science lab to do something about my dress.

"Here," Noah said, stumbling in behind me, "let me help."

"You cannot help me," I told him. "Okay?"

"You don't have to be a bitch," he snapped, still reaching around to the back of my dress, his hand brushing my skin. "You know, you've changed so much since we went out."

"Whatever, Noah," I said. I needed a safety pin, badly. I could not go inside and moon my entire class, not even for Scarlett.

"You used to be nice, and all that," he went on, "but then you started thinking you were all cool, hanging out with Macon Faulkner and all. Like you were too good for everybody all of a sudden."

"Noah," I said. "Shut up."

"You shut up," he said back, loudly. Two girls in white dresses and heels looked over at us, trying to make us out in the dark.

I ignored him, reaching around the back of my dress again, when suddenly he was right up against me, his breath in my face when I turned around. I didn't remember him ever being so tall. He slid his arm around my waist, reaching back to the gaping fabric, and stuck his hand down my dress, brushing over my underwear. I just stared at him, dumbstruck, and watched his face get closer and closer, eyes closed, tongue starting to stick out—

"Get *off* me," I said loudly, pushing him away. He stumbled, tripped over a tree stump and landed on the sidewalk just as another group of people started to pass by. I leaned against the wall, not caring anymore about my dress, or this night, and tried to hide myself.

"Whoa," a guy in the group said as he stepped over Noah, who was still prone, blinking. "You okay, buddy?"

"She's just—she's such a . . ." Noah sputtered as he got to his feet, unsteadily, and started to weave back around the side of the building, muttering to himself. The guy and his date just watched him go, then laughed a little nervously and headed across the courtyard to Melissa Ringley and the cafeteria. And I was alone.

I thought about going home. I had money and could easily call a cab, or my father, and just give up entirely. But Scarlett would worry, I knew, so I bunched together the back of my dress, holding it that way, and went to tell her myself.

I found her on the dance floor, with Cameron. They couldn't dance that close but they did what they could, her stomach between them. All around her were these perfect girls, hair swept up and wearing lipstick and high heels, with their dates in dark tuxedos and dress shoes. I saw Ginny Tabor and Brett Hershey, wearing Prom King and Queen crowns, making out by the punch table. And Regina Little, one of the fattest girls in school, in a huge white dress with a hoop, dancing with a guy in a military uniform who looked at least thirty. And lastly, in the corner, I saw Elizabeth Gunderson and Macon, not dancing or smiling or even talking, just standing there staring at the crowd, same as me.

Macon saw me, and right then I felt it for the first time in so long, that rush and craziness, that feeling I'd had at Topper Dam. He looked good and he grinned at me, and I thought that in this desperate moment, alone at the prom, he could take me away.

It was too much, all of a sudden, everything rushing at me. The prom and Michael and my mother and the baby. Macon and Ronnie's house and that night in the car, with the glass shattering around my head. Elizabeth Gunderson and her sly smile, the cold of the woods as I'd gotten sick on New Year's Eve, Grandma Halley's hand, thin and warm, in mine. And finally, Noah coming closer and closer to me, his tongue sticking out, and now Scarlett on the dance floor, right before my eyes, swaying to the music and smiling, smiling, smiling.

I pushed through the crowd, still holding my dress, thinking only of getting out, getting away, something. I pushed past girls in their princess outfits, past clouds of cologne and perfume, past Mrs. Oakley, the vice principal, who was eyeballing everyone on the lookout for drugs and drunks. I didn't stop until I reached the bathroom door and ran inside, letting it slam behind me.

The first person I saw was Melissa Ringley, standing in front of the mirrors with a lipstick in her hand. She looked at the mirror in front of her, and me beyond it, and turned around, her mouth still in a perfect O.

"Halley, my goodness, what is wrong?" She put the lipstick down and walked toward me, lifting her dress off the ground so it wouldn't brush the floor. It was black, with a full skirt and a modest neckline. She had a small gold cross hanging from a chain around her neck. "Are you okay?"

I did look crazed, wild even. My hair, so carefully crafted into a perfect French twist by Scarlett, had somehow come untucked and was sticking up like a lopsided Mohawk. My face was red and my mascara smeared and that didn't even include my dress, which was bagging open in the back now that I had let go of it. Two other girls, checking their makeup, brushed past me, glanced at my exposed underwear and clucked their tongues as they pushed the door open, leaving me and Melissa alone.

"I'm fine," I said quickly, moving to the sink and wetting a paper towel, trying to do something about my face. I pulled my hair down, bobby pins spilling everywhere. "Just a rotten night, that's all."

"Well, I heard Noah was drunk," she said, whispering the last word and taking a furtive look around. "You poor thing. And what happened to your dress? Oh my God, Halley, turn around. Look at that!"

"I *know*," I said, my teeth clenched. I couldn't believe I was mooning Melissa Ringley. "I just want to get out of here."

"Well, you can't go out there like that," she said, moving around behind me. "Here, hand me some of those bobby pins, I'll see what I can do."

So I stood there, with Melissa behind me muttering to herself and stabbing bobby pins into my dress, all the while wondering how the night could get any worse. And then, it did.

Elizabeth Gunderson was wearing a tight black dress and spike heels that I could hear clacking outside before she even opened the door and came into the bathroom itself. When she saw me she narrowed her eyes and looked me up and down before moving to another sink and leaning into the mirror.

"Well, this should at least get you through the rest of the night," Melissa said cheerfully, coming out from behind me and tossing the extra bobby pins into the trash. "Just don't try any radical movements or anything."

"Okay," I said, staring at my reflection. I could feel Elizabeth watching me. I told myself it was only fitting she was with Macon; they deserved each other. This didn't really make me feel better. "Thanks, Melissa. Really."

"Oh, no problem," she said in her chirpy little can-do voice, fluffing her blond bob with her fingers. "It's all part of being prom chairwoman, right?" She waggled her fingers at me as she left, the sound of music—something slow and easy—coming in as the door opened and then drifted shut behind her.

Beside me, Elizabeth was putting on eyeliner, leaning in closer to the mirror. She looked tired, worn out, now that I was looking at her more closely. Her eyes were red and her lipstick was too dark, making her mouth look like a gash against her skin.

I took one last look at myself, decided there wasn't much I could do under the circumstances, and started to leave. I had nothing left to say to Elizabeth Gunderson. But then, just as I was reaching for the door, I heard her voice.

"Halley."

I turned around. "What?"

She pulled away from the mirror, brushing her hair over her shoulders. "So." She wasn't looking at me, instead down at the purse in her hands. "Are you having a good night?"

I smiled, in spite of myself. "No," I said. "Are you?"

She took a deep breath, then ran a finger over her lips, smoothing out her lipstick. "No. I'm not."

I nodded, not sure what else to say, and reached for the door again. "Well," I said, "I guess I'll see you later."

I was halfway out, the music loud enough that I almost didn't hear her when she said, "You know, he still loves you. He says he doesn't, but he does. He does."

I stopped and turned around. "Macon?" I said.

"He won't admit it," she said quietly, but her voice was shaky, and I thought of how I'd envied her that night at Ronnie's, stretched out across the bed examining her toes. I didn't now. "He says he doesn't even think about you, but I can tell. Especially tonight. When he saw you out there. I can tell."

"It's nothing," I said to her, realizing how true it was. It was just a feeling, a whooshing in my ears. Not love.

"Do you still love him?" In the bathroom her voice echoed strangely, louder and then softer all around us.

"No," I said quietly. And I caught a glimpse of myself in the mirror, my wild hair, my ripped dress. You could even see the scar over my eye where the makeup had brushed off. But I was okay. I was. "I don't," I said.

And Elizabeth Gunderson turned from the sink, her hair swinging over her shoulder just it had before she tumbled off a million pyramids at a million high-school football games. She opened her mouth to say something more but I didn't hear it, never got a chance, because just then the door slammed open and Ginny Tabor burst in with a blast of pink satin, her voice preceding her.

"Halley!" She stopped, fluttering one hand over her chest while she caught her breath. "You've—you've got to get out here."

"Why?" I said.

"Scarlett," she gasped, still breathing hard. She held up a finger, holding me there, while she gulped for air. "Scarlett's having the baby."

"*What?*" I spun around to look at her. "Are you serious?"

"I swear, she and Cameron were getting their picture taken and Brett and I were next in line and right when the flash went off, she just got this look on her face and then boom it was happening—"

"*Move,*" I said, pushing past her out into the cafeteria, around the dance floor and the people drinking punch, past the band and to the edge of a crowd gathered around the tiny wooden drawbridge where everyone had been posing for pictures. There was a buzz in the air and a photographer with a huge camera wringing his hands and finally, with her face bright red and way too many people pressed around her, Scarlett. When she saw me, she burst into tears.

"You're fine, you're fine," I said, sliding around to her other side, by Cameron who was looking kind of ashen. Someone was shouting about an ambulance and the music had stopped and I couldn't even remember the breathing patterns we'd learned in Lamaze class.

Scarlett grabbed me by the neckline and jerked me toward her; she was surprisingly strong. "I don't want an ambulance," she said. "Just get me the hell out of here. I am not having this baby at the prom."

"Okay, okay," I said, looking to Cameron for support but he was leaning against the edge of the drawbridge, fanning himself with one hand. He looked worse than Scarlett. "Let's go, then. Come on."

I helped her to her feet, her arm around my shoulder, and started to push through the crowd. Mrs. Oakley was on one side of me, saying she'd already called someone, to stay put, and somewhere in an explosion of pink was Ginny Tabor, yelling about boiling water, but all I could think of was Scarlett's hand squeezing my shoulder so damn hard I could hardly even see straight. But somehow, we were making headway.

"Where's Cameron?" Scarlett said between gasps as we burst out the door into the courtyard. "What happened to him?"

"He's back there somewhere," I told her, dragging her along beside me, her grip still tight on my skin. "He looked a little nauseous or something."

"This is no time for that!" she screamed, right in my ear.

"We're fine, we're fine," I said, and now that we were getting closer to the parking lot it suddenly occurred to me that we had no mode of transportation, since the limo wasn't due back until midnight. By now we'd lost most of the crowd, all of them hanging back by the cafeteria door with Mrs. Oakley shouting about how we should wait for the ambulance, it would be here any second.

"I don't want an ambulance," Scarlett said again. "I swear, if they put me in one I will fight them tooth and nail."

"We don't *have* a car," I told her. "We took the limo, remember?"

"I don't care," she said, clutching at my shoulder even harder. *"Do something!"*

"I will get us a ride," I said, looking around the parking lot for any poor sucker who just happened to be driving off at that moment. "Don't worry," I told her. "I have it under control."

But this was nothing *Seventeen* magazine had ever covered. We were on our own.

Just then I heard a car screech around the corner, and I leaned out and waved my arm frantically, as much as I could while still supporting Scarlett. "Hello!" I called. "Please, God, please stop."

"Oh, no," Scarlett said quietly. "My water just broke. Oh, man, what a mess. This dress is a goner."

"Please stop!!" I screamed at the car as it came closer, already slowing down, and of course as it slid to a stop beside us, engine rumbling, I knew who it was.

"Hey there," Macon said, smiling from the driver's seat as he hit the button to unlock the door. He was in a different car this time, a Lexus, Elizabeth next to him. "Need a ride?"

"Of course we need a ride!" Scarlett screamed at him. "Are you stupid?"

"That would be nice, thank you," I said smoothly as Elizabeth reached behind her to open the back door and we piled in, Scarlett all sticky and me scattering bobby pins everywhere because these were definitely radical movements. We were pulling away when Cameron ran up and we had to stop to let him in, too; he was huffing and puffing and still looked kind of pale.

"What happened to you?" I asked as Scarlett bore down on my bad hand, squeezing so hard my fingers were folding in on each other.

"I passed out," he said quietly.

"What did he say?" Scarlett bellowed from my other side.

"He didn't say anything," I said. "He's fine. Now, let's work on our breathing. Deep breaths, in and out—"

"I don't want to breathe," she said in a low voice. "I want drugs and I want them *now*."

From the rearview, I could see Macon grinning back at us, and I had a sudden flash of the last time we'd been together in a car, speeding toward town. But I couldn't think about that now.

"Breathe," I said to Scarlett. "Come on now."

"I'm scared," she said. "Oh, God, Halley, it *hurts*."

I gripped her hand harder, tighter, ignoring my own pain. "Think about what we learned in class, okay? Peaceful thoughts. Uh, oceans and fields of flowers, and country lakes."

"Shut *up!*" she said. "God, listen to yourself."

"Okay, fine," I said, "don't think about that. Think about

267

good things, like that trip we took to the beach in sixth grade, remember? When you got stung by the jellyfish?"

"That was good?" Her brow was wet, sweaty, and her hand in mine was hot. I tried not to look scared, but it was hard.

"Sure it was," I said, and Macon was still watching me as we sped down Main Street but I ignored him, going on, "and remember baking cookies in your kitchen all those summers, and dancing to the radio, and last summer with Michael, and going to the lake, and . . ."

"Kiwi fruit," she said, gasping. Beside me Cameron looked like he was ready to pass out again.

"Right," I said, ready to run with anything, "kiwi fruit. And remember the day you got your license? And the first thing you did was back into my house, right there by the garage door? Remember?"

"Your dad said most people stick to just hitting other cars," she said, her voice raspy, hand still gripping mine. "He said I was special."

The lights of the hospital were coming up now, closer. I could hear an ambulance, somewhere. "I know he did," I said, brushing the damp hair off her forehead. "Just hold on, Scarlett, okay? We're almost there. Just hold on."

She squeezed my hand, hard, and closed her eyes. "Don't leave me, okay? Promise you won't."

"I won't," I said as we pulled into the parking lot, past the front entrance to Emergency. "I'll be right here. I promise."

They put Scarlett in a wheelchair, shoved a bunch of forms in my hand, and pushed her through a set of double doors with a bang, leaving me and Cameron at Admitting with a bunch of Boy Scouts who'd had a camping accident, an old man with a bleeding forehead, and a woman screaming in Spanish with a baby planted against her hip. Cameron went over and sat down, putting his head between his knees, and after I scribbled what I could on the forms, I went to the pay phone to call Marion.

Of course she wasn't home. She was off jousting, or doing medieval dances, or whatever she and Vlad did on their theme weekends. The phone rang and rang before the machine came on, and I hung up and did what came instinctively. I called my mother.

"Halley?" she said, before I even finished my hello. "Where *are* you? Mrs. Vaughn just called and said Noah had been found drunk in the school parking lot and Norman had to go down there to pick him up from the principal, she's completely hysterical and no one knew what happened to you. . . ."

"Mom."

"I trusted you not to drink, and I don't know what got into Noah, he's never been in trouble before and John was just livid, apparently . . ."

"Mom," I said again, louder this time. "The baby's coming."

"The baby?" There was a sudden silence. "What, now? Right now?"

269

"Yes." Beside me the Boy Scouts were banging on a candy machine, grumbling about being gypped, and Cameron was a few seats down with his eyes closed, slumped in a plastic chair. "I'm at the hospital, they just took Scarlett away and I don't have time to explain about Noah right now, okay? I can't get in touch with Marion, so when you see her come home, tell her where we are. Tell her to hurry."

"Is Scarlett okay?"

"She's scared," I said, thinking of her alone wherever they'd taken her, and how I'd promised to stay right with her, no matter what. "I have to go, okay? I'll call you later."

"Okay, honey. Let us know."

"I will." I hung up the phone and rushed back to Admitting, my dress dragging across the floor, one lone bobby pin still holding it together in the back. As I passed the front entrance I saw Macon and Elizabeth still in the car. They were talking, Macon's mouth moving, one finger pointing, angrily. Elizabeth was just staring out the window, her arm hanging down the side of the car, a cigarette held loosely in her fingers. She didn't even see me.

I went to the Admitting desk, told them I was Scarlett's sister and Lamaze partner, and got led back through the double doors, past the emergency-room cots and curtains, to where they had Scarlett on a bed, the fetal monitor already hooked up and beeping.

"Where have you *been?*" she shrieked as soon as I came

around the corner. She had a plastic cup full of ice in her hand and a green gown on, her prom dress tossed over a chair in the corner. "I am *freaking* out here, Halley, and you just vanish into thin air."

"I did not vanish," I said gently. "I was calling Marion and handling things at the front desk. I'm here now."

"Well, good," she said. "Because I really need—"And then she stopped talking and sat up straight, holding her stomach. She made a low, guttural moaning sound, rising and rising louder and louder, and I just stared at her, not even recognizing her face, and knew all at once I was in way over my head.

The door opened behind me and the doctor came in, all cheerful and easygoing, taking her time walking up to the bed while Scarlett huffed and puffed and grabbed for my hand, which she immediately squeezed so hard I felt bone meeting bone, crunching.

"So," the doctor said easily, grabbing a chart off the end of the bed, "looks like we're having a baby."

"Looks that way," Scarlett said between gasps. "Can I have some drugs, please?"

"In a minute," the doctor said, moving to the end of the bed and lifting the sheet, moving Scarlett's legs into the stirrups attached to the side of the bed. "Let's see how far along you are."

She poked and prodded, and Scarlett ground the bones in my hand to powder.

"Okay," the doctor said, patting the sheet back down, "we're

271

getting close. It shouldn't be too long now, so I just need you to relax, and work your breathing with your partner here. Leave the rest to us."

"What about the drugs?" Scarlett said urgently. "Can I get the drugs?"

"I'll send someone in shortly," the doctor said, smiling like we were cute. "Don't worry, honey. It'll be over before you know it." She slipped the chart back into its place on the end of the bed, tucking her pen behind her ear, and walked out the door, waving as she went.

"I *hate* her," Scarlett said decisively through a mouthful of ice. "I mean it."

"Let's do our breathing," I suggested, pulling a chair up beside the bed. "Deep breath in, now, okay?"

"I don't want to breathe," she snapped at me. "I want them to knock me out, completely, even if they just hit me on the head with something. I can't do this, Halley. I can't."

"Yes, you can," I said sternly. "We're ready for this."

"Easy for you to say." She sucked down more ice. "All you have to do is tell me to breathe and stand there. You've got the easy part."

"Scarlett. Hold it together."

She rose up in the bed, spitting frozen shards everywhere. "Don't tell me to hold it together, not until you have felt this pain, because it is unlike anything—" And then she stopped talking, her face going pale again as another contraction hit.

"Breathe," I said, doing it myself, *puff puff puff,* inhale deep, *puff puff puff.* "Come on."

But she wasn't breathing, only moaning again, that low scary noise that made me back away from the bed, literally scared for my life. I was wrong. *We weren't ready for this.* This was big, and scary, and I understood suddenly how Cameron must have felt, woozy and terrified all at once. I wished I was out in the waiting room, with the Boy Scouts and the candy machine, pacing and waiting to light up a cigar.

"Stay here," I said to her, backing away from the bed, step by step, as she stopped moaning suddenly and watched me, eyes wide. "I'll be—"

"Don't leave!" she cried, trying to sit up straight, reaching for the sides of the bed. "Halley, don't—"

But I let the door swing shut behind me and I was suddenly alone, in the corridor, the cool wall pressing against my back where my dress was gaping open. I tried to shake the fear off. I could hear Scarlett on the other side of the door, moaning. Just when she needed me, I was falling apart.

Then, I heard it. The sound of footsteps coming closer, louder and louder, *clack clack clack,* all businesslike as they rounded the corner. I looked to my left and coming toward me, purse tucked under her arm and eyes straight ahead, was my mother.

"Where is she?" she said as she got closer, switching her purse to the other arm.

"In there," I said. "She's freaking out."

"Well, let's go." She reached for the doorknob but I hung back, pressing myself harder against the wall. "Halley? What's wrong?"

"I can't do this," I said, and my voice sounded strange, high. "It's too crazy, and she's in pain, and I just think—"

"Honey." She looked at me. "You need to be in there."

"I can't," I said again, and my throat hurt when I spoke. "It's too much to deal with."

"Well, that's too bad," she said simply, grabbing my shoulder and pushing me toward the door, her hand guiding me from behind. "Scarlett is counting on you. You can't let her down."

"I'm no help, she wouldn't want me there, I'm a mess," I said, but she was already opening the door, pushing it with her free hand.

"You are the *only* one she wants," my mother said, and then we were crossing the room, her arm clamped around my shoulders, back to the bed where Scarlett was sitting up, clenching the sheet in her hands, tears streaming down her face.

"Hi, honey," my mother said, crossing to the bedside and smoothing down Scarlett's hair. "You're doing great. Just great."

"Is Marion here?" Scarlett said.

"Not yet, but Brian is over at your house, waiting for her. She'll get here any time now. Don't worry. Now, what can we do for you? Anything?"

"Just don't leave me," Scarlett said quietly as my mother

settled in next to her, laying her purse on the chair with the prom dress. "I don't want to be alone."

"You won't be." My mother was eyeing the chair on Scarlett's other side, so I took my place carefully, ashamed. "We're here."

I looked across the bed, past Scarlett's tired, shiny face as my mother leaned close to her ear, whispering words I couldn't hear. But I knew what they were, what they had to be: the same ones I'd heard after all those bad dreams, all those skateboard and roller-skating accidents, all the times the little fiendettes chased me home on pink bicycles. I watched my mother do what she did best, and realized there would never be a way to cut myself from her entirely. No matter how strong or weak I was, she was a part of me, as crucial as my own heart. I would never be strong enough, in all my life, to do without her.

Chapter Nineteen

The doctor looked up at us, nodding.

"Here it comes, Scarlett, I can see the head. Just a couple more big pushes and it's out, so get ready, okay?"

"Not long now," I whispered to her, squeezing her hand harder. "Almost there."

"You're doing so great," my mother said. "Very brave. Much braver than I ever was."

"It's the drugs," I said. "Since then it's been a piece of cake."

"Shut up," Scarlett snapped. "I swear, when this is over, I am going to *kill* you."

"Give me another good push!" the doctor said from the foot of the bed. "Get ready!"

"Breathe," I said to her, taking a deep one myself. "Breathe."

"Breathe," my mother repeated, her voice echoing mine. "Come on, honey. You can do it."

Scarlett braced against me, her hand twisting mine, and I watched her face swallow up her eyes, her mouth fall open, as

276

she pushed harder than she had all night, with every bit of strength she had left.

"Here it comes, it's coming, look at that." The doctor was smiling from the end of the bed, excited. "Oh, push once more, just a little one, Scarlett, just a tiny one . . ."

Scarlett pushed again, gasping, and I watched as the doctor reached down with her hands, groping around, and then, suddenly, she was holding something, something small and red and slimy with kicking feet and a tiny mouth that opened up to wail, a tiny, tiny voice.

"It's a girl," the doctor said, and the nurses were wiping her off, cleaning out her mouth, and then they put her in Scarlett's arms, against her chest. Scarlett was crying, looking down at her against her skin, closing her eyes. She'd been with us since that summer, growing and growing, and now she was here, real as we were.

"A girl," Scarlett said softly. "I knew it."

"She's beautiful," I told her. "She has my eyes."

"And my hair," she said, still crying, her hand brushing the top of the baby's head and the red fuzz there. "Look."

"You should be very proud," my mother said, reaching to touch one tiny little hand. "Very proud." And she looked over and smiled at me.

"I'm going to name her Grace," Scarlett said. "Grace Halley."

"Halley?" I said, amazed. "No kidding."

"No kidding." She kissed the baby's forehead. "Grace Halley Thomas."

When I looked down at Grace, I was overwhelmed. She was our year, from the summer with Michael to the winter with Macon. We would never forget.

Scarlett was just beaming, rocking Grace in her arms and kissing the tiny fingers and toes, asking everyone if they had honestly ever seen a more beautiful baby. (It was agreed that no one had.) After we all cooed over her, and Scarlett nodded off to sleep, I went out to the waiting room to deliver the news. What I saw, as I rounded the vending machines and water fountains, was enough to stop me dead in my tracks.

The room was bright and packed. On one side, grouped around the Emergency Room door, was at least half of our class, all in dresses and tuxedos, leaning against the walls and sitting on the cheap plastic sofas. There were Ginny Tabor and Brett Hershey, girls from our Commercial Design class and their dates, Melissa Ringley and even Maryann Lister, plus tons of people I didn't even know. All in their finest, eating candy bars and talking, waiting for news. I didn't see Elizabeth Gunderson, but I did see Macon, leaning against the candy machine and talking to Cameron, who had finally gotten some color back in his face.

And on the other side of the waiting room, segregated by some chairs and modern time, were Vlad, a breathless Marion, and at least twenty other warriors and maidens, all decked out in full medieval regalia. Some were carrying swords and shields. One was even wearing chain mail that clanked as he paced back in forth in front of Admitting.

Then, all at once, they saw me.

Marion ran across the room, dress swishing madly across her feet, with Vlad and a handful of warriors right behind. The nurse at Admitting just rolled her eyes as I passed, with Marion approaching from one side and Cameron and Ginny Tabor fast closing in on the other, Ginny in her shrieking pink followed by a slew of girls in pastels and boys in tuxes, all crowding in. Everyone else had stopped talking, rising from their seats and gathering closer, watching my face.

"So?" Ginny said, skidding to a stop in front of me.

"How is she?" Marion asked. "I just got here, I was late getting home—"

"Is she okay?" Cameron said. "Is she?"

"She's fine," I said, and I smiled at him. I turned to the assembled crowd, the prom-goers and Cinderellas, the maidens and ladies and warriors and knights, not to mention the odd Boy Scout and security guard, all carefully keeping their distance. "It's a girl."

Someone started clapping and cheering and then everyone was talking at once, slapping each other on the back, and the tuxedos and warriors were intermingled, shaking hands and hugging, as Marion went back to see her granddaughter and

279

Cameron followed her and Ginny Tabor kissed Brett Hershey just for show. The Admitting nurse told everyone to quiet down but no one listened and I just stood and watched it all, smiling, committing everything to memory so that later I could tell Scarlett, and Grace, every single detail.

Much later, I sent my mother home and sat with Scarlett, watching her sleep. This had been our Special Night, just not the one we'd expected. I was so excited about the baby and what was coming next, I wanted to wake her up and talk about everything, right then, but she looked so peaceful that I held back. And as I left, I walked past the nursery and looked in on Grace, curled up so tiny in her bassinette. I spread my fingers on the glass, our signal, just to let her know I was there.

Then I walked downstairs and out into the night to go home. I didn't want anyone to start this journey with me.

I bent down and took off my shoes, hooking the straps over my wrist, and started down the sidewalk. I wasn't thinking about Macon, or my mother waiting at home for me, or even Scarlett dozing behind one of those bright hospital windows. I was only thinking of Grace Halley with each step I took, in my prom dress (safety-pinned tight, now), barefoot, heading home.

I wondered what kind of girl she'd be, and if she'd ever see the comet that was her name, and Grandma Halley's, and mine. I knew I'd try, one day, to take her and show her the sky, hold her against my lap as I told her how the comet went overhead, how it was clear and beautiful, and special, just like her. I hoped that Grace would be a little bit of the best of all of us: Scarlett's spirit, and my mother's strength, Marion's determination, and Michael's sly humor. I wasn't sure what I could give, not just yet. But I knew when I told her about the comet, years from now, I would know. And I would lean close to her ear, saying the words no one else could hear, explaining it all. The language of solace, and comets, and the girls we all become, in the end.

THAT SUMMER

I would like to acknowledge Doris Betts and Jill McCorkle, my teachers, for their support; Dannye Romine Powell, for granting permission for me to use the wonderful poem that inspired this book; my agent, Leigh Feldman; and Lee Smith, for her friendship, generosity, and practical wisdom. Thank you

PENGUIN BOOKS
An imprint of Penguin Random House LLC, New York

First published in the United States of America by Orchard Books, 1996
Published by Puffin Books, an imprint of Penguin Random House LLC, 1998
Published by Speak Books, an imprint of Penguin Random House LLC, 2004
Published by Viking, an imprint of Penguin Random House LLC, 2006

This omnibus edition published by Penguin, an imprint of Penguin Random House, 2019

Visit us online at penguinrandomhouse.com

THE LIBRARY OF CONGRESS HAS CATALOGED THE VIKING EDITION AS FOLLOWS:
Dessen, Sarah.
That summer / by Sarah Dessen.
p. cm.
Summary: During the summer of her divorced father's remarriage and her sister's wedding, fifteen-year-old Haven comes into her own by letting go of the myths of the past
ISBN 0-14-03688-2 (hardcover)
[1. Sisters—Fiction. 2. Interpersonal relations—Fiction. 3. Weddings—Fiction.] I. Title.
PZ7.D455Th 1998 [Fic]—dc21 97-50534 CIP AC

Omnibus Edition ISBN 9780593113585

Printed in the United States of America

1 3 5 7 9 10 8 6 4 2

To my parents, for their faith and patience,
and to Jay for everything else

THAT SUMMER

At Every Wedding Someone Stays Home

This one sits all morning
beside the picture window,
staring out at the lawn
which in these situations
is always under a sheet of ice,
even in June. The girl is wearing
her quilted robe, gloves,
fur-lined slippers. Still she can't
get warm. Her mother gets hot
just watching her, so she goes out
for groceries, makes a great show
when she returns of rattling
the brown paper bag she saves
to line the bird cage.
Now she is running water,
peeling melons, humming, arranging
daisies. We who are watching
want the mother to quit making noise,
to stop chopping fruit, to leave
the kitchen. We want her to walk
down the hall to the closet
where wool blankets are stored.
We want her to gather five or six,

the solids, the stripes,
the MacGregor plaids and tuck them
under her daughter's legs, saving one
for her feet and one for her thin shoulders.
Now we want her to heat water for tea,
bring in wood and quick
before her daughter freezes
seal all the windows
against the stray, chill peal of bells.

—Dannye Romine Powell

Chapter One

It's funny how one summer can change every-thing. It must be something about the heat and the smell of chlorine, fresh-cut grass and honeysuckle, asphalt sizzling after late-day thunderstorms, the steam rising while everything drips around it. Something about long, lazy days and whirring air conditioners and bright plastic flip-flops from the drugstore thwacking down the street. Something about fall being so close, another year, another Christmas, another beginning. So much in one summer, stirring up like the storms that crest at the end of each day, blowing out all the heat and dirt to leave everything gasping and cool. Everyone can reach back to one summer and lay a finger to it, finding the exact point when everything changed. That summer was mine.

The day my father got remarried, my mother was up at six A.M. defrosting the refrigerator. I woke to the sound of her hacking away and the occasional thud as a huge slab of ice crashed. My mother was an erratic defroster. When I came down into the kitchen, she was poised in front of the open freezer, wielding the ice pick, Barry Manilow crooning out at her from the tape player she kept on the kitchen table. Around Barry's voice, stacked in dripping piles, were all of our perishables, sweating in the heat of another summer morning.

"Oh, good morning, Haven." She turned when she saw me, wiping her brow with the ice pick still in hand, making my heart jump as I imagined it slipping just a bit and taking out her eye. I knew that nervous feeling so well, even at fifteen, that spilling uncontrollability that my mother brought out in me. It was as if I was attached to her with a tether, her every movement yanking at me, my own hands reaching to shield her from the dangers of her waving arms.

"Good morning." I pulled out a chair and sat down next to a stack of packaged chicken. "Are you okay?"

"Me?" She was back on the job now, scraping. "I'm fine. Are you hungry?"

"Not really." I pulled my legs up to my chest, pressing hard to fold myself into the smallest size possible. It seemed like every morning I woke up taller, my skin having stretched in the night while I slept. I had dreams of not being able to fit through doors, of becoming gigantic, towering over people and buildings like a monster, causing terror in the streets. I'd put on four inches since April, and showed no signs of letting up. I was already five-eleven, with only a few more little lines on the measuring stick before six feet.

"Haven." My mother looked at me. "Please don't sit that way. It's not good for you and it makes me nervous." She stood there staring at me until I let my legs drop. "That's better." Scrape, scrape. Barry sang on, about New England.

I still wasn't sure what had brought me down from my bed so early on a Saturday, aside from the noise of my mother loosening icebergs from our Frigidaire. I hadn't slept well, with my dress for the wedding hanging from the curtain rod, fluttering in the white light of the street lamp outside my window. At two P.M. my father was marrying Lorna Queen, of "Lorna Queen's Weather Scene" on WTSB News Channel 5. She was what they called a meteorologist and what my mother called the Weather Pet, but only when she was feeling vindictive. Lorna was blond and perky and wore cute little pastel suits that showed just enough leg as she stood smiling in front of colorful maps, sweeping her arm as if she controlled all the elements. My father, Mac McPhail, was the sports anchor for channel five, and he and the Weather Pet shared the subordinate news desk, away from the grim-faced anchors, Charlie Baker and Tess Phillips, who reported real news. Before we'd known about my father's affair with the Weather Pet, I'd always wondered what they were smiling and talking about in those last few minutes of the broadcast as the credits rolled. Charlie Baker and Tess Phillips shuffled important-looking papers, worn thin from a hard day of news chasing and news delivering; but my father and the Weather Pet were always off to the side sharing some secret laugh that the rest of us weren't in on. And when we finally did catch on, it wasn't very funny after all.

Not that I didn't like Lorna Queen. She was nice enough for someone who broke up my parents' marriage. My mother, in all fairness, always blamed my father and limited her hostility to the nickname Weather Pet and to the occasional snide remark about my father's growing mass of hair, which at the time of the separation was receding with great speed and now seemed to have reversed itself and grown back with the perseverance and quickness of our lawn after a few good days of rain. My mother had read all the books about divorce and tried hard to make it smooth for me and my sister, Ashley, who was Daddy's pet and left the room at even the slightest remark about his hair. My mother kept her outbursts about that to a minimum, but I could tell by the way she winced when they showed my father and Lorna together at their subordinate news desk that it still hurt. Before the divorce my mother had been good at outbursts, and this quietness, this holding back, was more unnerving than I imagined any breakdown could be. My mother, like Ashley, has always cultivated the family dramatic streak, started by my grandmother, who at important family gatherings liked to fake horrible incidents if she felt she was not getting enough attention. No reunion, wedding, or funeral was complete without at least one stroke, heart attack, or general collapse from Grandma at which time everyone shifted into High Dramatic Mode, fussing and running around and generally creating the kind of chaos that my family is well known for.

This always made me kind of nervous. I hadn't inherited that flair for the stage that Ashley and my mother had, this snap ability to lose control in appropriate instances. I was more like my father, steady and worried all the time. Back then, we had it down to a science:

Mom and Ashley overreacting, thriving on crisis, my father and I standing calm, together, balancing them out. Then my father left, and like a table short a leg, things had been out of whack ever since.

"So are you going?" That was Ashley, standing in the kitchen doorway in a T-shirt and socks. Just looking at her made me acutely aware of my own height, the pointedness of my elbows and hipbones, the extra inch I'd put on in the last month. At twenty-one my sister is a petite five-four, with the kind of curvy, rounded body that I wish I'd been born with; tiny feet, perfect hair, small enough to be cute, but still a force to be reckoned with. At my age she had already been voted Most Popular, dated (and dumped) the captain of the football team, and been a varsity cheerleader. She was always the one at the top of the pyramid, tiny enough to be passed from hand to hand overhead until she stood high over everyone else, a bit shaky but triumphant, before letting loose and tumbling head over heels to be caught at the bottom with a sweep of someone's arms. I remembered her in her cheerleading uniform, short blue skirt, white sweater, and saddle shoes, grabbing her backpack to run out to a carful of teenagers waiting outside, squealing off to school with a beep of the horn. Back then, Ashley seemed to live a life just like Barbie's: popular and perfect, always with a handsome boyfriend and the cool crowd. All she needed was the Dreamhouse and a purple plastic Corvette to make it real.

Now, my sister just scowled at me when she caught me looking at her, then scratched one foot with the other. She had a good tan already, and on the inside of her left ankle I could see the yellow butterfly tattoo she'd gotten in Myrtle Beach when she'd gotten drunk after high school graduation two years earlier and someone double dared her. Ashley was wild, but that was before she got engaged.

"No. I don't think I should go," my mother said. "I think it's in bad taste."

"Go where?" I said.

"She invited you," Ashley said, yawning. "She wouldn't have done that if she didn't want you there."

"Where?" I said again, but of course no one was listening to me. There was another crash as a block of ice fell out of the freezer.

"I'm not going," my mother said solidly, planting a hand on her hip. "It's tacky and I won't do it."

"So don't do it," Ashley said, coming into the kitchen and reaching across me to pick up a pack of frozen waffles from the table.

"Do what?" I said again, louder this time because in our house you have to make a commotion to even be heard.

"Go to your father's wedding," my mother said. "Lorna sent me an invitation."

"She did?"

"Yes." This fell into the category of whether Lorna, the Weather Pet, was either downright mean or just stupid. She did a lot of things that made me question this, from telling me it was okay to call her Mom once she married my father to sending my mother a framed picture of an old family Christmas card she'd found among my dad's junk. We'd all sat around the kitchen

• 6 •

table, staring at it, my mother holding it in one hand with a puckered look on her face. She'd never said a word about it, but instead went outside and ripped up weeds in the garden for forty-five minutes, handful after handful flying over her head in a massive horticultural tantrum. I believed Lorna was mostly mean, bordering on stupid; my mother refused to even voice an opinion; and because Ashley couldn't bear to criticize anything about Daddy she said Lorna was just stupid and left mean out of it altogether. All I knew was that I would never call a woman only five years older than Ashley Mom and that that framed Christmas card was what Ann Landers would call In Quite Poor Taste.

So my mother was not with us as we set off for the church that afternoon, in our matching shiny pink bridesmaid dresses, to see our father be bonded in holy matrimony to this probably stupid but quite possibly just mean Weather Pet. I'd felt sorry for my mother as she lined us up in front of the mantel to take a picture with her little Instamatic, cooing about how lovely we looked. She stood in the doorway behind the screen, waving as we walked out to the car, the camera dangling from her wrist, and I realized suddenly why Ashley might have wanted her to come, even if it was tacky. There was something so sad about leaving her behind, all of a sudden, and I had an urge to run back and take her with me, to pull that tether tight and hold her close. But I didn't, like I always don't, and instead climbed into the car next to Ashley and watched my mother waving as we pulled away from the house. At every wedding someone stays home.

* * *

As we got out of the car at the church, I saw Ashley's fiancé, Lewis Warsher, heading our way from the other end of the lot where he'd parked his little blue Chevette. He was fixing his tie as he walked, because Lewis was a neat dresser. He always wore shiny shoes and skinny ties in pastel colors. When Ashley saw him I swear she shrank about two inches; there is something about Lewis that turns my sister, who is tough as nails, into a swooning, breathless belle.

"Hey, honey." And of course they were immediately connected, his arms slipping around her small waist, pulling her close for one of those long, emotional hugs where it looked like he was the only thing that was keeping her from collapsing to the ground. Ashley and Lewis spent a lot of time hugging each other, supporting each other physically, and whispering. They gave me a complex, always with their heads together murmuring in corners of rooms, their voices too low to catch anything but a few vowels.

"Hey," Ashley whispered. They were still hugging. I stood there fiddling with my dress; I had no choice but to wait. Ashley hadn't always been this way; she'd had boyfriends for as long as I could remember, but none of them had affected her like Lewis. For years we kept track of major family events by who Ashley had been dating at the time. During the Mitchell period, I got my braces and Grandma came to live with us. The Robert era included my mother going back to night school and Ashley getting in the car wreck that broke her leg and made her get the stitches that left a heart-shaped scar on her right shoulder. And it was during the year-long Frank ordeal that the divorce came down, complete with law proceedings, family therapy, and the advent of Lorna, the Weather Pet. It was a boyfriend timeline: I could not remember dates, but I could place each important event in my life with a face of a boy whose heart Ashley had broken.

But this was all before Lewis, whom Ashley met at the Yogurt Paradise at the mall where they both worked. Ashley was a Vive cosmetics salesgirl, which meant she stood behind a big counter in Dillard's department store, wearing a white lab coat and putting overpriced makeup on rich ladies' faces. She thought she was something in that lab coat, wearing it practically everywhere like it meant she was a damn doctor or something. She was just coming out of the messy breakup of the Frank era and was consoling herself with a yogurt sundae when Lewis Warsher sensed her pain and sat himself down at her table because she looked like she needed a friend. These are their words, which I know because I've heard this story entirely too many times since they announced their engagement six months ago.

My mother said Ashley missed our father, and needed a protective figure; Lewis just came along at the right time. And Lewis *did* protect her, from old boyfriends and gas station attendants and bugs that dared to cross her path. Still, sometimes I wondered what she really saw in him. There was nothing spectacular about Lewis, and it was a little unsettling to see my sister, whom I'd always admired for being plucky and tough and not taking a bit of lip off anyone, shrinking into his arms whenever the world rose up to meet her face to face.

"Hey, Haven." Lewis leaned over and pecked me on the cheek, still holding Ashley close. "You look beautiful."

"Thanks," I said. Lewis had the arm clamp on Ashley, steering her towards the church, with me following. Even though we were wearing the same god-awful pink fluffy dresses, we looked totally different. Ashley was a short, curvy pink rose, and I was a tall, pink straw, like something you'd plunk down in a big fizzy drink. This was the kind of thing I was always thinking about since my body betrayed me and made me a giant.

When I was in first grade I had a teacher named Mrs. Thomas. She was young, sported a flip hairdo that made her look just like Snow White, smelled like Lily of the Valley, and kept a picture of a man in a uniform on her desk, staring stiffly out from the frame. And even though I was shy and slow at math, she didn't care. She loved me. She'd come up beside me in the lunch line or during story hour and smooth her hand over my head, saying "Why, Miss Haven, you're just no bigger than a minute." I was compact at six, able to fit neatly into small places that now were inaccessible: under the crook of an arm, in the palm of a hand. At five-eleven and counting, I no longer had the sense that someone like Mrs. Thomas could neatly enclose me if danger should strike. I was all bony elbows and acute angles, like a jigsaw puzzle piece that can only go in the middle, waiting for the others to fit around it to make it whole.

The church was filling up with people, which wasn't surprising: my father is the kind of person who knows everybody, somehow. Mac McPhail, sportscaster, beer drinker, teller of tall tales and big lies, the latter being told mostly to my mother in the last few months of the marriage. I can remember sitting in front of the TV watching my father on the local news every night, seeing the sly sideways looks he and Lorna Queen exchanged during the leads into commercial breaks, and still not having any idea that he would leave my mother for this woman best known for her short skirts and pouty-lipped way of saying "upper-level disturbance." She didn't know the half of it. There had been no disturbance before like the one that hit our house the day my father came home from the station, sat my mother down at the kitchen table right under the vent that leads to the floor beneath the counter in my bathroom, and dropped the bomb that he'd fallen hard for the Weather Pet. I sat on the side of my tub, toothbrush in hand, and wished the house had been designed differently so I wouldn't have been privy to this most painful of moments. My mother was silent for a long time, my father's voice the only one wafting up through the floor, explaining how he couldn't help it, didn't want to lie anymore, had to come clean, all of this with his booming sportscaster voice, so agile at curving around scores and highlights, stumbling over the simple truth that his marriage was over. My mother started crying, finally, and then told him to leave in a quiet, steady voice that made the room seem suddenly colder. Two weeks later he had moved into the Weather Pet's condo. He met me and

Ashley for lunch each Saturday and took us to the beach every other weekend, spending too much money and trying to explain everything by putting his arm around my shoulder, squeezing, and sighing aloud.

But that had been a year and a half ago, and now here it was wedding day, the *first* wedding I was dreading this summer. We walked into the lobby of the church and were immediately gathered up in the large arms of my aunt Ree, who was representing the bulk of my father's side of the family, most of whom were still upset about the divorce and sided with my mother, family loyalty notwithstanding. But Aunt Ree was ample enough to represent everyone in her flowing pink muu-muu, a corsage the size of a small bush pinned to her chest.

"Haven, you come over here and give your aunt Ree some sugar." She squashed me against her, and I could feel the flowers poking into my skin. She'd clamped Ashley in her other arm, somehow getting her away from Lewis, and hugged us both as tightly together as if she was trying to consolidate us into one person. "And Ashley, this should all seem pretty familiar to you. When's your big day again?"

"August nineteenth," Lewis said quickly. I wondered if that was the answer he gave to any question now. It was what I usually said.

Aunt Ree pushed me back, holding me by both arms as Ashley made a quick dash back to Lewis. "Now you are just growing like a weed, I swear to God. Look at you. How tall are you?"

I smiled, fighting the urge to slouch. "Too tall."

"No such thing." She tightened her grip on my arm. "You can never be too tall or too thin. That's what they say, isn't it?"

"It's too rich or too thin," Ashley said. Leave it to my short, curvy sister to correct even a misworded compliment.

"Whatever," Aunt Ree said. "You're beautiful, anyway. But we're running late and the bride is a mess. We've got to go find you your bouquets."

Ashley kissed Lewis and clung to him for a few more seconds before following me and Aunt Ree through the masses of perfumed wedding guests to a side door that led into a big room with bookcases covering all four walls. Lorna Queen was sitting at a table in the corner, a makeup mirror facing her, with some woman hovering around picking at her hair with a long comb.

"We're here!" Aunt Ree said in a singsong voice, presenting us in all of our pink as if she'd created us herself. "And just in time."

Lorna Queen *was* a beautiful woman. As she turned in her seat to face us, I realized that again, just as I always did when I watched her doing her forecasts in her short skirts with color-coordinated lipsticks. She was pert and perfect and had the tiniest little ears I'd ever seen on anyone. She kept them covered most of the time, but once at the beach I'd seen her with her hair pulled back, with those ears like seashells molded against her skin. I'd always wondered if she heard like the rest of us or if the world sounded different through such small receptors.

"Hi, girls." She smiled at us and dabbed her eyes with a neatly folded Kleenex. "Y'all look beautiful."

"Are you okay?" Ashley asked her.

"I'm fine. I'm just"— she sniffled daintily—"so happy. I've waited for this day for so long, and I'm just so happy."

The woman doing her makeup rolled her eyes. "Lorna, honey, waterproof mascara can only do so much. You've got to stop crying."

"I know." She sniffled again, reaching out to take my hand and Ashley's. "I want you girls to know how much I love your father. I'm going to make him just as happy as I can, and I'm so glad we're all going to be a family."

"We're very happy for you," Ashley said, speaking for both of us, which she often did when Lorna was concerned.

Lorna was tearing up again when a man in a suit came in through another door and whispered, "Ten minutes," then flashed the thumbs-up sign as if we were about to go out and play the Big Game.

"Ten minutes," Lorna said, her hand fluttering out of mine and to her face, dabbing her eyes. The makeup woman spun her back around in the chair and moved in with the powder puff. "My God, it's actually happening."

Ashley reached into her purse and pulled out a lipstick. "Do like this," she said to me, pursing her lips. I did, and she put some on me, smoothing it across with a finger. "It's not really your color, but it'll do."

I stood there while she added some more eye shadow and blush to my face, all the while looking at me through half-shut eyes, practicing her craft, her face very close to mine. This was the Ashley I remembered from my childhood, when the five-year gap didn't seem that large and we set up our Barbie worlds in the driveway every day after school, my Ken fraternizing with her Skipper. This was the Ashley who painted my nails at the kitchen table during long summers, the back door swinging in the breeze and the radio on. This was the Ashley who came into my room late one night after breaking up with Robert Losard and sat on the edge of my bed crying until I wrapped my arms awkwardly around her and smoothed her hair, trying to understand the words she was saying. This was the Ashley who had climbed out on the roof with me all those nights in the first few months of the divorce and told me how much she missed my father. This was the Ashley I loved, away from Lewis's clinging hands and the wedding plans and the five-year-wide impasse that neither of us could cross.

"There." She capped the lipstick and dumped all the makeup back in her purse. "Now just don't cry too much and you'll be fine."

"I won't cry," I said, and suddenly aware of Lorna looking at us behind her in the mirror, I added, "I never cry at weddings."

"Oh, I do," Lorna said. "There's something about a wedding, something so perfect and so sad, all at the same time. I bawl at weddings."

"You better not be bawling out there." The makeup lady dabbed with the powder puff. "If this stuff doesn't hold up you'll look a mess."

The door opened and a woman in a dress the same shade as ours but without the long flowing skirt came in, carrying a big box of flowers. "Helen!" Lorna said, tearing up again. "You look lovely."

Helen was obviously Lorna's sister, seeing as how she also had those tiny little seashell ears. I figured it had to be more than coincidence. They hugged and Helen turned towards us, clasping her hands together. "This must be Ashley and Haven. Lorna said you were tall." She leaned forward and kissed my cheek, then Ashley's. "And I hear congratulations are in order for you. When's the big day?"

"August nineteenth," Ashley said. It was the million-dollar question.

"My, that's soon! Are you getting nervous?"

"No, not really," Ashley said. "I'm just ready to get it all over with."

"Amen to that," Lorna said, standing up and removing the paper bib from around her neck. She took a deep breath, holding her palm against her stomach. "I swear I have never been so nervous, even when I did that marathon at the station during the hurricane. Do I look all right?"

"You look lovely," Helen said. We all nodded in agreement. An older woman appeared, gesturing franti-cally. Her lips were moving as if long, unpronounceable words were coming out, but I couldn't hear a thing she was saying. As she came closer I made out something that sounded like "It's time, it's time," but she was warbling so it could have been anything.

"Okay," the Weather Pet said with one last sniff. Ashley checked my face again, licking her lips and tell-ing me to do the same, and with Lorna Queen behind us, her sister Helen carrying her train, we proceeded to the lobby of the church.

We'd practiced all this the night before, when I'd been wearing shorts and sandals and the aisle seemed like a hop, skip, and jump to the spot where the minister had been standing in blue jeans and a T-shirt that said Clean and Free Baptist Retreat. Now the church was packed and the aisle seemed about a hundred miles long with the minister standing at the end of it like a tiny plastic figure you might slap onto a cake. We got pushed into figuration, with me of course behind Ashley since I was taller and then Helen and then Lorna, who was telling us all how much she loved us. Finally the mad whisperer walked right to the front of the line, waved her arm wildly like she was flagging a plane in to land right there in the middle of the church, and we were on our way.

The night before, they'd said to count to seven after Ashley left, so I gave it eight because I was nervous and then took my first step. I felt like the man on stilts in the circus who walks as if the wind is blowing him sideways. I tried not to look at anything but the middle of Ashley's back, which was not altogether interesting but somewhat better than all the faces staring back at me. As I got closer to the minister I got the nerve to look up and see my father, who was standing next to his best friend, Rick Bickman, smiling.

My father only does one impression, but it's a good one. He can do a perfect rendition of the munchkin who greets Dorothy right after she lands on the witch in the *Wizard of Oz*, the one who with two others sings that silly song about being the Lollipop Guild. They rock back and forth and their faces get all contorted.

My father only does this when he's drunk or when a bunch of what my mother calls his bad seed friends are around; but suddenly it was all I could think of, as if at any moment he might forget all this nonsense and start singing that damn song.

It didn't happen, of course, because this was a wedding and serious business. Instead my father winked at me as I took my place next to Ashley and we all turned and faced the direction we'd come and waited for Lorna Queen to make her entrance.

There was a pause in the music, long enough for me to take a quick glance around to see if I recognized anyone, which I didn't because all I could see was the backs of everyone's heads as they waited for Lorna to appear. Charlie Baker, Important Local News Anchor, was giving her away. There had been a long story in the paper this very morning about the novelty wedding of the sports guy and the weather girl, which went into detail about the mentoring relationship between Charlie Baker and the intern he'd taken under his wing during her first shaky days at the station. My mother had left the article out on the kitchen table, without comment, and as I scanned I realized it could have been about strangers for all the attachment I felt to my father's fairy-tale second marriage.

Lorna was beaming as she came down the aisle. Her eyes sparkled and the waterproof mascara wasn't holding up the way it should have but no matter, she was still beautiful. When she and Charlie got up to the front she leaned forward and kissed Helen, then Ashley, and then me, her veil scratching my face as it brushed against me. It was the first time I'd seen Charlie Baker, anchorman, close up, and I would have bet money he'd had a facelift sometime during those long newsdoing years. He had that slippery look to him.

The minister cleared his throat, Charlie Baker handed Lorna over to my father, and now, finally, it was really happening. Some woman in the front row, wearing a purple hat, started crying immediately, and as the minister got to the vows Helen was tearing up as well. I was bored and kept glancing around the church, wondering what my mother would think of all this, a fancy church and a long walk down the aisle, pomp and circumstance. My parents were married in the Party Room of the Dominic Hotel in Atlantic City, with only her mother and his parents in attendance, along with a few lost partygoers who stumbled in from a bar mitzvah a couple of doors down. It was low-key, just what they needed, seeing that my mother's father disapproved and refused to attend and my father's family couldn't afford much more than the Party Room for a couple of hours, a cake, and a cousin playing the piano; my father had paid for the justice of the peace. There are pictures of them all around one table together, my mother and father and grandmother and my father's parents, plus some white-haired man in Buddy Holly glasses, each of them with a plate of half-eaten cake before them. This was the wedding party.

I watched my father, thinking this as he said his vows, speaking evenly into Lorna's veil with his face very red and serious. My sister began to cry and I knew it wasn't for the happiness of weddings but for the finality of all of this, knowing that things would never go back to the way they were. I thought of my mother at home in her garden, weeding under a hot afternoon sun, away from the pealing of church bells. And I thought of other summers, long before my father lifted this veil and kissed his new bride.

Chapter Two

❧

Of all of Ashley's boyfriends, there were only a few that I can remember past the dates and events they represent. Lewis, of course, who would be the end of that line come August nineteenth. Robert Parker, who two months after breaking up with Ashley in my eighth-grade year was killed in a motorcycle accident. But of all of them, only Sumner really mattered to me.

Ashley met Sumner Lee at the beginning of tenth grade, before I turned ten. He wasn't like anyone she'd brought home before: Ashley was into well-formed boys, mostly athletes—wrestlers, football players, the occasional tennis guy, but that was rare. These boys with their thick necks and muscled legs traipsed up our front walks with my sister on their arms like a trophy. They were polite to my parents, uncomfortable around me, and drank all of our milk when they came around after school. They run together like a blur, these boys, their names three letters: Bif, Tad, Mel. My father liked them because he was on his home turf, with sports as a common ground. My mother eyed her dwindling milk supply but said nothing. We all pretty much saw this to be the norm, at least until she brought Sumner home.

It was right after a nasty breakup with Tom Acker, quarterback of the Lincoln High Rebels. He was skinny and fast and chewed tobacco but only when Ashley let him. When she broke up with him he lurked around the neighborhood after school, football tucked under his arm like Ann Boleyn's head, haunting.

But Sumner wasn't an athlete. He was skinny and smooth, with black curly hair and bright blue eyes that almost didn't seem real. He had a long, lazy Alabama accent and wore tie-dyes and beat-up Converse high-tops that thwacked when he walked. Sumner was the kind of person that you wanted to sit with in the sun and spend the day. He was interesting and hysterically funny and it just seemed like if you tagged along with him you'd never be bored because he never was. My mother said that Sumner was the kind of person that things just happen to, and she was right. Weird, amazing, incredible things. He led a charmed life, always stumbling into something interesting totally by accident.

One time right after he and Ashley started dating,

he took us to the mall because he had to buy a shoe tree for his father for his birthday. We were walking along looking for one when we bumped into this camera crew filming one of those taste-test commercials right there in front of Cheeseables, the gourmet cheese shop where they also sell that snobby expensive coffee. They had some guy tasting a piece of cheese and they were trying to get him to say something snazzy they could film for the commercial, but he was hemming and hawing and spending too much time staring at the camera.

"So you like the cheese?" a woman holding a clipboard said to him, prodding. "Would you say it's the best cheese you've ever eaten?"

"Well, it's good," the guy said real slowly, "but I've had better when I was abroad."

"But it's still pretty good?" the woman asked while the cameraman rolled his eyes. "Maybe the best you've eaten in a while?"

"It's good," the guy said. "I mean, I like it fine but I wouldn't say—"

"Just say it," the cameraman said in a low, growly voice. "Just say it's the best damn cheese you've ever eaten."

The man nibbled at the cheese a little more, taking his time. The woman with the clipboard glanced around, looking for other prospective participants, and all of a sudden Sumner says in this loud, happy voice, "This is the *best cheese* I've ever eaten!" And then he just smiled a big cheese-loving smile while the onlookers watched him and Ashley turned bright red and socked him in the stomach for saying anything in the first place. That was the thing about Ashley; she loved Sumner's craziness, but it embarrassed her no end.

The woman with the clipboard walked over to us and looked at Sumner. "Can you say that again?"

"This is the *best cheese* I've ever eaten!" He said this in the same bouncy voice and added for extra effect, "I swear."

The woman turned around and gestured to the cameraman. He made fast business of shooing the first cheese guy away and setting up a fresh plate for Sumner, who grinned at us as he was escorted behind the makeshift counter and took his place in front of the camera.

"I don't believe this," Ashley said to me.

The cameraman was talking to Sumner, who was nodding and saying at random intervals, "This is the *best cheese* I've ever eaten!" as if anyone was not clear on that point yet. They set him up with the cheese, which he took hesitantly at first, nibbled with an inquisitive look, and then let a big smile slowly work its way across his face before saying as if it had just popped into his head, with clear intonation and stress on all the right syllables, "THIS is the BEST CHEESE I have EVER eaten."

The woman with the clipboard smiled, the cameraman shook Sumner's hand, and everyone applauded except for Ashley, who just shook her head. Sumner collected a bunch of free cheese samples and gave them his name and number and signed an autograph for a little boy who had seen the whole thing.

We went on and got the shoe tree and thought little else about it, except that Sumner made it his signature line and said it whenever the mood struck him whether or not there was cheese in the vicinity. Then one evening we were all watching "Jeopardy!" and, right after we'd cleared a category on water fowl, who pops up on screen but Sumner, with his cheese and his big grin and of course the line, which was by that point known to the entire family and a few neighbors, all of whom called to make sure we'd seen the commercial. And suddenly, Sumner was the famous Cheeseables cheese guy. His tag line became very cool and they had him back to the Cheeseables in the mall to sign autographs and pose for pictures, and there was even talk of a national campaign, which never happened but was still very exciting. It wasn't that Sumner went looking for adventure on purpose, more that it just stumbled across him. And for Ashley and me and my entire family, it was fun just to be along for the ride.

The best time with Sumner was the summer after fifth grade, when all of us went to Virginia Beach for a whole week while my dad was covering a big golf tournament there. Mom let Sumner drive me and Ashley down in his old Volkswagen convertible, since he had to come late because he was working that summer selling shoes at the mall. Old-lady shoes, really, the kind with thick, springy soles in neutral colors and supertough laces that won't break under tension. The summer before, he'd sold aluminum siding over the phone, sitting behind a counter all day convincing people to make major improvements to their homes, sight unseen. He said he liked to try different jobs every summer, just to see what was out there. At the old-lady shoe store, which was formally called Advantage Shoe Wear, he'd already won salesman of the month. The only bad thing was that he had to wear a tie to work, which he got around by rummaging through thrift shops on weekends with Ashley for the widest, brightest, and plaidest ones he could find, clip-on preferred.

I can remember the tie Sumner was wearing that afternoon just as clearly as I can remember everything about that one week at the beach that summer when things were still good in my family. The tie was yellow, with big green shapes on it that from a distance looked like broccoli but up close were actually just splotches with no resemblance to anything. He pulled up in the VW still in his work clothes with that tie fluttering over his shoulder, flapping along. Ashley and I were sitting on the curb with all our stuff out on the lawn, chewing gum and waiting on him. Ashley leaned across the seat when she got in and kissed him, slipping her hand up to unclip the tie as she did so.

Normally Ashley wouldn't have stood for me coming along with her and her boyfriend, but with Sumner even she was different. He made her loosen up and laugh and enjoy stuff she usually didn't—like being with me. When he was around she was nice to me, really nice, and it closed up that five-year gap that had been widening ever since she'd hit high school and stopped looking after me and started slamming doors in my face whenever I got too close to her. It's strange, but over the next few years when things got bad between us I always looked back to that day, when we waited for Sumner on the grass, as a time when things had been okay.

We piled into the VW, which sputtered and spit as

Sumner tried to negotiate our cul-de-sac. The VW was old and faded blue and had a distinctive rattling purr to it that I could pick out anywhere. It woke me up when he dropped Ashley off late at night or cruised by just to see the light in her window. Sumner called it his theme music.

The trip to the beach was about four hours, and of course going down the highway in a convertible, you can't hear anything going on in the front seat. So I just sat back and stared up at the sky as the sun went down and it got dark. Once we turned off onto the smaller roads that wound along up the Virginia coast, Sumner turned up the radio and found nothing but beach music, so we sang along, making up our own words when we didn't know the real ones. The engine was puttering and my sister was laughing and the stars were so bright above us, constellations swirling. It was just perfect, just right all at once.

Ashley and I had one room, my parents had the other, and Sumner took the couch in the main room, which my mother made up for him every night. The couch was against the same wall that Ashley's bed was, and they knocked at each other through the wall all night because Sumner was sure they could make up a code and communicate, even though Ashley spent most of the time knocking just whatever and then opening the door and whispering "What?" to which Sumner would tell her what he'd just knocked and they'd both laugh and start the whole thing over again. Ashley never laughed before like she did with Sumner; she'd always been kind of pouty and quiet, always with a stomachache or some ailment, real or imagined. But Sumner made her happy and shiny all the time, her hair long and feet bare and a boyfriend driving a convertible. She became warm and easygoing, like summer itself.

When I think back to that week in Virginia Beach I can remember every detail, from the bathing suit I wore each day to the smell of the clean hotel sheets on my bed. I remember my mother's freckled face and the way my father could so easily slip an arm around her waist and pull her close, kissing the back of her neck as he passed. I remember steamed shrimp and cool, sweatshirt nights and the pounding of the waves in the distance lulling me to sleep. I remember the walks we took every night we were there, throwing a cheap Frisbee my father bought at a gas station on the way up and chasing each other across the sand in the dark, waiting for the moonlight to catch it as it sailed through the air. I remember that week in a way I can't remember anything else.

After it was over I rode back home with my parents, Ashley and Sumner staying for a last day on the beach. There was sand in my shoes when I got home and my suntan lotion spilled all out in my suitcase, carrying the smells and sensation of that week all the way back to my landlocked bedroom. Only the sound of Mr. Havelock's lawnmower in the distance reminded me it was really over, I was home. It was a different world and I sat in the quiet of my room that night, wishing I was back in the sand, with sky and ocean so close, lost in the thick of it all.

* * *

At the reception everyone was drinking and the band was playing and it took about ten years for me to finally locate my father in all the confusion. He was surrounded by a crowd, like he always is, his face red and beety, a drink in one hand. I waited until he saw me standing there and made a big production of putting his arm around me, always conscious of the fact that now I was edging taller than him, just a little. It is disconcerting to look down at your father, the one person you can always remember being bigger than the rest of the world.

"Haven." He kissed my cheek. "Are you finding everything you need? Did you get some food?"

"Not yet," I said. Another group of well-wishers passed by, practically yelling out encouragements. It was always a challenge to compete for my father's attention in public. "I'm really happy for you, Dad." This seemed like the right thing to say.

"Thanks, honey." He put his arm around my waist, that same simple gesture I associated with my mother. "She's really something, isn't she?"

Of course he was looking across the room at Lorna, who was surrounded by her own group of people, all admiring the ring, laughing, and looking at my father and me looking at them. Lorna was seated in a chair with a glass in her hand, fanning herself with a piece of paper. The reception was outside, under a big tent at Charlie Baker's house, and it was hot as blazes. Lorna Queen smiled at me, waggling her fingers, and blew a kiss to my father, who I am embarrassed to say pretended to catch it.

"She's very nice," I said, waving back at Lorna.

"It's real important to me that you girls are comfortable with this," my father said. "I know these past few years have been tough, but I know things are going to be smooth from here on out. I know your mother would want them to be as well."

I felt my stomach churn. I didn't want to think of her now, in this place with the white-topped tables and tuxedoed waiters and my father's new life. It seemed horribly inappropriate if not blasphemous in some way. I was trying to think about something else when Ashley and Lewis came up behind us.

"Daddy, I'm so happy," Ashley said, letting loose of Lewis long enough to throw her arms around my father. Her eyes were still red and puffy and my father didn't know that after the ceremony she and Lewis had driven around the block a few times so that she could gather her composure before going to the reception. I'd walked with Aunt Ree to Charlie Baker's and watched them make several passes, each time with Ashley wiping her eyes and Lewis wearing his most concerned expression. Now she just hugged my father and Lewis stared off across the room, holding her purse for her. Ashley kept some things to herself.

"Thanks, honey." My father kissed her on the forehead, then reached to shake Lewis's hand. "Not too long for you, eh, Lewis? Just a month or so away, right?"

"Twenty-nine days," Lewis, ever exact, replied.

"We'll be glad to have you in the family," my father said with his smooth drinking tongue, as if we as a family were still one flawless unit, without cracks and additions, the most recent of which was making her way across the room in a blur of white, throwing her arms around his neck while the rest of us stood and watched. Even Ashley, who had long been the only one who could stomach my father's new romance, looked somewhat uncomfortable.

I spent the reception listening to comments about how tall I was, everyone trying to make it sound like it was a good thing to be a giant at fifteen. I towered over everyone, it seemed, and Ashley kept coming up behind me and poking me hard in the center of my back, which was my mother's subtle and constant signal that I was slouching. What I really wanted to do was curl up in a ball under the buffet table and hide from everyone. After four hours, several plates of food, and enough small talk to make me withdraw into myself permanently, we finally got to go home.

Ashley had too much wine and Lewis drove us home, leaving her car in the parking lot to be retrieved the next day. She was talking too loudly and being all kissy with him while I sat in the backseat and thought about how quickly summer was passing. In a little over a month I'd be back in school with new notebooks and pencils, and Ashley would be gone from our house and the room she'd had next to mine for as long as I could remember. She and Lewis would be moving to Rock Ridge Apartments, off the bypass, into a two-bedroom place with peach carpet and a skylight and unlimited access to a pool that was within steps of their front door. She already had mailing labels, just sitting on her desk waiting to be used: Mrs. Ashley Warsher, 5-A Rock Ridge Apartments, with a little rose next to her name. She was ready to become someone else. She would take her dramatics and her tattoo and her legends of boyfriends to a new home, and we would be left to remember what we could as we passed by her empty room.

When we got home my mother was out in her garden. It was falling into dark and I could just see her hunched over her rosebushes, pruning shears in hand. Before my father left we had the perfunctory subdivision yard, with straight edges and our weeds whacked away from unwanted places. My mother had a few geraniums by the back door that struggled each year to bloom and failed, maybe a sprinkle of red and pink in the early season before giving up altogether. After the separation, however, my mother was a changed woman. It wasn't just the support group she joined, or her new interest in Barry Manilow, both of which she was introduced to by Lydia Catrell, our divorcée neighbor who moved in next door just about the same fall day my father moved out. Not two weekends later my mother was in the yard with a rented Rototiller and a stack of books on gardening, ripping up the ground with all the energy and abandon she'd controlled so well in the weeks since we'd found out about the Weather Pet. She bought seeds and raided nurseries and mulched and composted and spent full days with her hands full of earth, coaxing life out of the dry, dull grass my father had spent years pushing a mower over. All through the house there were seed packets and Xeroxed pictures of perennials and biennials and alpines and annuals and roses in every color you could imagine. I loved the names of them, like secret codes or magical places: coreopsis, chrysanthemum, stachys. The next summer my mother had the most beautiful garden on the block, far better than the evenly planned and scaled plots of our neighbors. Hers stretched itself across the entire yard, climbing over walls and across the grass, blazing out in colors that were soft and bright and shocking and muted all at once. There was always a huge bouquet on our kitchen table, overflowing, and the smell of fresh flowers filled the house the way a heaviness had since that October. I loved to see her out there, hair tied back and the world blooming all around her, the colors so alive and constant and all by her own hand.

"So how was it?" She smiled at me as I came walking up, my bridesmaid's bouquet dangling in my hand. I held it up as I got close and she examined it. "That's beautiful. You know what that's called? *Polemonium caeruleum.* I don't think I've ever seen it used in a bouquet before. Maybe I should try some of that next year." She bent over and tugged at a weed until it gave way, coming up with a poof of dirt around it.

"It was fine," I said, wondering what words I should use to describe such an event, the details I should go into. "The food was good."

"It always is at weddings." She reached down and picked a few shiny leaves, rubbing them together in her hand. "What do you think of this?"

I took them from her and held them to my nose when she motioned for me to do so. They smelled sweet and lemony, like the cough drops my grandmother always gave me instead of candy. "What is it?"

"Lemon balm." She picked some for herself, pressing it to her nose. "I just love the way it smells."

I could hear Ashley laughing from the front porch, where she was sitting on the steps, leaning against Lewis. "Ashley's drunk," I told my mother, who only smiled that sad smile again and yanked up another weed. "She had about a million glasses of wine."

"Oh well." She tossed the weed aside and wiped her hands against each other. "We all have our ways of getting through."

I could have said it all right there, all the Hallmark kinds of things that I felt I should say to my mother, words of support and solidarity and comfort. But with this opportunity so neatly presented I could do nothing but follow her down the stone walk past her rosebushes and flower beds and bird feeders to the back steps and into the kitchen. She went to the sink and washed her hands, and in the suddenly bright light I looked at her in her faded jeans and flowered shirt and thought how much she looked like Ashley: her long, dark hair done up behind her head, her tiny feet that tracked garden mud across the floor. They were both so small and precise. I wondered what she'd done that afternoon and watched my mother at her sink and said no right things, only pressed those shiny leaves to my face and breathed in their strong, sweet smell.

Chapter Three

∽

I woke up the next morning to a wedding crisis. By July I could sense one from miles off, but I didn't have to go that far thanks to the vent in my bathroom and the fact that all major family confrontations seem to take place in our kitchen below. I was lying in bed at eight A.M., already awake but staring at the ceiling, when I heard our neighbor Lydia Catrell knock at the back door and come in with a flurry of high-pitched chatter, matched by my mother's lower, softer voice as they sat at the table drinking coffee and tinkling spoons. I listened as they talked about the invitations and the guest list; Lydia Catrell had married off four daughters and was our senior advisor on Ashley's wedding. It was Lydia who arranged for the hall and the church and Lydia who recommended the flowers and Lydia who bustled around our kitchen acting important and dispensing advice, most of it welcome. And so that morning I knew even before Ashley did that she was about to have more problems from the troublesome bridesmaid.

The bridesmaid's name was Carol Cliffordson and she was twenty-one, a distant cousin who had spent one summer with us when her parents were splitting up; she and Ashley had bunked together and giggled and driven the rest of us crazy being twelve-year-old best friends. They were inseparable. At the end of the summer Carol returned to Akron, Ohio, and we never heard much from her again except for Christmas cards and graduation announcements. When Ashley picked her bridesmaids she was firm that Carol be included even though we hadn't seen her since she was twelve and even then only for that one summer. Carol accepted and then proceeded to cause more problems than you could ever imagine one little bridesmaid being capable of. It started with the dresses, which Carol objected to because they are low cut in front. Being that she is rather flat chested (although she would never admit it), she called Ashley to say they were too revealing and could she please wear something else. Lydia Catrell and my mother and Ashley all sat around for hours talking about that one five-minute phone conversation, dissecting it and discussing its issues etiquettewise, before Carol called again to say she didn't think she'd be able to attend the wedding at all because her fiancé's family would be in town that weekend and they expected her to partake in the annual family cookout and square dance. With this, it looked like we might have gotten rid of her altogether, except that the dresses (still low cut but a different style) had already been ordered and it was too late to find anyone else. This set off another round of arguing and consoling between my mother and Ashley, not to mention Lydia Catrell, who wondered out loud several times if this girl was raised in a barn. Finally it was decided that Carol would still attend the wedding with her fiancé, then leave immediately afterwards to make the square dance.

Now there was another problem. Apparently Carol had called early in the morning, hysterical, and cried and cried on the phone, saying her fiancé had decided he would not attend and neglect his own family for the wedding of someone he had never even met. They'd had a big fight and Carol had called to cry to my mother, who clucked sympathetically and said she'd have Ashley call back right away. Then Lydia came over, was filled in, and I lay in bed listening to them go on and on about it, fretting about what Ashley would do when she was clued in to the situation. I heard Ashley going down the stairs and then their voices suddenly jerked to a stop.

"What?" I heard Ashley say after a few solid silent minutes. "What's going on?"

"Honey," my mother said smoothly, "maybe you should eat your toast first."

"Yes," Lydia echoed, "have something to eat first."

Of course Ashley was suspicious. The toaster-oven

timer rang but I didn't hear her open it, only the scrape of a chair being pulled away from the table. "Tell me."

"Well," said my mother, "I got a call from Carol this morning."

"Carol," Ashley repeated.

"Yes," Lydia said.

"And she was very upset, because she and her fiancé are fighting and she said"—a pause here, as my mother prepared to drop the bomb—"that she will not be able to be in the wedding."

There was another silence. All I could hear was the sound of someone stirring with a spoon and hitting the sides of a mug. Clink, clink, clink. Finally Ashley said, "Well. Fine. I probably should have expected this."

"Now, honey," my mother said, and I could tell by the way her voice was moving around that she had probably gone to put her arms around Ashley, pinch hitting for Lewis. "I'm sure she didn't realize what a problem this would be for you. I said you'd call her back. . . ."

"Like hell I will," Ashley said in a loud voice. "This is just the most selfish, bitchy thing she could do. I swear if she wasn't in Ohio I'd go right to her and punch her face in."

"My goodness!" Lydia said with a nervous laugh.

"I would," Ashley said. "Goddamn it, I have had it, I can't take this anymore. No one can just do one simple thing that I ask them to do and this whole wedding is going to be a total disaster and it will all be her goddamn fault with her goddamn flat chest and her goddamn fiancé and who the hell does she think she is anyway

• 38 •

calling me crying when she's ruining my wedding and she's such a damn idiot!"

Lydia Catrell added, "You'd think she was raised in a barn. You honestly would."

"I hate her. I hate all of this." There was a crash as something fell to the floor. "I don't need her. I don't need anyone but Lewis and we're going to elope, I swear to God we are."

"Honey," my mother said, trying to be calm, but there was that crazy edge creeping into her voice, the family hysteria swelling to full force. "Ashley, please, we can figure this out."

"Call the wedding off," Ashley was saying. "Just cancel it all. I'm not going through with it. I'm calling Lewis right now and we're eloping. Today. I swear to God."

"Oh, don't be silly." Lydia Catrell had obviously not seen my sister in a fit before and so did not know to keep her mouth shut. "You can't elope. The invitations are already out. It would be a social disaster."

"I don't give a shit," Ashley snapped, and I sat up in bed. Lewis disapproved of cursing and it had been a good long while since I'd heard any four-letter word snap from my sister's lips. For a moment, she sounded like the Ashley I remembered.

"Ashley," said my mother quickly, "please."

"I can't take it anymore." Ashley's voice was tight and wavering now. "I'm so sick of everyone bothering me with their stupid details and I just want to be left alone. Can't anyone understand that? This is my own wedding and I hate everyone and everything involved in it. I can't stand this anymore." She burst into tears, still babbling on, but now I couldn't make out anything she was saying.

"Honey," my mother said, "Ashley, honey."

"Just leave me alone." A chair scraped across the floor and it was suddenly dead quiet, like no one was even there anymore. A few seconds later the front door slammed and I walked to my window to see Ashley standing on the front walk in her nightgown with her arms crossed against her chest, staring at the Llewellyns' house across the street. She looked small and alone and I thought about knocking on the glass to get her attention. I thought better of it, though, and instead went to brush my teeth and listen to my mother and Lydia Catrell cluck their tongues softly, voices low, as they stirred their coffee.

I waited until this latest storm of details had died down before I approached the kitchen and grabbed a Pop-Tart on my way out the door to work. Sunday one to six is the most boring of all the shifts at Little Feet, the children's shoe store where I worked at the Lakeview Mall. It's probably the worst job in the world, because you spend all day taking shoes off grubby little kids, not to mention touching their feet; but it's money and when you have no working experience it's not like you can be choosy. I got my job at Little Feet when I turned fifteen back in November, and since then I've been promoted to assistant salesperson, which is just a fancy title they give you so you feel like you're moving up even when you aren't. The first week I worked there I had to pass a series of lessons on selling children's shoes. They sat me in the back by the bathroom with a boxful of audiotapes and a workbook with all the answers already scribbled in by someone else until I worked my way through the whole series: "What's in a Size?," "The Little Feet Method," "Lacing and Soles," "Hello, Baby Shoes!," and finally "Socks and Accessories—A Little Something Extra." My manager was a man named Burt Isker who was older than my grandfather and wore old moldy suits and kept a calendar of Bible quotes next to the time clock. He was rickety and had bad breath and all the children were afraid of him, but he was nice enough to me. He spent most of the time rearranging everyone else's hours so he never had to work and talking about his grandchildren. I felt sorry for him: he'd worked for the Little Feet chain his entire life and he'd ended up at the Lakeview Mall shuffling saddle shoes around and getting kicked in the crotch by squirmy kids.

The mall was only a few blocks from my house, so I took my time walking, eating my Pop-Tart as I went. When I got to the main entrance I stopped to put on my name tag and tuck my shirt in before going inside. I worked Sundays with Marlene, a short, chubby girl who was in community college and hated Burt Isker for no particular reason other than he was old and cranky sometimes and always nagged her for not selling enough socks. They kept track of these things, and every once in a while on a Saturday a Little Feet manager came down from the home office in Pennsylvania and set a quota for each of us on shoes, socks, and accessories. It's hard to push socks on someone who doesn't want them, and Marlene was always getting reprimanded for not being aggressive enough about it. They wanted you to *hound* the customer, and on big sale days Burt would stand behind me as I came out of the stockroom with my shoes and hiss, "Socks! Push those socks!" I would try but the customers would always say no because our socks were so expensive and they didn't come in for socks anyway, just shoes. No matter what those higher-ups at Little Feet thought, socks just weren't an impulse item.

Marlene was already there when I walked in, sitting behind the counter with a donut in her hand. The store was empty like it always was on Sunday, the mall deserted except for some senior citizens from the nearby retirement home doing their laps, from Belk's to Dillard's and back, with a pulse-check break at the Yogurt Paradise. The Muzak was playing and Marlene was reading the *Enquirer* and grumbling about Burt Isker when our first customers appeared. Because of her seniority it was always my turn when it was slow, so I got up and went over to see what they needed.

"Hi, what can I help you folks with today?" I said in my cheerful-salesperson voice. The mother looked up at me with a blank expression on her face; the father was over by the sneakers, flipping them over one at a time to check the prices. The little boy they'd dragged in with them was sitting next to his mother and gnawing on his thumb.

"We're looking for some new sneakers." The father walked over to me, holding a popular style called Benjamin in his hand. All the Little Feet shoes had children's names; it was part of the gimmick. The Little Feet chain was full of gimmicks. "But thirty-five dollars seems kind of steep. Got anything cheaper?"

"Just this one," I said, holding up a model called Russell, which was cheap because it was an ugly bright yellow-and-pink-striped style from last year that never sold well. "It's on sale for nineteen ninety-nine."

He took the shoe from me and looked at it. It was blaringly bright, especially under the fluorescent lights. "We'll try it. But we're not sure what size he's up to now."

I went to get the measuring scale, then squatted down in front of the kid and unlaced his shoe. There was a small explosion of dirt and gravel as I pulled it off, at which his mother like all mothers looked embarrassed and said, "Oh, dear. I'm sorry."

"That's okay," I said. "Happens all the time." The little boy stood up and I fixed his foot in the scale, sliding the knob on the side to see where it reached to. "Size six."

"Six?" the mother said. "Really? My goodness, he was just a five and a half only a few months ago."

I never knew what to say to this, so I just nodded and smiled and went off to look for the ugly Russell shoe in the storeroom, where we had tons of them piled in stacks. Marlene was still in the same spot, licking her fingers and flipping through the glossy pages of the *Enquirer*.

While I was lacing up the shoe, sitting on the floor

in front of the little boy, he looked at me and took his thumb out of his mouth long enough to say, "You're tall."

"David," his mother said quickly. "That's not polite."

"It's okay," I said. I was used to this by now; kids are dead honest, no way around it.

Once we'd gone through the fitting and the lacing and the pinching of toes, and we'd all watched David walk around the store in his bright, ugly shoes, blaring pink and yellow against the orange carpet, the decision was made that they were a perfect fit and affordable. I watched the father sign his credit-card slip, his script looping and neat, then slid the old shoes into the new box and handed the kid a balloon and they were on their way. Little Feet was too cheap for helium, so all we gave out were balloons pumped from a bicycle pump, with a ribbon tied around them so you could drag them along behind you like a round plastic dog. There's something depressing about a balloon that just lies there, listless. I always felt apologetic as I offered them to the children, as if it was somehow my fault.

I told Marlene I was taking a break and went down to the Yogurt Paradise for a Coke. The mall was still dead and I waved to the security guard. He was standing outside the fake-plant store flirting with the owner, who had a beehive and a loud laugh that echoed along behind me after I'd passed them. I got my Coke and walked down a little farther towards Dillard's, where a stage was set up and some kind of commotion was going on: several people running around and hammering nails and one woman with a microphone complaining that no one was paying attention. I sat down on a bench a safe distance away and watched.

There was a sign right next to me that said LAKEVIEW MALL MODELS: FALL SPECTACULAR! with a date and a time and a graphic of a girl in a big hat looking mysterious. Everyone in town knew about the Lakeview Models, or at least about the very best known Lakeview Model, Gwendolyn Rogers. She'd grown up right here in town over on McCaul Street and gone to Newport High School just like me and was one of the very first of the models, which were basically just a bunch of local girls all made up and flouncing down the middle of the mall for the seasonal fashion shows. She was the closest thing we had to a local celebrity, since she'd been discovered and gone off to New York and Milan and L.A. and all those other glamorous places where beautiful girls go. She'd been on the cover of *Vogue* and did fashion correspondence on "Good Morning America," always standing in front of some fancy store with her hair all swept up and a microphone planted at her lips, telling the world about the latest in hemlines. My mother said the Rogerses had let Gwendolyn's success go to their collective heads, since they hardly spoke to the neighbors anymore and built a pool in their backyard that they never invited anyone over to use. I'd only seen Gwendolyn once, when I was eight or nine and walking to the mall with Ashley. There she was in front of her house, reading a magazine and walking the dog. She was so tall, like a giant in cutoff shorts and a plain white T-shirt; she didn't even seem real. Ashley had whispered to me, "That's her," and I turned to look at her just as she saw us, her head moving slightly on her long, fluted neck, like a puppet with strings that stretched all the way up to God. I didn't know what was in store for me then, what I would someday have in common with Gwendolyn other than our shared hometown and neighborhood. Back then I was still small, normal, and I just stared at her, and she waved like she was used to waving and went back inside with the dog, who was short and fat with hardly any legs to be seen, like a Little Feet balloon.

Because of Gwendolyn, everyone knew about the Lakeview Mall Models. She'd talked about them plain as day in all those interviews when they asked her where she got her start, and even came back one year to judge the contest herself. Everyone in town pooh-poohed it but still went to try out when they were old enough, even my sister, who was too short and never made it past the first round. The contest had just been held a few weeks earlier there at Dillard's and my best friend, Casey Melvin, had even gone so far as to sign us both up. I could have killed her when I found the confirmation card in my mailbox, all official on pink Lakeview Mall stationery. Casey said she only did it because I had the best chance of anyone, since being tall is 90 percent of modeling anyway. But the thought of walking alone in front of all those people while they all watched, with my huge bony legs and spindly arms, was the stuff my nightmares were made of. Like being tall is what it takes to be Cindy Crawford or Elle Macpherson or even Gwendolyn Rogers. I wasn't sure where Casey got her statistics or percentages, but it had to be from *Seventeen* or *Teen Magazine*, both of which she quoted from as if they were the Bible itself. I had no interest in modeling; attracting attention, on purpose, was the last thing I wanted to do. And so the day of the tryouts, while Casey went and got cut the first round, I stayed at home and hid in my room, drawing the shades, as if just by happening, a few blocks away, it could hurt me.

Ashley went too; as a Vive cosmetics girl she was required to stand at a booth and offer free Blush n' Brush gift packs to all the contestants. She said every butt-ugly girl from five counties around had showed up with too much eyeliner and lipstick on, posing up and down a plastic runway that was set up in Dillard's Sweaters and Separates department. The paper covered it and reported that there was crying, laughing, joy, and sorrow, as there always was at the Lakeview Model tryouts since most of the girls got sent home because they were normal looking, short and round and big and small and not Gwendolyn Rogers. They picked fifteen girls who could now proudly claim that they got to go to official mall functions like the Boy Scout soapbox car display and stand around smiling with twelve-year-olds or the garden and home show and do compost and recycling demonstrations. They also got to be in the Lakeview Mall fashion shows, the first of which was the Fall Spectacular!, which appeared to be in rehearsal that Sunday.

There was a woman in a purple jogging suit who seemed to be in charge, or at least thought she was since she was walking around yelling at everyone to be quiet. The Lakeview Models were all grouped around the edge of the stage, posing and giggling and looking important.

They were wearing red Lakeview Mall T-shirts and black shorts, as well as high heels that were clacking all over the place and making a huge racket. One of them, a brunette with her hair in a French twist, looked over at me, then poked the girl next to her so she turned and looked too. I felt myself slouching and imagined myself dwarfing the Lakeview Models in their heels and lipstick, a freak among fairies.

"Girls, girls, listen up." The woman in the jogging suit clapped her hands, bringing quiet except for the *pop pop pop* noise of the staple gun a guy on the stage was using to attach giant leaves to a backdrop. "Now, we have less than three weeks until this fashion show *must* come off, so we've got to get serious and get working. As the Lakeview Models it is critical that you present the best possible image to the community."

This seemed to calm everyone down but the staple-gun guy, who just rolled his eyes at no one in particular and hoisted another leaf up on the stage.

"Now," the woman continued, "we're going to do it just like we practiced last week: you enter, walk down the center aisle, across the stage, pause, and then go back down the way you came in. Remember the beat we learned last week: one, two, three." She snapped her fingers, demonstrating. One of the models, a short girl with long black hair, snapped her own fingers in time to make sure she got it. I finished my Coke and tossed the cup in the trash.

"Okay, let's line up and do it." The woman climbed down the small steps at the side of the stage, with the Lakeview Models clackety-clacking along behind her.

Their voices and hair tossing melded into one long stream of girl, a blur of makeup and giggling and clean skin. They lined up just to the right of me and I could feel my hipbones sticking out and wanted to cut myself to half my size, small enough to fit in a corner, under a table, in the palm of a hand.

I got up quickly as they were still shuffling into order, red shirt after red shirt, curve after curve, the same white toothy smile repeated into infinity. I turned and walked back to Little Feet while the purple-suited woman clapped out the beat behind me and the first girl started down the aisle, mindful of the pace: one, two, three.

Chapter Four

～

Lydia Catrell had changed my mother's life. With her tan and frosted hair and too many brightly colored matching shorts-and-sandals outfits, she had brought out a side of my mother that I believed would otherwise have lain dormant forever, never shown to the world. My mother, who had spent most of her life smiling apologetically while my father entertained and offended everyone around him, had to wait until he had stepped out of the spotlight before she finally came into her own. And like it or not (and I usually didn't), Lydia Catrell had shown her the way.

Lydia was a widow, like all women from Florida seemed to be. Her husband had been involved in the plastic utensil business and her house was filled with more colorful plastic bins and spatulas and bathtub mats than you could shake a stick at. She moved in with a flourish of bright furniture all making its way up the driveway right next to ours; a pink couch, a turquoise easy chair, a lemony-peach divan. My mother went over the next day with a mason jar full of roses and zinnias and stayed for three hours, most of it spent listening to Lydia talk about herself and her children and her dead husband. Lydia was all color and noise, in her bright pink shorts and sequined T-shirts with fringe, zooming through the neighborhood in her huge Lincoln Town Car that seemed to suck up the road as it passed. Lydia blew in like a cyclone, altering the landscape around her, and my mother was pulled in immediately.

Within a month you could see the change. My mother was wearing sandals and even the occasional sequined shirt, frosting her hair, and going out every Thursday night to Ranzino's, the bar at the Holiday Inn that featured easy-listening hits, dancing, and tons of paunchy men in toupees out for a good time. My mother came home with her cheeks flushed, tossing her newly frosted hair, saying she couldn't believe she'd ever go to such a place and Lydia was such a card and it wasn't her thing, not at all, only to head right back the next Thursday. I sat upstairs and listened to my mother pour her heart out to Lydia Catrell over coffee, thinking these were things she could never share with me. She cried and cursed my father as Lydia clucked her tongue and said Poor dear, it must have been so hard for you. Ashley had Lewis and my mother had Lydia but I was alone on Thursday nights, waiting for the rumble of the Town Car in the driveway and my mother's key in the lock on the kitchen door. I couldn't get to sleep until I heard her trying to tiptoe past my door in an effort not to wake me.

The newest thing was the trip to Europe. Lydia belonged to a travel club called The Old-Timers, which was a bunch of single women over forty who got a cheap group rate by taking trips together to exotic locales, usually Las Vegas. My mother had been on one of those trips a few months after Lydia moved in. I'd spent the weekend with my dad and the Weather Pet, picturing my mother playing blackjack, seeing Wayne Newton, and going to the Liberace Museum, all of which were listed on The Old-Timers travel itinerary. After three days and four nights my mother had returned with a new white shorts-and-sandals set, winnings of about fifty bucks, and a million stories about these middle-aged women taking Vegas by storm. She said it was the best time she ever had, so it was no wonder she was interested in the trip to Europe. That was a four-week extravaganza through England, Italy, France, and Spain, with stops along the way to see the bullfights, tour Buckingham Palace, and sunbathe nude in the South of France, the latter being something my mother chose to pass on. If she went, she'd be leaving two weeks after Ashley got married.

"Just think," Lydia was saying as I came in from work one afternoon, "four weeks in Europe. It's what you wanted to do in college but could never afford. Now you have the money, so why not go?"

"I don't have the money," my mother said. "With the wedding so close and Haven going back to school too, I just don't know if the timing is good."

"Haven is a big girl." Lydia smiled at me. "Look at how tall she is, for Godsakes. She can take care of herself for a month. She'll love it."

"She's only fifteen," my mother said, and I could tell by the way she was biting her lip that she hadn't made up her mind yet. I felt bad about it but there was some place in me that didn't want her to go. Europe seemed too far away. I couldn't picture her anywhere there, except standing in front of famous landmarks from my history books. My mother and Lydia, in front of the Eiffel Tower, Westminster Abbey, the leaning Tower of Pisa. My mother and Lydia, topless in France—the landmarks were easier.

I watched my mother from across the table as she talked with Lydia. Now and then I'd catch her eye and find her smiling at me, that same smile I remembered from when times were better and my father looped an arm around her waist, pulling her in closer the way I so often wanted to do now. To scoop her away from Lydia and the rest of the world and have her all to myself—if only for a while.

Meanwhile, the wedding continued to take over our lives. It hung over the house like a storm cloud, refusing to budge, promising possible disaster at any second. Every surface from the coffee table to the top of the television seemed to be filled with small scraps of paper detailing wedding reminders in my mother's small, neat hand.

> *Bridesmaids: orders in by?*
> *Ashley meets with caterer again July 30*
> *Haven shoes, pantyhose, hair?*
> *RSVP list, final version*
> *Europe???????????????*

She left them around like clues, a way I had of keeping up with her concerns from day to day. Just like I'd sat in my bathroom and listened through the vent to her crying to Lydia all those mornings. I was only able to share my mother's concerns from a distance, unknown to her at all.

Meanwhile my father had returned from honeymooning for a week in the Virgin Islands, with a tan, more hair, and a grin that seemed pasted on that my mother noticed even from the front window when he dropped me off after my weekly dinner with him. She tossed her hair and kept whatever sarcastic comment was twisting her face to herself before she headed out again with Lydia, the Town Car's horn beeping three times to summon her off to the Holiday Inn.

And then there was Ashley, who after dealing with Carol's on-again–off-again participation in the wedding (now back on, after many tears and much long-distance wrangling and a promise that she could leave immediately after the wedding pictures were taken) was on to another crisis, this being her first sit-down dinner with

Lewis's parents, the Warshers. I sat in my room and listened to her tearing through her closet, hangers clanking, until I was summoned in to judge which dress was best.

"Okay," she said from inside the closet, where she was busy bumping around, "this is the first option." She came out in a red dress with a white collar, tugging at the hem to make it appear longer than it was.

"Too short," I said. "Too red."

She glanced at herself in the mirror, then gave up on the hem and headed back into the closet. "You're right. Red is the wrong message to be sending. Red is a warning; it just screams out. I need something that makes me blend. I want them to welcome me into the family."

Ever since Ashley had met Lewis, she had taken to using what my mother called Oprah phrases. Lewis talked the same way; he was a placater, a peacemaker, the kind of person who would hold your hand on an airplane if you were scared, able to quote verbatim the statistics about how it was the safest thing, honestly. I could only imagine what an entire Warsher clan would be like. They were from Massachusetts: that was all we knew.

She came back out in a white dress with a high neckline and a long flowing skirt that rustled when she walked. "Well?"

"You look too holy," I told her.

"Holy?" She turned and looked in the mirror, to judge for herself. "God. This is awful. Everything is wrong." She sat down beside me on the bed, crossing her legs. "I just want them to like me."

"Of course they'll like you." This was one of the rare moments since her engagement when Ashley and I were just talking, not yelling or discussing the wedding or exchanging the odd nasty look on the stairs. I talked slowly, as if one wrong word might end it altogether.

"I know they'll pretend to like me; they have to do that." She lay back, stretching her arms over her head. "But they're normal people, Haven. Lewis's parents have been married for twenty-eight years. His mother teaches kindergarten. What are they going to think of Daddy if he gets all loud at the wedding and starts doing his Wizard of Oz thing? Plus I already told Mom she's got to keep Lydia under control because they just won't know what to make of her. I don't even know what to make of her."

"She's Mom's best friend."

"I guess so." She sighed, bouncing her feet against the edge of the bed.

"Do you think she'll go to Europe with her?" I asked.

"I don't know." She sat up and looked at me. "It would be good for her if she did, though. All this stuff with Daddy has been harder on her than she's let on to you. She deserves to treat herself."

"I know," I said, wondering how much she'd let on to Ashley. With that one sentence, I could feel the five years between us again. "I just think with the wedding and all . . ."

"Haven, you're in high school now. You should jump at the chance to stay alone for that long. I would have. God, I would have been wild." She stood up and went behind the screen, tossing the holy dress over the top a few seconds later. "But you won't, and that's good. You won't be like me."

I thought back to Ashley's long list of boyfriends from high school, all their names and faces running together until they ended with Lewis's skinny nose and constant look of concern. I thought of Sumner again, suddenly, and saw him clearly in my mind on the boardwalk at Virginia Beach, the sunset fading pink and red and purple behind him. I heard the doorbell sound from downstairs and Ashley said, "Get that, will you please? It's Lewis."

I went downstairs and opened the door. Sure enough, there was Lewis in one of his trademark skinny ties and oxford shirts. He was holding a bouquet of bright purple flowers with yellow eyes surrounded by some creepy kind of fuzzy foliage. It was easy to get a complex from bringing flowers to my mother's house, so Lewis usually stuck to exotic ones: orchids, tulips out of season. He wanted to bring Ashley things she couldn't get at home; with my mother's obsessive gardening, that left very little to choose from.

"Hey, Lewis," I said. "How are you?"

"Good." He leaned forward and pecked me on the cheek, something he'd taken to doing as soon as the engagement was announced. I was taller than him, and this made it awkward. He still did it, though, every time I saw him.

"You want me to put those in water?" I nodded to the flowers.

"Oh, sure. That'd be great." He handed them to me. "Is she upstairs?"

I watched him go up, taking the steps two at a time. He moved through our house now with the ease of someone who no longer considered himself a guest, no sidestepping knickknacks and perching on the edges of furniture but walking easily across the floors as if he belonged there. It hadn't taken long for Lewis to feel at home; he'd come along when we needed a man in the house. With my father gone and the three of us struggling to fill up the spaces he'd left behind, it was only natural that Ashley would find someone to hold her together, to take care of things. Maybe it was the very thing I hated about Lewis—his absolute dullness— that attracted Ashley most to him. After the divorce and all the craziness, she'd needed something normal and steady to ground herself. Maybe by then she didn't want any more surprises.

Ashley always turned to a new boy when things got sticky or hard, or lonely. But she was never alone. She called the shots, easing people in and out of our door and our lives with the wave of one hand. The ones I liked and the ones I hated, they came and went at her whim with little or no explanation to the rest of us other than a slammed door or a muted sniffle that I could only hear late at night. Ashley kept it all to herself, even when she wasn't the only one who was affected.

Ashley dated Sumner all that Virginia Beach summer and into the next fall, speeding around town in the Volkswagen and laughing all the time, filling the house with noise whenever they came breezing through. Whenever Sumner was over, everyone came out of their respective hiding places: my mother from the kitchen, my father from in front of the TV, all of us migrating towards his voice and laughter, or whatever it was that made everyone want to be around him. He and Ashley celebrated each month they'd spent together; he bought her a silver bracelet with a slender heart that dangled off of it and brushed against her watchband. I could hear them in the driveway just after curfew, their voices rising up to my window, and then the putter of the VW engine as he pulled away, that low, steady murmur that filled the entire street, humming. Ashley was happy and nice to me and things were good that fall as the days turned crisp and sharp and the weather on channel five was still being done by Rowdy Ron the Weather Mon, who was overweight, more than a little crazy, and no threat to my parents' marriage whatsoever. A new family moved in down the street and Ashley had a new best friend, a girl named Laurel Adams, with freckles and a long drawl. Ashley and Sumner gave her a ride to school every day that fall after Virginia Beach and introduced her around; pretty soon she was breezing in the back door with them. Sumner imitated her accent and she and Ashley traded clothes and I hung around the edges of rooms watching them, listening to their voices through the house. Sumner would always look up and see me and call out, "Miss Haven, stop hiding and show yourself," and Ashley would put an arm around me and tease Sumner about two-timing her with me. Laurel Adams would toss her long honey-blond hair and just say "Lawwwwd" the way she always did when she had nothing better to contribute. The weather turned colder and colder and my mother packed up all my summer clothes, shaking the sand of Virginia Beach from my shorts and tank tops before whisking them off to the attic until Memorial Day.

Halloween came and Sumner carved a jack-o'-lantern that was supposed to look like Ashley but turned to mush. Ashley's had one of Sumner's awful ties hanging off of it and dangling over the porch rail. Ashley went as Cleopatra, Sumner as a mad scientist, and Laurel Adams as Marilyn Monroe in a peroxide wig and a dress that I could tell my mother thought was entirely too tight. They took me around the neighborhood, house to house, and ate my candy; I felt like I was really doing something, being somebody, with them all around me. Afterwards they dropped me off at home and Ashley kissed my forehead, which she never did, and then they were gone, puttering down the street with the light catching the blond in Laurel's wig and turning it silver. I sat up and watched my father scare the hell out of all the trick-or-treaters with his monster mask until everyone had gone home and I got sent to bed and ate candy in the dark. I was just dropping off to sleep when I heard them outside.

First the car coming up the street and pulling into the driveway, and then Ashley's voice, harsh. "I don't care, Sumner. Just go, okay?"

"How can you do this?" He sounded strange, not like himself. I sat up in bed.

"It's done." A car door slammed. "Leave me alone."

"You can't just walk off like that, Ash." His voice

was bumpy, breathless, like he was moving around the yard after her. "At least let's talk about it."

"I'm not talking." Her feet were stomping up the front steps. "Let it go, Sumner. Just forget it."

" 'Forget it.' Shit, I can't forget it, Ashley. This isn't something you can just wipe away like that."

"Sumner, leave me alone." I could hear her fumbling with the key. "Just go. Please. Just go."

A pause, long enough for her to have gotten in the house, but she was still out there. Then, "Come on." It was Sumner.

"Go away, Sumner." Now her voice broke, a sob muffling the end of the words. "Go away."

The door opened, then shut just as quickly, and I heard her feet coming up the stairs and the door to her room shutting with a click. Silence. I got up and went to my window. Sumner was in front of the house, running his hands through his hair and staring up at Ashley's room. He stood there a long time in his costume, lab coat and stethoscope, no longer looking like a mad scientist but like one who was deeply perplexed about something, or lost. I pressed my palm against my window, thinking he might see, but if he did he never let on. Instead he turned to the VW and walked the short distance of grass to the driveway, taking his time. He started the engine and noise filled the air, his theme music humming as he pulled out, paused at the end of the driveway, and finally drove away. I got back into bed and stared at my ceiling, knowing he wouldn't be back. I'd heard Ashley dump boys before on the front porch and I knew that tone, that finality in her voice. By the next morning he'd be gone from conversation, wiped from our collective memories. There would be somebody new—soon, probably within the week. My sister, chameleonlike, would change her voice or hair overnight to match the mannerisms of whoever was next. Sumner, like so many before him, would drop from sight and join the ranks of the brokenhearted, dismissed with a wave of my sister's impatient hand.

Chapter Five

⁓

Every week, my father takes me out for dinner on Thursday night. It's our special time together, or so my mother used to call it right after the divorce, a term taken straight from *Helping Your Kids through a Divorce* or *Survival Guide for Abandoned Families* or any other of the endless books that grouped themselves around the house in those first few months, guiding us along unknown territory. Each time, he pulls up in front of the house and waits, not beeping the horn, until I come out and down the walk, always feeling uncomfortable and wondering if my mother is watching. Ashley used to come along as well, but with the wedding so close she'd taken to bailing out every week, preferring to spend the time being comforted by Lewis or fighting with my mother about appetizers for the reception.

There are always a few minutes of awkwardness when I get into my father's convertible and put on my seat belt, that exchanging of nervous pleasantries like we don't know each other very well anymore. I've always thought he must feel like he's crossing into enemy territory and that's why he stays in the car with the engine running, never daring to approach the front door full-on. He usually takes me to whatever restaurant he's frequenting that week—Italian, Mexican, a greasy bar and grill with cold beer and a bartender who knows his name. Everyone seems to know my father's name, and at every place he takes me there's always at least one person just dropping by, staying for a beer, talking sports and scores while I sit across the table with a ginger ale and stare at the walls. But I am used to this, have always been used to it. My father is a local celebrity and he has his public. At the supermarket, or the mall, or even on the street, I have always known to be prepared to share him with the rest of the world.

"So when's school start up again?" he asked after a man whose name I didn't catch finally got up and left, having rehashed the entire last four seasons of the NFL complete with erratic hand gestures.

"August twenty-fourth," I said. This week we were at some new Italian fresh pasta place called Vengo. The ceilings were blue, with clouds painted on them, and all the waiters wore white and whisked around the jungle of ferns and potted plants that perched on every table and hung from the ceiling.

"How's your sister holding up?"

"Okay, I guess." I was used to these questions by now. "She has a breakdown just about every other day though."

"So did Lorna. It must be one of those privileges of the bride." He twirled his pasta on his fork, splattering his tie. My father was a messy eater, a boisterous kind of person, not really suited to the fancy restaurants he liked to frequent. He was the perfect patron, though, with his long-winded stories and locally known sportscaster face, and now with a trophy wife to match. (Lydia Catrell's term, not mine. I'd heard it through the vent.)

"You know," he said after a few minutes of silence, "Lorna really wants to spend some time with you and Ashley. To get to know you better. She feels with the divorce and our wedding you three just haven't had much of a chance to bond."

I picked at my fettucine, not looking at him. I thought I'd done plenty with Lorna, with her bridesmaid fittings and showers and all the vacations she'd come along on even before they were engaged, plunking herself in all the places my mother used to go but not quite making it fit. Thursday nights were the only time I saw my father without her, because she had to do the six o'clock news, the nine-thirty WeatherQuick Update, and the eleven o'clock late-night forecast. Lorna was a one-woman weather machine on Thursdays. I said, "Well, Ashley's been really busy, and . . ."

"I know." He nodded. "But after the wedding, once things have calmed down, maybe you three can take a trip together. To the beach or something. My treat." He smiled at me. "You'd really like her if you just gave her a chance, honey."

"I do like her," I said, now feeling guilty. Suddenly I was mad at Ashley for squirming out of dinner and leaving me to make peace with Lorna through our father.

"Hey, Mac McPhail!" some big voice said behind me, and a huge guy clapped his hand down on my father's shoulder. "I haven't seen you in a million years, you sly dog! How are ya?"

My father stood up and shook the man's hand, grinning, and then gestured to me. "This is my daughter Haven. Haven, this is the craziest son of a bitch you'll ever meet, Tony Trezzora. He was the biggest linebacker they ever had over there at your high school."

I smiled, wondering how many crazy sons of bitches my father actually knew. It was how he introduced just about everyone that dropped by. I went back to my pasta as Tony Trezzora sat to join us, his big knees rattling the table so I had to steady my water glass with my hand. I was studying the size of Tony Trezzora's neck when someone was suddenly right beside me with one of those huge pepper grinders, wielding it like a magic wand right over my food.

"Pepper, madam?"

"Oh, no," I said, "I'm fine."

"You look like you need some. Trust me." Two twists and a small shower of pepper fell over my food. I looked up at the person holding the grinder and almost fell out of my chair. It was Sumner.

"Hey," I said as he whipped another grinder out of his pocket, this one full of some white substance.

"Cheese?" he asked.

"No," I said. "I can't believe—"

Twist, twist, and I had cheese. He was grinning at me the whole time. "You like cheese, Haven. I remember that about you."

"What are you doing here?" I asked him. The last time I'd seen him was at the supermarket a few weeks after Ashley broke up with him. He'd been working in produce bagging kiwis and had trouble meeting my eyes even as he joked with me.

"I'm the pepper-and-cheese man." He twisted the grinder again, just for good measure, then slipped it back into his apron pocket like a gunslinger after a shootout. "I'm also authorized to fill your water glass, if you so desire."

"No, thanks," I said, still staring up at him while he puttered around our table, removing empty plates and at the ready with the pepper and cheese grinders, while my father traded stats with Tony Trezzora and didn't even notice him.

"How's your mom?" He glanced around at the other tables, keeping an eye out.

I was so flabbergasted at seeing him, just popping up out of nowhere with cheese for my pasta. I said, "How long have you been in town?"

"Just a few weeks." He stepped out of the way as a

short girl carrying a huge tray on her shoulder staggered by, barely clearing a fern that was balanced on a ledge beside us. "I'm still in school up in Connecticut, but I'm thinking about taking some time off. I'm not sure."

"Really," I said, as he started to back away, off to cheese another table. "You should—"

He waved, doing some weird hand signal that I couldn't interpret, pantomime in retreat. I realized I was about to tell him he should call Ashley, and thought maybe it was best that he'd been walking away and hadn't heard. She could barely handle answering the phone now, much less any major blasts from her past.

I sat and watched Sumner work his way around the restaurant, wielding his cheese and pepper mills like a professional, laughing and joking at table after table, while my father stayed lost in sports talk with the giant next to me. I kept wishing I'd said something more important, something striking, in the short conversation I'd had with the only boyfriend of Ashley's I'd ever really liked.

Later, when I'd finished my food, I went to find the bathroom and saw Sumner sitting in a back booth eating and counting a pile of money. He waved me over, scooting aside to make room for me to sit down, so I did.

"So tell me what's going on with you," Sumner said, arranging his stack of bills in a neat pile. "Besides the fact that you are tall and gorgeous."

"Too tall," I said.

"You are not." He twirled some pasta around his fork and pointed it at me. "You should be grateful you're tall, Haven. Tall people are revered and respected in this world. If you're short and stubby, no one will give you the time of day."

"I don't want to be revered," I said. "I just want to be normal."

"There's no such thing. Trust me. Even the people you think are super-squeaky-clean normal have something about them that's not right." As he said this, a tall waitress with long, shimmering blond hair passed by, winking at Sumner. He waited until she was out of earshot, then said, "Take her, for instance. She looks normal."

I watched her disappear through double doors by the pay phone. "And you're saying she isn't?"

"Not specifically. I'm saying no one is. She looks like your typical blond beauty, right? But in actuality"— now he leaned closer to me, sharing secrets—"she has an extra toe."

"She does not," I said firmly.

"I swear to God, she does." He went back to his pasta, nibbling. "Sandals. Just yesterday. Saw it myself."

"Yeah, right," I said.

He shook his head. "Well, I guess those childhood full-of-trust days are over for you, huh? You don't believe me the way you used to."

I watched my father talking to Tony Trezzora, his face pinkish from a few beers and a good session of male bonding. "I don't believe a lot of things."

The extra-toed waitress passed by again, smiling a big warm smile at Sumner, who smiled back and nodded towards her feet. I was embarrassed and concentrated on the fern that was hanging over us.

"So," he said after a few minutes, "how's Ashley?"

"She's good," I said. "She's getting married."

He grinned. "No kidding. Man, I never would have pegged her for the early-married type. Who is it?"

"This guy named Lewis Warsher. He works at the mall." I wasn't sure what else to say about Lewis. It was hard to describe him to strangers. I said, "He drives a Chevette."

Sumner nodded, as if this helped. "Ashley Warsher. Sounds like you have a mouthful of marbles when you say it."

"He's okay," I said. "But now Ashley's miserable 'cause the wedding's so close and everything's going wrong."

"Ashley's getting married," he said slowly, as if it was a different language and he wasn't sure where the syllables fell. "Man. That makes me feel old."

"You're not old," I said.

"How old are you now?"

"Fifteen," I said, then added, "I'll be sixteen in November."

He sighed, shaking his head. "I'm old. I'm ancient. If you're fifteen, I'm a senior citizen. Little Haven. Fifteen."

My father was looking for me now, having noticed I was missing for longer than it takes to go to the bathroom. Tony Trezzora, undaunted, was still talking.

I took Sumner back to the table with me, and as we came up my father smiled and said, "There you are. I was beginning to think I'd been ditched."

"Dad, you remember Sumner," I said, and Sumner stuck out his hand as my father stood up to shake it. "He used to date Ashley."

"Sumner, how's it going?" my father said energetically, pumping Sumner's hand within his own large one. "What have you been doing lately?"

"I've been in school up North," Sumner said when my father finally let go of his hand. My father believed in the power of a strong, masculine handshake. "I'm taking the semester off, though. To work and take a break from school."

"Nothing wrong with that," my father said firmly, as if someone had said there was. "Working is the best learning you can do, sometimes."

"And that's the truth," Tony Trezzora added.

"Well, I should get going," Sumner said. "My next shift starts in about fifteen minutes."

"Here?" I asked.

"Oh, no, at my other job," he said. "One of my other ones."

"Now that's a work ethic," my father said. "Take care, Sumner."

"Good to see you again, Mr. McPhail." He turned to me as my father sat back down to his now-cold food. Tony Trezzora made his excuses and disappeared to the bar, probably in search of another audience. Sumner said, "It's really good to see you again, Haven. Tell Ashley . . . well, if it comes up, tell her I asked about her. And congratulations. On the wedding."

"I'll tell her," I said. "I know she'd want to see you." I didn't know this, but it seemed like the right thing to say.

He grinned. "Well, maybe not. But pass it on anyhow. Take care of yourself. Remember what I told you." He raised his eyebrows at the six-toed waitress as she swept past again, long blond hair shimmering. "See ya."

"'Bye, Sumner." I watched him walk towards the front of the restaurant and then out the door, onto the street. I thought about Virginia Beach and the ride in the back of the Volkswagen under the stars, so many summers ago. As I sat back down with my father I could have sworn I heard the soft putter of the VW, the theme music, curving above the noise and mingled voices of the restaurant, just as I'd last heard it outside my window on that night, long ago.

In the car on the way home I looked over at my father, his new hair fluttering in the breeze, and said, "Wasn't it great to see Sumner again?"

"You know, I'm not sure I remember which one Sumner was. Was he the football player?"

"Daddy." I looked at him. "I can't believe you don't remember him. You really liked him."

"Oh, honey, I liked them all. I had to." He laughed, taking the turn into our neighborhood just fast enough to squeal the tires a little bit. My mother said his personalized license plate should not read MAC, as it did, but MIDLIFE CRISIS. I tried to tell her that was too many letters, you could only have eight, but she said that wasn't the point. He added, "They all run together in my head now. There were too damn many of them."

"Sumner was different," I said. "He went to Virginia Beach with us, remember? When you did that golf tournament and we stayed in that nice hotel?"

He squinted, as if it took great effort to reach so far

back. Then he said, quickly, "Oh yeah. I remember that. He was a nice kid."

And that was all my father, with his selective grasp of the past, chose to remember. He was skittish whenever I brought up the past, our vacations, family events. He was eager to start over—brand-new wife, brand-new house, brand-new memories, the old carelessly tucked away.

We pulled into the driveway, right beside Lewis's Chevette, which was parked with the motor off and he and Ashley still in it. As we slid up beside them Ashley looked over, with a scowl that told me they were fighting and not to get involved. Unfortunately, my father is not skilled in reading my sister's expressions: he was waving at her. She just looked at him; Lewis slumped beside her.

"They're fighting," I explained. "Thanks for dinner."

My father sighed and put his car into reverse. "See you next week." He kissed my cheek when I leaned over. I waited a beat for what I knew came next. "Need any money?"

"No, I'm fine." I never took it, even when I did need it. Ashley always *said* she just couldn't take any even though it had been a hard month and her credit card was due . . . well, okay, just this once. She had it down to an art. I would have felt strange taking my father's pocket money, a twenty slipped here or there to make up for his day-to-day absence. Besides, I had my four twenty-five an hour at Little Feet, no big deal but enough to get me by. It would have been nice to have an extra bit, but whenever I felt tempted I thought of my mother's face and said no. The tether, stretching beyond my mother and out of the house, was always attached and I was ever mindful of where my obligations lay.

I stood in the driveway as my father pulled away hitting the horn twice, that happy *beep-beep!* as he turned out of sight. I started up the walk towards the door, Ashley's voice now audible without the rumbling of my father's car.

"Lewis, that's not the point. The point is that you didn't do anything to stop it." I recognized the tone, the clipped ends of each word, like speaking right into a wall. "I just didn't think you'd ever act that way. I assumed you'd defend me."

"Honey, I don't think it was as bad as you're making it out to be. They were only giving their opinion. They didn't mean it to be some kind of attack."

"Well, Lewis, if you can't even see why it was so upsetting to me, then I guess I can't expect you to understand why it bothers me that you didn't take the action that I thought, as my fiancé, you would take."

A silence, with just the cicadas chirping and the TV from our next-door neighbors, the Bensons, playing the theme song from "Bewitched." I kept walking until I was out of sight on the porch, then took off my shoes and sat on the steps.

"Well," Ashley said with the sort of finality she used whenever we fought and she was getting ready to stalk out of the room, "I guess we just can't discuss this anymore. This is a side of you I didn't know before tonight, Lewis."

"Ashley, for God's sake." I sat up. "I understand you

weren't in the mood for their input, but they're my family, flawed or not, and I'm not going to sit here and trash them to make you feel better. I'm just not." It sounded like Lewis was growing a spine, finally, right there in the Chevette.

I expected lightning to flash, stars to fall from the sky, the earth to shake and rumble at its core, but instead I heard only the slam of the car door and Ashley saying, "Then there is nothing left to discuss. I don't want to be with you right now, Lewis. I don't know when, actually, I'll want to be with you again."

"Ashley." And there it was, just as she was coming up the walk, the plaintive whine: Lewis lost his new bravado and returned to his old self. But it was too late. Ashley was In A Mood and he'd have to ride it out, like it or not, like the rest of us always did.

She came stomping up the steps, saw me, and stopped just long enough to shoot me a look. She was wearing the holy dress, and in the porch light she seemed to be almost glowing. She kicked her shoes to the far end of the porch and climbed into the swing, making quite a racket as the chains clanked before settling into a nice, smooth to and fro. Lewis was still out in the driveway, waiting in the car.

"What happened?" I asked after a few solid minutes of her heavy sighs overlaying the occasional yap of the Weavers' dog from across the street, a fat little sausage of a dog that had a bark like a duck. There was something wrong with it, some kind of vocal problem. My father had called it Duckdog, upsetting Mrs. Weaver, who liked to dress it in sweaters, galoshes when it rained.

Ashley leaned further back in the swing and waited awhile before answering, like she wasn't sure it was worth the trouble. "They hate me," she said simply. "They all ganged up on me when we started talking about the caterer and they all hate me."

The Chevette started up now, softly, and I wondered if Lewis was actually going to leave. I'd imagined him sitting all night in the driveway, sleeping upright rather than leaving angry. But there he was, pulling into the street with one last long pause in front of the house before driving off.

"I'm sure they don't hate you," I said, sounding just like my mother, who was too busy dancing with middle-aged men at the Holiday Inn to be here for this latest crisis.

"All I said was that I hadn't felt like arguing with the caterer about salmon. If it was going to be that much trouble, we'd have chicken. I mean, by this point I have to pick my battles, right? But with just the mention of the salmon issue the whole table looks at me and Mrs. Warsher says, 'If you wanted salmon, you should have pursued it. The caterer is working for you, not the other way around.'" Her voice was high and nasal, spiteful. She still had it in her.

"You fought with his family about salmon?" Now that I knew the core of the dispute was fish, it seemed less exciting. I'd expected something major, something involving sex or religion at least.

"Oh, not just salmon. Lewis decided to tell them about Carol, too. Oh, and the invitations and how the typesetter forgot to put the date the first time around. And that's not even counting what he said about Daddy."

"Daddy. What about him?"

"Well, they asked"—she waved her hand around in summary as if it would take too long to explain— "about the family and all, and Lewis tells them about the divorce, which is fine, but then he has to go into the whole Lorna thing, and the TV station thing and how she's a weathergirl and Dad's a sportscaster and on and on and on. It was just too much."

"Well, Ash, it is the truth," I said. "Embarrassing or not."

"But he made it sound so awful. I mean, there's Lewis's whole family all grouped around the table like the Waltons and he's telling them about Daddy and Lorna and I can only imagine what they'd think if they knew Mom was out dancing with Lydia Catrell. I mean, these people go to church, Haven."

"So? It doesn't make them better than you."

She sighed, blowing hot air through her bangs. "You don't understand. You don't have anyone you have to impress now. It's different when you're older. What your family does reflects on you a lot more, especially when it's as twisted as ours is."

"A lot of people get divorced, Ash," I said. "It's not just us."

She climbed out of the swing, leaving it to rock empty behind her. She leaned far over the edge of the rail and balanced her weight on her palms while the holy dress, translucent, blew around her legs. Her hair hung down over her face, hiding her mouth as she said, "I know, Haven. But no one else has our parents."

A car blew by on the street, radio blasting; a cigarette hit the pavement with a shower of sparks. Then it was quiet again, except for Duckdog's barking.

"I saw Sumner tonight," I said quietly.

"Who?" She was still leaning over, her feet dangling.

"Sumner."

"Sumner Lee?"

"Yeah."

A pause; then she righted herself and brushed her hair back. "Really. What'd he say?"

"We just caught up for a while. He asked about you."

"Did he." Her voice was flat. "Well. That's nice."

"He's working over at Vengo," I went on. "And some other job, too."

"What's he doing back in town? I thought he was in college."

"He's thinking about taking some time off."

"Dropping out?" she said.

"No." I spoke slowly. "Just time off. And anyway he hasn't decided yet." I was beginning to regret I'd even mentioned it. Ashley had a way of taking anything good and ruining it.

"Well, that sounds like Sumner," she said dismissively. "He never was very ambitious."

"He told me to congratulate you," I answered, suddenly wanting to keep talking. She didn't have to be so nasty. "He wishes you the best."

"That's nice." She was bored with it already. She

walked to the door, reaching for the knob. "If Lewis calls, tell him I'm sleeping. I don't feel like talking to anyone right now."

"Ashley."

She turned, having already opened the door. "What?"

"He was really happy for you." She had that look on her face, like I was wasting her time so late at night. "I thought . . . I thought you'd have more of a reaction."

She shook her head, moving inside. "Haven, I'm getting married in less than a month. I don't have time to think about old boyfriends. I don't even have time to think about myself."

"I was happy to see him," I said.

"You didn't know him the way I did." She rubbed one foot with the other, that classic Ashley gesture. "Just tell Lewis I'm asleep, okay?"

"Okay."

I'd let it go now, just like I'd learned to let all things go that brought out that tired voice and impatient gesture in my sister. Being in her good graces was still important to me. I sat out on the porch for a long time, not sure what I was waiting for. Not for the Town Car, which didn't come home with my mother tucked safely inside until much later, when I was in bed half-asleep, making myself stay lucid until I heard her key in the lock. Not for Lewis's call, which came and I let ring, on and on, long after Ashley had pretended to be sleeping or was asleep. There was time for waiting, even if I wasn't sure what to wait for. It was still summer, at least for a while.

Chapter Six

There *were two* homecomings in the first week of August for our neighborhood. One was little, not mattering much to anyone but me. And one was big news.

The little one was the return of my best friend, Casey Melvin, from 4-H camp, where she'd spent most of the summer letting boys go up her shirt and writing me long, dramatic letters in pink magic marker sealed with a lipstick kiss. She came back plumper, cuter, and wearing a green T-shirt that belonged to her new long-distance boyfriend, a seventeen-year-old from

Hershey, Pennsylvania, named Rick. She had a lot to tell me.

"God, Haven, you would just die if you met him. He is so much better looking than any of the guys around here." We were in her room drinking Cokes and going through what seemed like eighteen packs of pictures, double prints, all of smiling people posing in front of log cabins, bodies of water, and the occasional flag. They had to salute the flag three times a day, apparently. That seemed to be the only 4-H activity involved, at least for Casey. In the mere month and a half that she'd been gone, she had become what my mother would politely call "fast."

There were at least twenty pictures of Rick in the small stack I'd already gone through, half of which featured Casey hanging off of some part of him. He *was* good looking, but not stunning. Casey was lying on her stomach beside me, naming all the people.

"Oh, that's Lucy in the red shirt. She was so crazy, I swear. She was sneaking around with one of the counselors—this college guy? And she got sent home the third week. It was too bad because she was loads of fun. She'd do anything if you double dog dared her."

"Double dog dared?" I said.

"Yeah." She sat up, plunking another stack of pictures into my hands. "And Rick called me last night, can you believe it? Long distance. He said he misses me so much he wanted to go back to camp for the first time in his life. But I'm going up there for Thanksgiving; we already asked his parents and everything.

But that's four months. I think I'll die if I don't see him for four months."

I watched my best friend, boy crazed, as she rolled on the bed clutching the stack of Rick pictures to her chest. Sometimes love can be an ugly thing.

"So what did I miss here?"

I shrugged, taking another sip of my Coke. "Nothing. Dad got married. But that's about it."

"How was the wedding? Was it awful?"

"No," I said, but I was glad that she asked. Only your very best friend knows when to ask that kind of question. "It was weird. And Ashley's practically psychotic with her wedding so close. And my mother is going to Europe in the fall with Lydia."

"Lydia? For how long?"

"Months, I think. A long time."

"God." She pushed her hair out of her face. Casey was a redhead, actually an orange-head, with that brassy kind of pumpkin-colored hair. She'd had masses of freckles when we were little, which thankfully faded as she got older; but her hair stayed basically unmanageable, a mop of wild orange curls. "Hey, who are you gonna stay with while she's gone?"

"I don't know. We haven't talked about that yet."

"Cool, the whole house to yourself! Man, that will be awesome. We can have a party or something."

"Yeah. Whatever." I tossed the pictures back to her, all the strange faces tumbling together. I didn't know these people. It was like a whole world in a different language.

She got up and put the pictures on her desk, then

tugged on her cutoffs, which dangled fringe down the back of her leg. Suddenly she spun around and said, "God! I can't believe I forgot to tell you!"

"Tell me what?"

"About Gwendolyn Rogers." She jumped back onto the bed, shaking it so madly that the headboard banged against the wall. Casey was always taking flight or crashing into things. My father called her the whirling dervish.

"What about her?" I had that image again of Gwendolyn walking her dog, the leash reaching far up to her hand.

"She's back. She came home," she said ominously (I could always tell when something big was coming), "because she had a nervous breakdown." She sat back, nodding her head.

"You're kidding."

"Her mother is friends with Mrs. Oliver, who is in my mother's walking group and was sworn to secrecy but can't keep anything quiet so she told everyone but made them all swear not to pass it further."

"So your mom tells you."

"She didn't tell me. She told Mrs. Caster next door and I overheard because I was out on the roof smoking a cigarette. They never think to look up."

"You smoke now?"

She laughed. "I have since the beginning of the summer. I want to quit, but it's just so hard. You want one?"

"No," I said, still trying to catch up with all this new information. "Why'd she have a nervous breakdown?"

"Because"—she went over to her dresser, reaching

far under the sweaters she never wore to retrieve a box with a rumpled pack of cigarettes and some matches in it—"she was badly hurt by a man. And the modeling industry. It's a hard life for a small-town girl, Haven."

Something told me these were not her own words. "What man?"

"A photographer. He took all those pictures of her that we saw in *Cosmo*; you know, the ones in that tight red sweater that showed her nipples." She shook out a cigarette and put it in her mouth, then took it out. "She was going to marry him, but then she found him in bed with a sixteen-year-old girl."

"God," I said.

"And another man," she added with a flourish, popping the cigarette back into her mouth. "Could you die?"

"That's horrible," I said. I felt guilty knowing this about a stranger, some poor girl who knew no shameful secrets of mine. With Mrs. Melvin's mouth, it had to be all over the neighborhood by now.

"She flew in last Friday, and Mrs. Oliver said she took right to her bed in her old room and slept for forty hours straight. Poor Mrs. Rogers thought she was dying of some horrible disease 'cause Gwendolyn wouldn't say what was wrong or why she came home or anything." She reached over and opened the window, then lit a match and touched it to the end of the cigarette. "She woke up at four A.M. and made pancakes, and when Mrs. Rogers went downstairs to see what was going on, that was when Gwendolyn told her. Standing there at the stove flipping pancakes at four A.M. and telling this horrible story. She ate ten pancakes and burst into tears and Mrs. Rogers said she is just at a loss as to what action to take. And since then, Mrs. Oliver says, Gwendolyn hasn't said a word."

"Ten pancakes?" I said. This, to me, seemed like the most unbelievable part of the story.

"Haven, honestly." Casey hated when anyone tried to take away from whatever story she was telling. "And that was when Gwendolyn took to walking."

"Walking?"

She puffed on her cigarette, then blew the smoke out the window, where it circled across the roof and into the sky. "She walks all night long, Haven, through the neighborhood. She can't sleep, or won't, and Mrs. Oliver says she's like a ghost passing on the sidewalk, long legged and freaky looking. All night long."

Suddenly I had chills, the kind you get during the climax of a good ghost story, when you realize the scratching on the roof is the disembodied hand or that the ribbon holds her head on. I could see Gwendolyn loping along on her thin legs, casting a giant shadow across the green lawns of our subdivision. Gwendolyn Rogers, supermodel, wandering lost on the streets of her childhood and mine.

"Creepy, huh?" Casey said, taking another long drag off her cigarette and fanning the smoke outside. "Mom says she bets modeling made Gwendolyn crazy. It's a horrible industry, you know."

"So you said." I thought of the Lakeview Models in

their pumps and matching T-shirts, posing in front of giant fake leaves. And Gwendolyn, the town's pride and joy, walking mad in the streets.

"It'll be all over the papers, and *People* magazine, soon," she went on, waving her hand in front of her face to fan off the smoke. "You know, it's big news when someone like Gwendolyn goes nuts."

"It's so sad," I said again. If even supermodel and beautiful hometown girl Gwendolyn Rogers could crash and burn, what would become of me . . . or anyone? She'd been profiled in one of Casey's *Teen World* magazines just a few months before, sharing her Biggest Secrets: her favorite food (pizza), band (R.E.M.), and beauty secret (cucumbers on her eyes to reduce puffiness after long days of shooting). And we knew these things about her, just as we did about Cindy and Elle and Claudia, girls who didn't even need last names. Girls that could have been our friends by the details we memorized about them, or the girl next door. As Gwendolyn, supermodel and Lakeview girl, tall like me, had once been.

"Casey?" There was a sudden knock on the door and Mrs. Melvin's thick New York accent, which always made her sound irritated even when she wasn't, boomed through the wall. "It's time for dinner and it's your turn to set the table. Haven can stay if she wants to."

"Just a minute," Casey yelled, tossing the cigarette out the window, where it rolled down to the gutter and caught a wad of pine needles on fire. Casey, busy running around the room spraying White Shoulders on everything, didn't notice.

"Casey," I whispered, pointing out the window at the small blaze. "Look."

"Not now," she snapped in a low voice, still waving her arms. "God, Haven, *help* me."

"Wait," I whispered, getting up and going to the window. "Don't open the door yet."

"Can you smell it?" she said, whirling around. "Can you?"

"No, but—"

Mrs. Melvin knocked again, harder. "Casey, open the door."

"Okay, okay, one second." She put the perfume on the dresser and went to the door, passing the window without noticing the flame burning in the gutter. She unlocked the door. "God, come on in then."

As Mrs. Melvin came in I was leaning against the windowsill, attempting to appear casual with my Coke in my hand and trying not to cough as a thick cloud of White Shoulders settled over me. She took one step, stopping in the frame to take two short sniffs of the air. She was a small woman, like Casey, with the same shock of red hair, only hers was styled in a bob, ends curling down neatly over her shoulders. She wore stirrup pants and a long white shirt, with huge gold hoops dangling from her ears. Her eyeliner, as always, drew my attention next: onyx black, thick on upper and lower lids, curving out past her eye to a neat flourish that made her look like a cat. It must have taken half a jar of cold cream to remove and was a bit much, especially in our neighborhood, but it was her trademark. That and her incredible sense of smell.

She sniffed again, with her eyes closed, then opened them and said curtly, "You've been smoking."

Casey turned bright red. "I have not."

I glanced out the window. The fire was still burning, looking like it might spread to a wad of leaves nearby. I had to do something, so as Mrs. Melvin crossed the room, eyes closed again and still sniffing, I panicked and flung the rest of my Coke out the window, most of it hitting the glass with a splat but thankfully enough getting to the edge of the roof where it somehow, miraculously, doused the fire. I thought we were home free until I turned around to see Mrs. Melvin, hands on her hips, looking at me. Just past her was Casey, who threw her hands up in the air and shook her head, surrendering.

"Yes you have," she said, walking past me to the open window and glancing out at the smoldering gutter. "Look at that. You're setting fires and still lying to my face."

"Mom," Casey said quickly, "I didn't . . ."

Mrs. Melvin walked to the door. "Jake, get up here." Parenting in the Melvin household was a tag-team affair. Any conflict had to be dealt with in tandem, attacked from both sides. I heard Mr. Melvin pounding up the steps before he appeared in the doorway in jeans and loafers. My father called Mr. Melvin the consummate frat boy. He was forty-three but looked eighteen and was about as whipped as any man could be. One look, one call from Mrs. Melvin and he snapped to attention.

"What's going on?" He had a newspaper in his hand. "Hello, Haven. How's it going?"

"Good," I said.

"We have a situation here," Mrs. Melvin said, directing his attention out the window to the gutter, which was still smoking a bit and thus providing the proper dramatic effect. "Your daughter has taken up smoking."

"Smoking?" He looked at Casey, then out the window. "Is something on fire out there?"

"It's that 4-H camp, Jake, where she picked up every other bad habit this summer." Mrs. Melvin walked to the dresser and opened the box on top, taking out the pack of cigarettes. "Look at this. There are probably birth control pills in here too."

"Mom, please," Casey said, "I haven't had sex yet."

"Haven," Mr. Melvin said quietly, "maybe you should get on home to dinner."

"Okay," I said. This was the way I always seemed to leave the Melvins' house, under some sort of duress. Things were always exciting over at the Melvins'. During the divorce I'd spent most of my time there, sitting on Casey's bed reading *Teen* magazine and listening to arguments and situations that blissfully had nothing to do with my world whatsoever.

On my way out the door I saw Casey's brother, Ronald, on the porch petting the Melvins' cat, a hugely overweight tabby named Velvet. Ronald was only five, not even born when I'd met Casey the day they moved from New Jersey all those years ago.

"Hey, baby Ronald," I said.

"Shut up." He hated his family nickname now. At five, he was beginning to resent anything with the word "baby" attached to it.

"See you later," I said.

"Haven?" he called after me. "How'd you grow so much?"

I stopped at the end of the front walk to face his shock of Melvin red hair and his toughskin cutoffs, the cat shedding a cloud of hair all around him. "I don't know, Ronald."

He thought for a minute, still petting. He had the freckles, a faceful plus the ones Casey had lost once she hit fourteen. "Vegetables," he said slowly, pronouncing it carefully, then added, "probably."

"Yeah." I hit the sidewalk in full stride for the one hundred and fourteen squares of cement, cracks and all, that led to my own front walk. "Probably."

I saw Sumner again later that week at the mall, during my midevening break from Little Feet. It had been a long night, too many tiny shoes to put on smelly feet, too much pressure to move the socks, always the socks. I bought a Coke and took a seat facing the stage in front of Dillard's, now complete with its fall decorations, big leaves in all different colors, with black silhouettes of glam-looking girls interspersed. I was studying the sign sitting center stage that said FALL FASHION PREVIEW! FEATURING . . . THE LAKEVIEW MALL MODELS AND FASHIONS FROM YOUR FAVORITE MALL MERCHANTS . . . COMING SOON! with a hokey tear-off calendar counting down the days, as if anyone was that excited about it.

It was almost eight o'clock, which meant I had one more hour of Little Feet before I could leave. The mall was clearing out now that it was prime time, and I tossed my cup and was heading back to the store when I saw the little mall golf cart heading erratically my way. The horn was beeping. Loudly.

It whizzed right up in front of me, dodging ferns and benches and the fountain, skidding to a flourishing stop. Sumner, the Lakeview Mall Security Man. The uniform was too big, rolled up at the cuffs, and his name tag said Marvin. He was grinning at me.

"Hey there. Want a ride?" He extended one arm across the passenger seat, "Price Is Right" showcase style. "It's better than walking."

"Are you supposed to drive people around in that?" I asked, sure I'd never seen Ned, the other guard, taxiing the help up and down the mall.

"No." He grinned. "But you know me, Haven. I call it my Chariot of Love. Now get in."

So I did. He waited until I was settled, then turned us around and hit the gas, and we zoomed down the center of the mall with Yogurt Paradise and Felice's Ladies Fashions and The Candy Shack whizzing by in a blur. Sumner was laughing, barely dodging obstacles and people, yet managing to look official whenever we passed anyone who appeared to be important.

"If we get stopped by management," he yelled at me above the whirring of the engine as we blew past Little Feet and my boss, who was selecting socks for someone, "act like you're injured. Say you sprained your ankle and I'm rushing you to help."

"Sumner," I said, but he couldn't hear me. We did another lap, slowing down a bit for the scenic tour. Sumner beeped the horn occasionally, scattering groups of teenagers in front of the arcade or pizza parlor, before finally being flagged down by a woman in a flowered dress, towing a toddler.

"Yes, ma'am," Sumner said, pulling up smoothly beside her.

"I wonder if you could tell me where I might be able to buy a personalized letter opener." She had a high-pitched voice, and the kid was drooling.

Sumner reached to the back of the cart, pulled out a clipboard, and rifled through it, concentrating. "Your best bet would be Personally Personalized." He snapped a sheet of paper from the clipboard, drew a long winding arrow on it, and said, "Here's a map. We're here"—he put a black mark on one spot—"and it's there." Another mark. "Ought to be able to find it with no difficulty." He put his pen back behind his ear as he handed her the page, one smooth movement.

"Thank you," the woman said admiringly, map in hand. "Thanks very much."

"No problem," Sumner said. I expected him to salute or something. "Have a good evening and shop with us again." And we cruised off, maneuvering smoothly through a thicket of potted plants.

"You were born for this job," I told him. We took another pass by the stage, coming to a stop by the side steps.

"I was born for every job," he said with a smile, climbing out of the cart and onto the stage. He walked to the sign in the middle and reached for the calendar, pulling the top sheet so that six days were left instead of seven. Then he stood at center stage and took a long from-the-waist bow, low and dramatic, before an invisible adoring public.

After climbing back down the stairs he jumped back in beside me and handed me the seven. "For you."

"Thanks so much."

"So," he said, shouting over the sound of the engine. "Where do you work?"

"At Little Feet." I realized how stupid it sounded even as I said it.

"Selling shoes," he said, smiling. "I did that one summer. It sucks, huh?"

"Yeah." The mall was whizzing by again, storefronts and people blurring past. Traveling with Sumner next to me, the mall was like an undiscovered country. He'd always had a way of making even the ordinary seem fun; during that summer at the beach he stayed in the water with me almost all the time, bodysurfing and doing handstands, diving for shells and making up games. Ashley spent the whole week on the beach with her towel and sunscreen, tanning, while Sumner and I swam until our fingers were pruny and white. He was the only one who had time to play with me. If Ashley pouted and made a fuss when he tried to include me, he could usually get her to come around. And when he couldn't and we fought, he had a way of taking my side without it looking like he was betraying her. He stuck up for me, and I never forgot it.

As we zoomed past the fountain I looked up at the huge banners that hung from the ceiling, each with its community motif: a house, a school, a flower, an animal that looked like a goat but I figured was a deer. I had this sudden, crazy urge to stand on the seat and rip every one of them down as we passed. I could almost feel my fingertips on the sheer fabric, smooth and giving as I yanked them from their bases. Speeding through the Lakeview Mall, dismantling it as I went. I glanced at Sumner, thinking of how much had changed, with the visions of those tumbling banners still in my head. I almost wanted to tell him, to ask him if he knew how it felt to be suddenly tempted to go wild. But we were flying along, the engine drowning all other sounds, and I let it go, for now.

Chapter Seven

⤨

After my chariot ride through the mall it seemed like I ran into Sumner everywhere. This was partly due to the fact that he had so many jobs. Besides pepper-and-cheese man and mall security, he was also mowing the lawn at the cemetery and driving a school bus for retarded children. Sumner did not believe in idle time.

I thought it must be fate that I kept bumping into him, some strange sign that he was meant to come back into my life and fix or change something, a voice from the past arriving in the present with the answers to everything. I knew this was silly, but it was hard to dismiss Sumner's timing.

Lewis and Ashley continued to bicker and make up, almost daily. The moods she'd made a habit of inflicting exclusively on the family were now fair game to him as well, and as the wedding crept ever closer he approached our front door as if it was a bomb and the wrong word, compliment, or even expression could cause everything to blow. My mother and I commiserated silently, watching him climb the stairs to Ashley's room like a soldier going off to battle. I found myself liking Lewis more now that he was suffering with us; I imagined it being the way crisis victims bonded, joined by the unthinkable.

It was now an even two weeks until the wedding. My mother's lists had taken over the house, yellow stick-it notes flapping from anything that was stationary and big enough to hold them. They lined the bannister, grabbing my attention as I climbed the stairs. They hung from the fridge and the television, last-minute reminders, things not to forget. They were like caution signs, flagging me down and giving a warning to proceed carefully around the next turn. The wedding, so long churning over our house in a steady pattern, was beginning to whip itself into a storm.

"Where's that other package of thank-you notes?" I heard Ashley say from the kitchen as I got out of the shower one morning. "I need more than just the six that are left in this pack."

"Well, I put them in that same drawer," my mother

answered,, her shoes making a scuffling noise across the floor as she went off in search of the notes. "They can't have gone anywhere by themselves."

"Obviously not," Ashley growled under her breath, that same constantly grumbling, incoherent voice I seemed to hear behind me whenever I was in the wrong place at the wrong time.

I heard my mother come back and pull out a chair. "Here they are," she said in her singsong placating voice. "And I brought this list in so we could go over what needs doing today."

"Fine."

"Okay," my mother said, and there was a rustling of plastic that I assumed was Ashley ripping open the new cards. "First, there are the final fittings at Dillard's today at ten. I know Haven has traded shifts so she can be there, and I called this morning to make sure the head-piece was ready."

"She's probably grown another four feet and we'll have to get fitted again later," Ashley grumbled, and I stared at myself in my bathroom mirror, through the steam. I had almost outgrown my mirror, the top of my head barely within the frame. I examined myself, the geometry of my ribs, elbows, and collarbone. I imagined lines intersecting, planes going on forever and ever. My arms were long, lanky, thin, and my knees were hinges holding the bony parts of my skinny legs together. I was sharp to anyone who might brush against me.

"Ashley, you know your sister is sensitive about her height." This was the closest my mother came to scolding Ashley, who was old enough not to need it. "Imagine being fifteen and reaching six feet. It's very hard for her, and comments like that don't help."

"God, it's not like I'm saying it to her face," Ashley said bitterly, and I wondered if all those thank-you cards and all that gratitude were having an adverse effect, leaving no niceties for anyone in person. "Besides, she'll be glad later. She'll never get fat."

"That's hardly a comfort now." My mother cleared her throat. "After the fitting we can have our final meeting with the caterer. He called yesterday and said the appetizers are in order and you just have to make some final decisions about desserts."

"God, I am so sick of making decisions." A pause, during which I heard my mother stirring her coffee. "And writing these damn thank-you notes. Does anyone really think that I'm not grateful for their gift? Is it really necessary for me to state it in writing?"

"Yes, it is," my mother snapped, and I turned to look at the vent as the words came up through it, surprised at the impatience in her voice. "And I've been meaning to talk to you, Ashley, about your attitude lately concerning this wedding and those who are doing their best to make it a success."

"Mother," Ashley began in that bored voice. I could almost see her waving her hand, dismissing the words even as my mother said them.

"No, you're going to listen this time." My mother was hitting full speed now, gearing up. "I understand that you are under a lot of pressure and that it's hard being a bride. That is all well and good. But it does not, ever, entitle you to be rude, selfish, uncaring, and generally obnoxious to me or Haven or anyone else. We've been very patient with you because we're your family and we love you, but it stops here. I don't care if the wedding is two weeks or two hours away, you were never raised to behave this way. Do you understand me?"

And there it was. I stood naked, my eyes fixed on the steel grate of the vent that transmitted my mother's words, clear as bells, up to my own ears. It was quiet down there now, with only the sound of the ceiling fan creaking in slow circles.

Then, a sniffle. Another. A sob, and the floodgates opened. Ashley was wailing, her usual response to any justified attack. "I don't mean it," she began. "It's just hard, with my job and the Warshers and all the planning, and sometimes I just . . ."

"I know, I know," my mother said, having jumped back into her soothing mode, easing off the troops and letting the skirmish settle down. "I just wanted to let you know how it was affecting everyone else. That's all."

I combed my hair, put on deodorant and eyeliner, and got myself ready for work while the gushing and apologizing continued. By the time my mother had gently suggested that Ashley come up and apologize to me for her behavior of, oh, the last four months, I was fully dressed and waiting on my bed. I opened the door when she knocked, trying to act spontaneous.

"Hey," I said, making a point not to notice her red eyes and the crumpled Kleenex clutched in her hand. "What's up?"

"Well," she said, leaning against the doorjamb and rubbing one foot with the heel of the other, "Mom and I were just talking about how crazy everything's been with the wedding and all, and I wanted to come up and say I'm sorry if I've been a jerk lately. I mean, I'm sorry for taking it all out on you, you know, when I did."

"Oh." I sat on my bed, nodding. "Well. That's fine."

"I'm serious, Haven." She came in and sat down beside me. "I'm sorry. It's the last time we'll ever be living under the same roof and I've been impossible. So I'm sorry."

"It's okay," I said. "And you have."

"Have what?"

"Been a jerk. And impossible." I smiled at her. "But I'm used to that from you."

"Shut up," she said, staring at me. Then she looked down and added, "Okay. You're right."

"I know," I said.

She stood up and walked to the door, turning back to me as she stepped out into the hallway. "You know, you're going to be really grateful someday."

"For what?"

"Being tall." She looked at me, her eyes traveling from my feet to my face. "You don't think so now, but you will."

"I doubt it," I said. "But thanks for making the effort."

She scowled at me, halfheartedly, and I listened to her tiny feet patter back down the hallway to the stairs. Ashley had two weeks left in the bedroom beside mine, with a wall so thin between us that I always knew when she cried herself to sleep or had nightmares and tossed in her sleep. I knew a lot more about Ashley than she would have allowed me to if she could have controlled such things. There was a strange bond between us, however unintentional: the divorce, the wall, the years that separated us or didn't. My sister was leaving the house, and me, in just two weeks. And regardless of it all, good and bad, I would be sad to see her go.

The fitting that afternoon went the way they all had. I stood on a chair while Mrs. Bella Tungsten, seamstress, crawled around on the floor beneath me with a mouthful of pins, mumbling through her teeth to "Stand still, please." She wore a measuring tape around her neck that she could brandish in a second, slapping it against my skin or around my waist with one flick of her wrist. This was the fourth and final fitting, and we all knew Mrs. Bella Tungsten a little better than we'd ever thought we would.

"I have never in all my life seen a child grow so fast." That was Mrs. Bella, tape in hand, tugging at the hem of my dress. "It's gonna have to be shorter on her than on the rest. That's all I can say."

"How much shorter?" My mother got up from the one good chair in Dillard's fitting room and came over to inspect for herself. "Noticeably?"

Mrs. Bella tugged again, trying to make length where there wasn't any to be found. "There's nothing I can do. I can't let the dress down."

Ashley sighed loudly from the corner of the room, where one of Mrs. Bella's assistants was unfurling her train, her arms full of white, silky fabric.

My mother shot Ashley a look and squatted down beside Mrs. Bella, staring at my hemline. "No one will be looking at the bottoms of the dresses, anyway. Right?" She didn't sound so sure.

"Well," Mrs. Bella said slowly, spitting out a few pins, "I suppose. You can hope for that, at least."

Meanwhile I just stood there, arms crossed over my chest to hold the dress up, which was missing the zipper as well as the white ribbon edging and bow that Ashley had added to personalize the pattern. It was bad enough to be standing in Dillard's with my mother and Mrs. Bella tugging on my hemline and staring at my ankles; but the employee lounge was in the next room, so people kept passing through, carrying brown bags or cups of coffee and stopping on their way. They all knew Ashley, fellow employee, and stopped to coo and make a fuss over her and her dress. They just stared at me, the giant on the chair, too tall for the pretty pink bridesmaid dress that would now make me look like I was expecting a flood, not falling gracefully across my ankles as originally planned. I just stared ahead at a clock over the water fountain and pretended I was someplace, anyplace, else.

"Okay, Heaven honey, drop your arms so I can check this bodice." Mrs. Bella had been corrected several times about my name, to no avail. It was one detail too many to keep straight.

I dropped my arms and she slapped the tape across my chest, then pulled it around to the side. Her hands were dry and cold, and I felt goose bumps immediately spring up and spread, my snap reaction to any contact with Mrs. Bella. She was my mother's age but already had that thick, musty smell of old women and old clothes. She dragged a stepstool around to stand on and climbed up to inspect the tape.

"I do believe there must be tallness somewhere in your family, Mrs. McPhail," she said as she pulled the tape tighter, then let it drop. "Or maybe on your husband's side?"

"No," my mother said in the light voice she used whenever she wanted to encourage something to pass, "not really."

"It has to come from somewhere, right, Heaven?" She pulled a pincushion from her pocket and fastened the back of the dress, inserting one pin after the other.

"It's Haven," my mother said gently, trying to get me to look at her so that I could see her please-be-patient expression. I kept my eyes on the clock, on the second hand jumping around the face, and concentrated on time passing.

"Oh, right," Mrs. Bella said. "It's probably one of those—what do they call them, recessive genes? Only pops up every other generation or so."

My mother murmured softly, trying to move Mrs. Bella along. Ashley was walking around the room in her dress and bare feet while the assistant followed, fixing the train behind her. More employees were passing through now, with the clock nearing twelve-thirty. I could feel my face getting red. I felt gargantuan, my head almost brushing the ceiling, my arms dragging past Mrs. Bella to the pins on the floor. I had that image of pulling down the banners in the center court of the mall again, my hands clutching the fabric as it billowed before me. I imagined myself monsterlike, plodding like Godzilla through the aisles of Dillard's, searching out Mrs. Bella with her pin-filled mouth and recessive genes and hoisting her above my head in one fist, triumphant. I envisioned myself cutting a swath of destruction across the mall, across town itself, exacting revenge on everyone who stared at me or made the inevitable basketball jokes like I hadn't heard one ever before. My mind was soaring, filled with these images of chaos and revenge, when Mrs. Bella's voice cut through: "Okay, honey, the back's unpinned. With a little creative sewing I think we can get this dress to look right on you."

I looked down to see Ashley below me in her own dress, a vision of white fabric and tan skin, her face turned upward, hand clamping her headpiece. "Just don't grow for two weeks," she said to me, half-serious. "As a favor to me."

"Ashley!" my mother said, suddenly fed up with everyone. "Get out of the dress, Haven, and we'll go to lunch."

I went to change and slipped off the dress, careful not to stab myself with any of the hundreds of pins in the fabric. I put on my clothes and brought the dress out folded over my arm, handing it back to Mrs. Bella, who was now absorbed in sticking pins into Ashley, who deserved it. We left her standing there in all her white, as if waiting to be placed in the whipped-creamy center of a cake.

We had to eat at the mall, so we chose Sandwiches N' Such, which was a little place by Yogurt Paradise that sold fancy sandwiches and espresso and had little tables with white-and-red-checked tablecloths, like you were in Italy. We sat in the far corner, with the espresso machine sputtering behind us.

We didn't talk much at first. I ate my tuna fish on wheat and looked out at the crowd walking underneath the fluttering banners of the mall. My mother picked at her food, not eating so much as moving things from side to side. Something was bothering her.

"What's wrong?"

As soon as I asked she looked up at me, surprised. She'd never been comfortable with how easily I could read her, preferring to think she could still fool me by covering what was awful or scary with the sweep of her hand, the way she chased monsters out from under my bed when I was little.

"Well," she said, shifting in her chair, "I guess I just wanted a little time alone with you to take stock."

"Stock of what?" I concentrated on my food, picking around the mushy parts.

"Of us. You know, once the wedding is over and Ashley moves out, it's just going to be the two of us. Things will be different." She was working up to something. "I've thought a lot about this and it's best, I think, if I kept you apprised of what's happening. I don't want to make any major decisions without consulting you, Haven."

This tone, this jumble of important-sounding words, seemed too much like the kitchen-table talk we'd gotten the morning my father moved out. They'd come to us together, while I was eating my cereal, a united front announcing a split. That had been a long time ago, before my mother bought all her matching shorts-and-sandals sets and my father sprung new hair, a new wife, and a new beginning. But the feeling in my stomach was the same.

"Are you going to Europe?" I asked her.

"I don't know yet," she said. "I really want to go, but I'm worried about leaving you alone so soon after your sister moves out. And of course the fall, with you in school . . . the timing just isn't so good."

"I'd be okay," I said, watching a baby at the table next to us drooling juice all over himself. "If you want to go, you should go." I felt bad for not meaning this, even as I said it.

"Well, as I said, I haven't decided." She folded her napkin, over once and then again: a perfect square. "But there is something else I need to discuss with you."

"What?"

She sighed, placed the napkin in the dead even center of her plate, and said quickly, "I'm thinking about selling the house."

The moment she said it a picture of our house jumped into my head like a slide jerking up onto a screen during a school presentation. I saw my room and my mother's garden and the walk to the front door with day lilies blooming on either side. In my mind it was always summer, with the grass short and thick and the garden in full color, flowers waving in the breeze.

"Why?"

The hard part, the spitting out part, was done and now she relaxed. "Well, it's only going to be the two of us, and it would be cheaper if we moved somewhere smaller. We could find a nice apartment, probably, and save money. The house is really too big for just two people. We can't possibly fill it. Selling just seems like the logical choice."

"I don't want to move," I said a bit too loudly, and I was surprised at the sharp tone in my voice. "I can't believe you want to sell it."

"It's not a question of wanting to, necessarily. You don't know how expensive it is to keep it up, month after month. I'm only thinking of the best plan."

"I don't like the best plan." I didn't like any of it, suddenly, the changes and reorganizations and alterations to my life that were all in the control of other people and outside forces. I looked at my mother in her nice pink outfit and lipstick and Lydia-inspired frosted-and-cut hair and wanted to blame her for everything: the divorce and stupid Lewis and Ashley's wedding and even the height that set me to stooping and scrunching myself ever smaller, fighting nature's making my body betray me. But as I looked at her, at the concern in her face, I said none of this. I would push it back again, dig my heels into where I stood while the world shifted around me, what I'd considered givens suddenly lost to someone else's mistakes, miscalculations, or whims. A marriage, a sister, a house, each an elemental part of me, now gone.

"Haven, none of this is decided yet," my mother said, reaching across the table awkwardly to brush back my hair, her fingers smoothing my cheek. "Let's not get upset, okay? Maybe we can work something out."

"I'm sorry," I said, thinking of the tether again, pulling me back even as I strained to get away, to speak my mind. "I didn't mean to snap at you."

She smiled. "It's okay. I think we should all be allowed to yell at each other, at least once, before the wedding. It would probably do us all a lot of good."

Later, after we'd made small talk so that she could feel we'd ended on a good note, I sat alone at the table and stared out into the mall, putting off going to work. The Lakeview Models would make their first appearance the next weekend, kicking off the official start of mall season, each weekend an event or sales spectacular. It was a whole world, the mall, enclosed and safe, parameters neatly marked. Only Sumner seemed out of bounds, cruising in his golf cart wherever he pleased, keeping the peace and dodging the crowds. As I left I could see him over by the giant gumball machine, uniform on, looking official. He saw me and came over, leaving his cart safely parked by a row of ferns.

"You look upset," he observed, dropping into step beside me. His uniform cuffs rolled over his feet and hid his shoes.

"Well, it's been a long day," I said.

"What happened?" He waved at the owner of Shirts Etc., a round woman with jet black hair that had to be a wig. Her bangs were too neat, clipped straight across her forehead.

"I just had lunch with my mother."

"And how is she?"

"Fine. She's going to Europe." I was walking as slowly as I could, with the Little Feet sign looming up ahead.

The words were spelled out in shoes, just like on the boxes and the name tag in my pocket, which I would wait until the last possible second to put on.

"I love Europe," Sumner said, adjusting his glasses. "I went my sophomore year and had a grand time. Lots of pretty girls, if you don't mind underarm hair."

"Did you?"

"Did I what?"

"Mind underarm hair?"

He thought for a minute. "No. Not especially. But it depended on my mood and the extent of the hair itself. They have great chocolate in Europe, too. You should ask your mom to bring you some."

"I think we're going to move," I said, trying out the words for the first time. It felt strange. Again I saw my house, my room, the flowers. Maybe we'd end up in an apartment like Ashley's, all white paint and new carpet smell, with a splashing pool within earshot.

"Move where?" Now Sumner was waving at all the merchants. A few days on the job and he already knew everyone, exchanging inside jokes and winks as we passed each store. Again I felt that dizzying rush: of being with him, close to him, being taken along for the ride regardless of where he might be going; that hope that maybe somewhere in all this madness and confusion, he was the one who could understand me.

"My mother doesn't know," I said. "She just wants to sell the house."

"Oh." He nodded but didn't say anything right away. "That's tough."

"It's only 'cause of the divorce and Ashley moving

out," I said. "Just the two of us now, and all that. I don't know. Things have been so nuts lately."

"Yeah," he said. "When my parents got divorced it was really ugly. Everyone was fighting and I couldn't deal with it. I just packed up my car and took off. I didn't even know where I was going."

"How old were you?"

"I don't know . . . eighteen? It was the summer before I went to college. I just traveled around doing my thing, and by the time I got back everything had calmed down a little bit. And then I went off to college."

"I wish I could go somewhere," I said.

"I know what you mean. Sometimes, it just gets to be too much." Then he added, "Did you tell Ashley you saw me?"

"Yeah." I still had my mother on my mind, the house and the move and Europe all jumbled, and suddenly here Ashley was, the center of attention again. "I told her."

"What'd she say?"

I looked at him, wondering what was at stake here, then said, "She didn't say much. She's got a lot on her mind now."

"Oh, yeah." He shrugged it off. "Well, sure. I just wondered if she remembered me, you know. If she ran screaming from the room at the mention of my name."

"Nothing that dramatic," I said. "She just . . . she said to say hello if I saw you again."

"Really?" He was surprised. "Wow."

"I mean, it was casual and all," I said quickly, worried that this little lie might carry more weight than I meant it to. I couldn't tell him how she'd hardly blinked, hanging over the porch with her hair shielding her face. How it had barely jarred her mind from the wedding and Lewis and even the smallest thought she might have been thinking. No one wants to be inconsequential.

"Oh, I know," he said. "I just wondered if she even remembered me."

"She does," I said as we came up on Little Feet, with sneakers bobbing on fishing line in the window and paper fish I'd made myself stuck to the wall behind them. "You're not so forgettable."

"Yeah, well. I don't know about that." He stopped at the door to the store, sweeping his arm. "And here we are."

"Yeah." I looked in to see my manager folding socks. When he saw me he took a not so subtle look at the clock, craning his long, rubbery neck. I hated my job. "You know you could always drop in at Dillard's and see her. She works at the Vive cosmetics counter."

He smiled. "I don't think that's such a great idea. There's no telling what might happen when she saw me."

My manager was watching me, folding sock over sock. "You could at least say hello. I mean, it wasn't like you ever did anything to *her*."

Sumner looked up. He stared at me as if my face was changing before him, and then said slowly, "Well, no. I guess not. Look, I better go, Haven. I've got to get back to work."

"Me too." I pulled out my name tag and put it on, fastening the clip. "Think about it, Sumner. It's not like she ever hated you." I didn't know why this was so important to me; maybe I thought he could bring back the Ashley I liked so much, the one who liked me. Maybe Sumner's magic could work on both of us again.

He started to back away, hands in his pockets. He looked smaller to me now, lost in the green of his uniform. "Yeah. I'll see you later."

I stood there and watched him walk away, still stalling for time while the second hand of the store clock jumped closer and closer to two o'clock. The mall was noisy and busy now, with people and voices and colors all jumbled together, another Saturday of shopping and families and bright red plastic Lakewood Mall bags. Still I kept my eye on Sumner as he waded through the throngs past the potted plants and swaying banners overhead. He'd been where I was, once; he understood. I watched him go until he was lost to me, another green in a sea of multicolors, shifting.

Chapter Eight

⁓

In the time that she'd been home, Casey had managed not only to be grounded for smoking, but also to get caught making hour-long interstate calls to Pennsylvania, drinking a beer behind the garden shed during a family barbecue, and disappearing for an entire day. Mrs. Melvin was exhausted and sick of Casey's face, so she granted her a leave of two hours to come to see me, provided she called in every half hour and got home by six. She arrived two seconds after inviting herself over, breathless.

"My mom wants to kill me," she said as we set out

for a walk around the neighborhood and a chance to talk in private. "I heard her and my dad discussing my situation last night, on the back porch."

"And she said she wanted to kill you?"

"No, she said she was beginning to think the only solution was to lock me in my room." She pushed a mass of orange curls out of her face. "But then she lets me out today. I think she's up to something."

"You're paranoid," I told her.

"Last night when I called Rick he said he was getting it from his parents, too. He can't call for a while." She sighed, crossing her arms against her shirt, a long white polo ten sizes too big. I wondered if Rick had any clothes of his own left. I imagined him leaving 4-H camp naked, with Casey packing up everything he owned as a souvenir.

"It's only till Thanksgiving," I said, trying to be helpful. It hadn't happened to me yet, this swirling mass of emotions that made all the women around me behave so erratically.

"Thanksgiving is forever away," she whined as we took the corner and headed down the street parallel to our own. "I'm going nuts here and it's been less than a week. I've got to find some way to get up there."

"Get up where?"

She rolled her eyes. "Pennsylvania. God, Haven, aren't you paying attention?"

"Not when you start talking like a crazy person. You don't even drive yet."

"I will, in two and a half weeks." With the wedding so close, I'd forgotten her birthday was coming up. "Dad's been taking me out every night to drive around and I know they're going to give me my grandmother's Delta 88. They think it's a secret and I don't know why it's in the garage, but I know."

"Even if you are about to get your license," I said as a mass of kids on bikes passed us, all of them in helmets and knee pads, little punks terrorizing the neighborhood, "they'd never let you take off to Pennsylvania."

"Of course they wouldn't let me." She said this matter-of-factly, as if I was slow and just not getting it. Since Casey had gone wild at 4-H camp, it seemed like we had less and less in common. "But that doesn't mean I can't go. I just slip out, see, in the middle of the night, and call them the next morning when I'm in, like, Maryland. By then they're just so crazed with worry they're just happy I'm alive, so they let me go on. Then I come back and get punished forever but it's worth it because I get to be with Rick."

I looked at her. "That will never work."

She stuck out her bottom lip, something she'd gotten good at in the last week, and said, "Yes it will."

"Oh, like Rick's parents wouldn't send you home the second you showed up. They're not going to let you just hang out while your parents are sitting around here waiting for you to get home so they can kill you."

She was staring at the sidewalk as I said this, making a point of not looking at me. After a minute she said in a tight voice, "You don't understand, Haven. You couldn't. You've never been in love."

"Oh please," I said, suddenly fed up. I was sick of hearing about Rick and Pennsylvania and camp stories.

I couldn't talk to anyone anymore. Sumner seemed like the only one who listened at all, the only one who asked for nothing and took nothing from me.

"You know what your problem is," Casey began, her hand poised to shake at me, but then she stopped dead, sucking in her breath. She grabbed my shirt, tugging, and pointed across one of the yards.

It was Gwendolyn Rogers. Or at least the back of Gwendolyn Rogers. Her hair was pulled up in a high ponytail and she was wearing a black string bikini top, standing there in the backyard all by herself. She had her hands on her hips and was staring off across the yard, over the wall and into the next yard. She was standing very, very still.

I heard a woman's voice, suddenly, wafting out from the open downstairs windows of the house. "Gwendolyn? Gwennie, are you down here? Gwendolyn?" It was a mother's voice.

Gwendolyn didn't move, so still and tall, so much like the trees around her. She was enormous, and for the first time in so long I felt small, no bigger than a minute.

Casey was still pulling on my shirt, pointing like I hadn't seen anything and saying, "That's her, God, Haven, *look*."

I was looking. And listening to Mrs. Rogers's voice as it moved past one window after another, growing louder, then fading. Finally she came out on the back porch, where we could only see the top of her head over the wall, being that she was normal sized. Softly, she said, "Gwendolyn?" The top of her head moved across the yard, until it was flush with the middle of Gwendo-lyn's spine. I saw a hand come up, tiny, and take one of the long, thin arms. "Let's go in, honey, okay? Maybe you should lie down for a little while."

Her voice was very clear and soft, the kind you hear at your bedside when you're sick and throwing up and your mother brings cold compresses and ginger ale and oyster crackers. Mrs. Rogers rubbed her hand up and down Gwendolyn's arm, talking now in a low voice that I couldn't make out; but Gwendolyn didn't move a mus-cle. Finally, Gwendolyn turned. I saw her face then, the same one we'd seen on all those magazine covers and on MTV. But it wasn't the same: it wasn't bronzed, with pink lips and lashes a mile long; no hair blowing back in the wind, framing her face; no diamonds flashing out of the wild blue of her eyes. Instead, I saw just a tall girl with a blank, plain expression, thin and angular and lost. Her cheeks were hollow and her mouth small, not luscious, more like a slit drawn hastily with a marker or a child's crayon. I don't know if she saw us. She was looking our way, her eyes on us, but there was no way of telling what she saw. It could have been us or the trees behind us or maybe another place or faces of other people. She only looked at us for a few moments, with that haunted, gaunt expression before her mother prodded her along and she ducked into the doorway, vanishing.

"Did you see her?" Casey was standing in their yard now, craning her head to get a look inside. "God, can you believe it? She looks horrible."

"We should go," I said, now aware that they could

be in any of those windows, watching us. It seemed like too small a house to hold someone so big, like a doll's house with tiny plates and newspapers.

I practically had to drag Casey down the sidewalk. She was sure Gwendolyn was going to make another appearance, or burst out the door for another hysterical walk through the neighborhood.

"Come on," I said, then gave up trying to move her forcibly and just took off myself, much the way I always did when she was doing something that could get us both in trouble.

She came along, complaining all the way. "If we'd stayed, she might have come out and talked to us. She's probably lonely."

"She doesn't even know us," I said as we turned back onto our street. Mrs. Melvin's flag, emblazoned with a strawberry, flapped in the breeze a few houses down. The bike gang passed again, this time in the street, yelling and shooting us the finger. They were all elementary school kids.

"She knows we feel her pain," said Casey, who suddenly had personal insight into this herself. "I know what it feels like."

"You do not," I said as we came up to the Melvins' house. "All you know is loving some dumb guy in Pennsylvania."

"Love is love is love," Casey said, stubborn. "We women know."

We were passing her house anyway, so Casey stopped for the first half-hour check. Mrs. Melvin was in the kitchen, making some kind of fancy meal that required the peeling of an eggplant. Baby Ronald was at the kitchen table eating baloney slices and playing with his Star Trek action figures.

"Just to let you know I haven't run off to Pennsylvania," Casey said, heading straight to the fridge. The room smelled like burnt rice. I could hear Charlie Baker, news anchorman, talking about national affairs from the small TV that sat on the counter by the bananas.

"Not funny." Mrs. Melvin put down the eggplant, which was a sickly brown color without its purple skin. "Don't forget we have dinner at six-fifteen. It's family night."

Casey pulled out two cans of Diet Pepsi and made a face at me. "God, how much time do I have to spend with you guys, anyway?"

Mrs. Melvin went back to the eggplant, her mouth in that tight little line that meant she was cranky. "I'm not in the mood to answer that question."

"Hey, baby Ronald," I said, pulling out a chair and sitting down across from him.

He scowled, wrinkling his nose. Freckles folded in, then out. "Shut up."

"Ronald," Mrs. Melvin snapped. "That's rude."

"I'm not a baby," he protested.

"Yes you are," Casey said.

"Well, you're in trouble," Ronald said indignantly, slapping a piece of baloney on the table and marching a Klingon across it.

"And you're stupid," Casey said. "So stuff it."

"Casey," Mrs. Melvin said in a tired voice, "please."

I turned my attention back to the TV, where I could

see the entire Action News Team paired off at their two sets of desks. Charlie Baker and Tess Phillips on one side, grimly shuffling papers as we came back from a commercial; and off to the other, my father and Lorna, smiling and whispering to each other. My father had even more hair than the last time I'd seen him. He'd never had that much, even when I was little. Lorna was beside him, hands crossed on the desk in front of her.

"And now for the weather, let's check in with Lorna Queen's Weather Scene," Charlie Baker boomed in his big voice while the camera panned across to Lorna's smiling face. She stood up, today in a hot-pink miniskirt and jacket, and strolled over to the weather map.

"Thanks, Charlie. Today was gorgeous, right, folks? I wish I could tell you there was more of the same coming, but we haven't quite gotten over the heat yet. Let's take a look at the national map. You'll see that a front is moving over the mid-Atlantic states, producing some heavy showers. . . ."

I tuned Lorna out, instead watching her gesture her way across the fifty states, sweeping her arm over the map as if she could create showers or drought on a whim. I wondered if anyone ever really listened to her at all.

Now she was standing in front of the Five Day Forecast. ". . . right up until Tuesday, but I've got to say I can't promise much for Wednesday through Friday. Look for some high cloud cover, the normal afternoon thunderstorm, and of course high temperatures and Charlie's favorite, lots of humidity. Right, Charlie?"

The camera panned back to Charlie, who was caught playing with his pencil and mumbled something quickly before it zoomed back to Lorna. Now she was standing in front of a video of a bunch of children chasing bunny rabbits across the grass. "And finally, I just wanted to thank all the kids at the Little Ones day-care center, where I went today to do a Weather Scene Class. We talked about rain and snow and had some fun with the bunnies they have there, as you can see. Great kids." She waved at the camera. "A special hello to all of them. Thanks for having me!"

"Good God," Casey said dramatically, rolling her eyes.

"Casey," Mrs. Melvin said, throwing the peeler in the sink.

"I'm just saying."

Lorna was done waving now and took her seat next to my father again. Charlie Baker shuffled his papers around, looking official, and then said, "Thanks, Lorna. I'm looking forward to that humidity you promised me."

"A little late to get in on that joke," Casey said. "He's such a cheeseball."

Tess Phillips leaned across Charlie Baker, smiling her newswoman smile. "And I understand you have a special report of your own over there, Lorna."

Lorna blushed, pinkly, and I got that sinking feeling in my stomach again. "Well, yes, both Mac and I do. Right, honey?"

"That's right," my father said. He seemed bigger with all that hair.

"We're expecting!" Lorna squealed. "I'm due in March!"

On the television, in the Action News newsroom, there was an explosion of congratulations, slapping of backs, and general good spirits. In the Melvins' kitchen it was too quiet and everyone was suddenly looking at me.

"Expecting?" Casey said. "How is that possible? The wedding was less than a month ago; there's no way she could already be pregnant. Unless it happened *before*, but . . ."

"Casey," Mrs. Melvin said in a low voice. "Hush."

I stared at my father on the screen, watching him smile proudly at the viewing public before they cut to a commercial. Suddenly I wanted to go home.

"God, Haven. Why didn't you tell me?" Casey was standing behind me now, her hand on the back of my chair.

"Look, I better get going." I kept my eyes on the commercial for satellite dishes. Baby Ronald stomped his figures across the table, staging a war by the sugar bowl.

"I'll walk you," Casey said.

"No," I said quickly. "That's all right. I'll call you later."

"You okay?"

I could feel Mrs. Melvin, mouth of the neighborhood, watching me and taking notes for the next neighborhood gossip session. "Fine. I just forgot I had to be home."

"Okay, well, call me." She walked me to the door, holding it open as I stepped out onto the patio. "Seriously. I'm like a prisoner here." Mrs. Melvin still had her eyes on me, eggplant in her hand.

"I'll call." I started down the driveway, sucking in the thick, humid air of late summer, heavy in my lungs.

It was late afternoon and all the kids were out, bike punks and Big Wheels, and mothers with strollers grouped on the corner, no doubt passing the latest about nervous breakdowns and tuna casseroles and failing marriages, the goods on the neighborhood. I made it to the end of the driveway and hit the sidewalk, feeling each step in my shins as if by the sheer force of pounding my feet on the ground I could force the world out from under me.

As I walked I kept seeing my father in my mind, with his hair and that smile, proud and bursting, father-to-be. Lorna Queen with her little ears and blond hair. A baby with my father's round face and my last name. My father's new life was progressing as planned, one neat step at a time. And I felt it, again, that same feeling I got whenever another change or shift in my life was announced to me—selling the house, Ashley's tantrums, now the baby—that need to dig in my heels and prepare myself for the *next* shock and its aftermath. I was tired of hanging on, taking the torn pieces to make something whole with them.

I stopped suddenly, breathless, unsure of where I was. The houses in my neighborhood all looked the same, one floor plan reversed and then back again. More kids on bikes, more mothers on corners, flags with watermelon and sunshine designs hanging from front porches. I could have lived in any of these houses. Any of these families could have been mine, once.

The tight, throbbing feeling in my throat made me want to start sobbing, to break down, right there on an unfamiliar corner in front of a house just like my own.

Everything seemed so out of control, as if even running the streets wouldn't save me. I wondered if this was how Gwendolyn felt running wild at night, this lost, loose feeling that no consequence could be so harmful as the sense of staying where you were, or of being who you are. I wanted to be somewhere else, out of the range of my mother's voice and ears, of Ashley's pouty looks, of the News Channel 5 viewing area. Someplace where the sight of me sobbing would tie me to no one and no one to me.

I was going to let it happen, let the tears come and the sobs rise up from my chest. I imagined crying until I was exhausted, dry, finally letting it all go.

And then I heard that *blub-blub-blub* puttering around the corner where I stood. Sumner was behind the wheel, so busy adjusting the stereo that he didn't even see me at first. Just as I thought to call his name he glanced over his shoulder.

He backed up beside me, smoothly aligning with the curb. The passenger seat was filled with books, heavy black volumes with gold monograms. "Hey, Haven. What's going on?"

Even as he spoke I was doing it, breathing in and clearing my head, swallowing until the lump in my throat disappeared. Digging my heels in again, regulating myself. "Nothing," I said.

"Need a ride?" He started pushing books into the back.

"Sure." I climbed in and we were off, puttering along the short distance to my house, passing the Rogerses', familiar territory. Sumner pulled off his tie and reached across me to stuff it in the glove compartment.

"So," he said after a while. "What's wrong?"

"Nothing," I said. "It's just . . . my father and his new wife are going to have a baby."

"A baby?"

"Yeah. They just got married."

He smiled. "Wow. They didn't waste any time, huh?"

"I guess not," I said. "I mean, it's like this just makes it official. My father has completely begun his life over." We passed the Melvins', where baby Ronald was playing on the steps.

"Well, maybe he is. And that sucks. But it doesn't mean he's forgetting you or anything," he said, tapping his fingers against the steering wheel. "It'll work out, Haven. This is the worst of it."

I knew he was probably right. It seemed like every time I saw Sumner lately I was reacting to a crisis. And every time, he said the one thing, the *right* thing, that no one else could say.

"So," I asked him, "what are you doing around these parts?"

"Selling encyclopedias. It's a new job. My first day, actually."

"Did you sell any?"

"No, but three people invited me in for soda. One of them was really old, too old for encyclopedias, but we looked at all her photo albums and talked about the war."

"I didn't think you could ever be too old for encyclopedias," I said.

"Maybe not," he said, "but according to my marketing manual eighty-five-year-old widows with ten cats and a houseful of dusty antiques are not writing a lot of term papers. Heard some great war stories, though. There's nothing like a good war story."

He slowed down; we were coming to my house. Ashley was walking up the front steps, still in her work clothes. She wore that damn lab coat everywhere.

We pulled up to the curb just as she got to the door, but she was digging for her keys and didn't notice us. She didn't remember the sound of the car the way I did. I wondered how she could ever have forgotten, but Ashley was always good at that.

We watched her fumbling in her purse, which was balanced against her knee. She brushed her hair impatiently out of her face, then tucked it behind her ear. Under her lab coat she had on a red dress that showed off her tan and wore black sandals over her tiny little feet. I thought again of her Barbie adolescence and how I'd envied her, and I looked at Sumner, at the expression I couldn't read on his face. I wondered how she looked to him, if she was older or fatter or just the same as that last time he saw her on the porch, when she put a door between him and herself. Finally she found her keys, opened the door, and kicked it shut behind her, rattling the glass. I still hadn't gotten out of the car.

"Do you want to come in?" I asked him.

"Oh no," he said. "I have to get to work."

"At the mall?"

"No." He shifted in his seat, reaching behind to pull out a stack of records: Lawrence Welk, Jimmy Dorsey, the Andrews Sisters. "I'm getting fifty bucks to dance with old women at the senior center. They're having a nostalgia dance but they're short on men. I'm not supposed to tell them I'm getting paid, though. It would ruin the spirit of it all."

"You dance?"

He sighed. "Sure. My mother thought she was Ginger Rogers. Didn't Ashley tell you? I taught her every dance she knows."

"I didn't even know Ashley could dance."

"You should see her waltz," he said, putting the records back behind the seat. "She's incredible. Of course, she always wanted to lead. She's not much of a follower, you know."

"I know." I wondered if Ashley was looking out at us. "You sure you don't want to come in? My mom would love to see you."

"Nah," he said, shaking his head. "Not now. I gotta go."

I got out of the car, shutting the door behind me. "Thanks for the ride."

"Well, you didn't have far to go."

"No. But it was nice anyway."

" 'Bye, Haven. Hang in there." He started the engine and the blubbing built to a noisy peak before leveling off steady. I stood on the curb, watching him drive away, and just as he turned the corner I thought of my father and Lorna again, and the baby with its tiny ears. Even Sumner and his jobs and jokes couldn't make some things go away.

Chapter Nine

⌒

That *weekend was* the official premiere of the Lakeview Models in the annual Back to School Fall Preview Fashion Show. The name had been changed, however, to the Back to School Fall Preview Fashion Show Featuring a Special Appearance by Former Lakeview Model Gwendolyn Rogers; someone had gone around with a magic marker and added on to all the signs. I wondered how Gwendolyn was feeling, if she was still out staring in her backyard or pacing the neighborhood in the wee hours of the morning, or if she even cared about the Lakeview Models at all, in the midst of her rumored nervous breakdown. I'd been thinking about Gwendolyn Rogers a lot lately as I sat awake in my own bed, staring at the ceiling and wondering what could happen next. Sometimes I even listened for the sound of her feet on the pavement outside, the rustle of her passing, the shallow breaths I imagined of someone gone wild. I was sure I'd heard her, at least once.

The whole town turned out for the Fall Fashion Preview that Saturday; but since most people were not interested in buying children's shoes, Marlene and I took turns walking down to the main stage and reporting back on the activity. In the early part of the morning, there was a great racket of chairs being set up and people shouting to each other. Around noon, the models arrived and began to get ready in the store that had been Holland Farms Cheeses and Gifts until it had just recently gone out of business. Now it had a sign in the front window that read Model Prep Area, with the words Authorized Persons Only, Please written in firm little letters beneath it. They were in there, cooing and giggling. You could hear them from outside, where all the younger girls and those who hadn't made it were grouped, trying to catch a glimpse of Gwendolyn or the models or anyone even slightly related to the whole process. And of course Sumner was there in his uniform, carrying a clipboard and looking official.

I was off for the day at one-thirty because I had the early shift, so I got to see the entire production. Casey and I met by the stage and took seats in the back, behind the mothers of the models and the screaming children that fill the mall every day and all the people with cameras out to get a good shot of Gwendolyn Rogers, Supermodel.

"I can't tell you how I've been dying to get out of the house," Casey said as we sat down. She was in another big shirt, this time an old rugby with worn elbows. "My mother is driving me nuts. She won't let me near the phone or out the door without giving me the third degree, and I know she's been in my room." I was watching the stage as she spoke, which now had two white partitions covering the big leaves I'd seen a few weeks ago.

"You can't tell," I said.

"Yes I can, because I set traps for her." She crossed her arms against her chest, triumphant. "I left a hair shut in my dresser drawer and in the latch of the box I keep all my important stuff in, and when I checked after coming home the other day they were both gone."

I looked at her. "Hairs?"

"I saw it in a movie." She flipped her hair and rolled her eyes, a combination of moves she'd picked up at camp along with all her other bad habits. "It's drastic, I know, but something had to be done."

"But she still went through your stuff," I told her. "It's not stopping her, it's just proving the fact."

"Right. And I have ammunition when I accuse her of invading my privacy. I'll tell her I can prove it and then watch her squirm." She sighed. "It'll be ugly, but like I said, there's no love in war."

"It's not really a war, Casey."

"It's close to it. You know Rick's parents won't even

let him talk to me anymore? Every time I call they say he's busy or at practice or something. I haven't talked to him in a week."

"He hasn't called you?"

"He probably has and my parents don't tell me. I swear to it, Haven, they want me miserable. They hate Rick and they haven't even met him." Behind us some baby started howling.

It was amazing what a summer could do. Before camp my best friend, Casey Melvin, was a short, pudgy redhead who hung back at introductions, couldn't look a boy in the eye, and spent every Sunday afternoon taking tap-dancing lessons with her mother. Now she was at war with her parents, angry at the world in general, and more than a little bit paranoid. I wondered if the summer had changed me, if with one look the world could see a difference.

"Ladies and gentlemen, on behalf of the Lakeview Mall I would like to welcome you to the annual Fall Fashion Preview!" Everyone looked around for the source, since in years before, the show had relied on a woman with a loud voice to yell the commentary from side stage. The voice came from a speaker mounted on a plant right behind us: the Lakeview Mall had gone high tech. "And to begin our festivities, we have a very special guest. Please give a big welcome to our very own former Lakeview Mall Model and hometown girl, Gwendolyn Rogers!"

Now everyone looked at the stage, apparently thinking Gwendolyn would suddenly pop out of nowhere like the voice had, and there she was, tall and haunting, walking slowly up the center aisle as heads turned, row by row.

She looked terrible, her face gaunt, the famous Gwendolyn lips that pursed out from all those magazine pages now slack and thin, her hair lying flat on her head, even a bit stringy. She was wearing a short skirt and a silk tank top that was wrinkled, with sandals that scraped against the floor with each step she took. But it was the walk that was the strangest, after seeing her striding down runway after runway in music videos and on television, her head held high and hips swaying to the music, eye on the camera, as if she knew how you envied her. Now she was tentative, taking light steps and holding herself tight even though she had the whole enormous aisle to spread out in. We were all applauding because we had to, but she seemed lost and uncomfortable, and when she reached the bottom stair that led to the stage I felt myself let loose a breath, relieved she had made it. The applause died out as Gwendolyn climbed the steps. The official Lakeview Mall greeter was waiting with her clipboard. She had been beaming, but suddenly her smile died and she squinted at Gwendolyn uncertainly, as if expecting her to collapse on the spot.

The emcee shook her hand and led her to the podium. Gwendolyn, towering above her, stood behind the microphone and looked out at us with the same dim, lost look that I'd seen the other day. She cleared her throat once and then jumped a bit as the sound echoed from one speaker to another to another. I wondered if she was sedated.

"It's spooky," Casey whispered to me, and I nodded.

A woman in front of me said loudly, "She looks like she's on drugs or something. Damn good example to set for the kids here. She shouldn't even be on the stage."

"Hush," her friend said.

"I'm just saying," the woman replied, shifting in her chair. "And look at that hair."

We were all looking.

The emcee next to Gwendolyn stood on tiptoe and whispered something in her ear, but Gwendolyn's face never changed. She cleared her throat again, and we waited.

"Thank you for having me," she began slowly, and we all relaxed a bit. Things were going to be okay. "It's a real treat to be here overseeing a new generation of Lakeview Models."

The emcee began applauding, looking nervous, so we all joined in. Gwendolyn was still staring at the back of the mall.

The silence had gone on too long now. I wished for words to come from her mouth, any sound that might get her through this. Her hands were gripping the sides of the podium, the tips of her fingers white from the strain. It was as if the Gwendolyn we all knew and expected had been left behind on those glossy magazine pages—or had never existed at all. She opened her mouth, took in a breath; I closed my eyes until I heard her voice echo around me.

"So without further ado, let's begin this year's show." Her voice was flat, even, and as the woman ushered her off the stage to her seat of honor in the front row,

Gwendolyn ran her fingers over her long, stringy hair, obscuring her face as she passed by. Once seated, her head stuck up above the crowd, and I watched as the people behind her, no longer charmed, grumbled and rearranged themselves.

Suddenly there was a burst of music, so loud that a woman behind me actually shrieked. It was disco, a fast beat and lots of technological-sounding blips and beeps along with the occasional loud panting of a woman's voice. We all stared up at the stage, waiting for something while the music pounded on behind us. Then, the partitions slowly parted (with the help of Sumner and some other guy in a uniform, who tried hard to stay out of sight), revealing the leaves I'd seen before. Now, however, there were lights spinning across them, blue and green and red and yellow, catching bits of glitter that I hadn't noticed until now. It was all a bit overwhelming, a definite change from the show of last year, which consisted of one lone ficus tree that the models walked by, posed around, and then pulled to the edge of the stage for the big finale, where they threw its leaves on the audience to symbolize fall. That fashion show had been the most innovative, until this year.

Suddenly, the music stopped, and the lights fell steady on the leaves, each a different color. The disembodied voice came again. "Ladies and gentlemen, please join the Lakeview Mall Models as we journey into fall. A fall of expectations . . . of new ideas . . . and of potential. Come, come with us . . ."

"Oh, for Christ's sake," someone behind us said loudly.

". . . to a world of color and style, of tweed and tartan, of reality and imagination. Close your eyes and feel the cool air, the sharp colors of the leaves, and the dreams of winter. Come, come, and journey with us . . . into the Fall of Fashion."

The lights started swirling again, the music came on full blast, and suddenly the models began to walk up on stage, each of them smiling big toothy smiles and vamping like nobody's business. The first was a girl in a beret who flounced out on the runway, tossed her hat in the air Mary Tyler Moore style, and just let it fall on some woman in the second row who looked like she wasn't quite sure whether to throw it back or keep it. Beret girl was replaced by a girl in a long tweed jacket who took it off and dragged it dramatically down the runway with such abandon that someone behind me began to speculate about the cost of dry-cleaning it. The next girl clomped down the runway in torn jeans and combat boots, tossing her hair and gyrating suggestively, grinning out at us. A group of older women, probably remembering the tame ficus-tree show of the previous year, made a big fuss of leaving in disgust.

It only got worse. The music switched to just a woman moaning, over and over again, and one girl actually came out in hip-length black leather boots, which sent a flurry of exclamations down the crowd and another set of people packing up and leaving. The models were oblivious, most of them making a point of playing specifically to Gwendolyn Rogers as if to prove they were just like her, real *models*. Gwendolyn's head, however, bowed forward, as if even watching was too much for her.

For the grand finale, which was always a showcase of evening wear for Christmas balls and dances, the models came out in tight black dresses and spike heels, with their hair pulled straight back and lips bright red, the rest of their faces white and pale as if they were very sick. They stopped to pose, waiting for the applause to thunder down upon them.

We applauded, those of us who were left, and watched as the director of the show, a young guy in a purple suit with a walkie-talkie in his hand, came up for his bow. I wondered if he realized that the entire board of the Lakeview Mall was probably waiting for him offstage, ready to wring his neck. When they brought Gwendolyn back up to address the models there weren't that many people left in the audience, which was probably a good thing.

They stuck Gwendolyn in the middle and the models giggled and panted and shuffled around to get closer, their lips red and bright. As the photographer took pictures, she was pale in the center, towering above them all with their black dresses and pulled-back hair, their pale skin and scary Halloween lips, looking down at them as they crowded in around her. And then, just as they were all saying cheese once more, smiling for the camera on their big day, Gwendolyn Rogers burst into tears.

No one knew how to react at first; she was just suddenly crying, tears running down her face as she stood there, surrounded by these girls who wanted to be just like her. The models moved away, uncertain, as if by proximity they could catch whatever she had, as if sorrow was infectious. No one did anything to help her.

Then I saw Mrs. Rogers; she was coming up the center aisle, her purse clutched against her hip, almost running but trying to look calm. She climbed the stairs and came up behind Gwendolyn, who was making little whimpering sounds that embarrassed me for her. I didn't even watch, focusing instead on a wad of gum that was stuck on the floor. I heard them passing: Mrs. Rogers's voice soothing and calm, saying, "All you need is rest, honey," and Gwendolyn's jarred and ragged, replying, "It's so awful, they just don't know how awful it is, those poor girls."

Casey watched them, attentive, then tapped my shoulder. "Let's get out of here."

I nodded and followed her, and we wove our way down the middle aisle, which was now suddenly crowded with models' mothers (most of whom were biting their lips and looking irritated), a few men in suits with strained looks (I was sure they had to be the contingent of mall management), and a bunch of women talking in hushed voices about how shocking it all was. I lost Casey in the blur of perfume and general mayhem, then found her waiting for me by a planter full of ferns.

"Can you believe that?" she asked me as we started walking down in the direction of Little Feet. "A total breakdown, right in the middle of the Fall Fashion Preview. She has to have totally lost it. She's nuts."

"God, Casey," I said, suddenly nervous that Gwendo-lyn was still in earshot. "She's sick."

"She's nuts, Haven," she said with authority, pulling out a pack of gum and offering me a piece. "Beautiful and nuts. What a combination."

We were coming up on Sumner now, who was busy talking with some woman who had a baby attached to her hip and a toddler linked to her wrist by one of those baby leashes. The kid was straining on it, yanking towards the toy store, but kept getting jerked back, losing his balance, and crashing to the floor. The mother was too busy fussing at Sumner to even notice.

"I'm not the kind of person who usually complains," she was saying as we got within earshot. "But I really feel like that was just a disgusting display and completely unnecessary. Those aren't the kind of clothes a girl would wear back to school. What happened to plaid jumpers? To tights and slacks? To those nice sweaters with the reindeer prints on them?"

"I don't know, ma'am," Sumner said in a deep voice. "I can't really say."

"Well, it just upsets me." She yanked on the leash, plopping the toddler, who had managed to make some headway, back to the floor again. "I feel like it just sends the wrong message, you know? I don't associate gyrating with homework, myself, and I don't think any other mother who spends money at this mall does, either."

"I completely understand," Sumner said, and then saw me and smiled. "I would suggest contacting mall management. I'm sure they'd be very concerned about what you're saying. Here's the number right here, or if you'd like to write a letter—"

"Yes, a letter might be better," she said. "It's always better to put it in writing, isn't it?"

"It is indeed." Sumner wrote something on a card and handed it to her. "That's the man to address, right there. In case you decide to call, he's not in on Tuesdays."

"Thank you." She put the card in her fanny pack and leaned over the toddler, who was now sitting on the floor eating a dirty candy wrapper. We watched as she got him to his feet, adjusted the baby to her other hip, and they walked off down the mall together, the leash hanging between them.

"Hey," Sumner said, coming over to us, "quite a show, huh?"

Casey was just staring at him, with a sudden sparkle in her eye that I didn't like, so I said, "Sumner, this is Casey. Casey, this is Sumner. He's an old—"

"Family friend," Sumner put in. "I like to think I'm more than just one among the crowd of Ashley's ex-boyfriends. I want to believe I made my mark."

"You did," I said. He had to know how important he was. "You were the best of all of them."

He laughed. "I wouldn't say that."

"How old are you?" Casey asked him, her head cocked to the side like she was Nancy Drew solving a mystery.

"Twenty-one," Sumner said, glancing down at his uniform. "And it shows, doesn't it?"

"Not really," Casey said, and her voice was different,

long and drawling. And I didn't like the way she was standing, either, all cutesy in her big shirt and cutoffs, smiling at Sumner like he was some guy at camp.

"Well, we better go," I said, wanting to move on. Suddenly I wasn't so sure I wanted to share Sumner with Casey, who saw boys only as people to take shirts from and pine for. I wasn't sure I wanted to share him with anyone. "I've got to get home."

"You do not," Casey said, using that same voice on me now, high and flirty. "God, Haven's always having to go home and do something, isn't she? She's such a good girl."

I looked at her. "I am not."

"Oh Gawd," she said, "honestly. Anyone looks bad compared to you, Little Miss Do Whatever Anyone Wants You To."

Sumner looked at me, then said, "Ah, but you do not know Haven as I do."

"I've known her all my life," Casey said, now smacking her gum, which she thought made her look cool (she was wrong), "and I know."

"She's a wild one," he said, grinning at me, making it up on the spot. I loved it, every bit. "Maybe sometime she'll tell you about it."

Casey looked at me, still smacking. "You must have the wrong girl, Sumner."

"Nope. That's her," he said, pointing at me as he turned to walk away. "I know. Take it easy, Haven. Nice to meet you."

"You too," Casey called after him, waggling her fingers. She waited for him to get lost in the crowd and then said, "Why didn't you tell me about him? He's so cute."

"He's just Sumner," I said. "He dated Ashley forever."

"Well, he's fine as hell," she said, using another expression she'd picked up at camp. "All this time you're after some guy at the mall and you didn't even tell me."

"It's not like that," I said.

"Why not? You should be after him, big time. He seems to like you already. Can you imagine, you dating a college boy? That would be so cool!"

"He's my friend," I said, amazed that Casey could take Sumner away from me and twist him into something else, something almost dirty. That wasn't what he was to me.

"Whatever," she said, still smacking her gum. "If it was me, I'd be after him."

"You don't understand," I said quietly, not wanting to talk about it anymore. Me and Sumner—that was ridiculous. He was Ashley's old boyfriend, for godsakes. And Casey didn't understand because she couldn't. She hadn't seen her whole life change in the last few years, hadn't had everything taken away. His reappearing was proof that the time I looked back to had actually happened. This summer, Sumner was just what I needed.

Chapter Ten

∽

The wedding countdown, suddenly reduced to single digits, continued. With eight days to go to The Big Day, Ashley had her bachelorette party, which allowed her a full week to recover from the night of drinking, giggling, and general secret activity that her friends had been planning since the engagement. I'd overheard my mother saying something to Lydia Catrell about strippers and tequila, but since I was underage. I went along for dinner and then was dropped off unceremoniously on my front lawn while the rest of the group sped off to places unknown. I watched television until late and fell asleep on the couch, remote still in my hand, then woke up when I heard scratching at the front door. The doorbell rang, a few times, among an explosion of giggling, the slamming of car doors, and a beeping horn. I opened the front door and found my sister splayed out on the porch, missing a shoe, wearing what appeared to be underwear around her neck, and mumbling.

"Ashley?" I wasn't quite sure what to do. "Are you okay?"

"Mmmhpgh." She rolled over so that she was flat on her back; her face was red. "Haven."

I leaned over her, smelled her breath, and then took a few steps back. Across the street, Duckdog started barking. "Yes?"

"Help me inside." She reached up, waving her arm at me crookedly. I grabbed it and pulled her over the threshold, bumping her head on the door. "Ouch," she whined. "That hurts."

"Sorry." We were inside now, so I dropped her arm and kicked the door shut. I felt sorry for her, lying on the floor with her head by the umbrella stand, so I pulled her a little farther to the base of the stairs and arranged her in a half-upright position. It *was* underwear around her neck, a pink pair. Not a girl's, either. She also had a collection of swizzle sticks poking out of her hair, all different colors. She tried to wipe her hand across her face, hit her nose, then left her hand there and whimpered softly.

It had been a long time since I'd seen Ashley drunk. In her wilder years, back in high school, she was always getting busted coming in past curfew with a mouthful of Certs and her speech slurred. My mother was never taken in. The next morning Ashley would be grounded with a hangover, and my mother would vacuum outside the bedroom door bright and early, making a point of banging the vacuum against the wall in an effort to get those hard-to-reach spots. I'd woken up more than once to the sound of Ashley getting sick in the bathroom at two A.M., which she thought she was so cleverly hiding by running the shower and the exhaust fan. My parents were never fooled, not even for a minute. They locked their liquor cabinet and did a sniff test every night and eventually Ashley grew out of it, just like she did football players and short shorts and Sumner, not necessarily in that order. Lewis wasn't a drinker, or a druggie, or even bad tempered. Lewis was viceless, and Ashley gave up everything to become bland, just like him. At least, until tonight. Maybe her friends had known that this was her last gasp, her last chance at the wildness she'd once been famous for. Now I looked at my sister, prone at the bottom of the stairs, and thought how I would miss her when she was gone.

"Ashley." She still had her hand over her face, her eyes shut now. I reached down and shook her shoulder. "Come on, at least get on the couch." I crouched beside her, my tiny sister, and put an arm around her shoulders, helping her to her feet. We stumbled together into the living room, where I directed her to the couch and covered her with a blanket, taking off her one shoe and removing the swizzle sticks from her hair one by one. I left the underwear, just out of spite for all the times she'd been nasty to me in the last few months. Some things are deserved, between sisters.

I went to the kitchen and got a trash can, which I put by her head in case things got nasty later, and just as I was leaving to go upstairs she mumbled something, then said louder, "Hey."

"What?" She was just a blob on the couch now, in the dark. On the coffee table, by the swizzle sticks, I could see a pile of my mother's lists, all on yellow sticky paper, lying in the one slant of light that was coming in through the curtains.

"Come talk to me," she said, and I heard the couch creak as she slowly rolled over. "Haven."

I sat down on the chair beside the couch, pulling my legs up to my chest. I could remember when I'd fit in it perfectly, sinking into its deep cushions, when my feet didn't even touch the ground. Now I contorted myself, linking an elbow around a knee, just to fit in its small space. I didn't say anything.

"I'm gonna miss you, you know," she said suddenly, her voice clearer than before. "I know you don't believe that."

"I figured you couldn't wait to leave," I said.

She laughed, a long, lazy laugh. "Oh, yeah, I can't. I mean, I love Lewis. I love him, Haven. He's the only one who ever really cared about me."

This was old news. I nodded, knowing she couldn't see me in the dark.

"It's all gonna be okay, Haven. You know that, right? You know it." She was rambling now, her voice softer, then louder, falling off into sleep. "Mom and Dad and everything, it's all gonna be okay. And Lorna. And me and Lewis. We can't be sad about it forever, you know? We've got to think back to the good times, Haven, and just remember them; that's all we can do. We can't worry about the past or what happened at the end, anymore. I can't and you can't."

"I don't," I said softly, hoping she'd fall asleep.

"You do, though," she said quietly, her voice muffled by the blanket. "I can see it in your face, in your eyes. You gotta grow up, you know? It's nobody's fault. We had good times, don't you understand? Some people don't even have that."

I saw a shadow passing on the street outside, suddenly, and thought of Gwendolyn. Of going wild. I said, "Go to sleep, Ashley. It's late."

"We had good times," she murmured, more to herself now than to me, if she'd ever been talking to me, really. "Like that summer, at the beach. It was perfect."

"What summer?" I sat up now, listening closely. "Which one?"

"At the beach . . . you know. With Mom and Daddy, and the hotel, and playing Frisbee every night, all night. Remember, Haven? You have to remember that, and try to forget the rest. . . ." Her voice faded off, muffled.

"Sumner was there," I said to her, "remember, Ashley? Sumner was there the whole time and you guys were so great together, remember? He was the greatest."

"The greatest," she repeated in that same sleepy, soft voice. "It was the greatest."

"I didn't think you remembered," I said to her, leaning closer. "I thought you'd forgotten."

I waited, listening for her response, but she was out, her breathing steady and soft. "I thought you'd forgotten," I said again, quietly, before pulling the blanket tighter around her, smoothing my hand across her hair and sitting for a while in the dark, watching my sister dream.

The next morning Ashley spent three hours in the bathroom, moaning and flushing the toilet, while my mother and I stood outside the door wondering if we should intervene. Finally, in early afternoon, she emerged after a shower, looking kind of pasty but alive. Lewis showed up a half hour later, with Pepto-Bismol, ginger ale, and oyster crackers. He was quite a guy, that Lewis.

"I can't believe they just left me on the porch," Ashley was saying as I came into the kitchen later that afternoon. She and Lewis were at the table going over wedding details. She had her legs across his lap and he was rubbing her feet. "Some friends."

"They must have thought it would be funny," Lewis said in his soothing, even voice. He was wearing a pastel oxford shirt and madras shorts, a veritable explosion of color next to Ashley in her gray sweatpants and white T-shirt. She was nibbling on an oyster cracker, eating the edges.

"Well, it wasn't." She took another sip of ginger ale. "If it wasn't for Haven, I would have died, probably."

"No, you just would have woken up on the porch," I said.

"I'd rather die. Can you imagine what the neighbors would think?" Overnight, my sister had grown old again, worried about consequences. I missed the loopy silliness of her the night before, hanging off my arm with her hair in her face.

"Well, if you hadn't gone out drinking, and done what I did . . . ," Lewis said in a tsk-tsk voice, checking something off the list.

"Shut up," Ashley said, rearranging her feet in his lap.

"What did you do?" I asked, pulling out a chair and sitting down beside them.

"We went to a dinner, and then a baseball game," Lewis said smugly, "where I had two beers, and made it to my own bed without incident."

"And without underwear around your neck," I chimed in, reaching for an oyster cracker.

Suddenly I knew, without even looking up, that I'd said something wrong. Very wrong. I had the sensation of eyes boring into my neck, hard. As I lifted my head Ashley was staring at me, her mouth twisted in that tight line that meant I was in trouble.

"Underwear?" Lewis said, turning to face her. "What's this about underwear? I never heard anything about underwear."

"It's nothing," Ashley said, shooting me a death look.

"Underwear is not nothing," Lewis said, shifting in his chair so that her feet fell out of his lap to the floor. "You said you just went to dinner and had too many margaritas. You didn't say anything even remotely related to underwear."

"Lewis, please," Ashley said. "We went to this place, right before we came home. We didn't stay long, it was stupid, but they told the guy I was getting married and then he . . . ."

"Oh, God," Lewis said, throwing down his pencil. "Strippers? You were with strippers last night?"

"Not strippers, Lewis," Ashley said in a tired voice. "They're exotic dancers, and I didn't even want to go. It was Heather's idea."

"I don't believe this." Lewis looked at me, as if I could help, and I looked back at the table. "We promised each other we wouldn't do any of that traditional stuff, Ashley. You made a vow."

"Lewis, don't do this. It was just a stupid thing."

Lewis crossed his legs, a habit that always made my father cringe. "Did you touch him?"

Ashley sighed. "Not really."

There was a silence and I thought about making a quick exit, but as I moved to go I felt Ashley's foot lock around the bottom of my chair, holding it in place.

"Not really," Lewis repeated slowly. "So that would be a yes."

"It wasn't like I *touched* him," Ashley said quickly, "but he danced in front of me and I had to put money in his . . . , thing . . . because it's rude if you . . . ."

"His thing?" Lewis shrieked. "You touched his thing?"

"His underwear," Ashley said. "God, Lewis, his underwear, for Christ's sake."

"The same underwear that was around your neck, right?" Lewis stood up, pushing his chair out. "I don't want to hear about this, okay? A week before my wedding and my fiancée is out putting her hands on strange men . . . I just can't think about it right now."

"Lewis, don't be like this," Ashley said, too tired and hung over to get into a big fight. "Like I said, it's just a dumb thing."

"Well, obviously *that* vow didn't mean much to you," Lewis snapped. "So I wonder if any of the others will."

"Oh, please," Ashley said, rolling her eyes. "I'm too tired to deal with your dramatics, Lewis. Let's just forget about it."

Lewis just looked at her, in his pastels and madras. "I think I need some time away from you, Ashley. I have to go now." And with that he walked stiffly to the door, opened it, and left with a great flourish of shutting it behind him. Ashley just watched him go, then turned her gaze on me.

"Thanks a lot, Haven," she said icily. "Thanks a whole lot." She stood up and slammed her glass on the table, then went out the same door, calling his name.

I sat at the table knowing I should feel bad. But I couldn't do it. I knew I owed Ashley somewhere for something nasty she'd done to me; there had been enough over the years. It was exhilarating in a way, this feeling of wrongdoing, of making things even. I listened to them arguing outside and thought of Ashley the night before, telling me to remember when things were good. I sat back, listening, and concentrated on this moment, my last act of revenge against my sister, and savored it.

It was later that night that I got the call from Casey. I didn't even recognize her voice at first, a voice I'd heard all my life. She sounded like she was choking, or had a cold.

"I need to talk to you," she said as soon as I picked up the phone where Ashley had left it dangling on the floor with a glare at me. She was still mad, even though Lewis had forgiven her before he even made it down the driveway. "It's important."

"Okay," I said. "Should I come over?"

"No," she said quickly, and in the background I could hear baby Ronald hollering. "Meet me halfway. Right now, okay?"

"Sure." I hung up, found my shoes, then walked to the living room, where my mother, Lydia, and Ashley were watching "Murder, She Wrote" and making lists. "I'm going for a walk with Casey."

"Fine." My mother hardly looked up, her mind on the band and the ushers and the flower arrangements. "Be back by ten."

As I stepped into the thick summer air I heard only cicadas, screaming from the trees around our house. It was warm and sticky and I left my shoes on the porch, walking barefoot down the sidewalk, past houses with their lights burning, the sound of televisions drifting from open windows. I could see Casey coming from the other direction, walking quickly and brushing her hair out of her face. We met halfway, by the mailbox in front of the Johnsons'.

"It's horrible," she said to me, breathless. She was sniffling—no, crying—and she kept walking, with me falling into step behind her. "I just can't believe it."

"What?" I'd never seen her like this.

"He broke up with me," she said, sobbing. "That bastard, he broke up with me over the phone. Just a few minutes ago."

"Rick?" I pictured him from all those packs of glossy three-by-fives, always grinning into the camera, a stranger from Pennsylvania.

"Yes," she said, wiping her nose with the back of her hand. "I have to sit down." She plopped herself on the curb and pulled her knees to her chest, burying her face in her hands.

"Casey." I reached to put my arm around her, unsure of how to act or what to say. This was the first time it had happened to us. "I'm so sorry."

"I'd been calling so much, but he was never home, right? And I was leaving all these messages. . . ." She stopped and wiped her eyes. "And his mother kept saying he was out, or busy, and finally he called me back today and said she made him call me. Haven, he'd been telling her all along to say he wasn't home. He just didn't want to talk to me."

"He's a jerk," I said defensively, hearing that judging tone in my own voice, the one I recognized from Lydia Catrell talking to my mother all those mornings.

"He was hoping I'd just lose interest. . . . He didn't even have the guts to call me and tell me he had a new girlfriend. He had his mom lying to me, Haven." She made little hiccuping noises, bumpy sobs. I kept patting her shoulder, trying to help. "God, I was so stupid. I was going to go up there."

"He's an asshole." I could see Rick, someone I didn't

know, lurking at the end of a telephone line, mouthing the words *I'm not here.* I hated Rick, now.

"It's so awful," she said, resting her head against my shoulder and sobbing full strength, while I cupped my arm around her head and held her close. "It hurts."

I'd never been in love, never felt that surge of feeling or that fall from its graces. I'd only watched as others weathered it; my mother in her garden, Sumner on the front lawn all those years ago, Ashley sobbing from the other side of a wall. I sat curbside with my best friend, Casey Melvin, and held her, trying to shoulder some of the hurt. There's only so much you can do, in these situations. We sat there together in our neighborhood and Casey cried, a short distance down from halfway.

Chapter Eleven

We were down to three days and counting. Things around the house were getting crazy, with the phone ringing off the hook and travel arrangements for the incoming relatives and Ashley having a breakdown every five seconds, it seemed. My mother and Lydia had set up headquarters at the kitchen table, with all the lists and plans and last-minute invitations covering the space entirely. I had to sit on the counter, with the displaced toaster oven, just to get my Pop-Tart in the morning.

Meanwhile, the rest of the world went on, although it was hard to imagine how. Casey was still suffering, having locked herself in her room and refused to eat for three days, until her mother took her shopping, got her hair permed, and signed them up for another tap-dancing class. Life would go on for Casey, with Rick retreating to just pictures in a photo album.

My father and Lorna had returned from a News Channel 5 promotional trip to the Bahamas, where they'd accompanied a group of viewers who'd won a contest involving sports and weather trivia. My father came back with even more hair, a sunburn, and a set of shell windchimes for me, which I hung outside my bedroom window, where it clanged all night until Ashley claimed it was ruining her sleep and demanded I take it down. I did, but I resented it. I resented everyone lately.

It had started soon after Ashley's bachelorette party and Casey's dumping. It was a feeling I'd woken up with one morning, a kind of whirring in my ears and an instability of the world, like things were coming to a head. I faced myself in the bathroom mirror and looked into my eyes, wondering if I would see something new in them, something crackling and different. I felt strong, as if every muscle in my body was taut and lean, not creaky and bony anymore. As if I was growing into myself, finally. I heard things differently, the sound of the neighborhood and the cicadas at night and my own breath, even and full. Everything was heightened, from the blazing blue of the sky to the feel of slippery grass under my feet to the sound of my mother's voice calling my name from across a room. It was both scary and exhilarating, unsettling and amazing.

The day before Ashley's wedding was also the first

day of the Lakeview Mall Hot Summer Deals Sidewalk Sale, which basically consisted of all the stores taking all the junk they couldn't sell and putting it outside, slashing the prices in half, and then watching as shoppers gobbled it up. I had to be at work extra early, at seven A.M., to help put one half of every ugly pair of shoes from the storeroom on a table out front, where it was my job to stand and watch for shoplifters while my boss, Burt, shuffled back and forth to the storeroom to find the mates for the shoes on the table. It was loud and crazy in the mall, with people digging through all the merchandise and pushing up against me in their mad dash to find a bargain. But even in all this craziness— with Burt saying in my ear that my sock quota was low so Push Socks, Push Socks and the mall Muzak blaring Barry Manilow and all the hands, all colors and sizes, grabbing at the shoes in front of me—I felt that eerie calmness, that floating feeling, that had followed me for the last few days. It was like I was just above it all, hovering, and nothing affected me.

Out of the blue, a woman grabbed my hand and said, "You call twenty bucks for a kid's shoe a good deal?" She was wearing a bathing suit with shorts over it, flip-flops, and a big straw hat.

I just looked at her.

"Do you?" She picked up a shoe, one that was yellow and blue and pink, with what looked like Smurfs on it. "I'll give you ten bucks for this pair. If you have a five and a half."

"I don't know . . . ," I said, looking for Burt, who had

disappeared for a bathroom break a good twenty minutes ago. "We don't really bargain on shoes."

"You don't, huh?" she said in a nasty voice, like I'd been rude to her. "Well, that's just fine. Just find me a five and a half, would you?"

Burt appeared next to me now, smelling like the hand soap we used in the bathroom. "Is there a problem here, Haven?"

"Five and a half," the woman said loudly, shaking the shoe in my face. I watched the Smurfs blur past, blue and pink and yellow.

"Find the woman a five and a half," Burt said to me, prodding me in the back with one hand. "I'll deal with the table for a while."

I went back in the storeroom and climbed up to the discount shelf, looking for the ugly Smurf shoe. There was a six and a four but no five and a half, of course. I went back out to the table.

"Sorry, it's not in," I said.

"It's not in," she repeated flatly. "Are you sure?"

"I am indeed," I said, realizing that I was being a smartass and not really caring. Burt was looking at me. I felt that whooshing in my ears, that powerful evenness. I imagined myself floating down the Lakeview Mall, tied to nothing, the silk of those banners brushing my shoulders.

"Haven, perhaps you can interest the woman in another style," Burt said to me quickly.

"I want this one," the woman said, shaking the shoe in front of my face again. Behind her, someone else was saying, "Miss? Miss? I need some help with this shoe, please?"

"We don't have that shoe in, ma'am," I repeated to her in a singsong voice, my customer-pleasing smile stretching across my face.

"Well, then, I think I should get another shoe at the same price." She put one hand on her hip and I watched as the fabric of her bathing suit scrunched, folding over itself at her stomach. People just shouldn't wear beach attire in public. "It's only fair."

"Ma'am, it's a sale item, we're out of that size, and I'm sorry," I said, but already my mind was drifting. Burt was busy untying a bunch of shoelaces and the people were all around me and the Muzak in the mall seemed louder, suddenly. I wondered if I was going to pass out, right there in the middle of the Hot Summer Deals Sidewalk Sale.

"Well, that's just fine," the woman snapped. I watched as she tossed the shoe at me. She meant for it to hit the pile probably, but it bounced off a stray saddle shoe in the bin and nailed me in the head, a direct Smurf hit. I was hot all of a sudden, the whooshing in my ears loud and calming, and I felt awake, my skin tingling.

She was walking away, flip-flops thwacking against the floor, as I grabbed the shoe, ducked around the table, and went after her. I could still feel where the shoe had hit me, but that wasn't what spurred me on and made me rush through the crowd of bargain hunters, following the pudgy lady in the straw hat. It was something more, a giant mass of Ashley's snide remarks and tantrums, of

Lorna Queen's tiny ears and my father's new hair, of Sumner standing on our front lawn, abandoned, all those years ago. It was the tallness and Casey's Rick and Lydia Catrell and Europe, and my mother standing in the doorway watching me leave for my father's wedding. It was the whole damn summer, my whole damn life, leading up to this moment with this stranger in the middle of the Lakeview Mall.

"Excuse me," I said loudly as I came up behind her, gripping the shoe in my hand so tightly that I could feel the plastic ends of the laces pressing into my palm. "Excuse me."

She didn't hear me, so I reached forward and tapped her shoulder, feeling the smooth rubberiness of the bathing suit beneath my finger. She turned around.

"Yes?" Then she saw it was me, and her eyes narrowed, nasty.

I just looked at her, not sure at all what words would come out of my mouth. We were in the middle of the mall now by the giant gumball machine where the ceiling is high and glass. The sunlight was pouring in across the center court, hot and so bright I was squinting. The noises and voices were loud and rising above me, pushing their way to the skylight and the world outside. People were rushing by and the banners were floating above me as I faced this woman, this stranger, every inch of me tingling, electric.

"You forgot this," I said to her, in a voice that didn't sound like me, and threw the shoe back at her, hard, and stood watching as it hit her square in the forehead, the same spot where it had hit me. Then it fell to the floor, bounced once, and landed upright, as if it was waiting for a little foot to wiggle into it.

She was stunned, staring at me open-mouthed. She had gold fillings on two back teeth. I noticed this offhand as the crowds pressed around us and the sun beat down and I was suddenly tired, sure I'd never make it the short distance back to the store.

"I'll have you fired," she snapped, squatting down to grab up the shoe, and then added on the way back up, "and I'm calling mall security and reporting this. This is an assault." She looked around at the few people who had seen me throw a shoe at this woman, and pointed to each of them as she added, "Witnesses! You are all witnesses!"

Everyone was looking at me, suddenly, and the place was too bright, and so hot, and all I could see was her face and her open mouth, yelling. I spun around, reaching out like a blind person in the hot glare of that skylight, pushing people aside, and I began to run. I ran down the middle of the Lakeview Mall with those banners swishing overhead, seeing the shocked expressions of people as they jerked out of the way, yanking children and strollers aside. I could hear her yelling behind me, but I didn't care, couldn't think of anything as I burst out the main doors into the parking lot and kept running, my feet pounding the pavement. I wondered if this was how Gwendolyn felt, searching the streets for some kind of peace. If at fifteen she'd ever felt the same way, tall and lost, not fitting in or finding a place for herself, anywhere.

I was still running, nearing the edge of the parking lot that led to the road home, when I thought I heard someone—Sumner—yelling my name. I couldn't stop, not even for him, as I took the turn and headed into my neighborhood, slowing my pace and breathing heavily, the wind swirling in my ears.

I found myself at the neighborhood park, still trying to figure out what had come over me. I walked past the swings and the jungle gym to what was called the Creative Playground, built by a bunch of hippie parents when I was in grade school. It was made of wood, with slides and hiding places, and tires stacked one on top of the other creating vertical tunnels. I crawled underneath the main slide and folded myself small, as small as I'd been in second grade when I first discovered this space. I barely fit now, my knees at my chin, but it was mossy and quiet and somehow right then it seemed like the perfect place to be.

I was fired, obviously. No more Push Socks, Push Socks. I took off my name tag and stuck it in my pocket, wondering what kind of charges would await me when I got home. I wondered if you could get arrested for an assault with a Smurf shoe at a mall. If I'd go to jail. If I *could* go home.

But soon I wasn't thinking about that anymore, or about the woman or the Hot Summer Deals Sidewalk Sale. I leaned my head against the slippery wood behind me and thought of better times, of that summer in Virginia Beach. I thought about Sumner running through the sand, chasing a Frisbee as it flew over his head.

About the way he made Ashley human and shrimp cocktail at the hotel restaurant and my father's pink cheeks, his grinning as he slid an arm around my mother's waist, pulling her close. I thought of Ashley's high, singsong laugh and that ride down in the Volkswagen with beach music on the radio and the stars overhead, the summer so new with so many days left, each sliding into the next. I wished I could go back somehow and start it all over again, with me and Ashley by the curb waiting and listening for the putt-putt of the Bug to come around the corner. I'd live each of those days the exact same way, when I was no bigger than a minute. When my parents were still in love and Sumner held us all together, laughing, until the day Ashley sent him away without even thinking of what would happen once he was gone. No more laughing, no more drawing together from the opposite sides of the house, all coming together to Sumner's voice, his laugh. I missed who we all were then. One summer and one boy, and suddenly things weren't the same.

I walked home. I'd fallen asleep under the slide, dozing off in the mossy quiet, only to wake up confused, having forgotten where I was, the sun slanting down hot on my head. Some little boys were sliding down above me, their voices high and giggly, calling out to their father to watch. He was wearing sunglasses, reading a paper by the tire tunnel, and looked up each time they told him to. I waited until they were gone before I slipped out and unfolded myself to my true size.

I went into the house through the back door, hoping

to avoid seeing anyone; but of course there was another power meeting going on at the table, with Lydia and my mother hunched over the clipboard that seemed attached to my mother's hand lately and Ashley sitting in the doorway that led to the living room.

"Well, obviously we'll have to replan the whole wedding party," my mother was saying as I stood on the other side of the glass, invisible. "We can't have five ushers and four bridesmaids. Somebody's got to go."

"I've seen it done before," Lydia said, tugging at her sequined shirt. "Four bridesmaids, three ushers. But it never looked right to me. You need symmetry in a wedding party. You've just got to have it."

"I still cannot believe this," Ashley grumbled into her hair, which was hanging down one side of her face. "I'm going to kill her, I swear."

"There's no time to think about that now," Lydia said in her loud, brassy Floridian voice. "We can hate Carol later; now we've got to come up with some kind of a solution. Quickly."

"Okay," my mother said, flipping through some pages on her clipboard. "How's this: we just find another bridesmaid. Ashley, you could ask one of your friends, right?"

"Mother," Ashley said in that annoyed voice that I'd heard way too much of in the last six months, "the wedding is tomorrow."

"I know that," my mother said wearily.

"There's no time to get a bridesmaid, get a dress, get it fitted. . . . We can't do it. There's no way." Ashley picked at the fringe of her cutoffs.

"How about bumping an usher?" Lydia suggested. "There's got to be somebody we can ask to bow out. For the sake of evenness."

"We can't throw someone out of the wedding," Ashley said. "God, that would be so horrible. 'Oh, thanks for renting the tux and everything, but we won't be needing you. Get lost.'"

"Of course we wouldn't say it like that," Lydia said sullenly, and they all got quiet, their minds working this over.

I figured this was the best time of any to come in, so I headed straight across the kitchen, over Ashley in the doorway, and made a quick dash for the stairs.

"Haven?" My mother was already after me. I heard her pushing her chair away from the table, that familiar scrape, and then her footsteps coming down the hallway behind me. "Haven, I have to talk to you."

I stopped in the middle of the stairs and turned to look down at her. She seemed very small. "What is it?"

"Well," she said, starting to climb up, step by step, "I got a strange call from Burt Isker. Did you have some sort of problem at work today?"

"No," I said, turning back around and taking the rest of the stairs, then heading to my room only a few paces away.

"Whatever happened, we can talk about it," she said quietly, still following me. I felt that stab of guilt, but pushed it away because I was tired of protecting her from my father, forgiving him for leaving us for the pregnant Weather Pet, giving Ashley free reign to hurt me because she was The Bride.

"I don't want to talk about it," I said, and even as the words came out I knew the look I'd see if I turned around, the hurt like a slap spreading across her face. But I didn't turn around, didn't even stop walking, until I was in my room with my hand on the back of the door, closing it.

"Haven," my mother said in a louder voice, trying to be stern, "we're going to talk about this. If you're accosting the customers and running out on your job, obviously something is going on that we need to discuss. Now I know it's been hard this summer with the wedding, but this isn't—"

"It's not about the wedding. It's not about the goddamn wedding or Ashley. For once this isn't about her. It just isn't," I said, now looking at her face closely as it changed from authoritative to lost. And then I slammed the door in my mother's face, so hard it shook the pictures in their frames on the wall of my room. I could hear her breathing on the other side of the door, waiting for me to open it, apologize, pull her close, and save her from everything just like I always did. But I didn't. Not this time.

A few minutes later, as if conceding defeat, she just said, "Well, don't forget your father is coming over. You told him you'd go shopping with him for a gift for your sister." Her voice was soft, and she was trying to sound like she wasn't upset. She waited another minute, as if this might bring me out, and then I heard her going slowly down the stairs.

I walked to my bed and stretched out across it, symmetrical, with my feet pressed to the bedposts and my head locked against the headboard. I closed my eyes and tried to block it all out, the mall and the bathing-suit woman and my mother's face as the door swung to close on her. I tried to think about anything to block out the sound from my vent, so clear, and what I knew they'd be saying about me as soon as my mother got back downstairs.

"What's wrong?" That was Ashley.

"Nothing." My mother didn't sound like herself, her voice quiet and even. "Let's get back to this bridesmaid problem."

"What did she say to you?" Ashley said, protective now. "God, what is her problem lately? She's impossible to deal with. I swear, it's like she's purposely doing it so close to the wedding just to ruin it. . . ."

"It's not about the wedding," my mother said quietly, echoing my own words. "Just leave it alone, Ashley. You've got enough to worry about."

"I just think she could wait to have her nervous break-down until next week. I mean, it's not like we don't have enough on our hands, and it's pretty selfish, really."

"Ashley," my mother said in a louder voice, sounding tired. "Leave it alone."

I lay there and listened as they talked about Carol, the difficult bridesmaid, who was supposed to fly in that afternoon but apparently had called earlier to say she had broken off her own engagement just this morning and was therefore too hysterical to attend. They went round and round, coming up with plan after plan, none of which would work. I looked at the clock. It was only eleven-fifteen.

And I was still expected to go shopping with my

father, to pick out the Perfect Gift for the Perfect Wedding. It was too late to cancel; my father had his faults, but he was always punctual. I went to my bathroom and washed my face, looking at myself under the greenish fluorescent light. I looked sick, haunted, which I felt was appropriate so I just left my face as it was, without applying any makeup or touching my hair. I was still in my work clothes as I crept downstairs, and out onto the porch to wait for him.

I heard the car before I saw it, the purring of the engine as it zipped around the corner and onto my street. He pulled up in front of the house like he always did and then beeped twice. I sat in the swing, watching him without moving. I wasn't sure if he could see me.

He sat in the car a few minutes longer, fiddling with the radio and smoothing his hand over his new hair. He beeped again. Still I sat there. I wanted him to come up to the house. I wanted him, I realized, to finally approach it and cross that imaginary line that had been drawn the day he packed a suitcase and left while I was at school, taking with him all his sports stuff and clothes and the stereo, which left a big hole on the wall of the living room. I wanted to watch him walk up the front steps, across the lawn he'd kept so neatly mowed all those years, to our front door and to be a man about it, not a coward who sat in his shiny new car at the curb, outside it all. I sat and watched my father, daring him to do it. To come claim me as he'd never done since that day, not lurking on the outskirts of what had once been shared property, waiting for me to cross the line myself, the line I hadn't even drawn.

He beeped again, and I saw my mother's face appear in the window beside the door, peering out at him. He backed up and turned the car around in our driveway, his head still craning to see if I'd appear—*whoosh*—suddenly, like a bouquet of roses from a magician's hand. My mother held the curtain aside, watching. I watched too, hidden in the shadows of our porch, as he slowly pulled out, coasted by with one last searching look, and then gunned the engine before disappearing. *Whoosh.*

Chapter Twelve

⮌

The first thing I felt when I woke up was that it was hot. Very hot. It was the middle of August and every day was hot, but there was something about that day that made it stand out. I'd napped without covers, having kicked off my light blanket and sheet, but still felt sticky and warm even with my fan pointed right at me. Outside, the sun was still blazing. I'd woken from a bad dream, one of those confusing ones where nobody is who they start out to be. Someone was leading me down my street, showing me things. First it was Lewis, in one of those skinny ties, but then his face changed to Sumner's. Then, as I turned away and then back, it switched again, to Lydia Catrell's, only she was very old and tiny, hunched over, and shrinking before my eyes. I woke up suddenly, confused, and remembered everything that had happened earlier in one great rush of colors and images flying past in a blur. I curled up smaller, pulling my pillow in close, and buried my face. This had been the longest day of my life. Everything was loaded with consequences, the wedding and the weeks to come; I wanted to sleep through it all. But the sun was spilling through the window, shiny and hot, and it was already one o'clock. It felt like forever since I'd climbed into bed after my father drove away, locking my bedroom door and ignoring my mother's voice as it whispered in the hallway outside. The earlier part of the day was fuzzy and distant, like the dream that was fading quickly from my head.

I stayed in bed for another hour, listening to the noises of my house. I heard Ashley next door, rustling around, doing the last bits of packing. Every once in a while it would get very quiet, and I wondered if she'd stopped to think about leaving. I wondered if she was sad. Then I'd hear her taping another box shut or making another trip downstairs, dragging something behind her. My mother and Lydia were in the kitchen, their voices high and chatty, against the tinkling of teaspoons and that humming excitement of something big getting ready to happen. I lay in my bed, feet to bedposts, head pressed to headboard. I lay as still as possible, pushing my back into the damp sheet beneath me. And I tried to think of the quiet that would come later, after tomorrow and the honeymoon and Europe, when there would be only me and my mother treading these floors and everything would be different.

I got up and showered, ran my hands across my body under the stream of water. Since I'd grown taller I hated looking down at myself; at my skinny legs, the knees poking out; my big feet splayed flat against the floor like clown shoes, ten sizes too big. But now I drew myself up to full height, pulling in a breath that spread through me. I thought of giraffes and stilts, of my bones linked carefully together. Of height and power, and gliding over the heads of the Lakeview Mall shoppers to touch those fluttering banners. As I stepped out to face myself in the mirror, reaching a hand to smooth away the steam, I saw myself differently. It was as if I had grown again as I slept, but this time just to fit my own size. As if my soul had expanded, filling out the gaps of the height that had burdened me all these months. Like a balloon filling slowly with air, becoming all smooth and buoyant, I felt like I finally fit within myself, edge to edge, every crevice filled.

"Hey," Ashley called out as I passed her open door on my way downstairs. "Haven. Come here a second."

I went in, immediately aware of how small her room looked with the dresser almost bare; the closet door open revealing empty shelves and racks; the bright spots of wallpaper where things had hung contrasting now to the faded rest of the wall. She was standing by her bed, folding a dress over one arm. She said, "I need to talk to you."

I stood there, tall, waiting.

She looked closer at me, as if she'd suddenly realized something she'd missed before. "Are you okay?"

"Yeah," I said. "Why?"

"You look different." She put the dress down in a box at her feet, kicking it shut. "Do you feel okay?"

"I'm fine."

She was still watching me, as if I couldn't be trusted. Then she shrugged, letting it go, and said, "I want to talk to you about earlier."

"What about it?"

"Haven," she said in that voice that meant she was feeling much, much older than me, "I know it's been hard for you with the wedding and all, but I'm concerned about how you treated Mom. It's hard enough for her right now without you freaking out and turning on her."

"I'm not freaking out," I said curtly, moving back towards the door.

"Hey, I'm not through talking to you," she said, walking quickly to block my path. I looked down at her, realizing how short she really was. She was in shorts and a red T-shirt, with a gold chain and matching earrings. "See, that's just what I'm talking about. It's like all of a sudden you just don't care about anyone but yourself. You snap at Mom, and now this attitude with me. . . ."

"Ashley, please," I said in a tired voice, and noticed how much I sounded like my mother.

"I'm just asking you to keep whatever is bothering you to yourself, at least until after tomorrow." She had her hand on her hip now, classic Ashley stance. "It's very selfish, you know, to pick these few days for whatever adolescent breakdown you're choosing to have. Very selfish."

"I'm selfish?" I said, and found myself actually throwing my head back to laugh, Ha! "God, Ashley, give me a break. As if everything in the last six months hasn't revolved around you and this stupid wedding. As if my whole life," I added, the light, airy feeling bubbling back up inside me, "hasn't revolved around you and your stupid life." It didn't even sound like me, the voice so casual and cutting. Like someone else. Someone bold.

She just looked at me, the gold engagement ring glinting on the hand she was shaking at me. "I'm not going to let you do this. I'm not going to let you get me started on this day, because I have too much to deal with and I'm not in the mood to fight with you. But I will say this. You better grow up and get your shit together in the next five minutes or you will regret it, Haven. I have planned this day and done too much for too long for you to decide to ruin it purely out of spite." Her hand went back to her hip, her lip jutting out.

"Oh, shut up," I said in my bold voice, stepping around her and out the bedroom door, then going down the stairs before she even had a chance to react. I was floating, the air whooshing through my ears all the way to the kitchen, where I found my mother and Lydia drinking coffee. They both looked up at me as I came drifting in, with the same expression Ashley had when she'd first called me into the room: as if suddenly I was no longer recognizable.

"Haven?" my mother said, turning in her chair as I reached for the Pop-Tarts and broke open a pack. "Is everything okay?"

"Just fine," I said cheerfully, lining up my tarts on the rack of the toaster oven. Upstairs Ashley was banging around, boxes crashing to the floor.

My mother and Lydia exchanged looks over their coffee, then went back to watching me. I concentrated on the toaster oven. After a minute or so Lydia asked, "Why don't you sit down and eat with us?"

"Okay." I took my tarts out and then sat down across from them and started eating, aware that they were still staring at me. After a few seconds of self-conscious nibbling I said, "What? What is it?"

"Nothing," Lydia said quickly, shrinking back in her chair. I thought about my dream where she'd been tiny tiny tiny.

"You just seem upset," my mother said gently, scooting her chair a little closer to me to suggest allegiance. "Do you want to talk about it?"

"No," I said in the same gentle voice. "I don't." And I went back to my Pop-Tart, envisioning that tether stretched to the limit, fraying from the strain, and then suddenly snapping into pieces, no longer able to hold against the force of my pulling away from it. I looked at my mother, with the same hair and same outfit and same expression as Lydia Catrell's, and thought, You go to Europe. You sell this house. I don't care anymore. I just don't care.

"Haven," my mother said in a pleading voice, placing her hand over mine. "It might make you feel better."

I don't care, I don't care, I don't care, I was thinking, stuffing pieces of Pop-Tart into my mouth one by one by one. Her hand was hot and snug over mine as I pulled it away and pushed my chair out from the table. "I don't want to talk about it," I snapped as Lydia Catrell pulled further back in her chair. "I don't care, okay? I just don't care."

"Honey," my mother said, and I could tell by the strain in her voice she was really worried now.

"I'm sorry," I said to her, unable to meet her eyes. I ran to the back door and out into the garden, slipping across the pathway past the blazing colors and smells, the tendrils reaching out to touch my skin, the mix of everything so sweet and humid, thick and stifling. I hit the edge and kept going, down the street past the Melvins' and out of our neighborhood altogether, past the Lakeview Mall with all the cars lined up in its parking lot in nice, even rows. I was someone else, someone bold, my feet finding the ground beneath me as I thought only of putting distance between me and what I'd left behind.

I didn't know where to go, or what to do. I had no job and only three dollars in my pocket, so I spent an hour walking around downtown. I bought an orangeade and spent a half hour on a bench sipping it, wondering if there was ever going to be any way for me to go home. I imagined the house itself in pieces, brought to the ground by my bad attitude. I imagined a crisis meeting convening as I sat there in the park, with Ashley and Lewis and my mother and Lydia and my ex-boss Burt

Isker and my father and Lorna, all of them debating the question What on Earth Has Happened to Haven? Only Sumner would be on my side. Over the space of just one summer he'd managed to breathe life into me again, just as he had all those years ago. And now I was playing hooky from my life there on that bench, on the day before the biggest day of my sister's life, and I didn't even care. I imagined their faces as they sat around that table, voices clucking with concern. I was causing a Crisis.

I called Casey. She was off phone restriction and back in her mother's good graces after tap-dancing lessons and family therapy. When she heard my voice she said, "Hey, hold on. I'm switching phones."

I was at a pay phone, watching a crazy man talk to himself on the bench I'd just left. I held on.

"Haven."

"Yeah."

"What the hell is going on with you?" She sounded incredulous, even as she whispered. "Your mom called here three times already, looking for you. They're freaking out over there."

"She called you?" I said.

"She thought you'd come here. She told Mom everything, and I overheard. My mom talks so damn loud."

"What'd they say?" I was the center of serious mother talks.

"Well, your mom asked if you'd been around and my mom said no, so then your mom goes into this whole thing about you freaking out at work this morning and then fighting with Ashley and running out of the house, and she's just frantic because she thinks you must be on drugs or something, she's not sure. . . ."

"Drugs?" I repeated. "Did she really say that?"

"Haven," Casey said matter-of-factly, as if she knew so much about these things. "They think everything is drugs. They do."

"I'm not on drugs," I said, offended.

"Well, that's not the point. So apparently your sister is going ballistic and your mom and Lydia are combing the neighborhood looking for you and the rehearsal is at six-thirty and they think you might ditch that too, so it's just imperative that they find you before then."

"The rehearsal dinner," I said. Of course. I was a bridesmaid. If I hadn't been, I doubted an all-points bulletin would ever have been issued.

"So what is going on?" Casey demanded. "Where are you? Tell me and I'll come meet you."

"Nothing's going on," I said. "I'm on my way home." I didn't know if that was true, but I didn't want Casey meeting me. I liked this freedom and I wasn't ready to share it.

"Are you sure?" she asked, sounding disappointed.

"I'll call you later," I said.

"Wait. At least tell me what happened at work. Your mom said she thought you'd assaulted a customer or something—"

"Later," I said to her. "Okay?"

"Okay," she said sullenly. "But are you all right? At least tell me that."

"I am," I said. "I just have some stuff to work out."

"Oh. Okay. Well, call me if you need me. I'm just here practicing my tap dancing."

"I will. 'Bye, Case." I hung up and glanced around the small park I'd been hiding in. There were families out with their kids, college students throwing a Frisbee while a big, dumb-looking dog chased after it. I wondered if the Town Car was cruising the streets downtown, Lydia hoping to catch a glimpse of me so that I could be rustled up and dragged to the rehearsal dinner. I was throwing everything out of whack, and I knew it. I was like a fugitive, running from some indefinable force made up of my mother's worried eyes and Ashley's whining and Lydia's Town Car, sucking up my steps even as I took them. It was late afternoon now, and hotter than ever. My shirt was sticking to me and I needed somewhere better to hide.

I was standing at the crosswalk, squinting, when I heard it. That humming of a car, coming around the corner behind me and then down the street, with Sumner behind the wheel. He stopped at the light, too far away to hear me even if I'd had time to yell his name. The light changed and he pulled away, one hand balanced on the steering wheel, the other arm hanging down the side of the car, drumming his fingers. He took off, I watched him go, blending with the other traffic until he turned onto a side street just a little way down. I started walking.

I found him at the senior center, a small building at the end of a long street of minimalls and office complexes. Everything looked very new and very clean, as if it had been hastily assembled the day before. Sumner's car was parked right next to the door, in a space marked FRIENDS.

I pushed the door open and went inside, looking around. I was still in my fugitive mode, suspicious, as I passed a group of tiny old women, all of them hunched over and white haired. They wore shiny Nike walking shoes with their skirts and sweaters. As I passed by them, my eyes averted, I heard one say in a quiet, musical voice, "What a beautiful, beautiful girl."

I turned, trying to catch another glimpse, but they had vanished around a corner. I could hear the soles of their shoes brushing the floor and the sound of music just down the hallway. I kept walking, past rooms with walls of bright, happy colors like Easter eggs. In one a group of people were busy painting, each behind an easel. One man glanced over his shoulder at me as I passed, holding his paintbrush in midstroke. In front of him was a half-finished canvas showing a beach scene, the water a mix of a million different blues, the sky a blaze of oranges and reds. I passed a sunroom where a woman in a wheelchair was reading a book, the light slanting through a window just enough to make her almost transparent, and came to a large room with a high ceiling and a shiny floor. In one corner was a record player, and a man shuffling through albums, while in front of him about ten couples danced in slow, even time. A woman in a long blue dress had her eyes closed, her chin resting on the shoulder of her partner as he carefully twirled her. A man with a flower in his button-hole was bowing to his partner as she smiled and took his hand for another dance. And in the far corner, by a table lined with cups and a punch bowl, I saw Sumner, his head thrown back in a laugh as he led a small, wiry woman with a crocheted shawl around their part of the dance floor. The woman was talking, her cheeks red, and Sumner listened, all the while spinning her slowly around, his feet moving smoothly across the shiny floor. He was in a red dress shirt with a blue tie and old black oxfords. His jeans were rolled into uneven cuffs, and his shirttail hung loose over the waist. When the music stopped, the couples broke up and applauded while the record guy picked out another song. Sumner bowed to his partner and she smiled, pulling her shawl closer around her.

People were milling around now, pairing off into new couples, and Sumner hung back by the punch bowl, waiting until the new song had begun. Then he crossed the room to a woman in a yellow pantsuit who was standing by the record player, arms crossed and watching the dancers with a half smile on her face. He came up to her grinning, extended his hand, and asked her to dance. She ran a hand through her short white hair, then nodded once before taking his hand and following him onto the floor. He slipped an arm around her waist, old-time style, and they began a neat box step, one-two-three-four. The music was cheerful and happy and everyone was smiling in this shiny room, where time could stop and you could forget about aching joints and old worries and let a young, handsome boy ask you to dance. I stood in the doorway and watched Sumner charm this woman as he had charmed me, and my sister, so many years ago. And I saw him through several more songs, each time waiting until everyone else was paired off and picking a woman who was standing alone watching the others. A wallflower wanting to join in but with something stopping her.

After a half hour the record man leaned into a microphone and said in a deep voice, "Last song, everyone. Last song."

I waited for Sumner to repeat his ritual for this last dance on this summer afternoon. He skirted the edge of the dancers, flitting in and out of my sight, a red blur among the shifting shapes. Then he cut right through the crowd, past women with their eyes closed, lost in the music, and walked a slow, steady pace right to me. He held out his hand, palm up like expecting a high five, and said, "Come on, Haven. It's the last dance."

"I don't dance," I said, my face flushing when I noticed all the couples on the floor were looking at us with that proud, attentive look of grandparents and spinster aunts.

"I'll show you," he said, still grinning. "Come on, twinkletoes."

I put my hand into his and felt his fingers fold over mine, gently leading me to the edge of the floor. I was about to make some joke about how I dwarfed him but he put his arm around my waist and pulled me closer and suddenly I didn't feel like joking about anything. He held my hand and concentrated on the music before saying, "Okay. Just do what I do."

So I did. I've never been a dancer, always too clumsy and flailing. Dancing was for tiny girls and ballerinas, girls the size to be hoisted and dipped, easily enclosed in an arm. But as Sumner led me around the floor, my feet slowly getting used to the curve and glide of the steps, I didn't think about how tall I was, or how gawky, or how I stood so far over him, his head at my neck. I closed my eyes and listened to the music, feeling his arm around me. I was tired, after this long day and it suddenly seemed like I wouldn't even be able to stand up without Sumner there supporting me, holding my hand. The music was soaring, all soprano and harps and sadness, mourning some lost boy away at war, but still I kept my eyes shut and tried to remember every detail of this dance, because even then I knew that it wouldn't last. It was just a moment, a perfect moment, as time stood still and fleetingly everything fell back into its proper place. I let him lead me around the floor of the senior center and forgot everything but the feel of his shoulder beneath my hand and his voice, saying softly, "There you go, Haven. That's great. Can you believe it? You're dancing."

When the music stopped and I opened my eyes, all those elderly couples were grouped around us, applauding and smiling and nodding at each other, a silent consensus that what I'd felt wasn't just imagined. There was something special about Sumner, something that spread across rooms and years and memories, and for the length of a song I'd been part of it once again.

"So," he said once we were in his car and pulling out of the parking lot, "tell me what's wrong."

"Nothing," I said, holding my hand out and letting the warm air push through it as we went down the street, back to the boulevard.

"Come on, Haven." We were at a stoplight now, and

he turned to look at me. His eyes were so blue behind his glasses, which were lopsided. "I know what happened at the mall."

I kept my eyes on the light, waiting for the green. "That was no big thing," I said, trying to conjure up my bold self, to hear that whooshing again that made me rise above it all, immune. "I quit anyway."

He was still looking at me. "Haven. Don't bullshit me now. I know when something's wrong."

And still we sat, at what had to be the longest light in the world, with him staring at me until I finally said, "I'm just pissed off at Ashley, okay? And my mother and all this wedding crap." I sat back in my seat, balancing my feet on the dashboard the way I'd seen Ashley do all those years ago. "I really don't want to talk about it."

The light changed and we turned right, heading towards the mall and my neighborhood. "Well," he said slowly, shifting gears, "don't be so hard on Ashley. Getting married must be kind of stressful. She probably doesn't mean to take it out on you."

"It's not about the wedding," I said, realizing how tired I was of repeating these words and this sentiment. "God, Ashley did exist before this wedding, you know, and she was my sister a long time before she became the bride, and we have problems going way back that have nothing to do with this goddamn wedding anyway."

"I know she existed before this," he said gently. "I knew her once too, remember?"

"Yeah, but when you knew her she was different," I said. "God, Sumner, you made her different. You changed her."

"I don't know about that," he said. "It was high school, Haven. It was a long time ago."

"You made her happy," I told him. "With you she was nice to me and she laughed; God, she laughed all the time. We all did."

"It was a long time ago," he said again. This wasn't what I wanted from him; I'd expected sympathy, shared anger, something. Understanding and encouragement. I wanted him to rage with me against everything and everyone, but instead he just drove, saying nothing now.

We were getting closer to my neighborhood, and I said, "If you're planning to take me home you can just drop me off here. I'm not going."

"Haven, come on." He turned to look at me. Over his shoulder I suddenly noticed storm clouds, which seemed to have popped up from nowhere. They were long and flat, full of grays and blacks, and hadn't yet reached the sun blazing above us. "Your mom is probably worried about you and it's getting late. Just let me take you home."

"I don't want to go home," I said again, louder. "And it's only five-fifteen, Sumner. If you're going to take me home to my mother like I'm still eight years old, just stop the car and I'll get out here."

He pulled over to the side of the road, right next to the mall. "Okay, Haven. I won't take you home. But I'm not dumping you on the side of the road, either. So it's up to you what we do now."

We sat there, with cars passing and the sun beating down, while he watched me and I stared at my reflection in the side mirror. My face looked dirty and hot. "You don't understand." I wondered if I was going to start crying.

He cut off the engine and sat back in his seat, jiggling the keys in the ignition. "Understand what?" He sounded tired, fed up. This wasn't going the way I'd thought it would. I wanted to be back on that dance floor with his arm around me, surrounded by all those old, crinkly, smiling faces, safe and perfect.

"Any of this," I said. "You don't understand what's happened since you left."

"Since I left?"

"Since Ashley sent you away," I said, still focusing on my own face in the mirror, my own mouth talking. "That Halloween. A lot has changed."

"Haven . . . ," he said, drawing in a breath as if preparing to say something a parent would say, something sensible that cuts you off with the wave of one hand.

"My father ran off with the weathergirl, Sumner," I said, and suddenly the words were rushing out crazylike, jumbled and fast, "and Ashley didn't like me and my mother was so sad, it just broke her heart. And then Lydia moved in with her Town Car and Ashley found Lewis at the Yogurt Paradise and nobody was who they'd been before, not even me. When you left—when she sent you away—it was like that started it all. When you were there, remember, everything was still good. We were all happy, and then Ashley was such a bitch and she sent you away and everything fell apart, just like that. God," I said, realizing how loud my voice was, and how jagged I sounded, "it was just like *that.*"

All this time he was staring ahead, Ashley's first

love in a wrinkled red shirt and Buddy Holly glasses. He shook his head, gently, and said to the road ahead, "There's a lot you don't understand, Haven. Ashley—"

"I don't want to hear about Ashley," I snapped, tired of her name and her face and the way she took over everything, even this moment, controlling it all. "I hate Ashley."

"Don't say that," he said. "You don't know." Now he sounded like everyone else, passing judgment, making assumptions. Not listening to me at this moment when it suddenly mattered so much.

"I know plenty," I said, because this sounded final. I wanted him to agree with me. To believe me. But he only sat there and shook his head, his fingers on his keys, as if the very words I'd said disappointed him.

The storm clouds were moving fast, piling into a dark heap that was spreading across the sky. The wind picked up, a hot breeze blowing across us, and I could smell the dirt and the road and my own sweat.

"It was her fault," I said quietly, seeing him again on the front lawn that Halloween, watching her window, "it was her fault you left. She sent you away."

"Haven, I can't deal with this," he said, hitting his hands on the steering wheel, suddenly angry. "I don't know what to say to you—"

"You don't have to say anything," I said, surprised to hear him raise his voice, lose patience with me. This wasn't how I remembered him.

"Look, Haven," he said, "what happened with me and Ashley . . . well, it wasn't like you remember it. There was a lot involved."

There always is, I wanted to tell him. These were the same things my mother said to me after my father left, trying to convince me it wasn't all the Weather Pet's fault.

"I've got to take you home," he said. The storm clouds were grouped high above us, black and foreboding with a blue sky peeking out behind. It was still sticky and hot, but the breeze was changing, now cooler and heavy, sending grass clipping swirling by the side of the road.

"I'm not going home," I said again as the clouds slipped over the sun, amazed at how fast the weather can change, a front blowing in a matter of minutes.

He started the engine, ignoring me, and put the car in gear. We slid away from the curb just as big fat drops began to fall, splashing across the windshield and my face. The cars coming towards us were turning their lights on, all at once. I opened my door and jumped out, slamming it behind me as my feet hit ground.

"Haven!" Sumner yelled at me, stopping the car again as I cut across the side of the road to a path, the back way we'd always taken to the mall to buy candy and Slurpees when I was little. "It's getting ready to pour; don't be stupid. Come on, get back in the car."

"No," I said softly, knowing he couldn't hear me. It was really raining now. I kept walking, hearing Sumner yell my name but knowing I couldn't go back to him, that he wasn't what I'd wanted him to be. Maybe he never had been.

As I got farther down the path I couldn't hear the traffic anymore, just the rain and thunder. I cut across a small creek, on a plank stretched across it, and saw the first flash of lightning shining suddenly above and then disappearing. It was followed by a crack of thunder that seemed to come from right behind me, pushing me forwards. The path was different than I remembered it, twisting around trees and rocks I didn't recognize, but then it had been a long time. Everything looks different when you're older, not staring up at the world but down upon it. Another clap of thunder boomed over me. I was sure the path came out in my neighborhood somewhere.

I couldn't see houses or lights, just trees followed by more trees, stretching into the distance. Suddenly I wasn't even sure if I was still on the path at all, and that made me panic and start to run, brushing branches out of my face as the rain pelted my back and dripped into my eyes, slippery and cold. The sky was black above me now and I started to think about tornados, the world swirling around and me with nothing to hold on to but trees, and this pushed me to run faster, the sound of my breathing hoarse in my ears. I couldn't see the path anymore in the rain and the dark, and everything was slippery beneath me as I ran harder, towards what had to be a clearing ahead. I thought of the houses on my street with their warm lights and the even, green lawns and all the landmarks, so familiar I could find them in my sleep. I ran to that clearing, sure that I could see it all in front of me—until I reached the last set of branches and pulled them aside to reveal more branches, and leaves dripping with rain, and pushed through with all my strength to burst out into open space, my heart racing in my chest, and kept running until I hit something, hard, something that moved and jumped back, its own breath hitting my face.

It was Gwendolyn.

She was sopping wet, her hair sticking to her forehead, in a white T-shirt with a red tank top showing through beneath and black running shorts. A pair of headphones hung around her neck, attached to a Walkman clipped to her waist. She was breathing hard, her face flushed and beaded with raindrops, and she was the first person I'd met in a long, long time who stood taller than me and looked down into my eyes. The thunder boomed around us, with another flash of white light, and Gwendolyn Rogers and I, breathing hard, stood still in that clearing, close enough that I could see the goose bumps on her flesh. She stared at me with her big, sad eyes as I stared right back, unflinching even when she raised her hand to my face and brushed her fingers across my cheek as if she wasn't sure I was real.

It seemed like we stood there together forever, Gwendolyn and I, two strangers in a clearing with the rain pounding down, inexplicably brought together in a summer storm. I wanted to talk to her, wanted words to come so I could say something that would make this all real. Something about what we had in common: a neighborhood, a summer, a revelation about a belief once considered sacred. But she only stared at me, her face wistful, a small smile creeping across it as if she knew me, had lost me along the way and only now found me again, here. I think she knew it too in that moment. She knew *me*.

Then I heard my sister's voice.

"Haven!" A car door slammed, hard, and then again, "Haven! Are you there?"

"I'm here," I said to Gwendolyn, and she pulled back from me, dropping her hand. I turned to look for my sister, who was still calling through the rain and the trees. "I'm here," I said again.

Ashley was coming through the brush now. She was bare-legged, wearing a yellow raincoat like the Morton Salt Girl, pulled tight. The trees were bending overhead, wind whistling through as the rain blew across me. I turned back around: Gwendolyn was already running down the path the way I'd come, a blur of white and black.

"Haven?" Ashley was closer now and I turned to the sound of her voice. Her raincoat was dripping wet, shiny and bright among all the green. I could see the headlights of her car now, beaming into the clearing. "Are you okay?"

"I'm fine," I said. "I got lost on this path."

"We were so worried," she said, coming to stand in front of me and wiping her hair out of her eyes. "Mom's practically hysterical calling everyone, and then Sumner Lee shows up and says you went running off into the woods back here."

"He talked to you?" I asked.

"He was worried too," my sister said, so small and wet in front of me. "We all were. God, Haven," she said softly, "what happened to you today?"

"I don't know," I said, and I was tired and wet, thinking only of crawling into my warm bed and putting this whole day behind me forever. But I had one more thing to say, to ask her, before I could do that. "Ashley."

"Yeah." She had turned to walk out of the clearing, and I faced the back of her raincoat.

"Why did you dump Sumner?"

She stopped and turned to face me. "What?"

"Sumner. Why did you break up with him that Halloween?"

"I dumped him?" she said. "Is that what he told you?"

"No," I said. "But I saw you do it. That Halloween when he was the mad scientist, remember? I saw you from the window."

"Haven," she said slowly, shaking her head. "I didn't dump Sumner. I mean, I did, but only because he cheated on me. With that girl Laurel Adams; remember her? I walked in on them that night at the party. That's why I broke up with him." She watched me as she said this, her voice even and sad. "All this time you didn't know, did you? God, Haven. He broke my heart."

I stood there and faced my sister, thinking back to that Halloween when I watched them driving down the street, Sumner in the front seat with Ashley beside him, and Laurel Adams in back with her hair shimmering silver under the streetlight. "That's not true," I said, thinking of Sumner as he held me on the dance floor earlier that afternoon. "It isn't."

"It is true. I loved Sumner and he hurt me badly." She reached up to brush my hair out of my face, an awkward gesture, a try at tenderness. "It's not always so simple, Haven. Sometimes there isn't a good guy and a bad guy. Sometimes even the ones you want to believe turn out to be liars."

"But he was so sad, and he kept coming around," I said, still not wanting to believe it was possible. "He begged for you to come back."

"That didn't change what he did." She shook her head, smiling sadly at me. "Haven, I know you don't like Lewis, but you have to understand how important it is to me to be able to trust someone I love. After Sumner and after Daddy, I was beginning to lose faith in everything. Lewis might not be Sumner, but he would never hurt me. Never. Sometimes things don't turn out the way you want them to, Haven. Sometimes the people you choose to believe are wrong."

"He loved you," I told her. "He still does, I think."

"He doesn't love me," she said, crossing her arms against her chest. "He might still love me as I was at fifteen, when I didn't know any better. When I trusted everyone. I'm not that person anymore." She started walking, holding aside the branches so I could get through. "He's just a boy, Haven. He was the first to really hurt me, but he's just a boy. There were a lot of them."

"Not like him," I said softly, although I knew that after today I'd never see him, or that summer at the beach, the same way.

"Maybe not," she said as we came to the car. "But maybe that isn't so bad. You can't love anyone that way more than once in a lifetime. It's too hard and it hurts too much when it ends. The first boy is always the hardest to get over, Haven. It's just the way the world works."

She held my door open for me as I climbed in, wet and sticky and tired after a day that was now a blur in my head, stretching back into forever. I watched her come around the front of the car and climb into the driver's seat and shut the door behind her. We didn't talk, me and my sister on the day before her wedding. She drove through the rain down those familiar streets, the houses all shiny and bright, and I thought about Sumner and that first summer, when everything was different. He'd affected both of us in separate but similar ways. He was the first to break her heart, and the first boy to let me down, to take something from me that I'd clung to so closely. A myth. Maybe Ashley was right, for once.

I thought about telling her this in the quiet of the car with only the rain drumming overhead. I looked over at her and thought better of it. Some things you don't have to tell. Some things, between sisters, are understood.

Chapter Thirteen

"*It's time.*" My mother was standing in my doorway, in a new pink dress with a corsage pinned below her right shoulder, a group of pink zinnias ringed with blue phlox. The entire house smelled like flowers that morning, from the bouquets that were lined up on the kitchen table, each constructed by her own hands.

I turned away from the mirror and she sighed, clasping her hands in front of her. "You look beautiful," she whispered, having broken into sobs so many times that morning that she had Kleenex poking out of her pocket, ready. "The dress is perfect. It looks just right."

Lydia Catrell popped into the doorway and promptly burst into tears. "You are a vision," she said, sniffling, as my mother offered her a damp Kleenex, which she waved away. "Isn't she something?"

"She is," my mother said softly, coming forward to hug me, her corsage pressing against my chest. She took my hand and we started down the stairs, with Lydia chattering ahead of us.

"I just know I'm going to bawl," she said loudly, the waterworks having passed. "I always cry at weddings, don't you?"

"I do," my mother said, squeezing my hand. "But Haven will be the strong one. Lucky for her she didn't inherit her mother's emotional tendency."

"Oh, there's nothing like a wedding for a good cry," Lydia said, clomping down the steps in her huge white slingbacks. "Everyone needs a good cry now and then."

My mother was still holding my hand as we walked through the hallway and out the door to the car. When I'd come home with Ashley she'd only hugged me so tight it hurt before letting me go upstairs for a shower and a long nap, skipping the rehearsal dinner altogether. When I woke up I found her and Ashley at the kitchen table, drinking wine and laughing, their voices drifting up like music. I sat in my nightgown and drank ginger ale with them, and we talked about the old times: when Ashley was ten and almost burnt the house down with her Easy-Bake oven, and when I was six and decided to run away, packing my red patent-leather suitcase with nothing but washcloths and underwear. My mother was laughing, her face flushed pink like it always was when she drank, telling the stories that for so long had remained in the no-man's land of the divorce, uncomfortable for what they no longer represented. Now we laughed about my father's hair and about Ashley's boyfriends, the timeline of boys, each with a quirk we remembered better than his name. And we laughed while it rained and the air smelled sweet blowing in the back door, like the flowers that bloomed just outside. The kitchen was warm and bright and I knew I would remember this night, in the same misty way I'd remembered all the good things, as a time when things were as perfect as they could be. Another summer to reach back to, that week in Virginia Beach now tucked away with the other, older memories. Later, when Ashley was gone and my mother and I tried to fill this house ourselves, I'd look back to that night and remember every detail, from Ashley's ring glittering as she sipped her wine to my mother's bare feet beside me on the chair, flecked with grass clippings. It would be a good place to start over.

I held my mother's hand as we walked to the car, knowing that things would be different now. My mother and I would have to start our own memories, maybe in a new setting. She'd go to Europe, because I'd make her, and I'd get another job, away from the mall, and start again with the fall and my junior year. My sister would be with Lewis and I would know that she was happy, there in her new apartment, without me on the other side of the wall. I'd have to let her go. And I would start my own timeline now, with the faces of my own boys marking the days and months and years.

I kept wanting to find Ashley, to tell her these things, but at the church it was crowded and crazy, with everyone running around and Ashley always behind a closed door or being whisked past in a blur of white. I stood in line with the other bridesmaids, Carol Cliffordson nowhere in sight, symmetry be damned. I held my bouquet and said I was fine, really, it was just a twenty-four-hour bug. I'd been a bridesmaid before: I knew what to do. And when the music started I stepped forward and followed the girl before me to the end of the aisle, past Casey and her parents and Lorna Queen and finally my mother and Lydia, all the while wishing I'd had time to say something to Ashley. Something about the day before, and how I was sorry. About how I would miss her and that I understood now about Sumner, and how he had brought us back together and given us something in common again. The night before, we'd been so caught up in the past that I couldn't make myself think ahead to this day and what came next, for either of us. I'd gone to bed and listened to her in the room beside me just as I had every other night of my life, not realizing that the next morning would be too late.

The organist started "Here Comes the Bride" and we all turned to the back of the church, expectant, and there she was. My father was grinning, his arm linked with hers as they took the first step together. Everyone was oohing and aahing because she was beautiful, white and gliding and perfect, and I watched her come towards me, a small smile on her face. I saw Lewis blushing and my mother dabbing her eyes and I thought about all we'd been through, my sister and I, the fights and the good times and every day we'd had that led up to this one and suddenly I was crying. I knew my mascara was running and I was the only one up there in front so close to bawling, but still the tears came, rolling down my cheeks as she got closer and her own eyes met mine from beneath her veil. I wanted to say it all then, but before I could speak she stepped away from my father and put her arms around me, hugging me tightly, her bouquet against my neck. I smelled flowers, my mother's garden, as I held her and knew I didn't have to say anything. My sister was wiser than I ever gave her credit for. She held me and whispered she loved me before pulling back, wiping her own eyes.

I knew it then. For me and Ashley, there wasn't any time left to think back to that summer and the beach and a boy who charmed us and disappointed us. There was only what stretched out ahead, years full of new summers and promise, with all the time in the world left to start again. My sister, who never understood most of the things I wanted her to, might have been able to understand what had happened to me in this summer of weddings and beginnings. And she was right. The first boy was always the hardest.